overwinter

also by david wellington

Monster Island

Monster Nation

Monster Planet

13 Bullets

99 Coffins

Vampire Zero

23 Hours

Frostbite

Overwinter

a werewolf tale

david wellington

 THREE RIVERS PRESS · NEW YORK

Copyright © 2010 by David Wellington

Published in the United States by Three Rivers Press, an imprint of the
Crown Publishing Group, a division of Random House, Inc., New York.

www.crownpublishing.com

Three Rivers Press and the Tugboat design are registered trademarks of
Random House, Inc.

Library of Congress Cataloging-in-Publication Data
is available upon request.

ISBN 978-0-307-46079-0

Printed in the United States of America

Design by Maria Elias

10   9   8   7   6   5   4   3   2   1

First Edition

For Adelaide

Tucker's Last Stand was the rowdiest bar in the town of Menden, Alaska, but when the naked woman staggered in through the front door it was still enough to make Greg Thomas's jaw drop. He was the town doctor, and had seen some pretty crazy things in his time, but *still*.

From her post behind the bar, Margie Hurlwhite let out a low whistle and put down the glass she'd been filling. The four men at the bar turned to look all at once and none of them said a word. Three of them were old fishermen with hands so cut up and weathered they could barely hold a knife anymore. Thomas, the fourth, stood up so fast he knocked over his stool. The noise was loud enough to drown out the radio, but nobody bothered to look away from the naked visitor.

Thomas wiped his hands on his pants. "Well, hi there," he said, when it was clear no one else was going to welcome the newcomer.

She looked him right in the eye and smiled. Didn't say a word. She was beautiful, he thought, far lovelier a creature than any woman in Menden had a right to be, with long red hair that fell across her eyes and shaded her face but totally failed to cover her breasts, not to mention the rest of her. She looked like she might be twenty, or maybe younger. Just a girl. He wiped his hands on his hips again, because suddenly they were sweaty. It had been a long time since his wife had died and he'd never bothered much with women since then, but this one . . . except maybe it wasn't exactly lust he was feeling in his heart at that moment. There was something about this girl. Maybe it was that she wasn't making any effort to cover herself up. That she wasn't shivering, even with snowflakes flecking her hair like glitter. It was just below freezing outside, and her feet were wet, as if she'd been walking in the snow, but she looked as though if you put a hand on her arm you might just get burned.

"You got a good enough look, Doc, to make a diagnosis?" Margie asked, rushing around the end of the bar to drag the girl inside, away from the door. She stopped before she could touch the girl's skin, though, and mostly just waved her toward the back and the pair of red leather booths there.

Margie's tone had been thick with sarcasm but Thomas shook his head and answered anyway. "Hypothermia's my guess. We got to get her warm." He stripped off his parka and wrapped it around the girl, which got him another smile, this one warm with gratitude. "Margie, make some coffee, will ya?"

"Got a pot brewing right now," Margie told him. She busied herself behind the bar while the three fishermen turned on their stools to face Thomas and the girl. They were blinking and rubbing their faces like they couldn't quite believe it.

"What's the matter, miss?" Thomas asked. "You in an accident or something? Where'd you come from?"

She tilted her head so the red hair fell away from her eyes and looked up into his face. "No accident, *m'sieur.* I have come from the water, just now, on a boat."

"You have people around here, someone I can call?"

The smile faded a bit. "Not so close, but people, yes. I have come for my man, who I have not seen for a very long time."

"What's that accent?" Margie asked, bringing the coffee. She set it down on the table in front of the girl with shaking hands. "Sounds like Quebec, maybe. You a Quebecois, dear?"

"Je suis française, but I have been abroad. Just now I am coming over from Russia."

Well, Thomas thought, that made some sense, anyway. Menden was on the west coast of Alaska, near about as close as you could get to Russia without going for a swim. Boats went back and forth between the two landmasses all the time. Of course, most of the people on those boats dressed for the climate.

"What's your name?" Margie asked, and Thomas felt like a cad for forgetting to ask that, himself.

"I am Lucie, thank you."

Thomas waved Margie back. The bartender was leaning so close she was blocking the girl's air. "Find some blankets, a tarp, anything. And turn the heat up in here. She's probably so cold her brain's froze. We have to—"

"I am altogether fine, sir," Lucie said, and she reached out to grab Thomas's hand. He flinched, expecting her touch to scorch him. Her skin was warm, it was true, though no more than normal body temperature. Her lips weren't blue or even chapped, and her pupils were normal, he noted. "But can you, please, tell me one thing? That clock, there. Is it accurate?"

He looked up at the old cuckoo clock above the bar mirror, mounted between a pair of antique snowshoes. It said it was a quarter to nine. "I suppose," he said, though it did seem like that must be wrong.

"No, honey, that's bar time," Margie supplied. "About fifteen minutes ahead. That's so when closing time comes I can get these sorry fools moving toward the door faster. Why do you need to know? Are you meeting your man soon?"

Lucie shook her head prettily. "Not yet. I merely wish to know, because the moon is due up at eight and the half tonight."

Thomas frowned. There really was something about this girl. Something off. "You know when moonrise is off the top of your head?"

"I should be very surprised to find her up without me," Lucie replied. "So it is just about now half past the eight? Yes, I can feel it is so." She shrugged her shoulders and the parka fell away. *"Merci.* You have all been so very kind."

Thomas grabbed for the parka and realized, too late, that she hadn't pushed it off herself. It had collapsed around her. Or—through her. She was becoming intangible, her flesh transparent so he could see the red leather of the banquette right through her white skin. "Holy mother," he said. "Like a—a ghost."

"No, *m'sieur.* Not like a ghost at all."

There was a flash of silver light, a shimmer like moonlight flickering on choppy water. Then in his arms was an explosion of fur and spittle and many huge teeth. Blood spattered the dusty floor of the bar and Margie screamed, but Thomas barely heard her. He never heard anything again.

great bear lake

1

Cheyenne Clark was, for the first time in her life, almost happy.

It wasn't something she liked to admit to herself. She had plenty of reasons to be miserable, depressed, even pissed off. But those reasons felt very far away.

There had been a time, before, when things had gotten bad. Very, very bad, and she hadn't come out of it innocent. She—or rather her wolf— had done things she didn't like to contemplate.

An agent of the Canadian government had tortured her. He'd been using her as bait to draw another werewolf to his death. The two werewolves had retaliated, and things had gotten out of control. She'd gone a little crazy. Maybe a lot crazy. She had killed some people. Or, as she wished she could put it, her wolf had killed some people.

But that was in the past.

Now she wasn't alone anymore. Chey and Montgomery Powell—she still called him Powell, though he'd told her she was a friend of his now, and could call him Monty—were together now, together in a way she'd never experienced with a human being. It was more like the bond wolves share in a pack. They'd headed north, away from anyone who might be looking for them. Away from people they might hurt, and people who might hurt them. People who had easy access to silver bullets.

Those people were a long way away. In the Northwest Territories of Canada, there was a lot of empty space to escape into.

Starting from Port Radium, a ghost town so polluted nothing could live there, they'd followed the sinuous curves of the shore of Great Bear Lake, staying close to the water where the hunting was still good. Summer was over, and though the ground was still soft and the wind didn't bite too hard yet, most game animals were already migrating south. There were fewer snowshoe rabbits every day and even field mice were becoming scarce. When Powell caught his first lemming—like a big mouse with a red back and a short tail—he brought it back to their camp and studied it as if he were reading a newspaper. "It must be September," he said.

He took a buck knife out of his pocket and started to skin the animal, preparatory to cooking it over their fire. Chey winced and turned away. She could feel him watching her, feel his surprise, but there were still some things her wolf handled better than she could.

"You're going to eat this once it's roasted, aren't you?" he asked her.

"Yes," she told him. She was always a little hungry these days and she knew once she smelled the cooking meat she wouldn't be able to resist. "I just don't want to see it cut up, that's all."

"You should learn how to skin one of these. Pretty soon we'll be living off them. You'll need to know, then."

She shook her head. Their wolves were perfectly capable of hunting for themselves. Powell and Chey didn't need to eat at all—what nourished their wolves nourished them. Powell insisted on cooking, though, because it was a human ritual and it made him feel like he was still in control of his destiny. She . . . respected that in him, that he still thought of himself as a human with some kind of disease. Something that could be managed. She was under fewer illusions, herself. "I'll just let my wolf do it," she said.

Her wolf loved it up here. Her wolf thrived on the constant cold, on the silence between the trees. On the clean air. And because there was no way for Chey to get rid of her wolf, she was just going to have to make do. Her wolf hated human beings and would attack them on sight, whether it was hungry or not. She didn't want that to happen. Didn't want to live with the consequences. The only option left to her was to live up here where people were scarcer than palm trees. Powell had figured that out decades earlier, after exhausting every other possibility. She had chosen to come with him, to learn from him, to live with him so that she didn't have to be completely alone.

When the lemming was cooked he carved off a fillet and brought it to her. The meat was stringy and gamy but her stomach lurched happily when the first drop of its grease touched her tongue. She gobbled it down without bothering to chew too much.

"So?" he asked.

"You overcooked it," she told him. He sighed and started to turn away, but she shot out one hand and grabbed his arm. "Is there any more?" she asked.

He stared at her with his big cold green eyes. Eyes she saw sometimes when she was about to fall asleep, eyes she couldn't not see. His eyes were searching her face, looking for something. Not validation, she knew. He was too tough to need that. Not an apology, because he knew better than to expect that from her.

She'd been hard on him, she knew. Harsher than she'd meant to be. He'd hurt her badly, once, and she'd never fully forgiven him.

But maybe . . . maybe she didn't have to be such a jerk about it. Things had changed. Were continuing to change, especially between the two of them. And all the bad things, the bad history that had led her to this point, seemed very far away indeed.

She took a step toward him. It was all he needed. He stepped toward her as well, then wrapped his arms around her and pulled her to him. Part of her wanted to push him away. Part of her wanted to lash out, to hit him, to scream in his face and rake her fingernails across his eyes.

Instead she nestled her face into the crook of his neck. His flannel shirt smelled like woodsmoke, from the fire. Underneath that she smelled his own personal scent. It was a good smell. She closed her eyes and relaxed into his embrace. "Thanks for breakfast," she said.

"You're welcome." His voice was gruff, as always, but he couldn't mask all of the relief in it.

2

They packed up their things and headed north again, on foot as always. To Chey it seemed like they'd always been moving north. Her legs didn't get tired, not the way they would have if she'd still been human, but after eight hours of walking she still thought she deserved a break. Powell made her walk another couple of kilometers, though, before he suddenly and without warning called for a stop.

Chey didn't argue. She sank down on a lumpy mat of yellow grass and took her shoes off. Her toes thanked her.

"There's something here you should see," Powell said, standing tall and straight like a park ranger showing off a scenic vista.

Chey grunted in response.

It was enough to keep him going. Like every man she'd ever met, Powell relished a good excuse to give a speech. "This is what's left of Fort Confidence," he told her, tapping a bit of stone with his boot.

"There's a fort here?" Chey asked, looking around. She couldn't see much but scrub grass and a couple of trees. On the ground there were a couple of square piles of stones that looked a little too regular to have just gathered naturally, she supposed. If you squinted at them.

"Back when the fur traders came through here," he explained, "there was. Jules Verne wrote a book about it. The fort burned down, though. So they rebuilt it. It burned down again. Nothing left but these chimney stones." He gave her one of his thoughtful looks. "This is what happens when people try to build on this land. The land always wins."

She bit her lip and tried to figure out what she was supposed to learn from this. "Are you saying we'll be safe here? That nobody's going to come this far north just to bother us?"

He shrugged. "It's the safest place I know. For a while, anyway, we can stay here. Make a camp. Maybe we'll even be allowed to overwinter here before they catch up with us again."

"So you think they will find us. Eventually."

He shrugged again. "I'm over a hundred years old, Chey, and for most of that time I've had people hunting me. I'd be at odds and ends if one day they just stopped. Running away from people is what I do best." He stared hard at the land around them, especially down the slope that led to the lake. "Still, it would be nice to rest awhile. Build a shelter, get a fire going. Sit for a while and . . ."

She waited for him to finish his thought.

"In the spring," he said, "when it's warm again. We can get to work on . . . the other thing."

"You're seriously still thinking about that?"

It had been a common enough topic of conversation on their long trek north. There had been a lot of time to talk of many things while they marched, or, after their wolves had come and gone, when they backtracked, looking for the clothes their wolves had left behind.

"You honestly think there's a cure," she said.

He wouldn't look at her when he answered. "There must be. There has to be a way to break the curse. There has to."

Who did he think he was fooling? The ground under her was wet and muddy. She moved over to sit on one of the chimney stones. Moss made a cushion for her. "How long have you been looking for this supposed cure? Fifty years?"

"More like seventy."

She knew all the things he had tried so far. He'd studied the old legends of werewolves and other shape-shifters from around the world, learning how people had supposedly turned themselves into animals and, more important, how they'd changed back. He'd spent decades reading old legends and folk-tales, hoping there was a grain of truth in them somewhere. He had made wolf straps—belts of skin, either wolf hide or human skin he'd cut from his own body, studded with silver nails that burned him every time he touched them. He had cultivated the flowers of wolfsbane and purple aconite, hoping to brew some kind of potion that would release him from his double nature.

None of it had ever worked.

"There's an answer," he said, sounding like he was trying to convince himself. "And it has to be here. This is where the curse began, did I tell you that?"

"A couple of times."

He shook his head. "Somewhere here in the north, in the New World. We know that this is where the first lycanthropes came from. If we can find the place where the curse originated, we'll find the answer. You and me. Together."

"And then what?" she asked. "We walk south again, through all this country without the wolves to keep us alive? We walk into the first big city we find and we turn ourselves in, say, 'Hi, we're the ones who killed Bobby Fenech and the Pickersgill brothers, but it's okay because we were wolves at the time, and now we're cured?' You think they won't lock us up? You think they won't send us off to prison?"

"A human prison. Where we can live safely with other human beings. Jail can't be worse than this existence."

She doubted that. Almost as much as she doubted there was a cure, of any kind, except the one that came from being shot multiple times with silver bullets.

"The two of us will succeed where I failed alone," he went on. "We'll be able to . . . to . . ."

"What?" she asked.

"Blast."

She knew the tone in his voice. It was time, again. She didn't bother putting her shoes back on. The moon must be just below the horizon, just about to peek up over the edge of the world and bring on the change. He had a way of knowing just when it was going to happen, a kind of internal alarm clock that went off just before it was time. She'd never known him to be off by more than a few minutes.

They each looked around them, memorizing landmarks. They would need to find this place again when they changed back—their clothes would still be here. It was a routine they'd established early in their trek north, and she did it automatically. But just like every time before, she was thinking, *Remember what this looks like with human eyes.* Because every time it felt like she might never see anything that way again.

"See you when we're—" he began to say, but he was interrupted as the moon came edging over the line of trees to their east.

Silver light dazzled Chey's eyes, blinding her. She felt her clothing fall away as she became as intangible as a ghost. And then there was nothing; there was the wolf.

The two of them were still finding each other in the dark, in many ways. Their wolves were working out their own relationship, every time the moon came up. Chey had seen the movies, but now she knew it wasn't true, that thing about werewolves only changing under the full moon. Chey and Powell transformed every time the moon rose over the horizon whether it was full or new, whether it happened in the middle of the day or only after midnight.

The change was ecstatic. For the wolves it felt like being joyously reborn. They had spent the long hours when the moon was down trapped in bodies that were fragile, slow, and half-blind—at least compared to the glorious forms the wolves possessed. The wolves emerged from flashes of silver light into a great symphony of smells and sounds, into wind that had more colors than their eyes could see, into bodies that were strong and sleek and fast.

The wolves ran and played and sported—and hunted. With flashing jaws they snapped at the snow on the ground, snatching up the little bright warm things that burrowed underneath. Blood flecked their muzzles and their paws and their bellies, finally, were full. The cold night air was bracing, not frigid, and the stars overhead were bright enough to see by, even when the imperious moon grew dark.

They marked their territory. They considered digging snug dens in the earth while it was still soft, and decided against it. The air was still warm enough, the days still long enough, that there was time to play.

How they played. The two of them danced about each other, ran arcs around each other, leaping sideways to keep their eyes locked even as they spun and turned. They snapped and nipped at each other's snouts, feinted with slashing paws and butted each others' sides with their heads, their powerful necks craning to try to get at each other's bellies.

He was stronger, and slightly bigger than her. Still he won only by trickery, by dashing up along a high tussock of grass and then crashing down onto her shoulders, spilling them both across the snow-strewn ground, sending them rolling. When she tried to right herself, to get her broad paws back down on the earth where they belonged, he was on top of her, pinning her with his weight across her chest, his jaws hovering over the soft flesh of her belly.

She wrestled and fought and scratched, mewled and whined and screeched in an agony of excitement and pleasure and the need to break free, to get out from under. He kicked at her hind legs with his own.

She sank her teeth deep into his throat.

With a cry he jumped straight up in the air, off of her, leaving nothing in her mouth but his torn-out fur. She spat it out and rolled effortlessly to her feet, spreading her legs wide to get a firm grip on the ground. His forelegs came down across her shoulders and she bucked him off, then spun around and slammed into his side with the bony part of her haunches, knocking him away. She spun again to face him where he crouched low and with his forelegs stretched out across the snow, in a courteous bow.

They were both panting. Their eyes were wild. The hair between their shoulder blades, a darker patch of fur called the saddle, stood up and puffed out to make them both look even bigger than they were. Their tails were up and lashing at the air. It was a signal any wolf could read instantly, any dog the world over, a warning, a threat, a promise, a demand to know what the other wanted.

That signal could be answered with growls or with sighs. In a moment they could be mating—or tearing each other's throats out. She watched his eyes, his tail. He watched hers. Neither was willing to make the first move, to break the spell, the staring contest, the ritual clash of wills.

Then—as suddenly and dramatically as ice breaking on a frozen pond—his head went up. His nose scanned the air and his eyes narrowed. He had something, something serious enough to be a distraction.

He sat down hard on his haunches and lifted his nose higher. His ears swept back and he closed his eyes, every iota of his perception committed to his impossibly keen sense of smell. She took a few tentative sniffs herself but couldn't find what had distracted him. Annoyed that the confrontation had finished without proper resolution, she took a step toward him, her body low to the ground, and then another. She lifted one paw to bat at his face but held back when she heard what came next.

His jaws parted slightly and a high, long keening came out, a bloodcurdling sound that made her teeth ache and her heart race. He let the sound slide out of him, a long descending yowl that broke up into a series of growling yelps. She'd heard him howl before, of course, but never with such nuance, with so varied a call. He was communicating something very specific but not something she could understand.

She lifted her own nose to the air, let out her own preliminary cry. He opened his eyes and stared her into silence. For a time they waited.

Did he expect a reply to his howl?

None came.

Eventually he rose to all fours again and trotted away, in the direction of the water. His tail rose again and started to waggle back and forth and she sensed a change in him, a slackening of tension. Had he been glad to get no reply? She could not know, but she understood that whatever had elicited that call was gone now. Everything was back to normal. She was glad for it. Still panting from their exertions, they sought out a place where the water had cut away a section of bank, forming a shallow overhang of frozen dirt, a bit of shelter from the wind. There they curled up together, sharing their warmth, recovering their energy for whatever came next. They dozed, their eyes drifting shut then snapping open again, still alert, still aware even as their muscles relaxed and their minds drifted into dreams.

When the moon set the next morning, the silver light of transformation found them there, her foreleg draped across his neck.

Chey's eyes opened slowly. It felt like her eyelids were made of sandpaper. Her mouth tasted stale and her tongue was stuck to the inside of one cheek. Her entire body ached.

It was never easy coming back.

She stirred a little, lifted her head, but that hurt too much, so she let it fall back. She opened her eyes enough to see that she was sheltered under an overhanging bank of earth, just enough to keep the wind off. Then she noticed how she was lying. She was naked, of course—her clothes had fallen away when she transformed, and they didn't magically follow her around—but unlike most times she had woken up naked on a pile of dirt, this time she wasn't alone. She and Powell were spooning, her breasts crushed against his back and one of her arms wrapped around his chest.

He seemed to be asleep. Slowly, careful not to wake him, she started to draw her arm away. If she could roll away from him before he woke, if she could get a little distance between them, she could pretend it hadn't happened.

She had known for a while now that their wolves were getting more than friendly with each other. More than once she'd woken with the impression that the wolves had been courting each other. She would come to still heavily aroused, her body aching for a male touch, and she knew it was the wolf's heat she was experiencing. It was just a matter of time, she supposed, before they started mating.

Chey didn't know what would happen then. Powell had told her she couldn't get pregnant, even by another werewolf, and he should know—he'd been mated to two of them, once, in both forms. For years he'd been the lover of a pair of female lycanthropes in France and though by his own admission there'd been plenty of sex, no one had ever conceived. It wasn't that which worried Chey, however. If she and Powell started mating when the moon was up, she would have to make a decision about how she felt about him when she was human. About whether the attraction she felt toward him was okay, and whether or not acting on it would betray her inmost being.

"Hello," Powell said, rolling over.

Her heart skipped a beat. She'd only managed to half extract her arm from their embrace, and when he turned to look at her like that she was still, technically, hugging him. She could still feel his body heat bathing her chest and legs. And now she had to accept the fact that he had an erection. And that it was pointing at her.

She forced herself not to look down. That meant, unfortunately, that she had nowhere to look but into his eyes. Eyes that were already searching hers, as if he was trying to decide what he was allowed to do next.

He shifted slightly, moving their faces closer together. Was he going to kiss her?

"We should get back to the fort," she said. She'd meant it to sound like a firm decision, a spur to get them both up and moving and out of each other's arms. Instead it came out faint and halfhearted. Like she was asking if they had to, or if it was okay to lie here a while longer.

He licked his lips. If his mouth tasted as bad as hers, she definitely didn't want him to kiss her, she decided. Then he opened his lips as if he were about to say something. Luckily he was interrupted as a fat, greasy drop of water splashed on Chey's cheek just then and she scurried backward, suddenly terrified.

There—up on the bank above them, leaning over the edge. Someone else was there, a stranger leaning over them, watching them.

Her hands grabbed at rocks and tree roots, looking for something she could throw. The figure above them was humanoid in shape, wrapped in thick furs. Its face was obscured by a long white wooden mask with square eyeholes and an elongated carved nose. With one hand the figure reached up and tilted the mask back, revealing a smiling gnomic face.

Not a stranger at all.

"Dzo!" she screamed, and jumped up to spread her arms and catch him as he leapt down to her level. "Where have you been? Where did you come from? What have you been doing?"

"I thought you could use these," Dzo said, and he pulled two bundles of clothing out from under his furs. He tossed them down on the ground and then hugged her back. His furs were damp with freezing-cold water, but she didn't care. "It took me a while to find you," he went on.

She was so excited to see him that she kissed his cheeks over and over. It wasn't just because he'd broken up a very awkward moment.

She had thought she had lost him forever. When she had followed Powell into Port Radium, Dzo had explained that the waters in that cursed place were too polluted to allow him to follow. Months ago she had said good-bye and assumed she would never see him again.

She was very glad it was otherwise.

"Good to see you, old man," Powell said, and shook Dzo's hand firmly.

"You too," Dzo agreed. "Hey. You got anything to eat?"

5.

A helicopter came in off the ocean, from the west, and half the town of Menden came out of doors to see what it meant. The harbormaster stepped out of his office with a cup of coffee in his hand and shielded his eyes to watch the helicopter approach for a landing. Then, with a deep sigh, he jumped in his jeep and headed out to meet it.

Not many helicopters came to Menden. It was a place where boats pulled in, dropped off their cargo, and left before the tide changed. There wasn't even an airstrip within close range of town—what little air traffic came through tended to land on the water. Adding to the strangeness was the fact that this particular aircraft was a decommissioned Russian attack gunship. There were people in Menden who might still take a Russian aircraft entering U.S. airspace the wrong way, even if it was repainted in civilian colors. This helicopter had a filed flight plan and official clearance, however, so somebody had to be on hand to do the official honors.

The harbormaster was seventy-two years old and had a beard that went halfway down his chest. He wore suspenders over his thermal shirt and a captain's hat on his head. He was not the kind of person who stared at people in the street based on how they looked. He was far more used to being the object of scrutiny. Besides, people in Menden tended not to get hung up on appearances.

The visitor who jumped down out of the helicopter's belly would have attracted second looks anywhere, though. He was a middle-aged man, in good physical shape, wearing a dirty flight suit and ear protectors. And his skin, what could be seen of it, was a deep blue verging on purple in places.

"My passport," he said, holding it out to the harbormaster. "And here is that of my pilot. Will you confirm that my papers are all in order?" The newcomer had a thick accent but his English was fluent. The harbormaster took one last look at his blue face, then opened the man's red passport and glanced at the photo page. The owner was named Yuri A. Varkanin, he read, born in Leningrad. In the photo he wasn't blue, though the face looked the same otherwise.

"Now, I'm not sure what the protocol is, but—"

"Ah," Varkanin said. "You are confused by my coloration. I am a sufferer of a condition known as argyria. A kind of heavy metal poisoning, which has had the effect of changing me into this." Varkanin waved a hand over his face. "I can produce documents from a physician proving this, if necessary."

"I don't suppose it is." The harbormaster fumbled a stamp out of one of his own pockets and held it above a blank page. "Business or pleasure?"

The Russian's face darkened. "Business. I am carrying out an investigation."

"Oh?" the harbormaster asked.

"I wish to learn something," Varkanin said, "of the werewolf."

"Oh."

"I understand she murdered four of your fine citizens before disappearing," Varkanin went on.

"It's not something we really like to talk about," the harbormaster said. "After the government and the media came through here, I guess we figured we were done with all that. We're still grieving for some good people, but that's private."

"Believe me, I understand this pain," Varkanin said. There was something soulful in his eyes that made the harbormaster believe him. "I am very interested in two things only, and when I learn them I will go and leave you in peace."

"Alright. That sounds fair. Why don't you start by asking me?"

The Russian nodded agreeably. "First I would like to know if you ever learned where she came from."

"Well, we think from your country. From Siberia, I guess. We found a boat we think she used, because nobody else could account for it. The whole thing didn't make any sense."

"In what fashion?"

The harbormaster shrugged expansively. "It was a twelve-foot dory, not much more than a rowboat. It had no motor and no sails, not even an oar. No food or water onboard either. The best guess we have is that she put to sea in Russia and just floated over, hoping she would hit land eventually. You'd have to be crazy to try that. It must have been well below freezing in that boat even when the sun was shining, and there was no source of heat onboard, nothing warmer than a couple blankets."

"I have reason to believe that she may be that crazy," Varkanin offered. "And a werewolf could survive the voyage without nourishment or protection from the elements."

"Alright, fine," the harbormaster allowed. "But then—why? She got bored over there in Siberia and decided she'd try picking on us for a change?"

"I do not pretend to understand the thinking of a crazy werewolf," Varkanin said. "My second question, then, is which way did she go?"

The harbormaster frowned. "Away from here was good enough for most of us," he said. "But I did hear one or two things. Some hikers claimed they saw a naked lady walking in the woods, about fifty miles up in the hills, heading due east. About a week later a forest service man said he saw her and she was still heading in that direction."

Varkanin nodded. The harbormaster could tell the man had known all this long before he came to Menden. He had just been looking for confirmation.

"So, now, that's all you wanted? Really?"

Varkanin smiled. The harbormaster felt his heart going out to the Russian, just seeing that smile. There was something of intense sadness in the man, and also compassion. The Russian smiled like a saint. "Really and truly. I do not wish to take up any more of your time. And besides, I have a long way to fly tonight."

The harbormaster frowned. "Where are you flying to?"

"The east," Varkanin said, and offered a good-natured shrug.

"Business, you said. You're here on business. What exactly is your line, Mr. Varkanin?"

"I am a hunter," the Russian said.

6.

Dzo's return eased the tension between Chey and Powell—without an exchange of more than a dozen words the three of them fell back into a familiar rhythm and Chey felt like her life was back to normal. Well, normally weird, anyway.

The three of them hiked back to the remains of Fort Confidence in a companionable silence marked by lots of shared smiles and the occasional laugh. It was a warmish day, considering how far north they were, and the sun was shining bright. The wolves hadn't run very far before the moon went down, so the walk wasn't too brutal. Sighting on the outcropping of rock, they found the site easily and when Chey saw the chimney stones she almost felt like she was coming home.

She wanted to lie down in the grass, roll around in it until it took on her own shape and just go to sleep right there, but of course Powell was already thinking about what they should do next.

"We can clear out some of those trees, there," he said, pointing downhill, "and have a clear view of the water. That way we'll know if anyone comes in by boat. And we can use the wood we fell to build a cabin."

"Okay," Chey said. "You got it. How do we do that?"

He blinked as if she'd surprised him. "We cut them down, of course."

"With our teeth?" Chey scratched her head. "When we left Port Radium, we didn't bring anything but the clothes on our backs. As far as I know you don't have a chainsaw hidden in your coat, and I know I forgot to bring any hatchets."

"We'll need to make our own tools."

"Out of what?"

"Rocks. Just like the cavemen did." Powell shrugged. "How hard can it be, for supernaturally strong lycanthropes?"

"Or I can go fetch some real axes," Dzo suggested. "I could even go back to our old place, gather up what we need, and bring it back in my truck."

"I loved that truck," Chey mused, with a little laugh. "And you can't deny it would be a handy thing to have up here."

Powell shook his head. "They might be watching there. I don't think it's worth the risk."

"You really think they're sitting around waiting for us to come back?" Chey asked. She picked a long stalk of grass and twiddled it between her fingers. "Maybe they'll just let us be, now."

"That's just wishful thinking," Powell said. He made it sound criminal. "No, they won't give up just yet. We made a mess back at Port Radium. Killed a government employee—"

"Who was trying to kill us! Who wanted to take me back to a lab and dissect me!"

"—and governments have very long memories," Powell finished, as if she hadn't spoken. "I'm not even sure that we're safe here. I really would have liked to get farther north before we stopped, honestly."

Chey shrugged. "Okay. I guess you're right. So why stop here at all, then? Why not press on?" She was loath to think about hiking any more, but she knew he was right. Knew they were still in danger, although it was hard to feel scared on such a nice, quiet day. "Why not keep moving until we know we're clear?"

"You don't know this country," Powell said. "Winter is coming, and it'll be here sooner than you expect, and a lot harder. If we had to, we could survive out here naked, in the open—but personally I prefer to be inside in the warm when it starts to snow. We need to start preparing now if we want to be ready. I want to have at least some kind of shelter before it really starts freezing up."

"Okay," Chey said, and rose wearily to her feet. "How do we start?" She suddenly realized that Dzo was staring at her. That he had, in fact, been watching her closely the whole time Powell was talking. "What?" she asked. "Is something wrong?"

"Well, no. It's just—your shoes," Dzo said.

"Huh?" She looked down and saw them dangling in front of her. She'd tied the laces of her boots together and hung them around her neck, with the socks balled up inside them.

"I don't claim to understand you wolves so good," Dzo said, scratching at one ear. "But I always assumed you wore those on your feet."

Chey frowned. "The grass felt good between my toes."

"Yeah, but—did the snow? Half the way back here we were trudging through old snow. And you never did put them on."

Chey blushed. She hadn't really thought about it. Her body, even in its human form, was a lot tougher than it used to be. Still, it was weird that she hadn't just put the boots on automatically. She'd never been a big fan of walking over rough ground barefoot before.

Powell shot her a look she didn't like. It was far too worried. Too paternal.

"I'll put them on now, okay? It's no big deal," she said.

But she could tell by the faces of the men that they didn't agree.

Dzo and Powell set to work right away, making stone axes of the kind people hadn't used in a couple thousand years. The trick seemed to be to find two nice sturdy rocks and hit them against each other until they split open. If you did it just right one of the rocks would be left in a sharp wedge shape that was still strong enough to cut through wood. Doing it right, though, was a long, slow, repetitive process, and you ended up ruining most of the rocks you tried it on.

At first they wouldn't let Chey help. "You can weave grass together to make lashings, and find good sticks to use as ax handles," Powell suggested.

"What, because that's woman's work?" she asked, smirking. "I know you've been living alone for most of the twentieth century, so you probably missed a few lectures on gender equality," she said, and grabbed a pair of stones for herself. She knocked them together so hard that the bones in her forearms vibrated.

"It's all in the wrist," Dzo said, and showed her how to hit them together in a shearing motion. A long thin chip came off the top of one of her rocks. It was too small and thin to work as an ax, but it was a start. "Boy," Dzo said, laughing, "I remember when we used to do this all day. Then somebody invented iron and you can't imagine the sighs of relief."

"Exactly how old are you?" Chey asked. She'd never gotten a good answer out of him on that issue.

"That's kind of hard to say," he told her, shrugging. "Time's funny," he added, after a while. "You know?"

"Sure." She brought down her rock with a clang. Tiny chips flicked off, joined a pile of the same between her feet.

She knew very little about Dzo, other than that she trusted him.

She knew his name was pronounced like "Joe," except not really, that was just the closest her Anglo tongue could get to the sound.

She also knew that he was not human.

Instead he was some kind of animal spirit, the incarnation of the musquash. He was immortal and he could travel between one place and another, even into locked and hidden places, as long as there was some water there. He could swim through water in a way that she could not, in some kind of mystical fashion where all water was one. She didn't claim to understand it at all, but she had relied on this ability often.

More important than all that, he was a friend. He'd been Powell's only friend for decades before Chey came along, following the werewolf as he migrated north, away from human habitation. Unlike every human being on the planet, Dzo had nothing to fear from a werewolf. When Chey had become a lycanthrope herself he had saved her life a few times—and helped her find her way when she needed it the most.

"Okay. Maybe let's try something easier. Where were you born?"

Dzo grinned. His teeth were big and brown and she would have preferred if he'd kept his mouth closed. "I'm not sure if I was. If I really think back, really, really far back—I used to live somewhere up there." He pointed north. "Good people up there. They worked hard but they laughed a lot, too. And there was always music. They didn't look like you two."

The rocks slammed together with a resonant sound. Like the world's most primitive drum band. "Were they Indians? I mean, Inuit?" she asked.

He had to think about that for a while. "No," he said. "Before they came along. I think they were, you know. Whatchamacallems."

Chey squinted as she tried to remember her social studies classes from grade school. Because she wasn't paying attention she missed as her rocks came together and one of them skidded off the top of the other, flying off into some bushes. Sighing, she reached for another. "Before the Inuit there were just the Paleo-Indians," she said. Which would make him at least six thousand years old. "You're telling me you used to live with the Paleo-Indians?"

He shook his head. "Nah. Before them. What did they have before them?" He turned to look at Powell, who was sucking on a bleeding thumb. "Remember, we talked about this once? The first people up here. The first ones who could talk."

Powell pressed his lips together as if stifling a laugh. He glanced at Chey and rolled his eyes. "Nowadays we would call them Neanderthals."

Eventually they had three decent axes. Dzo's was the best, the blade thin and tapering to a slick edge. The stone he'd used was flecked with mica and streaked with darker stone. It looked like a real tool when he'd lashed it firmly to a handle as thick as his thumb. Chey's ax looked more like a rock tied to a twig. She was at least pleased to see that Powell hadn't done much better than she had.

The next step was to take down some trees. Chey was enough of a twenty-first-century eco-liberal to feel real guilt at chopping down any growing thing, but she knew they needed the wood if they were going to build themselves a house. She picked a thin sapling that was kind of dead on one side, figuring she could put it out of its misery. Then she took a good stance, brought her ax up like a baseball bat, and brought it swinging down toward the tree's trunk in a perfect arc.

The head of her ax collided with the tree trunk—and tore out of its lashings. It spun away from her and bounced off another tree before crashing into a pile of dead leaves. She was left holding a broken stick.

She looked around quickly to see if Powell had seen that. He was facing away from her, so maybe he hadn't. He was smashing away at his own tree, a big old larch so thick he wouldn't have been able to get his fingers around the trunk. So far he'd managed to make a tiny dent in the bark.

Forcing herself not to curse or even sigh, she went to find the ax head so she could re-lash it to her stick.

8.

By nightfall they had, between the three of them, brought down two trees and started to strip off the branches. Dzo assured them that wasn't a bad showing for stone ax work, and that they could be proud of themselves.

Powell muttered something under his breath that didn't sound as if he was very pleased with himself.

The work had been hard. Chey's muscles were tight and sore. She hadn't got as tired as she'd expected, though she had built up a pretty nasty sweat. She stripped off her clothes—both men had seen her naked plenty of times before, so she didn't bother with modesty—and ran down to the lake to jump in and wash herself off. The water was frigid and she started shivering instantly, but it felt so good that she didn't care.

She ducked her head under and scrubbed out her hair, then surfaced and started swimming slow circles around the water, just stretching out her muscles, letting the soreness and stiffness of the day ease away. Eventually even her supernaturally tough body started to get really chilled, so she swam back to shore. The bottom was jagged with small rocks and she picked her way carefully along toward a place where the shore didn't look too muddy.

A noise from up on the eroded bank startled her and she spun around, splashing. It had sounded like someone stepping on a twig.

Her first reaction was to cover her breasts with her arms. She looked up at the shore but couldn't see anyone there—it was a jutting outcrop of mud that leaned over the water, an eroded bank thickly overgrown with small evergreens. "Powell?" she called. "Is that you?"

There was no reply, but she saw branches up there moving, as if someone were stepping back into the shadows.

"Did you want to come swimming with me? Or maybe you're just being a gentleman and bringing me my clothes," she said, laughing. Still there was no reply. She stared into the clump of trees, trying desperately to see him up there, but it was getting dark. The last blue light of the day was lying in great ragged sheets on the water and she could already see stars overhead.

Was Powell spying on her? Was he watching her, too embarrassed to say anything?

She looked straight into the trees, as if she could see him plainly, and lowered her arms, exposing her breasts. Then she took a long stride toward the water's edge, straight toward him. As she came closer the water got shallower and she could feel water streaming from her hips and belly. If he wanted a good look, she would give him one.

It was a dangerous game she was playing, she knew. Feeling very wicked, she reached up and laced her fingers behind her neck, then slowly, sinuously, arched her back.

From the tree line came the smallest of sounds. The noise of someone delicately adjusting their weight.

Like a wolf, she pounced, leaping up the side of the muddy bank, grabbing wildly at tree branches to haul herself up. She would pounce on him, she thought, laughing, pin him down to the ground and—and then—she would tickle him, yeah, until he begged for mercy.

But when she rushed into the little stand of trees, her eyes flashing, there was nobody there. She reached down and patted the ground and found that it was still slightly warm, as if someone had been crouching there for a while, but there was no other sign of anybody having been there.

"Lousy jerk," she said, mock-pouting.

She found her clothes where she'd left them, in a heap near the camp, and put them on hurriedly. Dzo had a pretty good fire going by the time she arrived, made out of the branches they'd stripped off their two paltry logs. Powell was crouched on the far side of the blaze, roasting a squirrel on a long stick. Dzo had some roots and berries mashed up in a cooking pot—where he'd got that she had no clue, maybe he'd had it the whole time hidden away in the bulk of his heavy furs—and was making his own nasty dinner, since he was a vegetarian.

She walked up to the fire and let it steam the water out of her damp hair. "Come clean," she said to Powell. "Did I catch you peeping back there, or what?"

"What are you on about?" he asked.

"Back by the water. Was that you in the trees?"

He frowned and shook his head. "I've been right here the whole time. With Dzo."

Dzo looked up from his cookery and nodded. "I saw him catch that varmint. It was gross, the way he snapped its neck."

"It was humane," Powell insisted.

Neither of them seemed very concerned that she'd seen someone down by the water. Then again, she told herself, she hadn't seen anyone either. She'd just heard something. It could very well have been an animal. She blushed a little to think she'd just given Bambi a free show.

Embarrassed now herself, she reached across the fire and grabbed the squirrel off Powell's stick. "You're going to burn that," she said, and tore off a piece of meat, still a little bloody, to shove it in her mouth.

9

In Toronto there was a very exclusive club, a little place above a bookshop. The club did not advertise. It had no sign out front and no one watching its door. To get in you had to possess a key that fit into the lock of a cheap metal fire door with cracked gray paint.

The rooms beyond that door were sumptuously appointed in dark, polished wood and green leather. Gathered around roaring fires were massive armchairs where members of the club could doze all day if they wished, or smoke cigars, or drink single malts carried to them on silver platters by servants dressed in livery. For those who didn't drink, coffee or bottled water were cheerfully provided. No music played and no newspapers were allowed inside. There were certainly no televisions permitted anywhere on the premises.

Beyond the open common rooms out front there were a few private rooms, small, cozy spaces containing little more than a table and a few chairs. There was a bedroom for anyone who'd had a few too many tumblers of whisky. And that was all.

The club's dues were fifty thousand dollars a year. Most of that money went to a private security firm, which routinely swept for listening devices and subjected every member and employee to a rigorous background check. The hushed conversations taking place around the roaring fires were of the kind that were not meant for too many ears. The club provided seamless, invisible discretion of a kind the twenty-first century was all too short of.

In one of the private rooms at the back of the club, a man named Preston Holness sat waiting to have just such a conversation.

Holness worked, technically, for the Canadian Security Intelligence

Service, the governmental organization responsible for identifying and neutralizing threats at home and abroad. He was what was called, in his line of work, an undeclared asset. This status meant he could operate with a certain degree of latitude that more public figures did not enjoy.

Enjoy was probably the wrong word. Holness did not sleep well at night. He did things, for a living, that the Canadian government tended to deplore and condemn in public. Should he be caught doing them he would be disavowed, the government denying all knowledge of his activities. He would probably go to jail for the rest of his life. He was expected to take this in his stride, but in fact it had given him ulcers.

And this meeting might just give him a coronary, he thought. He did not expect it to go well. He had prepared for it carefully. He'd had a manicure and a haircut, and he had dressed in his best Armani suit and silk Hermès tie. His shoes, which could not be seen under the table, were worth more than a thousand dollars.

Holness liked to dress well. It was a passion, one that made him feel good about himself and gave him a certain amount of confidence in an uneasy world. Still, when he heard a knock at the door, he jumped in his seat.

The door opened silently and a young man stepped through. He was perhaps half of Holness's age, with whitish blond hair and a pair of wire-framed glasses with rectangular lenses. His suit was made of silk. Holness didn't recognize the cut, but he knew quality haberdashery when he saw it. The young man looked like a very sharp, very tough lawyer, which he probably was.

"Hello," the young man said. "My name is Demetrios."

It was not his real name, of course. "Demetrios" was a code name used by a certain oil company that did business with the Canadian government. A lot of business. The company pumped billions of dollars and thousands of jobs into the Canadian economy every year. That meant the government wanted to keep this young man happy, no matter what the cost.

Things were already off on the wrong foot.

Demetrios's company had bought up a parcel of land in the Arctic, beneath which lay one of the largest oil deposits in the Western hemisphere. Before they could start exploiting the deposit, however, the lycanthropes had moved in. Now work crews couldn't be sent in to drill, because the lycanthropes would just kill and eat them. The CSIS had been given the task of removing the lycanthropes, and in this they had failed. If Demetrios wanted someone to blame for that failure, it was Holness's head on the chopping block.

Holness guided Demetrios to a seat on the far side of the table before sitting back down. "I'd really like to apologize on behalf of—"

"Robert Fenech fucked up," Demetrios said.

"Fenech is dead." Holness frowned in mock compassion. "He will be missed. He was a true patriot, and an excellent operative."

"He was a pathetic little boy, who thought he was James Bond." Demetrios folded his arms in front of him. "You should never have sent him on this mission. We asked for something very simple. There was one lycanthrope you needed to kill."

"Not an easy task, under any conditions," Holness said. "And given the lycanthrope's location—the country up there in the Northwest Territories is notoriously treacherous, even in good weather . . ." He gave Demetrios a little smile and spread his hands in resignation.

"You could have sent in troops to do the job properly. Instead you sent in a subcontractor and a civilian. The civilian was infected by the lycanthrope. Now there are two of them for us to worry about."

Holness couldn't deny that. He could only try to explain himself. "It was felt, at the time, that sending in troops would be too great a risk. Public opinion is already so divided about the wars in the Middle East. If we sent in our boys and some of them got killed—well, the prime minister is going to have a hard enough time getting re-elected already. He doesn't need that kind of bad press."

Demetrios fumed in silence for a minute. Then he leaned forward and spoke very slowly and very carefully, as if he thought Holness might have trouble understanding him. "We like Canada."

Holness smiled. "We aim to please," he said.

Demetrios shook his head. "We like Canada because we like doing business with civilized people. We would very much like to keep our business here. But I can assure you there are other oil deposits, in Venezuela, in Iraq, in Indonesia. Places we could learn to love, if only because there are no lycanthropes there. Now, if we have to resort to moving our business out of this country a significant part of your nation's gross domestic product will evaporate overnight. So it seems you and I have a mutual problem. So far I haven't heard of any possible solutions."

Holness fought down the urge to adjust his tie. He had one card left to play. "I have someone in the field right now," he said.

Demetrios didn't smile. He didn't look like the kind of man who ever did. But his posture changed, he relaxed a fraction of a degree, and he nodded in such a way as to suggest he was willing to listen.

"Let me tell you about a man named Varkanin." He reached down into his briefcase to take out the blue-skinned Russian's dossier. "I think you'll be pleased."

Demetrios leaned forward to see the photograph stapled to the front of the file folder. Holness couldn't help but notice the way the younger man's suit draped as he moved.

"Do you mind my asking?" Holness said. "Is that Dolce and Gabbana?"

Demetrios plucked at his own sleeve. "Savile Row. I have them made custom."

"It's . . . gorgeous," Holness said. "If this all works out, maybe you'll give me the name of your tailor."

"Don't get ahead of yourself," Demetrios told him.

10.

The temperature started to drop even before they'd finished their paltry dinner. The air got crisp and thin and suddenly Chey was hugging herself, pulling her parka closer around her. It was the first time in a while she remembered being truly cold.

It got dark in the little camp, too, even with the fire's embers popping and flickering merrily away. Exhausted by the day's labors, Dzo curled up near the ashes and pulled his wooden mask down over his face. In a moment he was snoring, a discordant rhythm of wheezes and grunts that made Chey laugh.

She was tired, herself, but there was no point in going to sleep now. In a few hours the moon would rise. She never liked going to sleep as a human and waking up naked and sore in a snowbank—if she was going to transform into a wolf, she preferred to be prepared. So she rose stiffly from her place by the fire and brushed off the seat of her pants, thinking she would have an easier time staying awake if she was at least standing up. Powell was staring into the coals, toying with a splinter of wood in his hands, tearing off fibrous chunks of it and throwing them into the dying light. Chey cleared her throat until he looked up, then gestured with a nod of her head toward a nearby copse of trees.

"You don't need to let me know that you're going off to heed the call of nature," he said.

She sighed dramatically. "I'm taking a walk," she told him. "I'd like your company, if you don't mind."

He muttered in frustration, but eventually he got up and followed her. They headed into the near-perfect darkness of the trees, lit only sporadically by a ray of starlight that managed to wind its way down through the sparse branches of the pines. "I wanted to tell you about something that happened earlier. I guess I was too embarrassed to say it in front of Dzo," she said, her voice startlingly loud in the otherwise flawless silence. She grabbed a branch of a birch tree and pulled at it until the entire tree swayed, then sighed again before telling him about how she'd thought she was being watched when she took her bath.

"You're probably right," he said, when she'd finished. She could just see the white plume of his breath streaming out away from him with each word. "Just an animal. I haven't seen any trace of people in this area. If I had, we would already be moving again."

"I know. I just figured it was the kind of thing I should share."

She could barely make out his silhouette nodding in agreement. "That's good. Good thinking." He took a step closer to her and without warning he was touching her face. She started to flinch away and she felt him tense up. It could have ended there.

Instead she forced herself to relax, then leaned into his touch.

His fingers traced the curve of her cheek. Brushed her temple. They were quite warm, which was nice in the cold night. Very nice.

"You were giving me a show, hmm?" he asked.

"What?"

"In the water. When you thought I was watching you."

"It felt like the right thing to do at the time." She reached up and took his hand off her face. But she held onto it, inside her own. His hand was rough with work and very large, the fingers thick and square at the tips. She couldn't remember ever holding it before. "Now I'm not . . . sure."

"You're not?" he asked. "You've been acting so strangely," he said. "Are you alright? It's just—"

"I'm attracted to you," she told him. "Lord knows I have plenty of reasons not to be." She felt her face harden in bitterness. "You made me what I am today. You killed my father. You hurt me, and gave me your curse in the process. I wouldn't be here right now, having this conversation, if you hadn't fucked up my life so badly."

"That was my wolf, not me."

"And sometimes I can believe in the difference."

He dropped his head. "When we're just human again. After we find the cure—"

"What exactly would that change, even if it was possible? We'll still be us. Just all the time. I like you, Powell. That's the hardest part of this. I think if I could hate your guts, really detest you, it would be a lot easier to let you touch me. Things would be less complicated. As it is I keep second-guessing myself."

He pulled his hand away from hers. "Don't," he said.

She was confused. "Huh?" she asked. Her breath came out in a broad pale cloud as her question crystallized in the air before her.

"Don't toy with me," he told her. He sounded a little angry, she thought. "If you want to be with me in . . . that way, then fine. You know I have no objections."

She pressed a hand over her mouth to keep from laughing. *In that way? No objections?* Sometimes she forgot how old he really was, and how old-fashioned. What a prude he could be.

"But if you're going to change your mind halfway through, don't even start."

Jesus, she thought. He was more sensitive than she'd been willing to believe. He had actual feelings, even if he rarely let them show. It was making him a little stupid, she thought. If he'd been another kind of man— the kind she'd known far too often, the same kind as every lover she'd ever had—this would be easy. Her flirting would be enough of a signal. He would have taken what he wanted. And the force of his desire would be enough to melt through any doubts she might have. For a while, at least.

"Are you seriously going to wait for me to make the first move?" she asked.

"I've never been any good at this," he grumbled. He turned away from her and took a step back toward camp. "I was a virgin when I got this curse. Since then every woman I've ever been with has initiated things. Chey, you should know something." He turned back to face her and she could see starlight glinting in his eyes. "I haven't had . . . relations with a woman since nineteen fifty-four."

If she said anything in response she thought she might crack up laughing, and she knew he would take that the wrong way. So she kept her mouth shut.

"I imagine I remember how. But the rest of this, the game we're playing, the little courtesies I'm supposed to make, *gah!*" She heard a nasty snap and realized he must have broken a branch off of a tree. "Am I supposed to bring you posies of wildflowers now? Are we supposed to dance under the aurora borealis? I don't know how it's done. I want you. I do know that much. But you have to tell me what you want."

"Okay," she managed to say. "When—if—the time comes. I'll make sure you know."

He turned and strode away from her, as if she'd frightened him off. She followed him back to camp more slowly, taking her time.

They didn't so much as look at each other again before the moon rose and silver light scrubbed away their confusion.

11.

The wolves might have settled the question. There were no moral conflicts in their streamlined minds, no doubts in their legs and their stretching muscles. The ineluctable pleasure of transformation gripped them both and they circled each other hungrily, wanting, desiring, nothing more.

Except—

There was a distraction. The female wolf couldn't place it at first, but she could see in the male's eyes that he was suddenly alert, suddenly very much on his guard. His hackles slicked back and his ears stood up very rigid.

Slowly, cautious not to make a sound, she turned to look about her. To smell the world, the best way she knew to identify threats. Her long lungs drew in the air, her sensitive snout decoding every molecule that streamed in through her skull. Her nostrils were specially designed for this, with flaps that slammed closed on every indrawn breath, trapping the scents inside her where they could be analyzed and logged.

The world had frozen since last she'd stood on four legs, that much was evident at once. The ground here was hard with permafrost all year round, frozen down to a depth of several feet, but since the moon last rose the ice had gone deeper, the groundwater hardening in long sharp crystals pointed like arrows at the planet's core. The trees were creaking and groaning with the extra weight of frost.

Next she caught a human scent, that most hated of stenches. In an abstract way she understood she was smelling her own human form, and that of the male. But there was something else, something human she could not identify. It wasn't the musquash spirit, either. The fur-covered, wooden-masked enigma lay by the remains of a fire, as inscrutable to her nose as to her brain. She'd never understood what he was, but she'd never needed to, either. He was a familiar presence, a friendly one.

No, the smell she had picked up belonged to a stranger. Which worried her very much.

The male nudged her side with his nose. He lifted his head and together they padded silently around the camp, their snouts dipping to the ground time and again. There were trails of scent all around them, circling them again and again. The stranger had been close all day, it seemed, but their stupid human bodies had lacked the necessary senses to detect it. Its footprints positively glowed in their brains, lighting up danger signals, triggering little jolts of adrenaline every time they found a new sign.

The wolves had never been afraid of something human before. Human things were to be hated, to be destroyed with a vicious bloodlust whenever they were encountered. But the presence of this human was different, somehow.

For one thing, its trail circled the camp three times and then—vanished. There was no sign of the human left nearby, but nor was there any sign of its leaving. No trail led away from the camp. Where was it?

The male started panting then. He turned in quick circles, spinning around to see in every direction at once. The female knew that could mean nothing good, but she couldn't detect what had agitated him so.

With a yelp he dashed away from the camp, into the trees. She could only follow.

Their legs pistoned at the hard ground, launching them from one solid footing to the next. Their tongues lapped at the air, dragging oxygen deep into their lungs, making their blood fizz and run fast. He was running at full clip now, as fast as his body could go, and it was all she could do to keep up with him as they wove their way through the trees, slipping around tree trunks so close that their fur stripped off pieces of fragile bark, ducking under low branches that chimed with cracking ice crystals.

They came to a clearing and he stopped suddenly, his four legs digging deep into the resisting earth. She didn't manage to stop in time and ended up skidding, her claws snatching at thin tree roots and small stones frozen stiff to the ground. Her hindquarters swung out and she came to a stop half facing him, squatting low to keep her balance.

He wasn't even looking at her. Sitting up with his forelegs very straight, he lifted his head high in the air and howled.

It was the same strangled yelping howl, desperate and sad and lonely and frightened, that he had given the last time they'd been out together beneath the moon. Only this time it was redoubled in strength, so loud it shook the branches of the trees, drawn out and long and more painful, more plaintive.

And this time, it was answered.

The call that came back was very similar to his own, a piercing wail trailing off into small yelps, but the emotion behind it was different. His howl was the cry of a being in distress, torn apart by feelings it could not contain.

The answer was almost joyous, and the crescendo of yelps that ended it sounded like cruel laughter, almost like mocking bells hung up high in the air.

At the sound, he was off again, his tail straight out behind him as he ran. She followed once more. Because she didn't know what else to do.

They were a pack of two. They were a family, and more than a family. They were hunters who relied totally on one another for their survival, two beings joined inseparably. But now—but now—he wasn't looking at her. He didn't even seem aware of her. He was like a creature possessed.

She followed. And when he stopped again, she was ready this time. She dropped to the ground just as he planted his legs, her muzzle tight against the frozen earth, her eyes looking up and around.

The trees had given way to a rise in the earth, a slope too gradual to call a hill but too high to be just a rough patch of the forest floor. Ahead of them, just outside of striking range, a sloping ridge of broken rock stuck up from its summit like a stone finger pointing at the Northern star.

Atop it stood a wolf, not a timber wolf but a dire wolf like them. Her white fur shone like cold fire as a narrow crescent of moon rode over her back like a celestial crown. Her eyes were in silhouette but her ears and tail stood up, the latter waving slowly back and forth, now to one side, now the other. She made no sound at all, barely stirred the air around her.

She licked her jowls and let loose the call again. And this time there could be no doubt. She was laughing. In triumph.

12.

Harsh red light streamed in through Chey's eyelids. She whimpered because her body hurt so much. What had her wolf been doing? She felt like she'd run a marathon.

At least she wasn't so cold anymore. She remembered how cold it had been the night before, just before the moon rose. It felt like the chill had lifted a little. It also helped that someone was snuggled up against her, spooning her from behind. That would be Powell, she thought. His arm was wrapped around her, holding her close, and his face was buried in the nape of her neck. It was unbelievably comforting to have him so close, as long as she didn't think about what it meant.

Then she felt his erection poking her in the back.

Her immediate reaction was to pull away, to get away from him as quickly as possible. But he was so warm, and his arm felt so good around her. And she had to admit she was tempted. Her wolf had been turned on, she could feel. Normally she remembered nothing of what it had thought or done when she was away, but sometimes she picked up on subtler things. Its emotional state, the raw open needs and wants and hatreds it felt. At that moment she could still feel the wolf's lust burning in her human veins. There was a dampness between her legs she couldn't deny.

And if she just shifted up a few centimeters, if she hitched her hips up and pressed back just a little, she could scratch that itch. Once it went that far, well—there weren't many more obvious ways to make the first move.

It would end the confusion between them, the tortured wondering and the constant feints back and forth. It would make so many things easier. And all she had to do was wiggle her butt a little.

Did she actually want it, she wondered? Or was she just ridiculously horny? The question seemed more academic the more she thought about it. Slowly, making no noise so she didn't wake him too soon, she started to squirm backward.

It would be a decision she couldn't unmake. But even if it was the wrong decision, that was maybe better than making no decision at all.

He sighed in his sleep. Happily. Yes. He would go along with this. Once he woke and found himself making love to her, he wasn't about to stop and demand to know what she thought she was doing. He would grab her, pull her close. Give in. He wanted this as much as she did, she knew, he would—

—There was someone looming over her, she suddenly realized. The two of them were not alone. She opened her eyes and looked up, saying, "Dzo? You've got lousy timing, buddy."

Except it wasn't Dzo. She just had time to see a snarling face, a pale naked human body. White hands reached down and grabbed Chey's hair, hauling her roughly away from Powell.

13

The stranger dragged Chey up to her feet and then shoved her forward, kicking her at the same time in the back of her left knee so she stumbled as she lurched toward a tree trunk a few feet away. Chey threw her arms up to protect herself as the tree loomed large before her. A broken-off stub of a branch, its end jagged and rough, came flying up toward her eyes as she tried desperately to get her balance back. She just managed to throw her head to one side as her chest collided with the trunk.

The breath was knocked right out of her. Chey saw spots swim in her vision and her ears rang with the force of the collision.

Had she still been human, that would have been the end. Instead she reached deep inside herself and found a growling roar there that vibrated through every cell in her body. It gave her strength to pivot sharply around so she could face her opponent, legs bent in a fighting crouch, hands up to counterattack.

It was a woman who had attacked her, a pale, slender woman with long red hair and a face contorted by rage. She was just as naked as Chey was, but she held a rock as big as her head in both hands. She brought it up high and then hauled it back, crashing down, aimed right at Chey's forehead.

Chey batted it out of her hands like it was a beach ball. She listened to it thud off the ground to her left, but never took her eyes off the other woman's face. She had no idea who this person was, or where she'd come from, or why she was naked, but none of that mattered. Something very old and strong and wild was filling her up, so big it felt like it was stretching out her skin. She opened her mouth to shout a question, but all that came out was a vicious snarl.

The redhead leaned hard to one side and aimed a kick at Chey's stomach. Chey grabbed the foot as it came slicing toward her and twisted, hard. The other woman grunted in pain and dropped to the soft covering of dead pine needles on the ground. Chey jumped on top of her and started punching her face and neck, with her right fist and then her left, over and over.

Spitting with rage, the redhead brought her knees up hard into Chey's chest and shoved her loose. Rolling to her knees, she grabbed for Chey's hair again. Chey reared back to avoid the snatching fingers.

It was a bad mistake. It left her throat vulnerable. The redhead jabbed hard at her windpipe and suddenly Chey couldn't breathe. She managed to scramble up to her feet and stagger away, but instantly her overworked muscles started demanding more air, air she couldn't get down her throat.

Her vision started to go dark as the other woman grabbed her from behind, pulling Chey's arms behind her and locking them there. Chey could only struggle feebly against the hold. Moving fast, the redhead marched her down the slope toward the water, and it was all Chey could do to keep her feet underneath her as they accelerated downhill.

Then the water hit her face and her body spasmed in terror. Water streamed up her nose and filled her mouth as she tried desperately to take a breath that just wouldn't come. Bubbles clouded her vision. The redhead shoved down hard on the back of Chey's head and pressed it into the rocky mud bottom of the lake. She wasn't even bothering to hold onto Chey's arms anymore, but it didn't matter. The fight, the animal anger that had given her such strength, was gone, whimpering in terror as her body signaled again and again that she was about to die.

She couldn't see, smell, or hear anything. Her tactile sense started draining away as well. It felt almost like no one was touching her anymore, as if the redhead had relented and walked away, leaving her for dead.

Then a new pair of hands grabbed her shoulders. Male hands, heavy and rough, with none of the supernatural strength the redhead had possessed.

The fingers dug deep under her armpits, then strained to heave her up, out of the muck.

Chey was rolled over on her back. She still couldn't see anything, but she could hear someone calling her name. Hands pressed down hard on her stomach and she vomited up lake water and mud that splattered all over her chest and face. When it was out of her, air surged back in and her lungs erupted in chilly fire as she took a breath for the first time in far too long.

She could do nothing at first but lie there and let life flood back through her sore limbs. Eventually she mustered the strength to reach up and wipe the mud out of her eyes. Dzo was staring down at her, his face open in terror.

"Do you need the kiss of life?" he asked, looking horrified at the prospect.

"I'm . . . okay," she croaked. It felt like a lie, but she knew that in a few minutes it would be true. Her body was a lot tougher now than it looked. Slowly—because even the simplest, smoothest motion was a jarring agony—she sat up and looked around her. She saw the redhead right away, standing a few meters apart with a look of deep concern and sympathy on her face. That made no sense. Even worse, she was wearing Powell's heavy wool coat like a dress, leaving the top button undone to show off some ample cleavage.

Powell stood to one side but between the two of them, as if ready to step in if they attacked each other again. He was buttoning up his own flannel shirt and already had his pants on.

Which left Chey the only one who was still naked. And hurt. And covered in mud, slime, pine needles, and dead leaves. She must look like hell, she thought.

The redhead walked over to peer down at her. Powell flinched, but he made no move to stop the stranger from bending down to place the back of one slender hand against Chey's cheek.

Chey considered grabbing that hand and breaking every dainty little bone in the redhead's wrist, but she didn't know if she had the strength for it.

"*Cherie,* you must accept my apologies," the redhead said, in a soft, cooing voice that probably made boys melt. "I am so very, very regretful that I attacked you. I didn't know you were one of us. I saw you there, oh! And I think, all at once I think, she is hurting my man."

"Powell," Chey mewled, "who the fuck is this?"

"Um," he said, as if unsure how to answer.

"Pardon, please," the redhead said. "I am Lucie. I am his wife."

14.

"No, of course we aren't really married!" Powell muttered. "She just likes to say that. To—to hurt me, to—"

"To fuck with your head," Chey supplied.

He glared at her obscenity but then shrugged and nodded. "Sometimes your foul mouth manages to say things we didn't have proper words for in my day," he conceded. "Yes. Indeed. To . . . fuck with my head."

They were whispering together, back at the camp, while Dzo and Lucie chopped industriously away at a tree down by the water. The redhead and the . . . whatever the hell Dzo was were making a lot of noise and talking a blue streak. Every so often Chey could hear Lucie laugh, a fluttery little pretty sound that made Chey's spine ache. There was no way Lucie could hear what they were saying, but still they kept their voices down.

Chey knew a little about Lucie already. Powell had told her something of the history he shared with the redhead before. Lucie, Chey knew, was the werewolf who had given the curse to Powell back during the First World War. She was several centuries old and batshit insane. She had trapped him in a silver cage, then transformed while he watched—and in the process she had scratched him, while making sure he survived long enough to see the moon rise with her the following night. At the time Lucie had been living in France with another werewolf, whom Chey had only ever heard referred to as the Baroness de Clichy-sous-Vallée. The two of them had kidnapped and cursed Powell because they wanted a mate.

He had, by his own account, served them both in that capacity with some distinction.

"The Baroness isn't going to show up next, is she?" Chey asked.

"No," Powell said, with definite finality. "She won't."

"I thought you got away from Lucie, back in nineteen twenty-one," Chey went on, because clearly he wasn't going to elaborate. "That's what you told me."

"I did. Then she found me again, in the Thirties. We had a very unpleasant reunion in Manitoba back then. We fought—I mean, we spoke harshly to one another—and she disappeared again, and I assumed I was quit of her. Then every few decades after that she would show up again. Sometimes things were almost cordial, but always, eventually, she would get bored or annoyed with me and leave without warning, and I was always glad to see her go. It's been a long time since I saw her, though, and I certainly wasn't expecting her now. I wasn't even sure she was still alive. Wherever she goes she has a habit of convincing villagers that it's time to get out the torches and pitchforks. That's one reason I broke things off with her."

Chey thought of something. "She was Miss Nineteen Fifty-four, wasn't she?"

He looked away from her. "I don't know what you're talking about."

Chey laughed bitterly. "The woman you had, uh, ah, intimate, er, relations with the last time," she said, mocking him.

"I don't need to stand here being quizzed about my love life," Powell told her. Though he made no move to walk away from her. If he did that he would probably have to go talk to Lucie instead.

Chey leaned back against a tree and rubbed at her throat. Her crushed windpipe had healed just fine but it still hurt a little. That had been a nasty punch Lucie had given her. She did not relish the prospect of fighting the redheaded werewolf again, but she would if she had to. "So what are your intentions?" Chey asked.

"What?"

Chey scowled. "Are you going to shack up with her again, now that she's back? Throw me aside in exchange for the sure thing?"

Powell kicked at the dirt. "Damn you, Chey, there's more going on here than this silly little game you and I are playing."

Chey winced. Surely he had just spoken thoughtlessly, she told herself.

"I don't even know what she wants, this time," he went on.

"Have you tried asking her?"

It was his turn to laugh. "Sure. We can try that."

"You don't think she'll tell us the truth?"

Powell shook his head. "With Lucie it's not a question of truth or lies. She isn't sane enough to understand the difference."

15.

"Take a break, Dzo," Powell said.

The spirit looked up and shrugged.

"Okey-dokey," he said, and swung his axe over his shoulder before marching off into the woods.

No one watched him go.

Chey had always considered herself attractive, and she'd never had any problem getting men to pay attention to her. She had an athletic body and a cute upturned nose. Her brown hair fell a little past her ears, a practical cut for life in the woods that didn't need a lot of maintenance to look good.

Lucie, on the other hand, was some kind of goddess. She looked like she was nineteen years old and her creamy skin was flawless, untouched even by freckles. Her red hair fell in cascading waves around her shoulders and showed no sign of the fact that she was hundreds of kilometers from the nearest beauty salon. Powell's shapeless wool coat managed to hug her curves fetchingly, falling to mid-thigh like a short kimono. She was smiling warmly and her eyes twinkled with merry intelligence. Usually when Chey met a beautiful woman, a woman more attractive than herself, her first thought was that they must be dumb as a stump. That nobody could look that good and actually be able to glance away from a mirror long enough to have an original thought. The look in those eyes told her otherwise.

Chey wanted to hurt her. Badly.

Powell cleared his throat before either of them could speak. Chey stopped where she was and realized that she'd been circling the other woman. The way a wolf circles an animal while trying to decide if it's prey or a threat. She folded her arms across her chest and looked down the hill, toward the water, even though the sunlight off the lake was dazzling enough to hurt her eyes.

"Lucie," Powell began, "it's been a long time. I don't think I expected to see you again."

Lucie laughed politely, as if he'd made a joke. "My dear," she said, "we may be separated by time or fate. But you and I shall never part forever. Haven't you learned this simple thing, yet? We're bound, you and I."

Powell waved a hand in the air, dismissing what she'd said. Or at least tabling it for further discussion. Chey, for one, fully intended to explore that subject.

"Maybe you could tell me what you're doing here," Powell said. "I mean, why you're here right now."

"Is it such a mystery? The whole world, he knows your story this time. I was living in Russia, being very good, as you asked me to be the last time we spoke. Keeping to myself, minding first my own business, yes? Do you remember when you asked this of me?"

"I remember," Powell said.

"Russia—Siberia—was such a dismal place, but it was lonely. The kind of lonely place you like. I was hoping, truly, that you would come to me this time. That we could be a family again. I kept watching the trees for you to emerge, dear. Kept listening at night for the sound of your whistling—ah." She turned to face Chey, who quickly looked away. "Cheyenne," she said, making Chey's name sound like "chain," but in an irritatingly lilting French accent, "do you know this habit of my husband? How he whistles to himself old songs, when he thinks no one can hear?"

Chey frowned. "No. I can't say I've ever caught him . . . whistling." The Powell she'd always known didn't seem the type. Most of the time he was far too miserable.

"Ah, perhaps someday you will hear this sound, you will look up from what you are doing and you will think, he is coming home."

"Lucie," Powell warned. "You're getting off track."

"Am I? How like me that is. I am ever the dreamer. As I said, I was living in Siberia, with no one there to talk to. I happened across a newspaper left by some wandering woodsman and I read about the werewolf attacks in Canada. Five dead. Who else could this be, I thought, but my Monty? So I came at once, thinking you are in trouble. That you should not be alone at this dangerous time. I did not know you had found another lover to replace me."

"She's not—she—" Powell ran one hand through his hair. "Chey and I did just fine on our own. We didn't need your help then, and we don't need it now," he said.

"Chain," Lucie said, turning to Chey again, as if for aid, "do you agree with him? Are the two of you truly safe?"

"I get to talk now?" Chey asked.

Powell shrugged.

"First off, don't call me Chain. Call me Chey."

Lucie smiled prettily. "If you like, Shy."

Chey rolled her eyes. "Powell's told me all about you, Lucie," she said. "There's no need to spin this line of bullshit about listening for his whistle and staying out of trouble. I know what you are. You're a murdering sociopath of a werewolf. For some reason you got this idea that Powell owes you something. That's crap. You kidnapped him during the war and turned him into a monster. He's spent the last hundred years running away from all human contact because of what you did to him."

Lucie's face was as innocent as clean sheets on a motel room bed. Her lower lip quivered a little, as if Chey had truly injured her, and she glanced at Powell as if looking for sympathy. He didn't provide it, though his shoulders did slump a little as if he were melting.

"Well," she said, very softly. "I suppose this is deserved, this hurt. But I will point out—he did the same to you."

"Totally different. I came hunting for him, came into his territory when the moon was up. It was my fault. He actually tried to save me after he realized what he'd done, when he was human again, but it was too late. He's a good person."

She glanced at Powell. He was watching Lucie as if she might attack at any moment.

"You are not. I want you to answer one question, I want an honest answer, and then I'm going to ask you to leave. To leave us alone. Okay?"

Lucie lowered her eyes demurely. She wasn't going to crack any time soon, Chey saw. She would keep up the act no matter how rude Chey got. Damn. "What is your question?" Lucie asked. "I will try to answer it, if I can."

"You said, back when we were first introduced—you said you were Powell's wife. What exactly did you mean by that? Was there a ceremony? A ring?"

"Oh, for the love of Mike," Powell said, throwing his hands up.

"A ring of gold?" Lucie asked. Her face grew wistful as she looked across at Powell. "No . . . he never gave to me a ring. And wisely so, really. For it would only fall away every time I changed. Silly me, I would lose it, again and again, I am sure. And no, there was no church, no happy families watching. No priest, certainly, ever spoke words over us. Ours was a secret marriage, a marriage of the forest and the moon. An unspoken ceremony."

"Where I come from, we call that shacking up," Chey said. "So you were never married. You can't call yourself his wife. You have no right to him."

"We are wolves," Lucie said, as if that explained everything. When Chey just stared at her, she added, "Wolves mate for life. Did you not know that? Only death can part them."

"Wolves have a life expectancy of six to ten years," Powell said. It sounded like he'd said it to her before.

"You want me to go. I suppose I must," Lucie said. "Will you be so kind as to let me eat among you, before I head back into the wastes?"

Chey opened her mouth to say no, but Powell grabbed Lucie's arm before she could speak. "Lucie. Tell me the truth now. Why are you here?"

"I have said already," Lucie whimpered. She glanced down at Powell's hand as if he was hurting her. Powell didn't let go.

"Why did you come?" Powell asked again. "You've never shown up before unless you needed something from me. Or unless you were running away from something. That's it, isn't it? Things got too hot for you in Russia?"

Lucie threw her head back and sighed deeply. "A man. A hunter. He wanted my pelt."

"Uh-huh. An ordinary, everyday hunter. Who you couldn't handle."

"He was more tenacious than most. More committed to the hunt."

Powell nodded. "Okay. Now we're getting somewhere. Let me guess. You did something to this hunter, right?"

"Yes," Lucie admitted.

"You hurt him, bad. Oh, not physically—or he'd be one of us. Or dead. No. You—you fucked with his head one time too many, as Chey would put it." Powell looked like he'd heard this story before.

"Perhaps," Lucie said. "Perhaps a little."

16.

Preston Holness stared out the window of a seaplane as it skimmed just above the tree tops, looking for any sign of human life. "There," Holness said, when he spotted the cheery orange glow of a campfire in a clearing a little to the south. The clearing let out onto a long thin glacial lake that would make a perfect landing strip for the plane. The pilot nodded and nudged his stick to bring them around for a closer approach.

Almost before the plane had skidded to a stop on the water, Holness leapt out of its side hatch and stomped through knee-deep water toward the shore. He was wearing technical snow pants of the kind you could buy in a Toronto department store and were guaranteed against temperatures well below freezing, but the instant the water soaked through his shoes he knew he'd made a bad mistake. They were top-of-the-line Rockport hiking shoes, designed to let his feet breathe. They were not in the slightest bit waterproof.

Hopping and cursing, he headed up into the clearing, toward the fire. If he didn't get his feet warm soon he would risk losing some toes. Which, while it might make for a good story to tell back at the club, would not help him with the ladies.

The blue man sitting by the fire jumped up and brought him a dry towel. He didn't look surprised to see Holness there. "Varkanin, right?" Holness asked, rubbing vigorously between his toes. "My name's Preston Holness. I work for the government of Canada. Thought I'd drop by and see how you were getting along. Ask you a few questions."

"The hospitality of your nation touches me," the Russian said. His English was pretty good, Holness thought. "Perhaps you will take a cup of tea? I have some food as well."

"I already ate," Holness said. He took the cup the Russian handed him and looked around Varkanin's camp. It was about what he'd expected. A good but well-used tent, some piles of boxes full of supplies and gear. Standing on top of a wooden crate was an ornate but tarnished samovar as big as the Stanley Cup. A flickering can of Sterno kept it warm. Holness turned its spigot and poured the tea into his cup. It was hot enough to be uncomfortable in his hands, but he supposed the warmth would be good for him.

Jesus, it was cold. Holness always forgot how much he liked Toronto until he had to leave it. The rest of his country was full of blackflies, drunken cowboys, and fucking ice and snow. It was below freezing this far north and it was barely autumn. Best, he decided, to do this as quickly as possible.

Still, though. It had to be done right.

"You're an interesting guy," Holness said, when the Russian just went back to tending his fire and didn't offer any further conversation.

"You refer of course to the color of my skin," Varkanin said with a sigh. "I know it must seem strange to you."

"Nah. I already figured that part out. It did get my attention, though—when the Border Service sent me your picture I thought maybe here was somebody I should check out. So I called up some people I knew in your homeland and they sent over your dossier."

"I am pleased that you took such an interest." Varkanin sat down on a packing case and smiled as he stared into his campfire.

"Trained by the Spetsnaz," Holness said. "The Russian Special Forces. Decorated for bravery in Afghanistan. Served as a *polkovnik* in Chechnya. I'm sorry, I don't speak your language. What's a *polkovnik*? Is that like a colonel over here? One step below general, right?"

"That was my old life. I'm retired now."

Holness laughed. "Sure. You were discharged with high honors from your unit in, what, ninety-six? After the first Chechen war ended. You didn't retire then, though. You went to Magnitogorsk, where you were some kind of high-level policeman."

"My duties in that city were purely in a consulting role," Varkanin explained. "I never had a formal job description."

"Yeah. Which means what, exactly? You were working for the KGB?"

Varkanin shrugged. "Such an organization no longer exists, not since the end of the Soviets."

"Fine. So they changed the name, now it's the FSB. Putin's attack dogs."

Varkanin poked the fire with a stick. He was starting to look peeved. Good. Holness wanted to break the man's reserve. It was all part of the negotiation that hadn't even started yet.

Holness was a very nervous man, but that didn't mean he was bad at his job.

"You liked working for Putin? Crushing dissent, keeping people from complaining?" Holness asked.

"The work was not all like that," Varkanin said. It was almost an admission of guilt. "Much of what I did concerned public safety."

"Right. And that's how you got mixed up with the werewolf in the first place. She was hanging out in the woods near your city. Occasionally eating somebody."

Varkanin looked up at Holness for the first time. His eyes were hard, calculating. There was a little anger flickering back there, but maybe not enough.

"My father was a lumberjack. Not a very complicated fellow. He used to tell me what men did. What real men did, and what made them real men. Once he told me that a man," Holness said, "a real man knows what to do with a rabid dog. He shoots it right between the eyes. He doesn't ask anybody else to do it for him. Is that right? Is that how you feel, too?"

"The world is full of shades of gray," Varkanin demurred. "Sometimes things are not so clear."

"But sometimes they are."

Varkanin frowned. "May I ask what branch of the government you represent, Mr. Holness?"

"No, you may not."

The Russian nodded as if he finally understood something. "I see. I know how that works, very well. Alright. May I ask why you've come here, truly? It was not merely to assure yourself that I am capable of surviving alone in these woods."

"I'm not done with your story yet," Holness insisted.

"I suppose this is true."

"You went out on your lonesome to take down this werewolf. You had a high-powered rifle and some silver bullets. You tracked her for six days. When you finally found her, you shot her and then you went home. But that wasn't the end of it."

"It looked like a clean shot at the time," Varkanin insisted. "A kill shot. The bullet was small and I made sure to aim into her central mass, toward her heart, yes? All as I had been taught. The silver bullet should have lodged inside her rib cage. If it did not kill her all at once, it would have poisoned her until she finally collapsed and died. It did not work that way. The bullet passed through her body and out the other side."

"That must have hurt, all the same."

Varkanin nodded. "And in both our countries, I believe, it is understood that a wounded animal is not a safe animal."

Holness reached for his socks where they were drying by the fire. They were still kind of damp. At least feeling was returning to his feet. "She didn't die. She came back. Hurt some more people."

Varkanin's shoulders tensed up. "Yes."

"Not just any people. Your family."

"I had three lovely daughters," Varkanin said, and his voice sounded like it was being choked inside his throat. Holness watched as the Russian slowly unwound himself, relaxing his muscles one by one. This guy was good—that had to be some kind of yoga training. "Now I do not," Varkanin finished, once again in control of himself.

It was time to step up the attack. "You came to this country to find her and kill her," Holness said. "I understand that. I'm sorry I can't allow it."

"I beg your pardon?"

Holness shrugged. "Call it a territorial pissing match. Any werewolves inside Canada's borders are my responsibility, not yours. You've got no police jurisdiction here and I can't allow you to operate on my turf."

"You cannot—"

"I *can* stop you, and that's what I'm here for. Look at it from our side. If you get killed here—and going up against a werewolf, we both know that's a suicide mission—then Canada could be held liable."

"Liable."

Holness smiled in mock sympathy. "It's an insurance thing. I'm sure you understand."

"Insurance." Varkanin's eyes were almost blazing as bright as the fire, now. "I have spent ten years of my life following her from one bloodbath to another. You will give her sanctuary now? You will stop me from doing what I must do, on a technicality of insurance?"

"It's nothing personal. I'll take you back to the border, now, in my plane. If you prefer I can fly you to an airport and I'll buy you a plane ticket back to Russia. Economy, of course. Canada isn't made of money."

The Russian stood up. He didn't bolt up to his feet—the man was too tightly controlled for that. But Holness could see that Varkanin's hands were clenching into fists. Maybe he would attack Holness, and that was okay. Holness could use that as leverage. The Russian didn't attack, though. Instead he moved briskly around the camp, throwing open all his cases, lifting the lids on all his crates.

"I am here on a tourist visa. You have no reason to revoke that. Look at my things, if you like. There are no weapons here. I brought nothing illegal into your country, nothing of contraband. Do you wish to look?"

"I'm sure you would have been stopped at some point if you were carrying any guns," Holness said, agreeably. "It doesn't matter."

"How am I to hunt this werewolf, with no weapons?" Varkanin insisted.

He was trying to be logical. Holness almost wanted to laugh. This was a matter of internal security. Logic had nothing to do with it. He lifted one hand and pointed at Varkanin's exposed blue face and hands. "You're a weapon, just on your own. And that," he said, jabbing his index finger in the direction of the samovar, "is sterling silver, right? You could melt that down and make a lot of silver bullets out of it."

A connection was made inside Varkanin's brain. Holness could see it in the man's eyes. "Bullets," he said. "Of what use are bullets when I have no gun?"

Holness smiled. This was what he'd been waiting for.

"Not much," he said. "But . . ."

"Yes?"

"I have guns," Holness said. "A lot of them. As many as somebody like you could want. I've got men on my payroll, too. The kind of men who would love to go toe-to-toe with a werewolf, just to prove something. I've got vehicles: helicopters, snowmobiles, boats. Why, just today I got a new toy—a satellite cell phone. Works anywhere, even up in here in this frozen pisshole. Want to see it?" He took the phone out of his pocket. "It's got a solar charger so it never runs out of juice. It's even got my personal phone number recorded in its memory. All of these things seem like they might be useful to a man hunting a werewolf."

Varkanin stared into the fire. *He's just pretending not to be tempted,* Holness thought. Time to bring out the big prize.

He made a big show of it, unzipping a pocket on his snow pants, drawing out one crumpled piece of paper, smoothing it very carefully along his leg. "I also have this. I bet you could use this."

"I suppose I must ask what it is," Varkanin said, with a sigh.

"This," Holness said, flourishing it over the fire, "is a classified document. It's a report on satellite intelligence. Just showing this to you could get me arrested. It shows exactly where your lycanthrope is, right now. As in today."

Varkanin's eyes blazed as he stared at the piece of paper. "How far away is she?" he asked.

"You could get there this afternoon, if you hurried." Holness shrugged and started to crumple the piece of paper, as if he intended to throw it in the fire. "That would be pretty helpful, wouldn't it? Too bad you aren't a Canadian citizen, or attached somehow to my government."

Varkanin sat back down. "One moment, please," he asked.

"Sure."

The Russian closed his eyes and stroked his cheeks. He was thinking this through. Weighing the benefits of signing on with Holness versus trying to go it alone. Figuring out the best plan of action, the one that would lead him straight to killing his lycanthrope.

He opened his eyes again. "There is something you should know."

"Spill it," Holness said.

"I said she killed my three daughters. Any werewolf could do that. This one is different. She did not kill them at the same time. Do you understand?"

Holness shivered a little, and it wasn't just from the cold. "Yeah, I get it." Lycanthropes weren't *necessarily* evil, he knew. They didn't necessarily *want* to kill people—at least, their human halves didn't. It sounded like this one was more in touch with her animal nature than the others. If she had made a point of tracking each member of Varkanin's family, one by one, picking them off just to get back at him because he injured her slightly . . . Jesus. Holness was glad he wasn't the one who would have to face her in the woods.

"I understand what you're saying," Holness added, "but it doesn't matter."

Varkanin nodded as if his first chess move hadn't worked out and he needed to consider another. "You have some problem, something you need my help with. You are making me guess what it is. I can only guess you have another werewolf on your hands." He nodded again, decisively this time. "In exchange for your help, you want me to kill this other werewolf as well. I am aware of him. She considers him to be her mate. I have no grudge against this male, of course. But if it is the price I must pay, so be it."

He rose to lean over the fire, holding out a hand for Holness to shake.

Holness didn't rise right away.

"We are agreed? I kill one werewolf for you, that is what you ask?"

"Actually," Holness said, rising carefully to his half-frozen feet, "there's more than just the one."

"As many as you've got," Varkanin said. He thrust his hand forward again. "Shake this. And may God have mercy on me for it."

17.

The second that lunch was over, Powell asked Lucie to leave.

"But why?" she asked, her eyes very wide.

Chey wanted to laugh out loud. Did anybody ever fall for this little-girl-lost shtick, she wondered? One look at the redhead and you knew she was trouble. Even if they'd met in some alternate, totally human life, in some shopping mall in the suburbs of Toronto, she'd probably still have wanted to scratch Lucie's eyes out. Who wouldn't?

Powell. That was who. He'd fallen for her act at least once. When she cursed him. And maybe again, in 1954.

"I am being chased, and you turn me away. I come to offer to help you with your own troubles, and you send me out into the snow." Lucie dropped down to her knees and grasped Powell's belt buckle. "Is it because of her?" she asked, not even looking at Chey. "Can it be, *mon cher*? You have fallen in love with . . . someone else? But even this, even this . . . I can share you." She looked deep into his eyes. "I have before."

Chey's jaw dropped open. The shameless little . . .

"None of that," Powell said, his chin looking very square, "matters."

Lucie blinked. She slumped her shoulders and looked around as if seeing the rest of the camp for the first time. "How can you say this?" she asked, in a very small voice. "After what we have meant to each other. After what we did together."

Powell shook his head. Chey wished, and not for the first time, that she could read his mind. Figure out what he was really thinking. "You're being followed by some madman bent on killing werewolves." He grabbed her by the shoulders and yanked her to her feet. "What did you expect, when you came here?"

For a moment the French werewolf's body tensed. As if she were about to attack. Maybe, having run out of other options, she intended to force them, physically, to let her stay. But she was outmatched, two to one—even an absolute nut like Lucie must see that. Her body fell again and a shudder of abject sorrow went through her.

It was almost enough to make Chey feel sorry for her.

Well. Not really. Lucie had tried to kill Chey on sight. There had been no misunderstanding, either—Lucie had acted out of simple jealousy.

Which, Chey had to admit, she felt to some degree herself. But hers was different. It had to be different in some way. She needed it to be.

"I suppose I expected some warmer welcome," Lucie said, her sad eyes watching the ground. "But what more can I ask from him I have hurt so much?" She brushed Powell's arm with one slender hand. "Farewell, my love. I see you have found a replacement for me, and truly, I am glad. Glad that you will be happy, now. You, who for so long have deserved—"

"Yeah," Chey said. "See ya. Bye."

Lucie smiled, though her eyes remained fraught with sorrow. She studied Chey's face for a moment, as if memorizing her features. Then she turned and gave Dzo a big hug. Finally she walked to the edge of the camp and gave them one last lingering look over her shoulder.

"Drama queen," Chey muttered.

Powell never said a word. He watched Lucie go, but his body language said he wasn't having second thoughts on sending her out into the big cold cruel world. It said he didn't trust her not to sneak back the second his back was turned.

"Oh, I forget one thing," Lucie said, when she was about ten meters away. "I forget your coat." She unbuttoned Powell's wool coat and slid out of it with one lithe movement of her shoulders. It fell to the ground in a heap, where she left it.

Then, completely nude, she turned back to the game trail that led away through the forest. They all watched her until the trail curved around a boulder and she disappeared from view.

"Good riddance," Chey said.

"Yeah, Powell got his coat back," Dzo agreed.

Powell still didn't say anything. But he didn't follow Lucie, either.

"Come on," Chey said. "We need to get back to work. This log cabin won't build itself."

"Sure," Powell said. He was still watching the game trail. Maybe he expected Lucie to come back.

Maybe he wanted her to.

Chey grabbed an ax and started bashing away at a random tree. After every few chops with the ax she would look up and check on Powell, who was still watching the last place he'd seen Lucie.

"We're better off without her," Dzo said. He glanced meaningfully at Chey. Then he brought one finger up and rotated it around his ear. The international sign for a crazy person.

"She kills people," Chey said, loud enough that Powell would definitely hear. "She kills them for fun. If she can't kill you, she messes with your head."

"Hmm," Powell said. He wandered over toward them slowly and after a while picked up an ax as if he wasn't sure what he wanted to do with it.

"You're not pining for her, are you?" Chey asked. "Not remembering the good old days when you and she were together?"

"No," he told her. He sounded a little wistful.

"Not thinking you were maybe too harsh on her? That you could have let her keep the coat, at the least?"

"The coat?" he asked, as if he'd barely heard her. "Are you kidding? It would have fallen off of her the next time she changed, and she isn't the kind to double back on her trail just for a cast-off piece of clothing. No, that's not what I'm thinking."

"Then what, exactly, is?" Chey demanded.

"I'm thinking about how she just left. Without any kind of fight, and no manipulation. We asked her to leave and she did." He paused. Then he lifted his ax and slammed it into a tree trunk. "I'm thinking it'll be a miracle if she really lets us off that lightly."

18

Autumn, this far north, was a relative term.

The local Dene Indians recognized six seasons in the year, not the four southerners usually thought of. The fifth season was called *hhaiye t'azé,* or "freeze-up." It was the pre-winter phase when the ground grew hard with subterranean ice, when rivers and creeks flowed sluggishly and frost formed on their banks. The time when everything turned inward and grew ready for the coming winter.

It was a subtle season, and it bode little good.

It started to snow that night, for the first time. Fat snowflakes, fluffy and soft, drifted down all around the camp. They melted before they hit the ground and left no sign of their arrival. One landed on Chey's face as she was getting ready for the moon to come up. She held her hand up to the air and caught one on her palm, then turned to show it to Powell.

He just nodded. His mouth was a tight line on his face. He didn't find anything whimsical in the snow.

Not for the first time, Chey wondered just how bad winter was going to be in the Arctic. It was something she couldn't imagine, he'd told her. Something she couldn't prepare for.

She didn't get a chance to worry about it. The moon crept up over the horizon and silver light drowned out all of her thoughts.

In the next moment her wolf was running, eyes half-closed with the joy of metamorphosis, running to get away from the human smells of the camp. The wolf understood in a limited way that they were her own smells, the smells of the body she was trapped in until the moon had returned to free her.

She scented the wind and found the world subtly changed. Every smell was slightly muted—the air had grown cold enough that ice was forming anywhere water was exposed, and dry air couldn't carry scents as well as the moist summer breezes she'd been used to. It was as if the world had lost some of its colors, and the wolf swept her ears back, disheartened.

The male came trotting out from behind a stand of bushes and she padded over to meet him. He was looking all around himself, searching the air—perhaps he was feeling the same diminution of his senses that had so bothered her. His jaw opened and his tongue came out, panting at the air, his sides flexing to suck more air into his lungs, and then he turned to look at her with his ice green eyes. Something was bothering him, she could tell. What could it be? The world was freezing over, but still they were free, they were in their strong, fast bodies and there was hunting to be done, which was always joyful. She leaned forward to nuzzle him with her snout, pressing her wet nose against his shoulder.

He turned, slightly, to move into the gesture. But then he stopped and his whole body went rigid.

From behind the bushes the other wolf emerged. The white female.

Chey's wolf growled softly at her. The message was simple: go away. Underneath was a far more emphatic response. Adrenaline poured into her bloodstream and muscles tensed in her legs. She was ready to kill, if it came to that.

She would wait for a sign from the male. See how he reacted. When he made a decision, she would be ready to enforce it.

But he only watched the white female, as if he were entranced. He could not seem to look away from her.

The white wolf sat down a few feet away and started preening the fur on her forelegs, quite casually.

It was clear, without any communication necessary, that the white wolf planned on sticking around. Which could mean only one thing. If she was in the territory of the other wolves, she must become one with them. She intended to join the pack.

When the male neither attacked the white nor howled to drive her off, she rose to her four feet. She stepped easily across the broken ground, silent as her paws touched so lightly she might have been floating. Her eyes were focused on the male, but her ears twitched slightly back and forth. She was paying attention. Perhaps expecting something to happen at any moment.

Chey's wolf had a pretty good idea what the white female was waiting for. The two of them had met the previous night, but there had been no time then to establish the relationship that would define the two of them. There was a ritual that had not yet been performed, and neither could be easy around the other until it was done.

The male looked between the two of them, his eyes very wide. Confusion was written all over his features, and for a wolf confusion is the worst kind of pain imaginable. Until things were settled, he couldn't know how he should act around the two females. He couldn't hunt, or play, or court. So it had to be done. For the good of the pack.

Dominance must be established.

When it had just been the two of them, the male and the female, there had been no question of authority. There had been no pack, and so no order of authority had been required. The appearance of the white female changed that. One of them had to be the dominant female. The other would have to defer to the dominant in all things. She would eat last, play the weakest roles in the hunt, and she would only be allowed to mate with the dominant female's blessing.

The two females circled one another, studying each other, looking for signs of weakness that could be exploited. Had there been a clear difference in their sizes, or had one of them been injured or sick, the contest would have been over in a moment—the weaker of the two would have laid down with her legs in the air and let the dominant female lick her stomach—or sink wicked teeth into her throat. The gesture the dominant female chose would have defined their relationship for the rest of their lives.

In this case, though, the females were pretty evenly matched. The white female's coat was glossier than her rival's, which made her look healthier. Chey's wolf's fur was white and gray and brown, much like a timber wolf's, but it was thicker and better suited to the cold climate. The white female's body was sleeker, her legs slightly longer, but the gray's legs were thicker, stronger, better for leaping and pouncing. Neither immediately stood out as the dominant. That meant it would come down to a fight.

The gray started things out with a half-playful feint, lifting one paw toward the white's shoulders. The white twisted at the waist and danced away. Her ears twitched back and her lips drew away from her teeth as she snarled a warning. The gray barely had time to get all four feet back on the ground before the white slammed into her, face first, knocking her sideways. The gray managed to keep her footing—but just barely.

She reared up, trying to get her legs over the white's back. It was a gesture of purely symbolic aggression. There were rules to this competition, rules as complicated and specific as the rules of Sumo wrestling or Olympic fencing. The rules were encoded deep in the DNA of every wolf, and were known by all on an instinctual level, where no possibility existed of challenging them.

But that did not mean there was no way to bend them. It was possible, for a wolf sufficiently motivated, to change the very nature of the game. To take the competition beyond formal courtesy.

You could kill your opponent. Or hurt her so badly she could never be dominant again.

The white seized her chance to do just that.

When she'd reared up, the gray had exposed her soft belly. In most dominance fights that would be safe enough. But not when the white female was willing to step up the stakes. Diving low, under the gray's falling legs, the white ripped into the gray's belly with her teeth.

The gray's skin tore open and her blood and guts splattered on the cold ground.

It was a shocking move, a level of violence most true wolf packs would never have allowed. At the first sign of such cruelty the male would have jumped into the fray and pulled the combatants apart. But these weren't normal wolves.

The gray screamed in pain and outrage. She danced backward on her hind feet, desperate to get away from her enemy's teeth. She nearly slipped in her own blood as she darted around to a defensive position, showing the white only her bony flank. She wanted to run away. She wanted to go somewhere and lick her wounds, wanted very much to lie down.

The white female bowed low on her forelegs. Her snout was thick with gore and her eyes were very bright. The saddle of fur on her shoulders and upper back stuck straight up—an invitation for the gray to come closer, to be finished off.

The gray looked with terrified eyes between the white and the male, who sat on his haunches, off a little ways, his face impassive. His body language was quite clear: this was between the females.

19

The gray did not look down at her own belly. To do so would have been a fatal mistake. It would have signaled that she was, in fact, terribly wounded—which would end the dominance struggle then and there—and at the same time it would mean taking her eyes off her opponent.

The white, on the other hand, was happy to sit down and start cleaning her blood-splattered paws. As if she'd already won.

The gray took a deep breath. It hurt. Everything hurt. Her hind legs felt weak and distant. Her vision was starting to dim as blood rushed out of her body. The pain was beyond measurement or description. But she wasn't done yet.

She took a faltering step forward, quivering on legs that she could barely lift. Then another step.

The white, looking annoyed at the fact that she couldn't just get down to enjoying her victory, jumped to her feet and turned her head around slowly to look at the gray. Her arrogance was a mistake, a tactical error the gray could take advantage of—if she had possessed the speed necessary to capitalize on the white's lack of attention.

Every step she took brought new and terrible waves of agony to come crashing against the shores of her will. She couldn't run, not when half the muscles in her belly were severed. But she could still hit. She gathered herself together, arching her back, and then dug her stronger forepaws deep into the frozen dirt.

With everything she had left, she leapt forward, her forelegs propelling her by sheer willpower. It was not how a wolf would normally jump—that would have come from the bigger, springier rear legs—and so when the white tried to dash out of the way, she went the wrong direction.

The gray twisted in midair and brought her hindquarters around like a bludgeon. Her hard, bony hip slammed into the side of the white's head, instantly stunning the white and making her yelp in surprise and pain. The white slid to one side, desperately scrambling to keep all four paws underneath her so she didn't fall over. She managed to do so, but only by spreading her legs out as far as they would go, her chest touching the ground to add support.

It was an awkward, ungainly position and it did not allow the white to defend herself against what came next.

The gray snarled and snapped at the white's sensitive ears. When her teeth found fur she bit down hard and then shook her massive neck. It was an instinctual attack, one designed to snap the spines of small prey animals. The white was too big for the attack to be effective against her.

Normally.

Normally the gray would not have been so desperate in a routine dominance fight. Normally the gray would have reserved some of her strength in case this struggle went on longer than expected. Normally she would not have the strength born of knowing that if she lost now, she was doomed to an eternity of cruel submission, of slavery, at the jaws of this white interloper.

The gray twisted and shook so hard that she fractured her own bones. Tore her own muscles. The white jumped up and tried to run away—and only managed to drag the gray along with her, still holding on with perfect tenacity. The gray felt her feet come out from under her and every instinct in her body flashed warning signals, demanded that she instantly let go and find her balance again.

The gray ignored her body, her brain, and fifty thousand years of evolution. She held on. When the white's ear tore away from the side of her head, the gray snarled again and snapped for a better hold, her jaws grating against the armored plates of the white's skull. The white cried and mewled and smashed at the gray with her forepaws, batting at her enemy, scratching at the gray's eyes and soft nose. She danced and spun in circles and leapt into the air to try to buck the demonic gray, who held on for dear life.

Then she did the one thing none of the wolves would have expected of her. She lay down and tried to roll over on her back. The ultimate gesture of surrender.

At first the gray refused to believe it was true. It was a common ruse to start to lie down, then jump up as soon as your opponent tried to move in for the final coup. That kind of feint was a basic move, one pups learned before they even left the mother's den for the first time. The gray wasn't about to fall for it. She dug in deeper with her massive teeth. Those fangs had evolved to crunch caribou bones, to crack them open so she could suck out the rich marrow inside. If she'd been a little stronger, if she hadn't lost so much blood, she could have cracked the white's skull like an eggshell.

In the end, though, she just didn't have the strength. She'd suffered too much from her belly wound, which had been sorely aggravated as she was dragged and flung through the air. Eventually, she had to let go.

She closed her eyes and sank backward, her teeth so deeply imbedded in the white's head that they left grooves in her skull as they pulled free.

She slid back and found that she could barely feel her hind legs anymore. Sitting was out of the question, so she just propped herself up on her forelegs and tried not to look too undignified.

A true wolf, a timber wolf, even one of the extinct dire wolves she resembled, would have been dead many times over by now. She was barely able to hold onto consciousness. But she refused to pass out now.

Before her, the white was on the ground. On her back. Her paws slapped at empty air. Her head rolled on the ground, torn open and bleeding liberally. Her tongue slithered over her own fangs as her mouth opened and closed, seemingly beyond her control. If this was a ruse, it was an awfully good one.

The gray dragged herself forward, centimeter by centimeter. It was up to her how she finished this. She could tear the white's throat out, if she wanted to. It was what the white deserved, what she had opened herself up to when she chose to make this struggle a real fight.

The gray moved forward and stretched her neck out to get her jaws closer to the white's body. Then she stopped, perfectly still.

The male had padded over to stand above the submissive white. He was standing as tall as he could, ears up. His tail was held straight back, at the same level as his spine. It was a posture that would not have made sense to a human observer, perhaps, but to another wolf it was perfectly clear. This was what was called the "dominance parade." It was what the alpha did when it was time for him to receive respect.

His behavior sent a message the gray understood. He was saying it was his choice how the struggle would end. How the pack would align itself, in cruelty or in cooperation. If he turned around now and walked away he would be refusing responsibility for the white. Leaving her to her fate.

He did not turn away.

The gray howled and whined—she deserved the kill, she wanted it desperately—but in wolf hierarchies there could never be dissent in the ranks. Eventually she tucked her tail between her legs (or tried to—she couldn't feel her tail) and leaned forward to lick the male's chin and snout. He accepted this deference silently, gazing straight ahead of himself and not acknowledging either of the wolves beneath him.

The white, seeing her chance, lifted her head and started licking the gray's face as well. The gray couldn't refuse the submissive gesture, not without breaking her own submissive bond with the male. The struggle was over, the order of the pack decided. The male was the alpha of the pack. The gray was the dominant female. The white was the omega, the bottom of the pack. Over time these relationships would be cemented and reinforced, but it was extremely unlikely they would ever change.

At least, if they had been true wolves . . . but werewolves were another matter.

20.

The gray was badly injured. As a werewolf she could survive her wounds—but even a supernatural creature immune to all hurts save those inflicted by silver couldn't get very far with her guts trailing on the ground.

When the submissive displays were finished she crept away into the trees, away from the others. The male made no attempt to stop her. As long as she remained within range of his nose—which meant within a circle with a two-kilometer radius—he would let her be. She needed to lick her wounds, to recover a little strength. Maybe he would even bring her a little something to eat.

Maybe . . . maybe she would just sleep for a while.

The moon, in its course, never rose very high above the horizon that night. Before long it had settled back, like a cold woman in her bed, burrowing down under the covers until only the frozen stars peered down on the world.

When the gray woke the world was covered in snow. Just a fine powdering, a crystalline overlay that made the yellow grass twinkle in the sunlight and made the trees pale and heavy. It was beautiful, in a way a wolf could not appreciate.

Especially when she felt so awful.

The pain had transformed. It no longer sang and thrilled through her veins. Now it was deeper, a bone soreness that made her flesh stiff and loath to move. She crawled forward to the snow and licked at it to assuage a terrible thirst that chapped her lips and made her tongue swell. She barked and whimpered softly to herself as she tried to understand what had happened. Her legs felt wrong—like they'd been broken, and the bones set in new shapes. Her fur had all fallen out. Had the white torn it out while she slept, for revenge? Wolves rarely indulged in such sport.

Her face felt wrong. Her snout had shortened and it felt as if her teeth had broken up and fallen out of her mouth. She sighed and clutched at herself, rocking back and forth in fear and confusion. What had happened? What had . . .

Chey closed her eyes tight and fought against the thing inside her head. The wolf didn't want to leave. She had transformed, and the change had healed her body—she ran one hand down her bare stomach and couldn't even find a scar—but the wolf was still there, a presence crouched in the back of her head, howling to get out, desperate for the moon to come back.

She tried to talk and her mouth made strange shapes around her tongue. Her throat warbled and a choked howl came gushing out of her. Her fingers were curled like claws and she felt a desperate urge to scratch at the ground, to dig and bury herself in the frozen dirt. She wanted to make a den, she realized, somewhere she could hide until all the confusion and anger went away.

"St-stop it," she managed to spit out. "Just—g-g-go away."

In her mind's eye she saw the wolf staring back at her. She saw it panting and desperate. It didn't like being confined inside her skull. It didn't like being anywhere near her human form.

"Get out!" she screamed.

The wolf put its tail between its legs and padded off, into the darkest corner of her being. It was gone—for the moment.

She rolled over on her side in the snow and tried to just breathe for a while, tried to focus on just existing, on being a human being in a human body.

What had happened the previous night? Normally she could remember nothing of what her wolf did, only a few flashing impressions of sensory imagery that fled from her if she tried to study them or remember them more clearly. This time she was left with a scream in her ears, an echo of phantom pain that she knew wasn't real but that she couldn't choose to *not* hear. Her stomach—she'd woken up clutching at her stomach, terrified and searching to make sure it was still there. Had the wolf been hurt somehow? Had there been some accident so traumatic that the wolf had forced her to remember it, to have it so clearly that the wolf could manifest inside of her even when the moon was down?

This wasn't good.

She hurt all over. Well, that was the normal transformation hangover. She was used to it. It would go away by the time she finished breakfast. It didn't worry her. Not the way she was worried that her wolf had lingered on. Had stayed with her through the night and into the first stages of waking. That was something she'd never experienced before.

She would have to ask Powell about it. Or—did she really want to do that? What if he told her that what she half suspected now was right? She wouldn't be able to deny it anymore.

Don't think about that, she commanded herself. Think about how hungry you are. Which was very true. She was extraordinarily hungry.

Sitting up carefully, she looked around herself. There was no sign of Powell anywhere around her. She could smell a campfire nearby, though, and the tuneless sound of Dzo singing quietly to himself.

Time to get back to being human. Time to be Chey again.

21.

Back in the camp she gathered up her clothes and put them on quickly. She found Dzo tending to the fire, building it back up from the night's last embers. His furs were dripping with water and he had his mask down over his face—he often kept it that way when no one was around to talk to. When he saw her he lifted it and gave her a broad smile.

"You were up to some real hijinks last night, eh? You and Monty? Huh?"

His leer wasn't human enough to be annoying. What Dzo knew about mortal sex wouldn't fill a very long pamphlet. She shrugged and returned his smile. "You know I have no idea what my wolf gets up to when I'm not around. So I couldn't say."

"A lady never does," he said, and poked the fire with a stick.

She rubbed at her abdomen, wondering what had happened. Her abs didn't hurt anymore, they just twitched occasionally as if the muscles there couldn't believe they were whole again. "What did you see?" she asked.

"See? Nothing. The wolves were making so much noise that I went and slept in the lake." He twisted a piece of his furs in his hands and water splatted on the ground. "There's something there for your breakfast," he told her, pointing to a tree at the edge of the camp. "You hungry? I'll have this fire ready to cook on in a minute."

Chey's mouth watered so much that she had to tilt her head back to keep from drooling. Hanging from a low branch were three hares, strung up by their feet with their throats slit. A year ago, she thought, she would have found them repulsive. Now she tore one down and stripped its skin off with her fingers. She didn't wait for the fire. Her body demanded that she eat, and right away. The meat was stringy and bloody, but she gulped it down in huge bites without even bothering to chew.

Dzo gave her a searching look when she did that, but then he just shrugged and put a cooking pot over his fire. He filled it with lake water and then crumbled in pieces of bark and various plants, making his own vegetarian breakfast.

"Have you seen Powell?" she asked, wiping her bloody fingers on a clump of dry grass. The grass crackled with ice, but her fingers barely registered the cold. "He must have been around at some point to hang these up."

Dzo shrugged again. "Not this morning. Here, give me one of those—he'll want it when he does show up, and he takes his meat a little more done." Dzo spitted one of the hares on a long stick and propped it over the fire to roast. He might not eat meat, but he was happy enough to cook it for the werewolves.

Chey went back to her own meal, still not bothering with heating it up. She'd eaten most of the first hare by the time Powell came wandering into camp. His hair was mussed and he looked almost as tired as Chey felt. He was still buttoning his shirt as he came and sat down next to the fire.

"What I wouldn't do for a can of coffee beans," he said, and rubbed at his face with his hands. "Chey, do you have any recollection of what we did last night?"

She shook her head.

"I feel like it must have been important," he told her. "But of course—oh. I guess I should mention something."

A clump of bushes on the other side of the camp rustled and Chey stood up very fast, ready to fight. When Lucie came out, wearing Powell's woolen coat, she didn't sit down again.

"I woke up next to her," Powell explained. "It seems she ran with us last night. Her wolf didn't get the message about leaving."

"*Cher,* how many times have you said to me, we are not responsible for what they do?" Lucie asked. She came and sat down next to him. Reaching over she grabbed the roasting hare and tore off one leg. She ate it daintily, careful not to get too much grease on her little fingers.

"I don't think you ever understood what I meant by that," Powell told her. "We can't give in to the guilt of being responsible for the wolves. But we do have a duty as human beings to limit the damage they cause."

Slowly, still not feeling particularly at her ease, Chey sat back down. It was clear that Powell wasn't going to run Lucie off, at least until breakfast was over. She looked at his hair again. It looked almost as if someone had been playing with it.

She kept her thoughts to herself. She couldn't stop her stomach from making queasy flip-flops, though.

Powell reached for the roasting hare and took a bite for himself. He grimaced in distaste. "This is almost raw," he said. "It tastes funny, too. Chey, where did you find these?"

She stared at him, confused. She opened her mouth to say that she thought he had caught them and hung them up before she woke. But if he had been off playing with Lucie, then—who—?

Her voice wouldn't come. Her tongue felt dead in her mouth. She reached up to touch her lips and found them numb, even when she pinched them. When she brought her hand back down she could see blood on her fingertips. Her own blood.

Her stomach squeezed, hard. Painfully so. She leaned forward, trying to keep it from jumping out of her body.

Dzo leaned over to stir his pot. "I thought you caught them, Monty. No? Was it you, Lucie?"

"Not I," Lucie said. "I—I—ah." She tried to cover her mouth with her hands, but then without warning she spat up a thin stream of bloody drool. Her eyes were bright with terror as she looked up at Powell.

Powell looked at the haunch of meat in his hand and then tore it open, pulling shreds of flesh off the carcass to study them up close. "These little shiny flecks—they're silver," he gasped. "Poi—pois—" He rubbed at his lips with his hand, then threw the remaining portion of the hare into the fire. "Chey," he called out.

She couldn't respond, though. She was too busy rolling on the ground, the searing agony in her belly driving off all rational thought.

22.

Chey could hear voices but couldn't see a thing.

"Help me—get her on her side or she'll choke—come on, Chey—how much of this did she eat?"

Her vision had started to dim and then it had slammed shut like a pair of utterly black doors closing in front of her. She was left blind and terrified, trapped inside her body with no way out.

Was this how her wolf had felt, she wondered, when it woke up and found itself inside a human skull?

"Charcoal—get some charcoal from the fire—now!"

She felt air whistling in and out of her, felt her heart pounding away. But she knew she was dying. It scared the hell out of her, but she had no way to express that fear. She couldn't feel her hands or feet, couldn't talk. Couldn't even move. Her mind raged and tore and spat at the darkness, but there was nothing to grab or hurt or even swim through. She could hear the voices again, but she couldn't place who they belonged to.

"I have it—is this enough?—just—just get her mouth—"

"We have to go, *cher*! We cannot stay here. He will come, this was only a delaying tactic, a trick to slow us down. Can you not see it?"

"Here. Here! C'mon, get it in there. Chey. Chey! You have to swallow this. Just swallow—no—no, goddamn it, don't spit it up—hold her mouth closed—hold it!"

Her breath sputtered and wheezed and she felt like she was being buried prematurely. Well, not that prematurely. Death was all around her, in the dark. She couldn't see any hooded skeletons advancing on her, nor did her life flash before her eyes. Her death was fluid, like smoke. It stank of wood smoke. Of charcoal.

"We must flee. It is the only chance. Leave her!"

In a vague way she was aware that something was in her mouth. And that someone was stroking her throat, the way you got an animal to swallow a pill. She wanted to fight against whatever was choking her, but she was no longer connected to her body in any meaningful way. Even the sounds she heard herself making, the gagging and the retching, were just sounds. They might as well have been playing on a tape, a tape she didn't particularly want to listen to.

"Stand back—let her get it out. It has to come out again, it—oh, blast!"

"Oh, boy—all over your only shirt. I'm so sorry, Powell."

"It'll wash. Dzo, I need your help—she's dying, I know you don't understand that, but—get me more charcoal. More!"

It would be so easy to let go. To stop.

To just . . . stop.

Chey's eyes snapped open. Light burst into her darkness and blinded her. She squinted and tried to look around. She saw Powell and Lucie standing over her. Both of them had blood on their lips and they looked pale and sick. She looked down and saw wet black dust all over herself. It was all over Powell's shirt, too, and all over the ground around her. Dzo leaned into her vision with a double handful of charcoal from the campfire. What the hell was he doing? He shoved it in her throat, then held her jaw shut with both of his hands so she couldn't spit it out. Was he trying to kill her? There was no air in her lungs. She gasped for breath. Tried to growl. She was back—she was back in her body, and it was—it felt—

"She's drifting," Powell shouted. "She's going to—"

Her eyes fluttered closed and then she was just gone.

Gone away.

23.

The gray wolf woke up slung across Powell's shoulders. She felt weak and sick, drained of all her supernatural vitality and close to death. Worse—once again her body felt wrong, perverted, and she panicked, terrified at her helplessness. She bit and scratched and tore open the back of Powell's shirt. She wanted to kill him, wanted to tear him to pieces, though she lacked the strength to lift her head far enough to bite at his throat. Her teeth felt wrong, anyway, short and round, as if they'd been ground down to powder. She yelped and growled and twisted herself around as best she could to get loose, but to no avail.

"Quiet!" Powell hissed, in little more than a whisper. She could understand his words, though she didn't know how. "Chey—we have to be quiet. He's close."

She snarled and tried desperately to get her head up far enough to at least tear his ear off. It was no use.

"Come on, Chey, please," he begged.

They were moving through a thicket of trees, but even the trees were wrong—alders barely five feet tall, not like the towering pines where the wolf had first found her legs. The trees had lost most of their leaves and looked skeletal and sick, almost as bad as she felt. Ahead of them the white wolf was moving cautiously, testing her footing every time she took a step. She looked wrong, too—hairless and awkward, her body stretched out and upright, graceless and clumsy when she should be flowing along the ground like a sleek avalanche.

Dzo brought up the rear, holding branches away from his face as he peered behind them, looking for something dangerous. Dzo looked the same as he always did, mostly human, but just as always he didn't smell human. Didn't smell like anything she understood.

The wolf opened her mouth to howl, to call Powell's wolf to her side to save her. She couldn't lift her head very far, but she thought still he might hear her, might come rescue her. Before she could even begin her vocalization, however, Powell's human hand clamped tightly over her mouth. She tried to bite and chew at his fingers, but she lacked the strength—or the jaw muscles—to even break his skin.

"Chey, you have to fight this," he whispered in her dull ear. "You're a human being. Remember yourself!"

The gray wolf squirmed at the very notion—but then a strange thing happened.

Her forelegs were numb and useless. They hung down Powell's back like so much dead game strung up to ripen. When she shifted her weight, though, they flopped around and for the first time since waking she saw her own paws.

They were human hands.

Her eyes rolled, looking for the moon, but couldn't find it anywhere in the sky.

It made her want to howl again. This time Powell wasn't fast enough to stopper up the sound that made her chest resonate like a drum.

"Leave her!" Lucie said, turning to glare at Chey. "She's going to get us killed."

"I won't," Powell insisted. It sounded like something he had said many times.

"Her mind is gone. You must accept this, *cher.* You've seen it happen before!"

Powell started to draw breath to answer, but a sudden sound stopped him in his tracks. It was a flat, distant report, like the sound a frozen lake makes when it begins to thaw. An instant later the bark of a nearby alder split and splinters of wood jumped into the air.

"Damnation," Powell said, louder now. "Run!"

Then Chey was flopping around on Powell's back, her head glancing off his shoulder blade again and again. She couldn't catch her breath, couldn't fend off the wave of darkness that crashed over her once more, and carried away both the woman and the wolf.

24.

The next thing Chey knew she was lying flat on her back. Her parka was rolled up and tucked under her head like a pillow, and she could barely see.

She was enclosed in some kind of shelter. She could just make out a ceiling, a few feet above her head. It was made of close-packed earth, veined with tree roots. Occasionally a few grains of dirt would come loose and patter down on her face or body.

She felt sick. She felt like her insides had been burned out with a welding torch. She felt so weak that she could barely breathe. But she was alive. And she was human. Her wolf was nowhere to be found, not even lurking in the deepest subbasement of her brain.

"Powell?" she said, her voice very, very soft. The earth all around her soaked it up at once and she wasn't sure anyone could have heard her. She took a deep breath and tried again. "Powell? Where are we?"

The thought that he wasn't there—that she'd been abandoned somewhere underground—hit her like she'd been doused with cold water. Underground, in the dark, lying on her back. Was she . . .

Was she dead and buried?

Then a hand grabbed her arm and squeezed in reassurance.

"Oh, thank God," Powell said. "I thought we'd lost you." He scooted closer to her and she saw his face, almost completely lost in shadows. It was so dark. He could just about sit up in the close, mud-stinking place. His body filled up most of the air she'd been breathing.

"She awakens," Lucie said. The redhead was close enough to touch as well.

"Powell, I'm so sorry," Chey said. A tear welled up in her eye and blurred her vision. It was too small to escape and run down her cheek. "Powell, did I get us into this?"

"Hush," he said. "You need to rest. You nearly died."

"Or worse," Lucie suggested.

Powell's dark face grew stiff. "Don't worry about that now. Here, there's some water." He turned away for a moment and she was terrified he was going to leave her alone with Lucie, even for an instant. But then he returned and his hands were cupped, filled with water that smelled terrible. Her lips were so chapped, though, and her tongue so swollen that it felt like infinite mercy when he dribbled a little of it into her mouth. "No food, I'm afraid."

"Not hungry," she managed to say, while licking her lips carefully to get every tiny droplet of the water. Her tongue could feel how cracked and broken the skin there was. "I don't think I'll ever be hungry again."

"I'm unsurprised," Lucie sneered. "Considering how much of that tainted meat you gobbled down. It should have killed you."

Chey managed to turn her head a little to the side, so she was looking at Powell. "What happened?" she asked.

He rubbed at his forehead and eyes as if he was very tired. "We had to abandon the camp," he said. "Someone—a hunter—came after us. It was him who left those rabbits for us, of course. He must have been feeding them for days on a silver solution before he killed them and brought them to the camp. Their meat was full of silver. Enough to poison one of us. He didn't really expect to kill us that way, though. Lucie and I knew what had happened as soon as we tasted the meat. He just wanted to slow us down." He shook his head. "He's clever. And more than that—he's diabolically patient. Just to get to the camp, he must have waited nearby for days until we were all gone, our wolves out in the woods, Dzo in the lake. Then he approached from downwind, so our wolves wouldn't even smell him. He had the element of surprise—we had no idea he was there—but still. This one's something special. Not like those idiots who tried to kill us at Port Radium."

"Is he from the government?" Chey asked.

"I don't think so. I think this is the same guy Lucie was running away from when she left Russia."

"Impossible," Lucie said. "A man like that—your nation would never let him inside its borders."

Powell frowned. "Unless he made some kind of deal with them. They want us dead, he wants to kill you. Maybe they decided to strike three birds with one stone. Who is he, Lucie? What does he want, other than to kill us?"

Lucie answered the second question first. "Nothing. Nothing but oblivion. If it is Varkanin—and I think this very unlikely, no matter what you say—he has sworn to destroy me though it be the last thing he ever does."

"Sounds familiar," Chey said. There had been a time when that described her—when she had come tracking Powell, intent on killing him. She'd made a mess of that, certainly, and in time her feelings had completely changed, but she still understood the urge.

"What is he?" Powell demanded.

"He is only human, really. Nothing to concern us. But he is possessed of a certain persistence I do not find amusing."

Powell grunted in dissatisfaction. "This isn't good."

Chey let her head fall back. Even talking was wearing her out, but there were things she needed to know. "Where are we now?"

"We ran for it when he started shooting," Powell told her. "I had no idea where to go, but I knew he was behind us the whole time. I headed north, following a creek that had some pretty good tree cover. Eventually we found this place. Judging by the size of it, I'd say it used to be a bear's den. It hasn't been used in a while. We'll lay low here until we know he's gone, then look for a more suitable place to overwinter."

Chey couldn't nod. She didn't have the strength. Instead she bit her lip a little and then turned her face as far as she could toward him. She didn't particularly want Lucie to hear what she had to say, but she supposed it was unavoidable. "I remember something," she told him. "Right after I ate the rabbit. You and Dzo were doing something to me, shoving ashes from the fire in my mouth."

"Charcoal," he told her.

"I can still taste it."

He smiled at her. "You were full of silver and the only way to get it out was to make you throw up." He sounded apologetic, for some reason. "Charcoal absorbs the contents of your stomach so when you vomit it back up, whatever you were poisoned by comes up with it. It was the only way to—"

"To save my life," she finished. "Thank you, Powell. Thank you for not just leaving me behind, too. How many times have you saved me now?"

"I owed you," he said, though she couldn't imagine why.

25

Hours ticked by but Chey was barely aware of them—she was in and out of consciousness, unable to tell, sometimes, whether she was awake or dreaming. She was barely aware of what was going on when she heard Powell talking.

"When we change," Powell said, "which is going to happen very soon now—our wolves won't know why they're hiding in here. They'll run outside looking for game."

"They will find Varkanin," Lucie said.

"Exactly. Him and his high-powered rifle. So we need to keep them inside. I can only see one way to do that."

The two of them, Powell and Lucie, went to work right away, collapsing the mouth of the den. They had to do it carefully in such a way that the entire structure didn't fall in, crushing all three of them, but so thoroughly that the wolves couldn't dig their way out with just their paws. It took a while. Chey could do nothing to help, only watch silently as more and more of the light was cut off. Finally, when it was pitch black inside the den, she heard the two of them come back. They were breathing hard, and not just from the exertion.

"We won't asphyxiate," Powell assured Chey, "even though there's no air coming in. But it won't be comfortable. At least it'll be our wolves gasping in here, not us."

"You hate your wolf, don't you?" she asked.

She couldn't see the expression on his face, so when he didn't answer her she had no way of knowing what he thought.

They changed soon thereafter. Even in the darkness where the moon couldn't find them, the silver light shone.

What the wolves thought of being buried alive she would never know. She woke up desperate for air and scared, but her wolf didn't make another appearance inside her human body, as she had feared it might.

Powell went to the mouth of the cave and dug an air shaft through to the outside world. No one tried to shoot him even for the scant minutes he was partially visible, but he didn't take that as a sign that it was safe to leave.

That was another problem.

"How can we possibly know when it's safe?" Chey asked, her lungs sucking deep on the cold sweet air coming in, and her eyes lit up by the rare beam of sunlight that made its way down into the den.

"Dzo's out there, keeping tabs on the hunter. He'll let us know."

There were other problems, some of them less important than others, but far more insistent.

"The bear that hibernated in here," Chey asked. "Where did it go to the bathroom?" She was feeling a little better—it might have been a day or so, or maybe more since they'd been inside the den, but this was the first time the call of nature had made itself known.

"It didn't," Powell told her. "When bears sleep through the winter they don't eat, drink, urinate, or defecate. Just sleep. Lucie and I have been going over there," he said, anticipating the question she was really asking. "Do you need help?"

"No, thanks," she said. She shifted carefully, moving as gently as possible. It tired her out just to crawl over Powell to get to the lowest point of the den, a place where the ceiling was barely thirty centimeters from the floor. Getting her pants down was hard, harder than anything she'd had to do in a long time, but she managed.

When she crawled back she considered the biggest problem she faced, one she'd been far too frightened to ask about. It had to be done, though. Most likely, she thought, as soon as she asked Powell would tell her it was no big deal, that it happened to everybody sometimes. That she shouldn't worry. That would be an enormous relief.

She lay back down in her spot, in the groove her body had already worn in the muddy floor, and rested awhile until her strength came back. Then she rolled over to face Powell and just said it.

"My wolf keeps showing up. Even when the moon is down, I mean."

"I know," he told her.

"You do?"

He was between her and the light. She couldn't see his face at all. "When I was carrying you here, you tried to scratch me. You started howling. I knew for sure, then. I had already guessed it was happening before, though. That time you didn't put your shoes on. That could have been nothing. Now I know what it meant."

"Care to share with me?" she asked.

He was silent for quite a while. Maybe finding the right words. Maybe conserving their precious oxygen. Maybe he just didn't know what to say.

Lucie broke the silence. "I will tell her, if you will not, *cher*."

Powell stirred as if he'd been slapped. "No, you will not. She'll hear it from me. The best way I can tell it."

Chey managed to laugh a little, though it sounded more like desperation than mirth to her own ears. She hoped that the weird acoustics of the den would make it sound different to him. "How bad is it, doc? Will I ever play the violin again?"

He didn't understand the joke. "Chey, normally when a human being becomes a lycanthrope, they manage to find a balance. An equilibrium between the human being and the beast. It doesn't have to be an easy equilibrium. You asked me if I hate my wolf and the answer is that I do. I despise it, as much as it loathes me. When I'm human, I try to be as civilized and rational as I can because I dread the moment when I lose those qualities, when the wolf comes for me. Lucie has her own balance to maintain, which I won't even try to explain."

"It is only the contrast between vicious beast and innocent girl," Lucie suggested.

"Whatever," Chey said, wishing Powell would just get on with it.

"Sometimes," he said, "the balance is lopsided. Sometimes the wolf gets stronger with each transformation and the human . . . starts to weaken. The human becomes more and more wolflike. The wolf asserts dominance over the human. It can go the other way as well, which is maybe worse. I can only imagine what it would be like to wake up in the body of a wolf but with a human mind. It must be torture. But in the cases we're talking about, the cases where the wolf predominates, it eventually leads to—well, to the human losing. Dying, in every way that matters."

Chey's breath came fast in her throat. She felt like her heart might stop. "Okay," she said. "Okay."

"It gets worse when the human is under stress. When you were poisoned, your human half thought it was going to die, and it gave in. The wolf took over. Now you're getting better and you're stronger. You, your human self, is stronger."

"Alright," Chey said.

"You need to fight it as long as you can," he said.

And that was it. That was all he was going to tell her. He lay back, not even looking at her.

She couldn't let it go, though. "So—so—we cure this. We figure out a way to make this stop happening. I could do Zen meditation. I could do really highbrow mental human stuff, like, like listening to classical music or playing chess. You'll help me make chess pieces, right, Powell? You'll teach me how to play?"

"Chey, I—"

"You must know how to play chess. I mean, you look like the type," she said. She was starting to get hysterical, and she knew it. "Because we can beat this. You didn't say we couldn't, which must mean that we can. Right? Tell me how to beat this."

He reached for her hand. She pulled it away.

"Don't," she said.

"I can't lie to you, Chey. I've heard of this happening many times. I've never heard of anyone who recovered from it."

Chey sat up so fast that she hit the ceiling with her forehead. Cold, wet dirt cascaded down the neck of her shirt. *Come on,* she thought. *Give me something.* But she knew what he had said was true—he couldn't lie to her. He never had before.

"You've heard of it happening. You've heard stories. But there's more," she said. "Lucie said something, when I was on your back, wolfing out. She said—she said—God, what was it? She said my mind was gone. Which was a little fucking presumptive, lady." She turned and snarled at Lucie.

Snarled the way a wolf snarls.

Lucie's eyes caught the wan morning light, what there was of it, and *sparkled*.

"She said something else, too," Chey went on, trying to ignore the sound she'd just made. "She said—'Her mind is gone. You've seen it happen before.' " Chey rubbed the dirt off her face and chest. "You've seen it. Who? Who was it this happened to?" She considered the possibilities. Powell had told her many stories of Lucie before, but the only other werewolf he'd ever spoken of by name had been—"the Baroness." She shook her head. "Oh my God. This happened to the Baroness."

"Yes," Powell said.

"What happened to her? Where is she now?" Chey grabbed the front of Powell's shirt and tugged at it, demanding that he tell her more. "What happened to her?"

"That I won't tell you," he said.

Lucie laughed. "I will," she said. "I was there, also."

Powell made a warning noise, deep in his throat.

"Damn it, Powell. I have a right to know," Chey said.

He didn't deny it.

26

Lucie told her story, then, and Chey was rapt with attention.

"Some things you already know. In nineteen seventeen Monty came to France as a soldier to the Great War, and there I met him. I was living at the time with my great-great-grand-niece Élodie, whom you know only as the Baroness. We fell in love with Monty and made him like us so we could have him forever. But it was not to be.

"The story of what happened to Élodie takes place in the year nineteen twenty-one, when we were still living in our castle, at Clichy-sous-Vallée. During the war we were a most happy family together, the three of us. After the peace, though, things became very difficult for us, and we were forced to leave France owing to a grave misunderstanding."

Powell grunted. "The locals didn't understand why wolves kept eating their pigs when real wolves had been extinct in France for centuries."

"*Cher.* I am telling this, no?"

Powell raised one hand in apology. "Alright," he said, "go on. But don't lie to her. If you think she needs to know this, then fine. But tell her all of it."

"I will endeavor to speak only truths. In nineteen twenty-one I had been changing for some hundreds of years. Élodie and Monty were new to it. They had become *loups-garou* much at the same time—I had given to her the curse only days before I met him—and it was my duty to teach them all I knew of our ways. I taught them to hunt, and how to conceal their double nature when the moon was down. It was also my duty to introduce them to the society of the great families of Europe. When we closed down our castle at Clichy-sous-Vallée for the last time, it was a sad thing, but I knew we had many friends who would be kind enough to take us in as their guests. Élodie and I were of noble blood, you see, and so we had many cousins in the grand houses of Europe. Many of those cousins had wolves living under their roofs, and would understand our plight, I thought.

"We traveled into lands that had been stricken by the war, places where refugees were common and a man and two women traveling together were not so strange a sight. We even had a big motor truck which was always breaking down in the wilderness, but which had room in the back for a silver cage, so that when the change found us we could contain ourselves, and hurt no one—"

"My idea," Powell insisted.

"—which was Monty's clever notion, I was just about to say that. You must understand that at this time things in Europe were very different. Now you can travel from Paris to Berlin, and along the way you will never be away from a superhighway, and there are people and their ugly little houses the whole way. Back then it was different, and still much of the country was wild. There were river valleys and whole mountains where no one ever went, and forests whose trees reached higher to heaven than the spires of cathedrals, with branches so thick and so woven together that it was always night beneath them. The roads were often as not unpaved, and always bumpy. When we saw people, it was always a little family on a farm very far from any town. So it was safe for us to travel and we were able to keep our secret close.

"Our cousins were always gracious, and took us in out of courtesy and compassion—"

"Or fear we would come back and kill them if they didn't," Powell chimed in.

"*Cher!* You do them too little credit. In Spain we stayed with a great man who was one like us, who lived in a house made all of silver built in the courtyard of his castle. In Venice—oh, Venice!—we had a house all our own, with a door that let onto the canal, and boats at our disposal day or night. It was in Prussia, though—that is part of Germany—that our story takes its tragic turn.

"At first it seemed a dream come true. I had a distant cousin there, the Graf von Krafft-Ebing, a very important man. Until nineteen nineteen he had been one of the most important men in Germany, and even then, during the Weimar Republic, he was influential. And quite wealthy, of course. He had a big estate out in the country that was quite a fashionable place to be invited to dine. Writers, artists, decadents of all stripes would come there to be seen, though always they must leave before the moon rose. The popular opinion was that the Graf had lost his mind and developed a phobia of the moon, but of course you will have guessed the real reason. He had a son named Gustav—though we always called him Tavin—upon whom he doted, and who was one like us.

"The Graf welcomed us into his home with open arms. He was a portly man with a red face and bright eyes. He was very glad to have us, as we represented good society for his son. He thought we would be of an improving nature for Tavin and we did our best to teach him what we had learned. We had a suite of rooms all our own, with two beds—though we only ever used one—and a bath to ourselves, and any food or drink we desired any time of day or night. Best of all, we were given a little iron key which opened a silver gate at the back of the castle. Beyond that gate was a stretch of forested land many hectares in size, walled all around with stone, that was the Graf's private hunting ground. It was his gift to Tavin, and made perfect for such as us. It was stocked well with game for us to chase and catch, and where our wolves could run and be free as nature had intended, without possibility of reproach. The six months we stayed there were among the happiest in my life. How I wish they could have never ended. But of course for poor Élodie, it would not prove so pleasant."

Lucie's voice drifted off a little at the end and it was clear she didn't relish telling what came next. Chey took advantage of the pause to turn toward Powell and ask him a question. "How much of this is how you remember it?"

"Oh, she's telling it pretty straight," he replied. "Though maybe she makes the Graf sound better than he actually was. He loved Tavin alright, but when it came to other people . . . well, when she says he stocked that hunting ground with game, you probably thought of deer, or maybe rabbits, right?"

"Yeah."

"It was more like drifters, criminals, and people who owed him money."

27

"That's horrible," Chey said. "He let his son hunt *people*?"

"None of them were innocent," Lucie insisted. "These were rapists and thieves."

"For the most part. It didn't mean they deserved to die like that." Powell grunted in distaste. "Chey, you have to understand something about people like the Graf. The nobility in Germany back then didn't think of themselves as the same *species* as the peasantry. The artists and the courtesans who came to the Graf's party were like the prize-winners at a country fair to him, but his son was born to be a great man. Nothing Tavin ever did, or wanted to do, could be wrong."

"And you lived under this guy's roof?"

Powell shrugged. "I genuinely thought I could help the boy. Teach him better and break the cycle. Or maybe . . . if I'm truly honest with myself, maybe I was just tired of running. It was pretty comfortable there."

"Tavin was a sweet child," Lucie said, as if there had been no interruption. "How I remember the blush upon his cheeks. He would bring me posies of wildflowers picked from his private hills, and let me strew them in his long blond hair. He saved the best of the blooms for Élodie, however. He was under the impression that Monty and I alone were married, and that Élodie was like a sister to me. He could not imagine that we three were joined in union, because no such thing would ever have been allowed in the very proper society that raised him. So it could not exist. Élodie was the first werewolf he ever met whom his father considered eligible to mate with him. He was not likely to meet another for a very long time. Do you understand what must happen in this case? He fell in love. For the same reason any boy falls in love with any pretty girl. Because she was there, and because she did not instantly refuse him.

"Élodie was already mated, for life, to Monty. Yet she could not tell the boy as much. Certainly not when it would get back to his father. The scandal would be too much, and we three would be sent back out into the cold. If not worse. So we let young Tavin have his fantasies. It was a time of very long courtships, and it seemed the boy would take forever to ask for Élodie's hand.

"I think, had we led him to believe that I was the available one, things may have gone very differently.

"For poor Élodie knew so little of life. Before I gave to her the curse, she had been a sheltered girl, never allowed to stray from the castle where she was born. Now she was being asked to play a part beyond her abilities. She claimed she understood our ruse, but I wonder if she did not come to love Tavin a little bit. He was so very kind to her, which is ever the way to a woman's heart. That heart was not hers to give, and I believe the fracture between these two desires drove a wedge into her sanity."

Powell rolled over to face the two women. It seemed he had to interrupt. "Come on, we knew well before then she was having trouble. When I first met her she was clearly shell-shocked. She could barely speak. She was walking around with a candelabra that wasn't lit. Afterward, when I understood what had broken her sanity—because I was going through it, too—I tried to help her, but she would never talk about the things we did. And then she started to slip away. Become less human, and more wolf. She would wake up growling and for an hour or so in the morning she wasn't human at all. She couldn't bear to wear any underclothes because they just felt wrong against her skin. It was all we could do to keep her from going naked all the time. And then there was what happened in Venice. That should have been an obvious warning."

"Ah. Yes. Venice," Lucie said, as if his words had recalled to her something she'd forgotten from a shopping list. "But that was not so much. We had a room in a tower, there, where we would retire when the change was coming on us. It had silver bars on the windows and the door, so our wolves could not escape. There was a bed in the room, and the three of us shared it, and that one particular morning, when we woke together—"

"Élodie rolled over and bit my throat," Powell said. His voice was hollow, almost emotionless. "Took a chunk right out of it. There was blood everywhere. Lucie tried to pull her off of me and Élodie slashed Lucie's face with her fingernails. It took both of us to finally pin her down and all that day—until our next change—we had to hold her arms. She squirmed and shook and screamed at us. Howled at us, sometimes demanding that we let her go, sometimes just growling like an animal. We were humans and she was still a wolf, and she wanted nothing but to destroy us. When we finally changed it was such a relief. But then the next morning we were ready for it to start again. When we woke we were ready to fight her off once more. We didn't have to, though."

"What happened?" Chey asked. She had to know.

"I awoke," Lucie said, "and jumped out of the bed ready to restrain Élodie, only to find her sitting before a vanity mirror, carefully pinning up her hair. She gave me a warm smile and asked if there was any chocolate for breakfast."

"She had no idea that anything had happened," Powell went on. "She couldn't remember the day before at all. When we insisted, when we showed her all the blood on the sheets, she only blushed and looked away and claimed she'd had her—her, you know. That she'd gotten her monthly bill."

"Like, her period?" Chey asked.

"Don't be crass, *jeune fille*," Lucie said. "I will admit, it was a disturbing episode. But we did not want to believe it was part of an overall pattern. It happened rarely that she would fail to recover her humanity upon awakening, and I for one was polite enough not to make much mention of it.

"Yet when Tavin started to plead his love for her, and fall upon her knees and beg her to say she loved him too—"

"It started to get worse," Powell said, his voice very soft.

28.

"I—I can see where this is going," Chey said. She was terrified by the story Lucie was telling her, and she suspected that was the very reason why Lucie had chosen to relate it. Lucie wanted her to squirm. To live in terror of what was happening to her, now. "Every time she changed, when she woke up, she had a harder time shaking off her wolf, right? It was always with her."

"Sometimes . . . she would seem so normal. So human. She would be walking with Tavin and they would be talking like young people," Powell said. A deep sadness had entered his voice. "Or we would be taking a meal and she would be correcting my etiquette—telling me which spoon to eat my soup with." He sighed. "And out of nowhere it would come over her. Her face would change. She would stop talking. She seemed to lose the ability to speak. She would look around as if she had no idea where she was and her lip would curl back in a snarl. It was like her mind wanted to transform, even when her body wasn't ready."

"When the moon was still below the horizon," Lucie pointed out. "You know how good it feels to change. To become that thing, so powerful, so self-assured. Élodie's human life could not compare. It was a maze of confusions and little pains. Every little shock, every frustration she felt would send her running for the comfort, the peace, that only our wolves can know."

Powell cleared his throat. He hadn't wanted to tell this story before, but now it seemed like he needed to get it off his chest. "We hid it as best we could. The Graf had been pretty clear on one thing: we were welcome in his house only as long as none of his guests ever suspected there might be something different about his son."

"It was not easy. We kept Élodie apart from the Graf and his human servants, as much as possible. Especially at mealtimes. Élodie could not bear to have anyone touch her food but one of us. Should a footman attempt to clear her plate before every morsel was finished she would snap and bite at his arm. Should anyone be so clumsy as to drop a fork on the castle's flagstones, the noise would send her dashing for the hunting grounds, where she would strip off her clothes and run as best she might on all fours.

"Tavin was our great ally in this deception. When his father would ask why Élodie did not dine with him, or why her clothes seemed to fit her improperly, he would make up one thousand excuses, or simply say she chose to spend all her time with him. He believed so fervently in her love. In their future together.

"But then the time came, when we could pretend no longer. There was a ball, a formal event. Guests of great importance were coming. All the *avant garde* that the Graf wished to impress—millionaire heiresses from America, cabaret stars from Berlin, a cousin of the Czar of Russia who intended to raise an army and take his country back from Lenin. The cars that pulled up in front of the castle were like none we'd ever seen before, sleek, powerful things that throbbed with speed. The fashions the guests wore were daring or provocative but always so *chic*. The servants, so many servants for these wonderful people, so many they had to build a city of tents outside the castle wall for them to live in. It was like a great sparkling galaxy of light and color had descended on our tiny world in the country. There was music playing, all the time. Jazz! Hot jazz, of a kind we had never heard before. It stirred the blood. Excited all the passions."

"Which was a problem," Powell said, his voice a soft growl. He didn't like this part of the story. "The Graf had told his guests a little about us. Not everything. They had no idea what would happen to us when they'd all gone, and the moon rose. But he had hinted that we were afflicted by some mysterious, ancestral curse. A dark past no one could ever speak of aloud. Which meant every one of them would want to meet us and ask us leading questions. The men would all want to dance with Lucie and Élodie. The women would want to try to seduce me. So there were no more excuses to be made. Élodie had to appear for this party, no matter how 'sick' she might be, no matter how much we claimed she needed to be allowed to rest."

"And of course, there was another reason, which we were not told. Which Élodie had not spoken of, not to us," Lucie said.

"Tavin had asked for her hand in marriage. And she had said yes."

"You cannot imagine the mental strain upon poor Élodie," Lucie insisted. "She knew this could not be permitted. And yet she could not refuse her beloved. Their engagement was to be announced at the ball before God and everyone worth knowing. She and Tavin would have the first dance. It was to be a grand evening, indeed."

"I'm guessing it didn't go so good," Chey said.

"No," Powell agreed.

"We did what we could," Lucie said. "We spent all that day with her. Calming her nerves, soothing her little fears. Encouraging all that was still human in her. Then we helped her into a very fine if slightly old-fashioned dress and a pair of satin dancing shoes, and led her down to the hall. When she was announced, she made a perfect curtsy, and everyone applauded her entrance. While a famous musician played his latest composition on the piano, we drew her back to the edges of the crowd, and told her how well she was doing. How proud we were of her, and how she was a perfect mate for the two of us. How we would soon leave the castle and begin a life together where things were easier for her."

"I've always wondered if that's what did it," Powell said. "I think maybe she wanted, in the human part of her, to stay there. To really marry Tavin."

"Unthinkable," Lucie insisted. "She was ours."

Powell could only shrug. Chey knew that he would have found a way to break the bond, to let Élodie have her happiness, if it had been possible.

"While the music was playing, the servants were busy laying out a quite lavish dinner. There were oysters and canapés, and sausages of a hundred varieties, and many fish courses, and of course an enormous roast joint of venison.

"Élodie said the music hurt her ears. To be fair, it was an atonal composition in the most progressive style of that time. Not melodic at all, instead all brash, jarring chords and sudden changes of time signature. Élodie asked if she could be excused to use the necessary."

"The toilet," Powell translated, and Chey nodded in thanks.

Lucie wrinkled her nose, but went on. "We listened to the rest of the piece, and gave our polite applause. We were just about to go looking for her, to bring her back, when Tavin said he had an announcement to make. You know what it was. Yet he never had a chance to say the words. He asked us where Élodie was, and when we attempted to stall him, he laughed and said we must produce her at once. I looked to see the Graf, his face very pinched, and knew he was displeased. This made me very worried, of course.

"At that same moment, a sound was heard from the grand dining room. A sound that was as dismal as the tolling of a funeral bell.

"Perhaps what happened next could have been hidden, if we had been quicker. Alas, we could only stand there in horror and pretend nothing was happening when everyone in the room could hear growling and the sound of gnashing teeth. Everyone rushed in to see what was happening. We could not stop them. All those millionaires, painters, jazz trumpeters, servants, the Graf, Tavin—all of them saw it. They saw our Élodie, crouched on the table like an animal, tearing at the joint of venison with her teeth. Grease and gravy covered her hands and chest. Her dress had been torn off and discarded on the floor. Though she still wore her satin dancing shoes.

"The ball, needless to say, was canceled. Everyone was sent home at once, the servants abandoning their city of tents in place, the intellectuals and artists bundled off in long cars. Some of those people could be bribed to never speak of what they'd seen. Others were guaranteed to gossip, but it was unlikely they would be fully believed. It was nineteen twenty-one, a very wild time in that part of Europe, and many impossible stories were making the rounds. As for us, however—the Graf made things quite clear.

"We had disgraced his house. Abused his generosity. Worst of all, we had broken the heart of his beloved son. Tavin had fled to his tower room and locked himself in, and would not come out for days. Servants who put food outside his door said they heard him sobbing in there, and thought every so often they heard him calling Élodie's name, sometimes in despair, sometimes so he could curse her to damnation.

"This, the Graf could not accept. At once he made his decision known. Élodie was sent naked into the walled hunting ground, behind the gate of silver bars, and there she was locked away. We were not permitted to go in after her. No one was."

"Nobody ever spoke a word to her again," Powell said. "She never put on another dress. Or combed her hair. Or had a fire when it was cold." Emotion choked his voice. He had obviously cared for Élodie, in some capacity. Had he loved her? Chey couldn't know. "It's hardly a surprise that within a week her human mind was gone. Utterly submerged. There was nothing left of her but a wolf, a wolf that couldn't understand why it spent half its life in a body it hated. We could hear her howling, day and night. We could hear her screams." He turned away so Chey couldn't see his face, even in the darkness of the den.

Lucie was nearing the end of her story and the excitement in her voice was growing. "In time, it became necessary to—"

"Stop," Powell said.

"But, *cher*, I—"

"No! You're done. Chey, as far as I'm concerned, you don't need to hear the rest. It has nothing to do with you. And I am not going to lie here and listen to it."

"No! Come on, I need to know this. I need to know how it ends," Chey insisted. "If I'm facing the same thing."

"It ended in madness and howling," Powell said. "What happened after that doesn't matter."

"It became necessary," Lucie said, as if Powell hadn't spoken at all, "to put her out of her misery."

29

"**The Graf was** many things, but always he had a sense of style," Lucie went on. "He sent to another cousin of his, a Polish prince who had a grand collection of curios and artifacts from the Middle Ages. A wagon was dispatched, and in a few days it arrived. In the back was a thing about the size of a packing case. Or a coffin. It was very old, and made of base metal, much of which was red with rust. It was tapered, wider at one end than the other, and the narrow end was carved with the face of a howling wolf. It opened in the front, with a pair of doors that could be latched shut with a silver hasp.

"It was—"

"Stop!" Powell shouted. In the little cave the noise was enormous. Chey felt his breath stir the tiny hairs on her cheek. "If you won't stop for her sake, stop for mine. I can't think about this now. I can't remember it!"

"Powell," Chey said, very calmly, "I'm asking you, please, to let her speak. Because I want to know this. I want to hear it."

He stared at her and even in the paltry light of the den she could see his eyes burning. Then he turned away and buried his face in the wall of the cave, clutching his hands over his ears.

"I will whisper it, so as not to hurt him too much," Lucie said, and dropped her voice.

"It was called the *silber jungfrau*. The silver maiden. A device that had been built by the Prince-Bishopric of Mainz in the sixteenth century. A device of execution for werewolves. It had been used only a scant handful of times. Mostly the church was content to burn our kind at the stake, and bury us with silver crosses. The silver maiden was used only for private executions, for those werewolves who were discovered high within the church hierarchy, or for those of princely rank and above. It was in a way a great honor that Élodie should meet her end within it."

"How did it work?" Chey asked, almost breathless.

Lucie didn't answer her at once. "A team of liveried servants unloaded it in the castle courtyard. They opened the doors and then ran inside, to safety. Tavin went to the silver gate and unlocked it. He called to Élodie. When she did not come, he went to her. How he convinced her to emerge from her refuge, I do not know. But he was almost tender with her as he brought her, naked and covered in filth, into the courtyard. I watched it all from a tower window. Powell could not watch. He was chained in the castle's counting-house, under armed guard so he might not try to effect a rescue.

"Élodie had eyes only for Tavin. There was fear on her face, but not as much as you might expect. I think the wolf in her brain recognized him, still. He led her over to the maiden, and only then did she begin to tremble.

"Perhaps you have heard of the device called the iron maiden, and so you know already what was in store for her. The inside of the silver maiden was lined with spikes of silver, very long, like very sharp nails, polished to a high gleam. There was room inside for a small person to stand without being pricked—but only with the doors open.

"Tavin spoke very softly to her. I could not hear his words. She nodded, once, and then she stepped inside.

"Then he closed the doors. He did not slam them shut. He locked the hasp. And then he went inside and had his breakfast.

"We could hear her screaming, of course, but no word was spoken in the castle that day about what was happening. The Graf would strike any servant who so much as glanced toward the courtyard with the back of his hand.

"I do not know how long it took her to die. I do know that when they opened the doors again, and took out what was left of her, it was a wolf's body, not a woman's. Powell buried it inside the hunting ground.

"Then he threw a glass of wine in the Graf's face. And the two of us took our leave of that place, forever."

Lucie's tale was finished. Chey couldn't breathe. She could only stare at the redhead, and try not to shiver.

30.

Perhaps tired out by telling her story, Lucie went to sleep shortly thereafter. Powell still was turned toward the wall. Chey knew she wasn't going to sleep for a long time, so she scooted over toward him and reached for his shoulder. He shrugged her off.

For a while she just lay there, thinking about what was happening to her. Wondering how much longer she had before she, too, went mad. Before her wolf took over and drove away the last of her humanity.

She couldn't stand it. Couldn't stand living with that knowledge, couldn't stand not having anyone to talk to. "Powell," she whispered. "Are you asleep?"

He shifted slightly, curling up further around himself.

"Powell," she said again. "That was in nineteen twenty-one. The same year you left Europe—that's what you told me. Was this why you left?"

"Yes," he whispered back.

When he didn't say anything more she scooted closer to him, until they were almost touching. "You must have been very upset," she said, which sounded lame. "It must have torn you up inside."

"Élodie was my mate. How do you think that felt?" he asked. He didn't turn to look at her, but there was a slight relaxation of his shoulders that told her he was resigned to talking to her now. "Yes. That was when I decided to leave. Before then I guess I thought I could make a life with the two of them. That no matter what horrible things I saw—what terrible things I did—it was still better than being alone. When Élodie . . . died, that changed. Lucie didn't want me to go, of course. She didn't want to be alone and she fought me."

"You mean you argued about it?"

Powell's shoulders shook in mirthless laughter. "She tried to kill me. Said that if she couldn't have me, I didn't have any right to live. She had made me into this—this lycanthrope. She felt that I owed her something. I disagreed. So we fought like savages. It was brutal, and bad, and we both got seriously hurt. She wasn't able to walk afterward, and I was. So I walked away."

"And then you came home. To Canada."

"No," he said. "I understood that wasn't possible. I couldn't go home—I would just be putting my family at risk. I came here because here I couldn't hurt anyone. In the wild places, where there weren't any people, I couldn't kill anybody."

Chey rubbed at her face with her hands. "Did you ever think of going back? To Lucie, I mean? You must have been so lonely."

"I never even considered finding Lucie again. She found me instead. I did think about going back to Germany, though. I used to think all the time about finding the Graf and his son, and killing them. I thought about it a lot."

"But you didn't?"

"No. I didn't need to. Hitler took care of them for me. In the Thirties, after he took over in Germany, he put out an edict that every werewolf in Germany had to be euthanized. And anyone who harbored a werewolf got the same punishment. They were among the first to go. You can call that justice, if you want."

Chey didn't know what to think of that.

There was something she wanted to say, though. Something she didn't want Lucie to hear. "Listen," she told him. "It sounds like there's not a lot of hope for me. Like this is just going to get worse. When the time comes—when there's nothing of me left, I want you to—"

She stopped. Something had moved behind her. Something that wasn't Lucie. Something big was displacing most of the air in the den. She spun around, thinking the bear who built the den had returned—or maybe the Russian hunter had found them; he had entered the den and was going to kill them all.

Instead, it was Dzo.

"Hi," the spirit said. He was covered in mud and his mask was dripping wet.

His appearance didn't entirely surprise Chey. She was certainly startled by it, but it didn't confuse her as much as it might once have. She had seen Dzo pop up in some very strange places, places where nobody should have been able to go. Wherever there was clean water—even the slow drip of groundwater sweating from the walls of the den—Dzo had access.

Powell turned and half sat up. His face changed instantly when he saw his old friend. "Have you got some news for us, old man?"

Dzo scratched underneath his furs. "The hunter's gone. He left. He tried to fool me, but I was too smart for him."

"What do you mean?" Powell asked.

"He said he was going to leave three days ago. Promised me he wouldn't hurt you and that he was giving up. I was ready to come back inside and tell you—"

"Wait," Powell said. "You talked to him?"

Dzo nodded. "Varkanin? Sure. He's actually a pretty nice guy, if you're not a werewolf. He made me some tea and we had a pretty long chat. How else was I going to figure out when he was leaving?"

Powell shook his head. "I asked you to watch him discreetly."

"Oh, I minded my manners," Dzo said. "I even held my pinky finger up when I drank my tea."

"That's not what 'discreet' means," Chey said, and rubbed the spirit's fur-covered arm. It was good to see him. It helped get her mind off of . . . other things.

"Yeah, okay. Anyway," Dzo went on, annoyed at being interrupted, "he said he was going to leave, and that it was safe for you to come out. I believed him at first, but then I noticed that he just went a little ways down the lake and made a new camp. And that he was still watching me with a pair of binoculars. I remembered what you told me once, Powell. About humans, and how sometimes they make up stories to fool each other. I figured Varkanin might be lying to me. That's the word, right? So I went into the lake and watched him from there. I can see pretty good under the water. He stuck around another three days, but then he left for real. He's about a hundred kilometers away, now. You think we'll ever see him again? I liked him. I never met a blue human before."

"Blue?" Powell asked. Then he shook his head. "Never mind. You did a good job, Dzo. Thanks."

Lucie stirred. "This means we can leave?"

"Yeah." Powell moved to the mouth of the den, which was still partially collapsed. "Come on. Help me dig us out. Chey—you take it easy. You're still recovering from your injuries."

The two werewolves worked fast. They seemed more than eager to get outside of the den and back to the wider world. Chey could imagine why. As cool light streamed in through the widening mouth, her stomach started growling, and she realized she was hungry for the first time since she'd been poisoned.

"Come on," Powell said, and took her hand. He led her out of the den, and together they stood upright again, blinking in the sunlight.

There was an awful lot of sunlight. It took a while for Chey's eyes to adjust—and to see where all the glare was coming from.

The ground outside the den was covered in nearly a foot of crisp white snow. It must have fallen while they were inside. Winter had come to the north.

part two

the barren grounds

31.

Preston Holness was in his happy place.

That did not mean he was happy.

He was surrounded by silk ties, in every possible combination of colors and patterns. One polished oak table held an array of matching handkerchiefs, while a glass case displayed tie pins that ranged from daring Art Deco fantasias to patriotic enamel maple leaves to tasteful but very large pearls set in white gold. He was in a shop that catered to people exactly like himself—powerful men who liked to dress well, and were happy to pay for the privilege of doing so.

It was the kind of place where you could have a heated discussion on your cell phone, as Holness was doing now, and the shop clerks wouldn't even shoot nasty looks at you. They understood that your work must be very important or you wouldn't have come in the shop in the first place. They understood that if you were taking a call, it was because you had to.

"I think we can be cautiously optimistic about what happened. Varkanin engaged them for the first time. He didn't expect to get them right away." Holness considered, carefully, a lie, then went ahead and told it. "I didn't expect him to, either. These things aren't easy. They take careful preparation and there's the basic necessities of survival to consider. He's not going to do you much good if he freezes to death. Do you know how cold it is up there at this time of year?"

On the other end of the line Demetrios all but snarled. "I want results, not a status report. He saw them. He shot at them. They are all still alive. Every day it takes is another day we have to wait on sending our crews in. Do you know how long it takes to survey a drill site, much less build a pipeline? Our people don't give a shit how cold it is."

"I'm sure I'll have better news for you very soon. Varkanin is motivated. He isn't going anywhere until he—until he achieves a satisfactory result." Even in a store with this understanding of high-powered phone calls, Holness didn't want to say the phrase "until he kills our werewolves" out loud.

"He's motivated when it comes to the French one," Demetrios said. "Are you telling me that if he gets her first, he'll actually stick around to take care of the other two? They mean nothing to him."

"I personally met with him and brokered a deal," Holness assured the lawyer. "From my end, I'm providing all the support I can muster. On his end . . . well. I can promise you he is committed to this. He would have done anything I asked for a chance to—to close the French deal."

"Committed. He's committed to it," Demetrios said, sounding one shade less angry than he had before. "I need something to take back to my superiors. Tell me how committed he is. Give me some proof of his commitment."

That, at least, Holness could provide. "You've seen the picture in his dossier. You've seen his blue skin. It's no accident he looks like that. Have you ever heard of something called colloidal silver?"

32.

The three werewolves were intoxicated by their newfound freedom, after they emerged from the den. Lucie danced across the snow, stretching every muscle in her body, while Powell ran around looking for signs of danger. Chey wanted to join them, wanted to do jumping jacks or yoga or just anything that would get her body moving again, but she felt like just crawling out of the muddy den had left her exhausted.

Dzo stood by, watching it all with a vaguely amused look.

"By God, it feels good to walk again," Lucie exclaimed, stretching her arms up toward the sky. She was standing on top of a rock that had been cleared of snow by the wind. "Two weeks in that hell! I thought it would never end."

"Lucie," Powell said, "I'm pretty sure this is your name."

"To breathe clean air. To see the sun! I am overjoyed," Lucie went on, lifting one leg, then the other. "Cher, do you not feel this good?"

Two weeks? Chey had had no idea it had been that long. She must have slept through most of it while her body repaired itself. It still didn't feel all that great. Knowing she was on an express train to crazy-town probably didn't help, but she felt weak and lethargic. Two weeks? Really?

"Could you just come down here for a moment?" Powell asked.

"Are you okay?" Dzo asked, taking Chey's arm. She tried to smile at him.

"How I long to run beneath the moon. To stretch and leap and jump. How I—"

"Enough!" Powell shouted.

Everyone turned to look at him. He was standing next to a tree, just outside the abandoned den. It looked like the bark had been cut up by something with sharp claws.

"Dzo," Powell said, his voice lowered now. "You're sure you didn't tell Varkanin where we were?"

"Well, no," the spirit said, looking guilty.

"No what?"

Dzo shrugged. "I mean, he already knew."

Chey looked again at the scarred tree. The scratches there looked kind of like writing, if you squinted, but like nonsense writing, like someone who didn't know the alphabet trying to make letters anyway. Then her brain made the connection. The scratches were in fact letters, very neatly carved into the bark. They just weren't in the alphabet she was most familiar with.

"That's—what? Cyrillic? Is that how they write in Russia?" Chey asked.

"Yeah," Powell said. "I can't read it. Lucie? I'm betting you can, since this first part looks a lot like your name."

Lucie was still standing atop her rock, as if she was afraid to get her toes wet in the snow. For a moment she just stared down at Powell, but then she jumped to the ground and walked over to the tree.

"It's nothing," she said. "Just a sign of his frustration. He knows we are too quick for him, and—"

"What does it actually say?" Powell demanded.

Lucie looked straight into his eyes as she repeated the message Varkanin had left for her. "It reads, 'Lucie, you will never have a home.' It means—"

Powell held up a hand for silence.

Chey knew what he was thinking. She was thinking it, too. The hunter had known where they were. He must have watched them crawl into the den. He could have killed them in there, when they had no place else to run to. He must have had a good reason not to do just that, but Chey couldn't think what it was.

A shiver ran down her back that had nothing to do with the weather.

"It means you can't hide from him. That he isn't going to just give up." Powell shook his head. "I wouldn't have believed him if he said otherwise. Fine. We need to get moving."

"I could really use a break," Chey said. "I'm still not a hundred percent, and maybe if I could just sit for a while. You know."

Powell came over and grabbed her shoulders. "I'd love to let you rest. I'd love to build some kind of shelter and overwinter here. But we just can't. He'll be back, probably when we're not expecting him."

"Okay," Chey said, struggling up to her feet. "Maybe I'll feel better once I get some exercise. Just—walk it off, right?"

"That's my girl. Come on. Lucie—you take point. You've got so much energy, you run on ahead and see if he left us any surprises. We're heading north."

"North?" Lucie asked.

"North?" Dzo echoed.

"Seriously, north?" Chey laughed. "What, like, toward the pole?"

"North," Powell repeated. "Lucie—get moving. We only have a few hours before the moon comes up. We need to be well clear of this place by then. He may be gone now, but there's nothing stopping him from coming back at any time. Dzo, help Chey walk if she needs it."

Lucie shrugged and darted off into the willow bushes to the north, moving almost as fast as her wolf could have run. Dzo offered Chey his arm and she took it gladly. She could walk with his help, though she wondered how long it would be before she just collapsed in the snow and Powell had to carry her again.

She didn't doubt that they needed to get away. But she did wonder why Powell had chosen this direction. The snow was thick enough to make walking difficult already. The farther north they got the more of it there was likely to be. And while the cold didn't bother werewolves the same way it bothered humans, there was a limit even to lycanthropic toughness. They were heading north, in the Arctic, at wintertime. It was one of those things you just didn't do. When Chey had been younger she had watched more than one television documentary that started out with a bunch of hikers heading north in winter. Typically they were documentaries about how people lost toes and other body parts to frostbite.

"Where are you taking us?" Chey asked.

Powell shrugged. "I just want to get clear of this area."

"That's bullshit. Lie to Lucie if you want to. But not me, Powell. I don't have much time left, so don't waste it on garbage. You're headed somewhere. Somewhere specific. Tell me!"

"It's you I'm thinking of," he told her. His icy green eyes revealed nothing. "I'm going to save you, Chey. If I can. So trust me. Alright?"

"You're looking for the place where the curse started," she said, suddenly getting it. "Like we talked about, before. You said in the spring we would go look for it, because you thought there was a cure there." She shook her head. "We're going to tramp through the snow forever just in case you might be right?"

"It's your only chance," he told her.

33

Far to the north, on the edge of the Arctic Ocean, lay the community of Umiaq. It was not a very large town, even by the standards of northern Canada. It had a permanent population of less than two hundred people, though that could swell at times when there was work to be had. The town had a general store and a post office, and a place that was a bar in winter and a fish restaurant in the summer when the ice-breakers could make their way into the harbor. It had a community hall that also served as the health center, with one nurse in attendance five days a week. Beyond that it had about a dozen houses, all of them looking as weather-beaten and small of stature as the local residents, 90 percent of whom were Inuit. The town's mayor was Métis, since he had a white trapper for a grandfather. As he made his way down the one plowed street of his domain he waved at everyone he saw, and stopped to shake hands with people he knew he wouldn't be seeing for months. The season called freeze-up was over, and winter was coming down out of the north pretty fast. Like it did every year, winter was going to drive most people into homes as snugly shut up and cozy as animal burrows. For weeks now these people had been stockpiling food and fuel, knowing how difficult it would be to get to the store once the snow started piling up for real and every creek and waterway leading out of town froze solid.

The Mayor stopped in front of the store and knocked caked snow off of his boots. The man named Varkanin was there waiting for him, sitting on a bench out front. He didn't know what to make of this new fellow, the Russian. It wasn't so much his nationality that bothered the Mayor. He'd met plenty of Russians before, coming through town off oceangoing fishing ships. Besides, he'd done a little checking and found out the Russian was working on behalf of the Canadian government, though of course that was all off the books. The government had given Varkanin plenty of money—which would normally make him the most popular guy in Umiaq. But his bright blue skin was disturbing.

"Have you spoken with your people?" Varkanin asked. "Have you found any who might be willing to assist me?"

"Well . . ." the Mayor said, rocking back and forth on his heels. "You gotta understand, we're what you might call a *traditional* sort of people. We're a people who like to tell stories. And we got a lot of stories about people who look strange." The Mayor held up two mittened hands. "No disrespect meant, now."

"None was inferred." The Russian was polite enough, and he wasn't in town to get drunk, which was also a plus.

The Mayor frowned, though. "Most people here think you must be some kind of *angakkuq*. That's like a shaman, I guess you'd say. Now, the *angakkuq* in most of the stories is a good guy; he helps the community. But he's scary, too, because he can do magic and talk to the spirits. You probably don't believe in spirits, since you're a southerner."

The Russian smiled knowingly. "I drank tea with one a few days ago," he said.

The Mayor cocked one eyebrow. Now *that* was weird. The Mayor believed in spirits; there was no doubt in his mind that they existed. But the idea that you could actually meet one—much less sit down and drink tea with it—was a little beyond how he conceived of them. He'd always thought of them as one of those things that was real specifically because you never actually had to confront it. He could believe they would drink tea, though, if they drank anything. He was a coffee man himself.

"I am no shaman, though," Varkanin continued. "I am here with the implicit sanction of your government—"

The Mayor shook his head. "That's not going to hold a lot of water with this bunch, honestly. They consider themselves people of Nunavut, not Canada."

Varkanin folded his arms across his chest. "I understand. Sir, I am only a simple hunter. I have found that my game is too challenging for me to handle alone. I only require the help of a few other hunters, men like

myself, hardy, brave souls. Who preferably know how to operate a snowmobile. I assumed I could find such people here."

"Oh, sure. You came to the right place for that," the Mayor assured
him.

"Then the problem is simply one of psychology." Varkanin nodded to
himself. "I did not wish to reveal something to you quite yet."

"Oh?" the Mayor asked. He'd kind of known there was something
fishy about this guy. Now it looked like he might just find out what.

"It is a very dangerous hunt I am on. The creatures I track are not
human. But they are not entirely inhuman, either. They are supernatural
in essence and viciously cruel. They are impervious to most modern
weapons."

"What are you talking about? Werewolves or something?" The Mayor
laughed out loud. "Boy, howdy. You really think I'm going to find hunters
around here willing to tangle with the likes of them?"

Varkanin smiled. It was not a warm smile, but there was a certain sympathy in it. "I think that if you approach the right kind of man—a young
man, one who feels the need to prove his mettle, my offer will prove irresistible."

The Mayor's mouth fell open. The guy had a point, he had to admit.

"I think it will also help, if I say I am offering one thousand dollars a
day to anyone willing to take this risk."

34

The wolves were starving, but there was nothing to eat. No game at all.

With the first heavy snowfall the last straggling migratory animals had headed south. Those that remained either curled themselves up in their dens to wait out the weather, or were smart enough to get very far away at the first scent of wolves moving across their territory.

The gray female stood very still in the blowing snow, nothing of her moving but her nose. It twitched back and forth, searching. Finding nothing. Behind her the white used her teeth to dig an insect out of the fur around her tail. It might be the only protein she got that day, and she intended to savor it.

The male ran circles, widening his gyre with every pass. Looking for any sign of food. The gray female could hear his feet cracking the brittle snow with every step. Any game animal within a kilometer's distance would be able to hear that noise, she was sure. Anything that heard it would run away.

She lifted her nose to point at the sky. She could smell more snow coming. A storm was heading down toward them, and she just wanted to curl up somewhere underground and conserve her strength. For some reason she couldn't understand, the other two didn't seem to want to find a den. They seemed almost frightened by the possibility, and every time she had pointed out some good location where the ground wasn't quite frozen, somewhere they could dig, the white and the male had shied away, dancing away from her as if she were mad.

She didn't understand what they were afraid of. She couldn't remember all those weeks in the bear den. She had slept through them, mostly. So she couldn't understand how stir-crazy the others had gone, how desperate was their need to be outside and running and hunting.

The male stopped circling.

There was no warning. He stopped in mid-lope, one paw still lifted to take another step. His body could have been frozen solid in place, except that his tail moved back and forth, very slowly. He closed his eyes.

And then he pounced. He threw himself forward, into the snow, paws and snout buried instantly. He scrabbled forward on his belly, pushing himself along with his hind legs, his rump in the air. Then he stopped again. His tail started waving dramatically.

The females rushed over to where he waited for them. The snow around his face was red with blood and steaming in the cold. Something small and furry lay dead in front of him. He'd attacked it with such violence that the gray female couldn't even recognize what it had once been.

It didn't matter. She was hungry. She moved forward to eat—and the male growled at her.

She jumped back in surprise. He'd never done that before.

Carefully, almost daintily, the male tore out the animal's internal organs and swallowed them whole. Then he stepped away from the remains and turned his face away so he wasn't looking at them.

The gray looked around, wondering what was going on. She saw the white sitting on her haunches in the snow nearby. Licking her lips. Waiting. Waiting her turn.

The gray had never been part of a pack before. When it had just been her and the male, there had been no need for the carefully stratified social structures that wolves had evolved over millions of years. The elaborate set of rules that made them social animals, instead of just coarse brutes.

One of those rules was that everyone got to eat—but in the proper order. The male would always come first. He was the alpha of the pack. As the dominant female, she was permitted to eat whatever she chose of what he left. There would be no repercussions if she finished off this meal. If she left nothing for the white. But it would be bad form.

In some ways, wolf society was as complicated as that of humans.

The blood had stopped steaming when she bent to eat. The meat was already starting to freeze. She tore a few strips of muscle tissue away from the dead thing's skeleton and held them in her mouth, then padded away to chew them at her leisure. Once she had stepped away from the feast, the white female lunged in to gobble up everything that was left, including the bones.

When it was done, the male rose and walked back and forth stiffly, his tail up and his ears forward and alert. Once he had their attention he headed away from the bloodstained snow, looking for the next meal. The females followed and soon he had broken into a run, head held low and level, tail streaming out behind him.

The gray ran to catch up with him, exulting in the strength that flowed through her muscles. She was still sore from her long convalescence, and her body still pained her wherever even an atom of silver remained in her flesh, but she was mostly recovered now and back up to speed. She started running capers and leaping every once in a while, even when she didn't need to clear some rock or tree root or other impediment in their path. It just felt so good to run. She dashed up beside the male, intending to race him, intending to spur him on to greater speed. She came up level with him until they were running side by side, and then she poured on a little more velocity, pushed her legs just a little harder—

The male slammed into her from the side, knocking her off her feet. She rolled in the snow, flakes filling the air as she shook herself in surprise. She got her forepaws down on the ground and stared at him with wide eyes.

He growled and showed her his teeth.

Then he turned away from her, and started running again. Behind them the white had stopped to wait for them. She danced back and forth in impatience, but she would not approach the gray where she lay on the snow.

In a pack, the alpha always led the way. No other wolf was allowed to run in front of him. He would be the first to spot danger or prey, the first to pounce, always the one to decide where they ran to, and this duty could not be interfered with.

The gray got back on her feet and followed him, not quite as exuberant as before. She didn't know how to live in a pack, how to operate as part of a well-oiled team. She was paying for her ignorance, now.

But she would learn. It wouldn't be difficult. The rules were written on her bones. They echoed in the beat of her heart. They were coded for in her DNA, in the secret place in every one of her cells. In time they would seem as natural as breathing.

Which wasn't to say her feelings weren't hurt.

35

"Jesus, it's cold," Powell said, and hugged himself. He was shivering wildly, his teeth smashing together again and again as he stamped his feet, trying to generate any kind of warmth. "What's keeping Dzo?"

The three of them were standing next to a frozen pond, little more than a puddle of ice in the middle of a stand of willow bushes. They had left Great Bear Lake well behind them, and this was the only body of water they'd been able to find, which meant it was the only place Dzo would be able to reach them. Lucie squatted down by the edge of the pond, clutching herself for warmth. She giggled, but Chey didn't even bother wondering why. Lucie was just crazy—she was the kind of person who would just giggle for no reason while she was naked in the freezing cold, waiting for somebody to bring her clothes.

Not as crazy as me, though, Chey thought. She had her arms wrapped around her chest and her feet placed tight together on the snow because she didn't want the others to know her secret.

She wasn't cold. Oh, she could feel how frigid the air was around them. She could feel the icy wind blowing through her hair. But it didn't bother her.

She could almost hear her wolf panting inside her brain. It liked the cold. It had evolved to live in temperatures like this. With every second that passed, as Chey's human body demanded that she start shivering, that she blow on her hands, that she start cursing the goddamned weather—the wolf was enjoying this more.

"He's so funny like that," Lucie said. She tore a long stick off one of the naked bushes and tapped at the ice of the pond. "Don't you think?"

"What are you talking about?" Powell demanded.

Chey stepped over to the edge of the pond and looked down.

The ice was nearly opaque, full of bubbles and white streaks. She could just see through it to the water below—where Dzo was pressed up against the surface, slapping at the underside of the ice with his hands. Silver bubbles streamed from his mouth and nose.

"Jesus, Lucie! Were you going to tell us, like, ever?" Chey demanded. She climbed out on the ice and started pounding on it with her fists. "He's trapped down there!" The ice cracked under her repeated blows and once Powell started helping her, they quickly smashed open a hole that Dzo could crawl through.

The animal spirit emerged dripping and bedraggled. The water on his furs was already starting to freeze over. Icicles hung from his mask. "Brr," he said, and then shook himself like a wet dog. Freezing water splattered all over Chey and Powell. Powell jumped back, cursing, but Chey just stared at Dzo in concern.

"You okay?" she asked Dzo.

The spirit squeezed some water out of his furs and shrugged. "Sure."

"You could have suffocated down there," Chey said. "Lucie would have let you drown!"

"Always you are so dramatic," Lucie said. "He can't die. Don't you know that by now? He is not what you might call human, *jeune fille.*"

"It's true," Dzo said, with a shrug.

"How about those clothes, old man?" Powell asked. Dzo nodded in understanding and took three bundles of clothes from under his furs. They were perfectly dry. Lucie shrugged into the woolen coat while Powell and Chey pulled on their pants and shirts. For a while no one spoke. Lucie and Powell closed their eyes and looked like they were just enjoying being warm again. Chey stared at her shoes.

"Okay," Powell said. "Let's get moving. We'll warm up as we walk. I want to cover twenty kilometers today before the sun goes down. You see that line of hills up there?" he asked, pointing. Almost lost in the white sky, the hills looked to Chey like they were perched on the edge of the world. There were no trees on them, no cover of any kind. "That's where we get to rest."

Chey rose to her feet and started to walk, not even waiting for Powell to lead. She knew what would happen in a second, and she didn't want to deal with it.

"Chey," Powell said, from behind her. "Chey. Come on. Put them on."

"I can't," she told him.

"Please. For me."

She stared down at the shoes in her hands. She had tried to put them on her feet. She really had. It had felt wrong. It had felt like she was putting on chains. Or a blindfold. Her feet wanted to feel the ground. To know it. Putting the shoes on would have been a betrayal of her body.

On a conscious, rational level, she knew exactly how crazy that was. She understood perfectly that it was her wolf telling her these things, feeling these sensations. That her wolf was winning.

On an emotional level, she would rather have chewed off her own feet at the ankle than shoved them into the shoes.

"It may help you, if you force yourself to be as human as possible," Powell told her. "It might delay the transformation."

"Just—just let me do this my way," she told him. "I'm still wearing my parka, aren't I?" Even though she was sweating underneath.

She threw the shoes into a snowbank. She couldn't even bear to hold them.

"If she doesn't want them, I'd be glad for them," Lucie announced, and ran over to dig them out.

36.

They had no maps, nor any GPS system to tell them so, but sometime that afternoon the werewolves crossed the Arctic Circle. Even if they had known, they wouldn't have stopped to commemorate the fact. Powell kept them walking at a brisk pace without a moment's rest.

By the time they reached the hills, the sun was already setting. It had never risen more than a few degrees above the horizon and for much of the afternoon it had been touching the earth, its lower edge blobby and wavering. In the long shadows of twilight they made a fire out of the branches of juniper bushes.

Chey lay back on a long stretch of gray rock and stared up at the sky. The clouds that scudded by sedately overhead were painted a million shades of orange. They formed great ramparts and bastions, impossible castles that stretched on forever. Beyond them a few of the more robust stars flickered in and out of view.

How long, she wondered, would she be able to look up at a sky like that and marvel? How long would she be stunned by it, awed by its beauty? It would mean nothing to her wolf. When her wolf took over her mind completely, would she ever look up at the sky again?

There were bigger things to worry about. They needed to eat. They hadn't seen a single animal during their northward trek, but Powell had told her not to worry. Now, while she watched, he made a spear out of a long, straight twig. He put a point on the end by scoring it with his teeth and then snapping off the end of the twig on a steep diagonal cut. Then he walked over to an unbroken field of snow and just stood in it for a while. When she asked him what he was doing, he said he was listening.

She watched him stand there until she started to get bored. Then, just before she decided to walk away and see what Lucie was doing—which was bound to be more entertaining—Powell moved.

His arm came up and down in one very fast, very smooth motion. His twig stabbed down into the ground like an arrow fired point-blank at the snow. She thought perhaps he'd just gotten fed up with waiting, until she heard a very thin, very piteous shriek from under the snow.

"Lemmings," he told her. "They burrow through the snow the way moles burrow through dirt. They eat whatever seeds they can find frozen into the soil below, and they never come up into the sun until it's time to mate." He reached down and brushed some snow away from the point of his makeshift spear. The weapon impaled the body of a creature no bigger than a field mouse.

"Nice," she said. There was a lot of blood, far more than she thought such a small creature could hold. There had been a time when that sight would have nauseated her. Now it just made her mouth water. Was that the wolf inside her, or was she just hungry? "Catch about fifty more of those and we can actually feel full tonight."

He smiled at her, then went back out into the field with his spear. And waited.

By the time it was fully dark, there were a dozen little dead animals hanging from his belt. As cute as they were, the very sight of them made Chey salivate. She tried to grab one away from him to eat it raw, but he held her at arm's length. He wouldn't give her any until they were fully cooked.

They tasted burnt. That was the wolf talking, of course. In reality he'd cooked them until they were just barely medium rare. Hunger overrode her preferences. The cooked lemmings were full of savory juices, dripping with fat. She ate as much as he gave her, and wished she could have more.

37.

After they'd finished dinner they had about an hour to kill in the dark before the moon rose. None of them wanted to sleep. Powell, who seemed to always know exactly when the moon would rise and set, had told them what was coming.

Up in the Arctic the moon did strange things—sometimes it never got above the horizon, and there would be entire days when the wolves never came out. Sometimes it rose and then never quite set again, and for five days the wolves would have free rein. The moon was about to enter one of the latter cycles, at a time when they least wanted it. "If this Varkanin comes back to finish the job when our wolves are awake," Powell said, "we could be in real trouble. They're tough and they're smart enough to know he's a threat. But he's already proven how tricky he can be. Our wolves wouldn't know what to do if he poisoned them, and if he sets a really clever trap they'll wander right into it."

For five days they wouldn't be human, not even for a minute to figure out their strategy. They would have to surrender themselves to the wolves and hope for the best.

"You really think he'll come back now?" Chey asked.

Powell shrugged. "He can read an almanac like anybody else. He'll know we're vulnerable, and for exactly how long. If it were me, this is the time when I would strike."

"So maybe we should find another bear den and hole up," Chey suggested.

"No!" Lucie said, shaking her head from side to side. "This I will not do. It was agony, down there. Pure torture."

"We need to keep moving," Powell decided, looking both Lucie and

Chey in the eye. "We need to keep moving north. We can't afford to lose five days, not now."

They were all silent for a while as they thought about what he meant. *He means,* Chey thought, *that I can't afford to lose five days. When we don't know how many my human side has left.*

"I'll keep an eye on your wolves," Dzo promised. "If something happens—"

Powell shook his head. "I appreciate it, old man. But if something does happen, if he comes for us—there won't be much you can do."

Dzo shrugged. "Maybe I can warn the wolves away from danger."

Powell smiled at Dzo and grabbed his shoulder through his furs. "They won't listen to you."

"Then I'll—I'll—I don't know what I'll do. But something," Dzo promised. He looked scared, and Chey wondered why. Dzo had a very limited concept of human mortality. Death was something that just happened to people, from Dzo's perspective, something to be dreaded no more than a bad cold or a stubbed toe. Maybe he was just afraid of being alone.

Lucie seemed not to be worried at all, even though she must have known the hunter wanted her death the most. She sat by the fire and spoke quietly with Dzo about nothing in particular, while Chey and Powell headed off into the shadows.

"You're scared," Powell said. "I don't blame you."

"I think the worst part is that we'll never know," Chey said, when they were far enough away from the fire. "We'll know the change is coming. And then maybe we won't come back."

"Maybe that's the best way to go," he told her. He kicked at the snow and together they watched ice crystals glitter in the starlight. "While we were walking here, I spent the day talking to Dzo, trying to put a plan together," he told her.

"I have a plan, too. Want to hear it?" she asked.

He sighed. "Sure."

"We give him Lucie."

Powell turned his face away from her.

"Just listen. We know he wants her dead. That's why he came here. We figure the Canadian government is helping him out and in exchange he has to kill us, too. But think about it from his perspective. He doesn't know us. Doesn't care about us. We've never even been to Russia, much less hurt anybody over there, right? So if he found her, tied up and defenseless, like a birthday present—and at the time he found her, we were a hundred kilometers away, or whatever—what do you think he would do? I think he'll forget about us. Let us go our own way."

"I'm not sacrificing her to him," Powell insisted.

"I know it doesn't seem like the sporting thing to do," Chey said, as if she were agreeing with him. "But maybe it's the *smart* thing to do. That's our big advantage over the wolves, right? Our brains?"

"This isn't something I'm going to discuss."

Chey frowned. "I don't like her. I admit it. She tried to kill me. But that's not where I'm coming from now, I—"

"It's not going to happen!" he said, and grabbed her arms.

She stared up into his eyes. He was certain about this.

"Why?" she asked.

"Because we need her. Don't ask me what for, because I'm not going to tell you."

He still hadn't let go of her. Chey leaned her head back. "It has something to do with the cure. You need her to make your cure happen. But as long as she's around we're in serious danger, Powell. The cure won't be much use if we're all dead before we find it."

"Just trust me," he hissed. "Please."

She had a hard time reading his face in the dark, but she knew he wasn't going to change his mind. She thought about arguing more anyway, just on principle. She thought about pulling away from him and storming off in a huff, to register her dissent, at least. But there was something about his insistence, his certainty—

He was doing this for her.

"I do," she said. "I do trust you." And then she leaned forward and kissed him, softly, on the lips.

"What does that mean?" he asked.

"Excuse me?"

"Was that because you trust me, or . . . ?"

"Maybe it's because you took care of me. Because when Lucie wanted to abandon me back at Fort Confidence, you wouldn't. You took me someplace safe so I could recover. You saved my life. Like you always do."

"I thought I ruined your life. By making you a lycanthrope."

She didn't want to think about that. Sometimes it seemed there was never a time when she hadn't been cursed. Sometimes she didn't want there to have been.

So instead of thinking, or talking, she kissed him again. Harder this time. His hands released her arms and instead they wrapped around her back. She sank into him, pressing her body against his. Pulling him into her. Their mouths opened and their tongues met. Her breath came fast and hot and she felt her body curling around him, felt his body warm against hers, felt his desire. He still wanted this. Even if she was losing her humanity, he wanted what was left of it.

"Chey," he said, as she kissed his throat and his collarbone, "the time—"

"Don't stop," she said. His hands searched her back, his mouth ran down the line of her jaw. She could feel him getting distracted, feel him worrying about the fact that at any second they were going to transform. "Please don't stop," she said, and moaned as his hand slipped under her parka and found the sensitive skin of her belly. "Yes," she sighed, as his fingers slid upward, toward her breasts.

Then silver light flashed between them, an instant that stretched out to eternity. The pleasure of his hands on her body melted away in the overwhelming glory of the metamorphosis. The gray wolf howled in pure joy. The male grasped her with his paws as she squirmed around, pulled her back toward him.

This time, they did not stop.

38

It was a rare thing when the wolves went to sleep and woke still in their own bodies. They relished the morning light and rolled about in the snow, stretching their legs out as long as they would go, yawning great yawns so their pink tongues flapped in the air. The gray female got up to relieve herself. Marking territory was important, now—now that she was part of a mated pair.

Her body throbbed with the soreness of the night's exertions and she picked her way carefully out of the copse of stunted trees where they had sheltered for the night. Her pads barely broke the crust of the snow as she started on a looping trail, lifting her leg every few meters to put her scent on the land. Later on, she knew, her mate, the alpha male, would follow her path, finding each of her deposits and double-marking them. In this way he would advertise to the world that she was his.

Halfway along her route, however, she stopped and sat down on the snow. There was something wrong with the sky.

Normally wolves have no interest in meteorology. The weather is not something they can control, nor do they have the human time sense that allows them to remember past conditions and extrapolate predictions of weather to come. There are some instincts, however, bred so deeply into the wolf brain, that they can break through even the immediacy of hunger and the constancy of the hunt.

Overhead, to the east, the west, the south, the sky was blue, a fierce unclouded blue that went on in all directions forever. Except to the north. The sky there was black.

The wolf turned her head to one side. Whimpered a bit. This wasn't good.

The blue shaded almost imperceptibly down into solid night up there. The wind coming from that direction was not particularly strong, though it did smell a certain way that bothered her. It smelled like snow. Not the powdery, soft snow that covered the world around her. It smelled like particles of flying ice.

She yelped a little, without really knowing why.

The male and the white female came and joined her presently. They both took a look at the wall of darkness approaching from the north, and they both looked concerned. But none of them seemed to know why it scared them so much.

By noon a curving arm of cloud had emerged from the darkness. It stretched over their heads as if it were gathering in the air, the way a human in bed gathers the covers on a cold winter night, bunching them around her body. The smell of icy snow had grown sharper and the wind had picked up.

The wolves spent most of the day hunting for lemmings under the snow. They took no real precautions, though they kept eyeing the salient features of the landscape, looking for those that might provide some shelter if this wind really picked up. Their bones told them something was coming. That was enough. Their bones would get them through it. Wolves had been relying on those instincts for millions of years, and they rarely failed except in the most extreme of circumstances.

By late afternoon the black sky had gained shape and definition. It was a whole system of clouds, spiral in shape, that was bearing down on them at a steady clip. In the middle of the spiral the air seemed—disturbed, somehow. There were occasional flashes of lightning inside the cloud.

The wolves were well fed by that point. It was definitely time, their ancestral memories told them, to start looking for a place to ride this out. In a very abstract way they knew that this was a storm coming, and that it was going to be a big one. They started nosing around the trees, poking their paws between clefts in the rocks, looking for caves. There were none to be found, however. The hills were of glacial origin, not volcanic, so they were very smooth and had few cracks or crevices in them. Those that did exist had long since been filled in by permafrost too hard to dig through.

The females looked to the male, who just watched the storm coming.

They needed a plan, but he didn't seem to have one. The gray wolf started to really worry.

Her head sank between her shoulders and her ears went back. She grumbled, a kind of half-growl, half-barking sound that was quiet enough the male could pretend he didn't hear it. It was not the kind of sound a confident, well-fed wolf would normally make. The white responded by standing closer to the male, which sent the signal that she believed in his leadership and would follow him anywhere.

There was nothing in the storehouse of instinctual knowledge, though, that the male could drag up. No perfect plan for what to do next. They could try to hide in the trees, but any serious wind would cut right through the naked branches. They could try to dig down into the snow and curl up there, melting out dens for themselves with their own body heat. There was a risk, however, that if the storm dumped more snow on top of their snow dens, they would be buried under deep drifts and not be able to breathe.

The one other option was to run south, to flee the weather. The male seemed to resist this idea, though by the look on his face even he couldn't have said why. Anyway, by the time it was upon them, it was far too late to outrun the storm. It moved much faster than any wolf that ever lived, supernatural strength or no.

It hit them like a freight train, and they were not ready.

39

It happened more quickly than any of the wolves could have imagined. Even the male, who had lived in this part of the world for decades, had never been this far north. Not in wintertime. He was unprepared for what the land above the Arctic Circle could do.

Everything seemed hushed and waiting. There were a few lazy snowflakes, drifting in the air. The snow danced on tiny air currents, the frayed hem of the wind, as if gravity itself was holding its breath.

Then they heard a howling noise, like a beast in torment. A beast the size of a country. In an instant the squall was upon them. The wind slammed through the scrub forest, tearing branches from the trees, kicking up ground snow in enormous prismatic sprays. The squall brought with it a million tons of ice, ground up small and thrown at the wolves with the force of a sandblaster. It was all they could do to keep from being picked up by the wind and thrown about like the storm's playthings. They were forced to dig their feet into the snow and the frozen earth beneath, their heads blown sideways, their eyes smashed shut to keep the stinging crystals out. The gray wolf tried to howl, but the sound was torn out of her, ripped away and thrown high up into the air.

The constant beat of the ice crystals on her nose, on her eyes, on the sensitive pink flesh inside her ears was torture. The screaming of the wind deafened her. The gray wolf tried time and again to get her head around, to keep it from being tossed and blown back by the storm. Somehow she managed to face forward. To open her eyes, just a crack, so she could see what was ahead of her.

Through squinting eyelids she could just see the male ahead of her, tail held straight back by the wind. His fur was slicked back by the wind and he kept trying to raise one foot, only to have to put it down again to regain his balance.

He growled with effort. She felt the vibrations of his voice through the soil, rather than hearing it. Somehow he got one foot to move a few centimeters forward before he had to slam it back down. She saw the muscles of his hind legs bunching, getting ready to push him forward another step.

Behind her the white wolf curled into what little lee the gray's body made in the wind. The gray wanted to turn and snap at the white for being so close, but she didn't dare turn broadside to the wind. It would knock her over and send her rolling halfway down to America. She tried to shuffle her forepaws forward, tried to inch them ahead of her into the wind. It was like trying to press her body through a brick wall.

She was stronger than a normal wolf. She was stronger than any living thing on earth. She would take this step. When it was done she would take another. She would follow the male, her alpha, wherever he chose to go. She would follow.

She managed to get her forepaws a centimeter farther. She sank lower to the ground, spreading her legs a little for balance. She couldn't seem to catch a breath before the wind tore it away. It didn't matter. Another step, another centimeter—there. She braced her hind legs, as she'd seen the male do. Shoved forward with the thickest, strongest muscles in her body. The wind tried to push her down. Tried to shove her face into the snow. She refused to allow that. Lifting her muzzle was agony, but she got her nose up into the wind, like the prow of a ship steering into a massive ocean current. It wasn't easy. Nothing was easy.

She was panting from exertion. Her muscles cramped and begged her to stop.

She refused to listen to them.

Another step. Another centimeter.

Ahead of them, perhaps a hundred meters, she could just make out a place where the ground fell away between two rounded hills. The site offered no sharp cliffs to shelter underneath, but if they could just get into the softly sloped hollow, if they could get into some kind of windbreak, any kind at all—she understood that this was what the male wanted.

Where he was leading her. Knowing they had a plan helped. It gave her new strength. She took another step.

Another centimeter.

Behind her the white wolf scurried forward, drafting along with her, stealing forward momentum from the gray's strength. The gray barked in annoyance but kept moving forward. Every time she tried to lift a foot the wind grabbed it and tried to tear it off her body. It did not matter. She would beat this wind. She would hold out against it. Ahead of her the male took another step. Faltered, his chin grazing the snow, his forelegs sprawling sideways. His body shook with the effort as he pushed himself upward again, pushed himself into the wind.

She would do the same. He was her alpha. She would follow him.

Another step.

Another centimeter.

40

When they reached the hollow between two hills, the gray wolf wanted nothing more than to lie down in the snow and sleep until the storm went away. It wasn't an option. The snow down there was up to her chest and constantly getting deeper.

It was coming down so hard that she couldn't see anything but white. The male was a shadow in the glare, the sky a shade of white that deepened to almost perfect darkness overhead. The white female was lost altogether in the whiteout. Only her lolling pink tongue and her panting breath gave her away.

Snow crusted on the gray's muzzle and got between her toes, where it burned. She had evolved to live in this environment, perhaps, but this was the Arctic at its most harsh and nothing could survive its wrath for long without shelter.

At least they could move here. Not easily. Each foot had to be lifted clear of the snow, dragged forward, and then stabbed downward through what felt like shaved ice. But it was better than when they'd been out in the fiercest current of the wind.

The male refused to let them stop. He kept them trooping forward, deeper into the storm. He was heading north, still, regardless of conditions. The gray followed him because he was her alpha, but she didn't have to like it. She grumbled and growled and snapped at the snow around her face when it drifted up around her. Eventually the male got tired of her vocalizations and turned to snap at her. After that she was silent, complaining only with her eyes.

They followed a more sinuous course now, winding their way through the hills, staying out of the wind. Moving at least kept them warm—the work of just forcing their muscles to obey them was enough to generate plenty of body heat.

It got harder as they progressed, however. The snow kept piling up until it was at the height of their chins. The gray wolf found she had to lift her nose to the wind just so she could breathe. It became all she could do to keep pulling her legs out of the snowdrifts with every step. Did the male expect them to burrow through the snow once it was over their heads?

Apparently he did. She could understand, in an abstract way. There was nowhere here for them to rest, nowhere they could stop and wait this out. Their only chance was to keep moving and find such a place. A cave, an abandoned bear den, a place where the rocks formed an overhang they could shelter underneath. Anything.

Night came and found them still struggling along. The darkness was total. If the gray had thought whiteout conditions were difficult, she quickly found the pitch blackness inside a snowstorm at night was worse. She did not know where she found the strength to keep moving. Eventually she decided she did not have any strength left. She kept moving anyway, because there was no choice.

The snow piled up around her face. She held her neck up as far as it would go so she could still breathe.

It piled up over her nose. She burrowed forward through it, shoving her chest against the drifts like a plow. Her breath was close around her face, and she felt like she was swimming in snow. She felt like her feet weren't touching the ground anymore.

She felt like the whole universe had been filled up with fluffy white snow. That she was falling through it, falling forever, with no earth left to catch her, no sky to be above her. She tried to flail her legs, to find something to catch onto. There was nothing there.

And then . . . she couldn't move her legs.

The weight of the snow above her was pressing down on her so hard it prevented her from moving. She couldn't get the leverage to move her feet. Not even enough to turn her head from side to side. She could just barely open her mouth—which instantly filled with snow.

She couldn't breathe. Werewolves can't asphyxiate, not like that.

But the gray wolf didn't know that.

She panicked. Tried to scream. Snow packed her throat and she couldn't even scream. She couldn't see anything, couldn't smell, couldn't taste—felt only snow around her, only freezing cold—her brain bashed at the confines of her skull, desperate to escape. She was buried alive, she was buried, she was, she was buried and couldn't, she was buried, buried alive and couldn't escape, she couldn't, couldn't—

Fangs buried themselves deep in the fur of her neck. She tried to twist around, to fight. The white wolf must have taken this opportunity to kill her, she thought. The white wanted to seize dominance, to take her mate away from her! She fought and scratched and clawed, but her body refused to obey her commands. She had to fight back—had to—had to—

The jaws dragged her upward, to the side. The power behind them was enormous, its strength seemingly limitless. Her body was pulled along by the loose folds of skin at her neck, pulled out of the snow until freezing air screamed all around her. She howled and whined and snapped but the teeth in her neck wouldn't let go. They hauled her backward, hauled her around. A wolf's head butted her stomach and made her spit up snow she'd aspirated into her lungs. Another push and she was up on her feet, standing on a spur of rock that had been cleared of snow by the wind.

It was the male. Her mate, her alpha, had come to rescue her. She tried to lick his face, tried to thank him, but he was in too great a hurry. Leading her by shoving against her side and goosing her backside with his nose, he made her run forward, her feet sliding on the frozen rock, sinking through the snow around it. He shoved her forward another few feet and then saw her collapse in the comparative shelter of a fallen tree. Beneath its great mass the air was almost still. The snow that spilled over the top of it came down softly and with an almost pleasant pattering sound.

The white was already there, curled around a broken branch, fast asleep.

It didn't take the gray long to join her.

41.

The storm lasted for three days. The wolves had to move constantly to avoid being buried under all the snow. Shelter became harder and harder to find, and each time they moved to a new location they had to push harder against the wind. They couldn't tell the solid ground beneath them from the treacherous snowpack. When the gray female slid, flailing, into a ten-foot drift, the male grabbed her by the neck and pulled her out. Later, when the male fell, he managed to struggle his way out before the gray could come to his rescue. When she tried to lick his face afterward and show him her concern, he growled at her and trotted forward to the front of the pack again.

On the morning of the third day the sun managed to punch through the spiraling clouds, and they were blinded by snow glare, but the gray knew it had to mean they were reaching the edge of the storm and she was glad for it. By driving them northward, through the storm, the male had actually taken the shortest possible course out of the snow and wind—had he run south, as she had wanted him to when it began, the storm would have followed them as far as they could run. By the afternoon of that day, when the wind had died down to a roar in her ears and the snow had stopped falling, she was so happy to be able to stand upright again (instead of leaning constantly into the wind) that she raced forward, nipping at his heels. The white brought up the rear and barked so they wouldn't forget her and leave her behind.

The clouds broke, dissolving into long curving streamers of shadow that could no longer blot out the sun. Eventually even the sky grew clear and they found themselves atop a rocky outcropping blown almost clean of snow, looking out on an ocean of white.

The drifts were as high as the tops of the hills. All the trees and bushes that had dotted this land before, all the winding creeks and streams, were completely buried. There was nothing to see from horizon to horizon but snow—and each other.

The male let them rest, for a while. They lacked the energy to do more than drop to the ground and pant, stretching their legs out in the air every once in a while. They soaked up what little warmth the sun offered and simply breathed, simply let their bodies uncurl and let the ice around their eyes and muzzles melt in their body heat. Long before the gray was ready, the male signaled it was time to move on again. The females followed, because that was what packs did. They followed their alphas.

The male's path was not something they could see or smell, but they knew that as he weaved and cut capers ahead of them he was not leading them blindly. He was still following the line of the hills, still dashing from one rock to the next where there was safe footing. The going was slow, but much faster than it had been during the storm. By nightfall they had entered a narrow valley between two high rills, a place where the snow was only a few feet deep. He led them down between these arms of raised earth, headed north. Always north.

The gray's instinct was to trust him, and not to wonder why they kept to this same course. He must have his reason, after all. Yet she could not help but glance back over her shoulder now and again, and wonder why they were headed into ever colder, ever snowier places. The temperature didn't bother her, but she knew in her bones that they would find more game to the south, where the plants the small animals depended on could thrive. The farther north they went the hungrier they would become.

Because as a wolf she was less than a year old, she had never migrated before, nor did she know they were headed toward a caribou mating ground. She had never seen one of the huge deer—though if she had, her body would have recognized it immediately. Her genes knew exactly how closely tied the caribou was to the wolf, so that their lives were like two threads twined together to make a stronger rope.

She followed where the male led.

If the white had any questions, or doubts, she kept them to herself. She trailed behind the gray a certain minimum distance, and stuck to her appointed place.

Until they heard the machines.

42.

They were not, of course, true wolves. Their bodies were made in the form of extinct dire wolves, down to the genetic coding that taught them how to live in and with their world. But they were more than animals, and less, in some ways. There was another kind of instinct that waited always, crouched in the dark recesses of their brains. The knowledge the curse imparted, which had but one commandment.

When they first heard the sound, the male's ears perked up instantly and he half crouched as if he was going to sit down. He stayed frozen in that position, tensed and ready to pounce, while his head tracked back and forth, turning his ears to focus on the buzzing sound he'd heard.

Behind him the females moved in close, ready for his signal. Ready to attack.

It was not a sound native to that land. It was a human sound, a buzzing, droning whine of the kind human machines made. Soon they had human scent in their noses as well. People were close.

The commandment of the curse came to the forefront of their minds. It made them taste blood. Their eyes narrowed and their tails drooped. The white started a throaty growl that spoke of violence.

The commandment was simple, and it was this: thou shalt kill humans. There was an irresistible urge inside them, a fiery need, to destroy, to claw, to tear apart and rend anything human they came across. It was what they had been created for by the magic that gave them wolf bodies, the same magic that made them vulnerable to silver.

There was absolutely no questioning this need, as far as the wolves were concerned. You attacked humans on sight without thinking, without wondering why. It was as natural to them as breathing, as the beating of their hearts.

The noise was growing louder. They tracked it with their ears, their feet shuffling on the ground, their bodies curling around and around as they tried to decide which direction it was coming from. To decide which direction they would strike.

At the top of the ridge to their left, it appeared. A long sleek machine with a human holding onto its back. It throbbed with machine noise and stank with oil. It threw up a great plume of snow in its wake as it blasted across the heights.

And then it stopped. It rumbled to a halt and the human stepped off its back. He waved his arms in the air, taunting them.

The male growled for them to hold their ground, perhaps sensing a trap—but it was too late. The white female couldn't stop herself, even if she had wanted to. She shot across the snow, nearly invisible except as a ripple in the air. She was barking and growling at once, licking her lips and digging in deep with her claws spread out to find better purchase on the loose snow. The human climbed back onto his machine and turned it around, heading north, from whence he'd come. Running away from her—or leading her.

The male and the gray had no choice. They followed after the white, running as fast as their legs could carry them. There was something wrong here, something out of place. They were werewolves. They did what their curse commanded, and nothing else.

43

"They're reporting in now, boss," Sharon Minik said, peering through a very nice pair of binoculars. They had polarizing lenses that compensated automatically for ice glare. On a day like this you could go blind looking through binoculars in the wrong direction. Her new employer had all kinds of cool gear. "Jimmy's almost done." Out on the hills she watched as Jimmy Etok smoothed at the snow with his hands. "That's the last one buried," Sharon said, when Jimmy stood up and gave her a thumb's up, lifting his arm high over his head.

Behind her Varkanin lifted his radio. "Very good, Mr. Etok," the Russian said. "Return to the first rally point now, if you please."

Sharon lowered the binoculars and turned on the seat of her snowmobile to look at Varkanin. She had grown accustomed to his blue face and it no longer spooked her just to look at him. It helped that he was so nice. He'd never once given her a hard time about being a girl hunter, like the old fellas up in town always did. And he'd made sure she was okay with this hunt, instead of assuming she would do what he said just because he was paying her.

"You are certain," he had asked her one night, during the storm, "that when you see them, you will be able to kill?"

"Yeah," she'd said, looking away. "If what you say is true, then . . ."

He'd nodded and put a gentle hand on her arm. "They are killers. Each of them. Between the three of them they've slaughtered hundreds of innocent human beings."

So it wasn't like she was drawing down on *people*. These were monsters. Even the government had decided they had to die, for the common good. How could she refuse that kind of public service? "And you say I won't have to shoot them when they look human. Just when they look like wolves."

"We will complete the hunt before the moon goes down," he'd said. He'd been very clear on that part.

He'd walked her through every piece of the operation, from the planning stage to the kill. He'd shown her maps and satellite data the Canadian government had given him, tracking every move the lycanthropes made. He'd shown her the guns they would be using, and the silver bullets. Maybe she'd started getting a little scared, then, because he'd changed his tack. He'd told her about how important it was that the lycanthropes were put down—that was his term, put down, like what you did to a mad dog. He'd pointed out how it could be done mercifully, and without too much danger. Sharon had listened to every word. She'd even started to admire him for what he was doing. After all, the werewolves were heading right for the town of Umiaq, where all her people lived. If they weren't stopped now, who knew what they were capable of?

And yet . . .

Now, when it was really happening, she had to admit she did have one doubt left. She had started to think that maybe Varkanin wasn't doing this just out of the goodness of his own heart. "You got a real hate thing going with these wolves, don't you?"

"I have a job to perform, just like you do," he said, with a smile. "You remember our agreement, yes?"

"Sure," Sharon said. "I still don't think it's smart, though."

He handed her a pistol loaded with silver bullets. She ejected the clip and took a look at them. She had expected them to be shiny, but in fact they were black with tarnish. "If the gray one or the big one, the leader, get close, I plug 'em. But the white one—"

"Is mine to put down," Varkanin said, nodding. "No matter the cost. If she attacks me, you are not to intervene. If somehow she injures me, you are to keep your distance until you are certain that I am dead. Only then should you engage her."

Sharon looked away. This guy called himself a hunter, but . . . she knew about hunting. When she was a kid her mother had tried to teach her the arts—which in her town had largely meant sewing, creepy throat singing, and carving wood. She'd never been any good at that stuff. Her dad, who lived down in Yellowknife, had taken her hunting every summer since she was six years old. He hadn't cared if she was any good at it, because he said like anything important in life, if you did it badly long enough you'd eventually develop some level of talent. He'd been right, too. Now she was one of the very few Inuit women in Nunavut who actually made a living at it. She had a reputation for clean kills, for bringing back meat no matter how bad the weather was, and for not making stupid mistakes. Varkanin had told her that was why he had chosen her to be his second in command on this mission, and she'd felt real proud when he said that. Because he was supposed to be some big-shot hunter himself.

She'd had time to get to know Varkanin a little, now. During the storm they'd holed up in a one-room cabin plotting their strategy, and she'd seen something in him she didn't recognize. In her experience hunters killed because they needed to eat, or maybe because some southerner was paying them to help him take a moose head for his wall. Real hunters kept their cool and they never let the hunt mean anything personal.

She'd had time to see underneath his unnaturally calm exterior, though. She'd seen the hatred he hid behind his blue skin and his placid eyes. This Russian guy wasn't hunting today. He was here to do executions.

"Please remember not to underestimate them," Varkanin said. "If we stick exactly to plan, we will not be in any danger. But if we deviate—"

"I know! They're werewolves. They're crazy dangerous, sure," Sharon said. She slammed the clip back into her pistol and shoved it inside her coat, where her body heat would keep the oil in the gun's action from freezing. "We've got all kinds of stories about them. About how you never, ever mess with them. Some people over east of here, near Greenland, they say if you see a werewolf it means you're going to die. Over here we know better—we just run the other way, fast as we can."

"Yet you chose to join me, when I asked for your help."

Sharon shrugged. " 'Cause I figured you knew what you were doing. I'll keep my head screwed on straight, don't worry."

Varkanin gave her his chilly smile. She'd seen it a couple times before and she wasn't sure what to make of it. It was like he approved of her, sure, but also like he was remembering something very sad. There was a story there, but it wasn't one she wanted to hear.

The radio in Varkanin's hand crackled. It was Leonard Opvik, the crazy kid from Kugluktuk who always wanted the most dangerous job. Sharon figured he was compensating for something. "They saw me! Yee-haw, here they come!"

Varkanin laughed. "Good, it is beginning. But tell me, Ms. Minik, what does 'yeehaw' mean?"

"Probably something he saw on TV," she told him. Sharon gunned her snowmobile into life. "See you at the rally point, okay?"

"Remember what I said about being careful!" he shouted over the noise of her engine. Sharon was already gone before he could finish his sentence, though, glad to finally be moving. Excited, despite her doubts and fears.

This might actually be fun, she told herself.

44.

The wolves weren't running as a pack anymore. They weren't animals living according to carefully maintained social rules. They had become plain and simple monsters. This was what the curse had been created for.

The gray raced to keep up with the white. The male was slightly off to one side, loping alongside them both. Ahead of them the human machine whined and belched hellish fumes in their faces. The driver kept looking back at them over his shoulder. He didn't look nearly as scared as he should be.

No matter. Jaws dripped with slaver. Lips pulled back from enormous, bone-crushing teeth. Claws dug hard into the snow to propel the wolves forward, faster, ever forward. They were gaining on the machine. Soon they would be upon it. They would pull it apart with their mouths, smash it with their paws. The driver would be shredded—his skin torn off, his vitals consumed and then, then, they would howl to the moon, offering up their blood sacrifice to something none of them understood. As it had always been, how it must be. Closer—they inched closer to the machine, until the snow it kicked up behind stung their noses and flecked their eyelashes. Just one more sprint, one more ounce of power dug up from inside their hearts and delivered straight to their legs, one more lunge and—

The machine roared. The driver twisted his handlebars and smoke billowed out of the back of the machine. It shot forward over the snow twice as fast as before, much faster than the wolves could run. It tore a crazy zigzag path through the snow, cutting back and forth for no apparent reason.

The wolves followed, running as fast as their legs would carry them—straight into a minefield.

The first explosion caught the male, throwing him high into the air. Blood spurted from his throat and legs and he spun, flipping over twice before crashing back down to the snow. The white female skidded as she slowed down, trying to turn to see what had just happened. Her foot barely grazed another mine. It was enough.

Heat, light, and smoke washed over the gray like an avalanche, the pressure buffeting her ears. She curled around herself in midair, then slid across the packed snow of the machine's path, rolling on her side and wheezing as blood poured from her mouth and nose. She'd been at the edge of the explosion and still the blast had deafened and blinded her, completely thrown her mind off balance. She couldn't think, couldn't hear, couldn't get her feet underneath her.

When the ringing in her ears subsided she lifted her head and put her forepaws down on the snow. Slowly she rose to stand on all fours and look around. She saw the white wolf right away.

The white female was missing one foreleg, and most of her face on that side. She kept shaking her head and sneezing. Her remaining eye was rolling in her head.

There was no sign of the male.

Angry buzzing sounded from either side. The land rose in a mild incline to the gray's left. To her right it was flat and featureless. Humans on machines were coming from both of those directions. She thought her chances would be better if she took on the human on the flat stretch of ground, and turned to run that way—and then stopped.

She sniffed the air. It was foul with smoke and human stenches. She could barely smell anything under the snow. But there—yes, right before her, not three feet from where she stood—something hard and metallic lurked, just waiting for her to step on it. Now that she looked more closely she could see that the snow atop it had recently been disturbed, then smoothed back over by human hands.

She snarled and took a step back. The white, perhaps thinking she was trying to close ranks, trotted toward her, bobbing wildly up and down as she tried to move gracefully with only three legs.

The humans were getting closer. They had guns. The gray knew the smell of gun oil. She could smell silver, too. She could smell their silver bullets.

She backed up another step. And then realized there might be something buried in the snow behind her, as well.

There was no time to check. The humans and their machines were coming closer, coming toward her at full speed. This was where she would have to make her stand.

45

"Jesus," Sharon Minik said, looking down from the top of the hill. The two wolves standing there looked like they should be dead already. They were pinned down inside the minefield, both covered in blood. The white one looked like the only thing keeping her alive was sheer hatred and willpower. "They don't have a chance," Sharon said, taking the gun out of her parka. It was warm in her hand.

"Do not feel sorry for them," Varkanin said over the radio. "They would not show mercy if the situation were reversed. You must show none now. Close in. The gray female must be Cheyenne Clark, the youngest of the pack. Give her a quick death, please."

"Don't worry," Sharon said. "She won't suffer."

"I am less worried about this than I am of the belief that if it is not done quickly, we will lose our advantage." The Russian called out for Jimmy Etok and Leonard Opvik to check in. They responded instantly, as they'd been taught.

Sharon understood all the things that could go wrong on a hunt. All the different ways nature could make a joke out of your plans, especially up here where the weather was openly hostile to human life and the animals were all smarter than most people she knew. Still, this one looked like it was all over except for skinning the pelts. She had to admire Varkanin's planning. He'd thought of everything.

Sharon gunned her snowmobile into life and tore down the slope toward the mine field. The two wolves were back to back, turning slowly to face every possible angle of attack. They were smart enough not to move too far—Sharon hadn't expected them to figure out how mines worked so quickly, but it didn't matter. As long as they were trapped, and they knew it, it was going to be easy to just sweep in and pick them off.

"Who can see the male?" Varkanin asked, over the radio. "Where is he?"

"Looks like he landed in a snowdrift over here," Jimmy said. "He didn't look too good, last I saw him—maybe he's dead."

"No," Varkanin announced. "He is not. Be careful."

"Cover me," Sharon said. "I'm going in for the gray." With silver bullets you had to get close to be sure of a kill. Normal bullets, lead bullets, spun on their long axis as they flew through the air. It kept them flying straight. Silver bullets were different—they tumbled when they came out of a gun barrel. That meant they weren't as accurate as lead bullets, so at more than short range they were almost useless. She goosed her throttle and her machine covered the distance easily. Twenty meters away—probably still too far. Fifteen. She had to get as close as she could without actually entering the minefield. Theoretically she knew exactly where each mine was, but it would be far too easy to make a misstep and blow herself up.

On the other side of the wolves, she saw Varkanin moving in as well. She glanced at his hands and saw he didn't have his gun out. Instead he was holding a long, thin knife.

"Boss, what are you doing?" she asked. "You can just shoot the white, right now, and we're done."

"She needs to suffer, first," Varkanin said.

Sharon bit back the words that came to her mouth. That was a mistake, and she knew it, but she couldn't tell him that. Not when he was calling the shots. During a hunt, you never questioned authority. There was no time for thinking.

At ten meters away she killed her engine and jumped down into the snow. She knew there was a mine a few meters to her left, so she swerved a little out of its way as she closed the rest of the distance on foot. Five meters. Three. That was close enough.

"Got movement," Jimmy Etok said. "Something's coming out of the snow. Might be the male."

"I see it," Leonard replied. "I'm moving." Behind her Sharon heard the roar of Leonard's snowmobile. "Got you, dickhead."

Sharon lifted her gun and sighted along the barrel. The gray stared back at her with hate-filled eyes. The animal lowered its head and its ears swiveled back. Its paws stretched toward Sharon across the snow. It looked like it wanted to jump but didn't dare because of the mines.

Fear, real deep, made Sharon's head hurt. She knew that feeling, though—she'd felt it when hunting bears and even moose. This was a creature who could hurt you, even kill you, if you didn't respect it properly. If you didn't use your human brain to get the better of it. She had a perfect shot, though. This was over. She started to squeeze her trigger.

Behind her she heard Leonard Opvik scream. She heard it again in her ear, over the radio, and it made her wince. She dropped her arm and turned around to see what was happening.

She nearly dropped her gun.

It wasn't the male wolf. Sharon had no idea what it was, except that it was nine feet tall and covered in white fur. Or it could have been a fur coat. Its head was covered in a carved wooden mask studded with ivory spikes.

With a roar, it picked up Leonard's snowmobile with one hand and tossed it end over end.

46

The gray wolf stared up the mouth of the gun. She could smell the silver bullet in the chamber. She knew it was her death. Still her hatred of human beings would not allow her to surrender. She lowered herself into a crouch, the first step in launching a killing pounce. Every muscle in her body tensed, became a tightened spring ready to be loosed.

The human female started to fire—and then stopped.

So intent on her pounce, the gray wolf didn't see the thing that came out of the snow. When the human turned around to look, the gray jumped—all claws and teeth, all concentrated rage. She landed on the human's back and knocked her forward, sending her flying to the ground. The gray's claws tore through the human's parka and the layers of clothing underneath, ripping great gouges through the human's skin. The hit shattered some of the human's ribs and dug a deep groove into the pelvis. In time those injuries would be enough to kill any human being. Either the human female would bleed to death on the spot, or chips of bone, knocked loose by the impact, would enter her bloodstream and eventually her heart or lungs.

The gray was just getting started. She would tear the human female to pieces. She would swallow her flesh whole.

The blood fury inside her distracted her so much that she was barely aware of everything that was happening around her. It was chaos and fire, but her world had shrunk down to a narrow window. She could see nothing but her prey.

Had she been more aware of her surroundings, she might have seen the giant figure striding across the minefield, setting off explosions everywhere it walked. Smoke wreathed in the air; shrapnel cascaded down like vicious rain. One of the human males, the one who had been thrown off his machine in the moment the giant appeared, staggered up to his feet and fired his weapon again and again into the giant's face and chest. The silver bullets bounced off the white furs, the wooden mask. The giant didn't even seem to feel them.

Meanwhile the male wolf had struggled up out of the snow, lost in his own bloodlust. His body was ravaged, torn apart. One of his legs hung off his frame by tatters of skin. His viscera dragged steaming on the ground and all the fur had been scorched off his face. A piece of jagged metal protruded from his left eye.

It was enough to make him very, very angry.

Even on three legs the male wolf streaked through the minefield like a horizontal bolt of lightning. He intersected with one of the moving machines with enough force and speed to send it rolling across the snow while its human driver crashed with a thud to the ground. The driver tried to get up, but the male wolf tore him to pieces without wasting time to breathe. One of his arms came off—then part of his face. His hot blood hit the snow like acid, melting a great pool of it. The male wolf found his prey's heart and tore it loose, then gulped it down without chewing.

The white wolf had circled back along her own tracks—the only safe path, where there could be no mines—and had doubled around to where the giant had emerged. The sound of her footfalls was lost in the general din, so she was able to sneak up behind the other male human, the one who had tried to shoot the giant. She moved forward and nuzzled his calf, almost gently. He spun around and tried to shoot her, but by then his gun was empty.

The white female licked her lips.

Her prey threw down his gun, then raised his hands in surrender. Wolves cannot laugh. But they can smile. The white female took a step forward. Her prey took a step backward.

Right onto a concealed mine.

The explosion was loud enough to deafen the gray, but she was too fixed on her kill to care. She didn't need to hear her prey moaning for help or mercy. She wouldn't have understood the words it spoke, anyway. She padded closer and licked blood from the human female's back. She thought she would flip the prey over and tear its throat out. That would be enough to show her anger, wouldn't it? Perhaps she would urinate on the corpse afterwards.

She heard a buzzing sound behind her and for once it got through the red mist in her head. There was a machine behind her, and a human riding it. A human who smelled—wrong, somehow. Well, no matter. The human female on the ground before her wasn't going anywhere. She could be finished off at the gray wolf's leisure. First she would take care of this new threat. She whirled around and found herself face to face with another human.

A male. With blue skin. Her color vision was not as acute as that of a human being, but she knew that humans didn't normally come in that color. No matter. She reared up and lunged forward to bite his face off. He shoved a forearm into her mouth, as if he wanted her to tear him apart. Obligingly, the gray wolf bit down with all her bone-crunching strength. The muscles in her jaws and neck were capable of snapping through the femur of a caribou. One human arm would be nothing to even slow her down. Her enormous teeth sank effortlessly through the padded parka sleeve, the layers of flannel and thermal underwear beneath, even the plastic and metal of his wristwatch.

But when they touched his skin her teeth—shattered. She felt them collapse inside her mouth as if they'd been rotted through by decay. Where her gums and lips touched his skin they burned and shriveled away.

Gasping for air, the gray wolf pulled back, her mouth wide, her tongue lolling. She felt dizzy and sore and she could barely stand up. She could do nothing as she watched the blue human load the dying female human onto his machine and roar away.

47

"I'm going to die," Sharon Minik whispered to herself. She was bouncing along on the back of a snowmobile racing over the tundra, its suspension lurching every time it hit a buried rock or thick patch of snow. Her head kept colliding with one of the side panniers. It hurt, a lot.

But nothing could compare to the pain in her back. Her flesh there felt raw and hot and agony seared through her every time the wind touched her exposed wounds. She could feel sticky blood pooling under her clothes, could feel things tearing open inside her guts. "I'm going to die," she said again, because it didn't seem real. It didn't seem right. But she knew it was true. Nobody could survive what the wolf had done to her.

Behind them, as if in a dream, the giant was still chasing them. They were kilometers away from the minefield by that point, but still it kept after them. It ran on all fours, though she could see that its front limbs ended in hands, not paws. Its wooden mask was carved in the shape of a horribly grimacing human face. She had a pretty good idea what it was—who it was—but she didn't want to believe it. Like the mayor of the town of Umiaq, she believed wholeheartedly that such things existed. But you never actually saw one, not if you lived to be a hundred years old. And definitely none of them ever chased your snowmobile, clearly intending to kill you.

Perhaps it would be a mercy if it did, she thought. If it caught up to them and ripped them up like tissue paper, at least she would really be dead. She could stop waiting for it to happen. She could stop hurting so much.

Even that mercy was to be denied her, however. The snowmobile sped up and pulled away from the big thing's pursuit. It didn't stop chasing them, but little by little they gained ground until it shrank in the distance, still running toward them but barely visible.

Eventually she couldn't see it at all.

Sharon closed her eyes. She was crying, which was always a bad idea in the Arctic during the winter months. No matter how salty your tears were, when it was twenty below outside they could still freeze to your cheeks. She couldn't help it, though. As strong as she liked to think she was, as tough—and life had given her plenty of chances to prove that—knowledge of her impending death was the thing that had cracked her open like an egg and let all the insecurities and vulnerabilities come bubbling out.

"I'm going to die," she wept.

She felt one of Varkanin's hands reach for hers. He twined his gloved fingers through her own. "No," he said. "You're not. That's the problem."

48

Chey felt as if she were buried in layer after layer of gauzy cloth. She could almost see through it—though she couldn't make out any details she could sense light and shadows all around her. She tried to scrub at her eyes with her hands, thinking maybe she was just still bleary from sleep. She quickly realized that she couldn't feel her hands, or any other part of her body.

It was then she heard her wolf panting. The noise of it filled her head and made her want to scream.

That was when she realized she didn't have a voice, either. It wasn't her head she was in. It was the wolf's—she was just a passenger inside it.

There followed a long, confusing period where she tried to fight and break her way out of the wolf's head, a futile combat she would later be unable to explain in any detail. How did you smash at the walls when there were no walls, and nothing to smash against them with? No shoulders, no hips, nor arms or legs? How did you scream dire threats or shout commands when you could not speak? How did you struggle to maintain control when you had none to begin with?

When she realized she was having no effect she stopped fighting. It made a world of difference. The wolf didn't seem to mind her being inside its head, not when she couldn't do anything there. It let her be, and gave her a certain degree of freedom. It let her use its senses as long as she didn't try to direct them.

Slowly her eyesight sharpened, though still she couldn't make out many colors and details still eluded her. She was seeing things as the wolf did, through the wolf's eyes. She could not control where it turned its gaze, so she could only study the wall next to her, a massive construction of layered sod reinforced with giant bones. She wasn't sure if she was in a real place or some fantasy world concocted by the wolf—though she didn't know how a creature of such limited imagination could come up with that wall.

She could hear what the wolf heard, as well, though it was a maddening experience because the wolf's hearing was so much more directional than a human's. There were faint mutterings just on the edge of sensation that she would really have liked to explore. They sounded like human voices. But unless the wolf turned its ears around to specifically listen to those voices, she couldn't be sure.

She could taste what the wolf tasted, but this she did her best to ignore. The wolf's mouth hurt, a lot, and something was wrong with its teeth—they felt like they'd all been smashed in with a hammer. The pain was unbelievable, so she tried to distance herself from it, which kind of worked.

Eventually she was allowed to smell what the wolf smelled. And while that was the most beguiling of all its senses—her human knowledge of smells was so limited, so narrow, that she could identify only a tiny fraction of what she was receiving—it was also the most reassuring. She could smell the wall before her, smell the dirt and withered grass roots that comprised the sod, smell the ancient dry smell of the bones. She could smell dirty bed linen underneath her. This at least made her think she was in a real place, since she couldn't imagine the wolf dreaming of lying on a human bed.

Far more exciting to her were other smells. The smell of Dzo's wet furs. The smell of Lucie's clean hair. And the smell of Powell's skin, the musky scent of him, the smell of his flannel shirt and of his sweat, the smell of campfires they'd shared, the smell of his excitement the last time she'd seen him, when they'd kissed.

She could smell him coming closer to her. The smell of him grew more intense, and suddenly it was all around her. She heard him speak, and though the wolf couldn't understand the words, she got them just fine.

"You're awake, finally," he said, sounding a little peeved, but a lot more relieved. "I was starting to worry about you."

The wolf whimpered as he reached down to touch her. The wolf cringed away from him.

"What is it?" he asked. "Are you—"

She felt the wolf's anger explode all around her. Her vision went red and her consciousness was dragged around as the wolf flipped over, bringing its claws around to attack Powell. *No!* she thought, knowing no one would ever hear her. *No! Please! Don't!*

He grabbed at the wolf's forelegs and held them back. The wolf growled in frustration and rage, not just because it was pinned down but also because this forced it to acknowledge that its forelegs had been replaced by human arms.

The damn thing was taking over her body, Chey thought. Those were her arms. This was her time, the time when the moon was down—

"Chey," Powell said, in a firm voice. "Chey, come back to me. Chey—if you're in there, come back."

She fought the wolf again, giving it everything she had, and this time she was almost successful. Knowing that she was fighting for her own body helped. She couldn't stop the wolf from struggling against Powell's grip, but she was able to gain control of her voice.

"Powell," she gasped. "Powell, I'm not doing this!"

"I know," he told her. "Fight it. Fight it." He climbed into the bed with her and wrapped his arms around her, holding the wolf still. His scent made the wolf crazy, but it gave Chey strength. "Come on," he said. "You can do this."

She called his name, again and again. He whispered in her ear, talking her through it. Helping her come back. It was a long fight.

And while it was happening she saw Lucie, standing a few meters off. The redhead was watching her with a cool, analytical gaze.

After a while a sly little smile crossed Lucie's face. It flickered away almost as fast as it had come, but there was no mistaking this.

Lucie enjoyed watching Chey squirm.

49

The moon rose again before Chey had fully regained control of her body. She fought against the flash of silver light, but nothing could stop the transformation. When she woke again, many hours later, she remembered nothing of the intervening time, but at least this time she woke up human, fully human. She couldn't even feel the wolf hiding inside her head. Her mouth still hurt but she didn't care—she was just glad to be alone in her own body.

She finally had a chance to take a good look at her surroundings. The place where she'd woken up was a spacious dome. The walls were made of sod, with great arches of whale bones for support. The bones met near the ceiling and formed a ring around a narrow hole that let in light and air. It was cold in the dome, below freezing, but nothing like as cold as it had been outside. The dome was sparsely but comfortably furnished, with lots of shelves to hold supplies and woven grass mats covering the floor. There were a couple of beds, each big enough to sleep four people comfortably. There was a portable generator chugging away—its smoke wafted up toward the hole and away—and it was hooked up to a very large, very old television set. She remembered hearing muttering human voices when she woke up and she realized now that she'd been hearing the TV. Currently it was showing an episode of *Coronation Street*—the same soap opera Chey's mother had watched, when she was a kid. In the center of the dome, under the skylight, sat a single massive armchair, its considerable mass shored up by more whale bones. Slumped on top of the chair was the creature she assumed had to be the owner of the dome.

He was not exactly human.

He had to be nine feet tall, and five feet across the shoulders. A giant.

He was dressed in a loose fur cloak that was as white as snow in some places, in others stained a greasy yellow. On top of his head was a carved wooden mask studded with ivory spikes. It was tilted up to reveal his face, which was broad and moon-shaped. His eyes were very small, almost beady, and it had been a long time since he'd last shaved. His nose was running.

As Chey studied him he reached under his furs and scratched himself so violently that the chair creaked under his weight and nearly collapsed. He grunted in annoyance and then reached down into a bucket next to his chair that held chunks of blubber—thick white slabs of fat backed with sleek black whale skin.

"What?" he demanded, in a voice like sandpaper on a rough piece of wood.

Chey sat up slowly on the bed. Suddenly she realized she was alone in the dome with this giant. And that he was talking to her.

"I'm so sorry," she said. "I didn't mean to stare."

He sneezed three times in a row and then started chewing on his piece of blubber. "Then fucking don't."

Chey looked away. She found her clothes folded neatly under the bed. She didn't want to put them on—the idea of cloth against her skin just felt wrong—but she fought back that urge and dressed herself. The shoes weren't there. Lucie was probably wearing them, wherever she'd gone. So that was a small relief.

"You feeling better?" the giant asked, with a nasty guffaw. "You had one hell of a night." He scratched himself again, roaring a little as if it hurt him to do so but he couldn't help it.

"I'm . . . okay," Chey said. "How are you?"

"Nearly fucking extinct, thank *you* very much." He reached for another piece of blubber.

That seemed to be all he wanted to say. His attention was fixed on the TV, and Chey remembered how her mom hadn't wanted to talk much when her show was on, either. She watched the human faces on the screen go through various melodramatic changes that she could barely sympathize with. She tried to follow the action, but it just didn't seem very important.

"This one's focused on the Mortons. The fucking Mortons—who cares? The Barlows are the ones who have the best stories," the giant grumbled.

Chey tried to remember what she knew of the show, just to make conversation. "Did Deirdre ever get out of prison?" she asked.

For the first time he turned to really look at her. Just moving his head was enough to make his chair creak. "Where . . . the fuck . . . have you been?" He growled and his lips pulled back. His teeth were not human teeth. "That was like ten fucking years ago." He struggled up out of his chair and staggered over to the TV. With one massive hand he slapped the power button to turn it off. "You some kind of fucking moron?"

Chey tried to laugh.

He wasn't joking, though. "I asked you a question," he said. His minuscule eyes bored into her like drill bits. "Are you 'special'?"

"No," Chey said, quietly. "I'm not special, I just—"

Maybe he hadn't heard her. "Is that it? I went to all that trouble for some kind of retard?" He stomped toward her, leaving huge footprints on the woven mats. "They brought you in here—into my home—" He loomed over her, huge and implacable, and she scooted backward on the bed to try to get away from him. "Into my—my home, and—"

Then he started to cough. Big, chest-wracking, gagging, choking coughs. He gasped for breath and pounded on his chest with one fist and dropped to the floor, on his back. His tiny eyes stared up at the ceiling as if he couldn't see anything. Chey scrambled down off the bed and knelt next to him, wondering what she should do. She tried to loosen the fur cloak from around his throat, but it seemed to be sewn shut.

"Gah," he moaned, and then leaned over and spat nearly a gallon of mucus out onto the mats. "Fucking global warming. Can you get me something to drink?"

Chey nodded and ran over to a refrigerator standing against the wall of the dome. It wasn't plugged in, she noticed, but it didn't matter—the air in the dome was as cold as a refrigerator ever got, anyway. Inside she found nothing but a six-pack of Diet Pepsi. It would have to do, she supposed. She cracked one open and brought it over to the giant, who sucked it all down in one gulp.

"Thanks. That was—that was really nice of you," he said, his face softening. "You didn't have to do that."

"Anybody would have," Chey insisted.

"No. No, they wouldn't," he said. He was crying. "What's your name?"

"Chey," she told him. She rubbed one of his massive shoulders. It was like rubbing a side of beef covered in greasy fur. "What's yours?"

"Nanuq," he told her.

Her eyes went wide. "Nanook? Like . . . *Nanook of the North*?"

His face hardened again. "You gonna start something, now?"

"No . . . no no no," Chey said, trying to soothe him. "I just—when I was a kid, in school, we watched—"

"That fucking documentary. You know the whole thing was staged? Fucking humans. Can't even tell a story right. Factual fucking inaccuracies all over the place. I hate that movie." He shook his massive head. "It's *N-A-N-U-Q*, thank you very fucking much. It happens to be the Inuit word for 'polar bear.' "

"Oh! So you're the—"

"Guy whose favorite show is on in three minutes, that's who I am." He climbed back in his chair. "So don't fucking try my patience."

50.

The others returned a little later, Dzo holding up a flap of seal skin that was the dome's door while Powell and Lucie squeezed inside. Powell proudly brandished a string of lemmings, the great hunter returning. "Hungry?" he asked Chey.

"I'm actually kind of full," she told him. Truth be told, she didn't feel that great. Her mouth still hurt. It felt like she had gargled lye or something. Her teeth felt loose and fragile. "I had some . . . blubber." Saying the word aloud made her stomach turn. She still couldn't quite believe it. She'd told Nanuq how much her mouth hurt and he recommended she try some of the whale fat. It didn't require much chewing, he told her, which had turned out to be incorrect. Maybe if your teeth were the size of Chey's thumbs. Then there had been the taste. It had tasted a little like clams, but the consistency had made her want to gag. Somehow she'd managed to swallow several mouthfuls of it.

"She's been keeping me company," the giant said, struggling to rise from his chair.

Chey shot Powell a quizzical glance. She still had no idea how she'd ended up in Nanuq's dome house, or exactly what kind of creature the giant was.

"You're . . . probably wondering what's been going on," Powell suggested, and she nodded in agreement.

"Well," Powell said, sitting down on one of the oversized beds, "it wasn't good. Apparently there was a huge storm—the world out there is about ten feet deep in snow. Then we got in some trouble. When I woke up, when I woke up human, I found Dzo waiting for us and he brought us here. We were all hurt. Lucie and I weren't in great shape. Nanuq was kind enough to take us in. I'm still not entirely clear on what happened. It all occurred while the moon was up, so my memories are pretty fragmentary. But I know the hunter tried to kill us again."

"Lots of explosions. Like American TV," Nanuq said, nodding his big head. "Guns and snowmobiles everywhere."

"People . . . ?" Chey asked. "Like, multiple people? Not just the blue guy?" Her blood turned cold.

"Yep," Dzo said. "I was watching you three when it happened, just like I promised. And I told you I would do something to help. I went and found my old buddy here, because I thought he might be useful. At first he didn't want to help."

Nanuq shrugged. "I said what the hell did I care, but eventually Dzo convinced me you could use some help, so I pitched in."

"He saved your butts," Dzo said.

Nanuq shrugged again. "Mostly I think I just scared them. I didn't kill anybody."

"Oh, you didn't?" Chey asked, with growing hopes.

"Nah. That was all you three. You tore their guts out pretty good."

No. Oh, no, Chey thought. *No no no, not again.* After what had happened at Port Radium, she thought that kind of violence was behind her. She couldn't bear the thought of killing another human being. And yet she knew, with real certainty, that her wolf felt differently. That her wolf wouldn't miss the chance to kill a human being and probably eat them afterwards.

Just like Powell had killed and . . . and eaten her father. Or rather, just like his wolf had done.

"How many of them were there?" Chey asked.

"Three or four."

"Did we kill them all?" she asked.

Nanuq scratched his head. "Yeah, I think so. I mean they were all bloody or blown up or in pieces. Yeah, all of them. Except the blue guy."

"No?"

"Nah. Not a scratch on him."

Chey sat down hard on the mats that covered the floor. The leader, the one who wanted nothing but their destruction, was the only one that survived. "Great."

"Yeah, it was pretty cool," Nanuq agreed.

51.

Powell announced he had things to discuss with Nanuq, but first he wanted to eat. He and Lucie made a fire under the smoke hole and cooked their lemmings, while the giant watched, occasionally licking his lips. Chey took Dzo over to the far side of the dome, intending to ask him some questions.

"So he's like you, right?" she said.

"Who, Nanuq? No way. Nothing like me," the spirit told her.

Chey frowned. "I guess I assumed, with the furs and the mask, that he was an animal spirit."

"Right. Spirit of the polar bear."

Chey frowned in incomprehension. "But you just said he wasn't anything like you."

"Exactly. Totally different. He eats *meat,* for one thing. It's kind of gross. Look at his mask, too, and mine. Completely different styles. Mine has a sort of Dene feel, because the Dene people south of here were the last ones who really took me seriously. Up here, it's various kinds of Inuit, some of whom still pay tribute to Nanuq, so he wears their kind of mask." He seemed to think of something else. "Oh, and he's dying."

"That's not the word he uses. He says he's going extinct."

Dzo rolled his eyes as if she was completely missing the point. "Same thing, isn't it? We're *animal* spirits. We're connected to our animals. Not the individual ones, of course. There's musquashes dying and being born all the time. But they aren't dying out. Polar bears, on the other hand, there's less of them every year. Which makes him weaker. Soon enough there won't be any left."

"And he'll die, then?" Chey asked.

"Sort of. I mean technically, no, because he lives outside of time in some really important ways. Which, believe me, you do not want me to explain to you what that means. Because it would give you a really bad headache."

"I can believe that," Chey said. She had tried in the past to understand how Dzo could travel from one body of water to any other even if they weren't connected, or how he could dive into a single drop of water without actually shrinking himself. She assumed the spirits operated on some kind of magical level that didn't compute with human logic.

"So it's not like he'll cease to exist. Because he'll still be there in the past, like he always was. And people will still tell stories about polar bears, long after the last one's gone. So he'll need to be around to embody those stories. But—well, let me give you an example. There used to be this one kind of elephant. Except it was all covered in hair and it lived up north here with us."

"You mean the wooly mammoth?"

Dzo nodded. "So you've heard of it. Anyway, all of them are gone, but there was this spirit of the mammoth, really nice girl, really . . . sweet. Hair down to her butt and even taller than Nanuq. But man, the teeth on her."

Chey smiled, for the first time in a while. As confusing as it might be, she always felt better after talking to Dzo.

"She used to live on an island off Alaska," Dzo went on. "You know, a while back."

"A couple thousand years ago?" Chey suggested. "During the last ice age?"

"Yeah, well, I stopped keeping track of individual years. Now I just think of that time as 'a while ago.' The thing is, people still talk about her, or at least, about her mammoths. She's gone as far as you're concerned, because you live in time. You could go to her island and you wouldn't find her there. If *I* wanted to go visit her, though, I could. I couldn't walk there directly, but if I dove really deep through the water I could end up where she is, in the past."

"I read a while back that there are some scientists who want to clone a mammoth, like in *Jurassic Park,* but without all the people getting eaten.

They would take DNA from one that's frozen in a glacier and make an embryo, then put it in an African elephant so she would give birth to a baby mammoth. What would happen to your friend then? Would she come back to life?" Chey asked.

Dzo shook his head emphatically. "That's just it. No. Because she never really died. She just went extinct. So I guess that's the difference you were asking about." He grinned at her. "Does your head hurt yet?"

"Always," she told him.

Over by the smoke hole, Powell and Lucie had finished their meal. Powell went over to where Nanuq sat in his arm chair, watching a rerun of *North of 60*. Powell cleared his throat and started to reach for Nanuq's arm, clearly intending to get his attention.

"Oh, shit," Chey said, running toward him. She had a bad feeling about what would happen if Powell interrupted Nanuq while he was watching his soaps.

Rightly so, it turned out.

52.

When Nanuq had finally calmed down again—it was like a light switch had been turned off and he settled easily back into his chair to reach for his remote control—Chey helped Powell stand back up and dust himself off. "You alright?" she asked him.

He looked up at the curving wall of the dome. There was a significant dent in the sod wall where Nanuq had thrown Powell hard enough to break human bones. "I'll be okay," Powell said. "A little bruised. I didn't know he took that box so seriously."

Chey stared into his eyes until she got it. "That box. You mean his TV." She forgot, most of the time, that Powell had been born in 1895 and that he had been living alone in the north country for most of a century. "You've seen a television before, haven't you?" she asked.

"Sure," he said, but it sounded like he was trying to remember. "Of course I have. I just didn't realize how seductive it could be, for some people."

"Nanuq told me he used to hate TV. It was full of stories but none of them were about animals," she said. They'd talked about TV a lot when it had just been the two of them in the dome. "But there's not much else for him to do around here."

"Hmm. Maybe I should wait until his program is done," Powell suggested.

"Good idea."

When the rerun had finished, Nanuq muted the set with his remote and then looked down at the werewolves arrayed before him. It was hard not to think of him as a king sitting on a throne—even if that throne was covered in avocado green upholstery.

"We want to thank you, first," Powell told the spirit. "If you hadn't come along when you did, all three of us would be dead now."

"It looked like it was going that way, yeah," Nanuq told him. "Thank Dzo for that, though. I would have let you get pasted if he hadn't begged me like a little girl."

"I'll . . . do that," Powell went on. "Still. There's a very old friendship between lycanthropes and *tuurngaq*."

Chey glanced over at Dzo. "That's the Inuit word for an animal spirit," he whispered to her, and she nodded her thanks.

"I guess," Nanuq said. "You live a lot longer than humans, so we have an easier time relating to you. They come and go so fast they don't make any sense." The polar bear spirit shrugged and Chey heard springs snapping inside his armchair. "It's not the kind of thing you should push, really."

"I wouldn't dream of that," Powell said. "But I do want to ask you for a favor."

Nanuq growled. Then he reached under his furs to scratch violently at his thigh. "I'm not known for generosity. And anyway, it looks more like you owe me."

Powell nodded in agreement. "Absolutely. But I'm not asking for much. Just a little information on something that happened a long time ago. I need to know about what happened to Amuruq."

Dzo and Nanuq both straightened up a little when they heard that name. Neither of them spoke, though.

"She was one of you," Powell said. "A *tuurngaq*. The *tuurngaq* of the wolf. I looked for her for a long time. I thought maybe she could help me learn to control my wolf. I even spoke to other *tuurngaq* who knew her. But they refused to tell me what had happened to her. All I know is that she disappeared at the same time the first lycanthropes existed."

"That's not something we ever talk about with humans," Nanuq said. "It's forbidden." He didn't growl, though. He didn't look angry at all. He looked sad. Chey remembered his earlier mood swings and her heart went out to him. Nanuq wasn't well. He was nearly extinct.

"As I've already established, I'm not human."

"But you want to be," Nanuq said. His beady eyes blinked rapidly.

"That's what you're after. You want to know what they did to Amuruq so you can undo it. So you can shed your curse."

The cure, Chey thought. *Nanuq knows something about the cure.*

Except, apparently, he didn't. "I wasn't there," he told Powell. "I only heard about it afterward. Yeah, it happened up here. Exactly where I don't know—and you're going to need to know exactly."

He settled himself deeper in his chair. "What I know is a story. It's not likely true in every particular, but I'll tell it to you.

"What I was told is that an *angakkuq,* what you would call a shaman, tricked Amuruq into laying her body across a stone and showing him her belly. He told her how soft he thought her fur must be and how he just wanted to pet her, like his favorite sled dog, and feed her pieces of meat. She was very curious, Amuruq, and she'd always wondered what dogs found so appealing about human affection. She wanted to experience it for herself, so she lay down for him. Once he had her there he cut her into many pieces. Then he took the pieces and fed them to his warriors, who thus became her children. They became werewolves."

"This shaman killed her? Killed the wolf spirit? Why the fuck would he do that?" Chey demanded.

Dzo grabbed her arm and gave her a warning shake of the head. "That wouldn't kill her. Remember what I said about my friend the mammoth? Amuruq is still alive. She's just in pieces, one piece in every werewolf in the world. She even travels around, like when you scratch somebody and they get your curse."

Chey's head hurt. In that old familiar way.

"You want to know why," Nanuq said, sighing. "You got me. And you're going to have to find out before you get your cure. Now you have all I know, for whatever good it is to you."

Powell's shoulders slumped. "I see. I thank you."

"You want to know more, you want to know how to undo what was done, you're going to need to talk to Tulugaq."

That name got an extreme reaction out of Dzo. He flipped down his mask and stamped his foot on the floor mats. "No way. No way, nuh-uh, no. We're not going to do that. Forget it."

Powell licked his lips. "Dzo, just hold on a second." He turned to look up at Nanuq again. "Why can Tulugaq tell us, when you can't? Was he there?"

"Yeah," Nanuq said. "He wouldn't have missed it. Since the whole thing was his idea."

53

Chey tried to calm Dzo down, but it wasn't much use. He seemed intensely agitated just at the thought of talking about Tulugaq, much less going to see him. She tried to find out who this guy was but Dzo wouldn't answer any of her questions.

Powell wasn't much help either, when she asked him. "I know he's another one of the animal spirits. One of the really powerful ones. Beyond that, I'm as much in the dark as you are. I just know that if we're going to save you from your wolf, he's the one we need to find."

Nanuq wasn't in a mood to talk anymore after he'd finished his story. He suggested, not very politely, that he'd prefer it if the werewolves left him alone. "You want to find Tulugaq, that's on your heads. I've got shows to watch. If you miss one day of these shows, you can never catch up."

"But how do we find Tulugaq?" Powell asked.

The polar bear spirit growled in annoyance and climbed out of his chair again. "It won't be hard. He'll come running when he hears he's got a chance to screw with you. There's an *inukshuk* about thirty kilometers from here, west by a little north. You go there, you leave some food for him. You'll have to do better than a couple of lemmings. He likes bigger game, and dead meat is best. Then he'll come."

Dzo and the werewolves left the dome house then, Chey thanking Nanuq profusely for his hospitality. He waved her away with one massive hand.

They crawled through the flap of seal skin that formed the house's door, into the darkness outside. For the first time Chey got to see the exterior of Nanuq's house with human eyes. It was the kind of place that would be easy to miss if you didn't know it was there. Most of it was underground, so it looked like just a modest rise in the snowdrifts. The smoke hole was clotted with snow, and the door was hidden between two rocks. Still, there were signs that people had been there repeatedly. There were woven baskets stashed outside the door, some of them smashed to pieces, some still holding foodstuffs. Dzo had calmed down a little and now he explained that the local Inuit hunters left food there for Nanuq, who was too sick to hunt for himself.

"Like sacrifices for a god?" she asked.

Dzo actually laughed at the idea. "More like bribes. If you want to kill a polar bear, or you want to be safe from polar bear attacks, they think you have to appease Nanuq or he'll come for you in the night." He shook his head. "The ideas that humans get about us. Still, it's kind of nice, right? Nobody ever gives me presents just because they're hungry for musquash steak."

The four of them headed out, moving in single file so that Powell could check the snow with every step. It wasn't as bad as during the storm. The wind had cut the drifts down to a manageable depth. Still, if they stepped into the wrong snowbank they could find themselves hip deep in the powdery stuff.

"For now, let's just get far enough away that we don't annoy Nanuq. We'll head for this *inukshuk* tomorrow," Powell told them. That didn't make Dzo happy, but he seemed glad they weren't leaving immediately. "I'd like to make an earlier start, but the moon isn't being helpful."

October was half done. The moon was below the horizon only a few hours each night. That would change—before the end of the month it would linger for longer stretches out of sight, and eventually they would even get five days when it never rose, nearly a week of just being human. For the moment, though, they needed to obey its command.

The silver light came on them without warning. Powell didn't even bother to signal a stop. Their clothes fell empty to the ground and the wolves shivered with the ecstasy of being back in their own skins.

There was no open water around for Dzo to dive into, so he couldn't escape. He had to wait patiently while the wolves sniffed him warily. The gray was confused by him, as always. He looked somewhat human but he smelled altogether wrong and the fire that burned always in the back of her mind, the fire that urged her to destroy anything human, didn't leap to life when she looked at him. Eventually she lost interest and trotted away. Hunger was a much bigger motivator at that moment.

The wolves spent the long night hunting. When the sun rose they were still hungry, having found little to eat. The gray looked longingly toward the south, toward the softer land where there had always been plenty of animals to chase and kill and devour, but the male, her alpha, kept them moving northward. She wasn't permitted to question his decisions, so she kept her doubts to herself.

In the afternoon they came over a low rise where a few skeletal bushes dotted the ground, mostly buried in the snow. The wind from the north brushed back the fur on her face, then, and she smelled something interesting—something she had never smelled before as a wolf. The frigid wind carried traces of salt and iodine, the smells of the sea.

They were no more than fifty kilometers, then, from the northern coast of the Arctic Ocean.

54

Sharon Minik woke lying on a cold wooden floor, completely naked. A silver collar was locked around her throat. Wherever it touched her it burned like winter ice. She felt like she'd been beaten and then left for dead.

It was not the best morning of her life.

She reached up for the collar and felt its catch. It was held shut by a simple cotter pin, and when she pulled it free the collar fell away to clank on the floor. At least that was something. She shifted away from it, because just the smell of it was enough to make her feel sick. She couldn't remember ever thinking silver had a smell before, but it did now. She thought maybe her sense of smell had somehow dramatically improved and she tried to sniff the iron door of the little room, but it didn't seem to have an odor.

While she was sniffing the hinges of the door, someone knocked on it. She jumped back and wrapped her arms around her chest and groin. There was a clanking noise like a heavy lock being turned back, and then the door opened. Varkanin was there, smiling down at her.

Sharon had never been so glad to see anyone in her life. She started to weep, and then to sob, as the blue Russian came and put a blanket around her shoulders. "It's alright," he said.

She stared up at him with wide eyes. Was he serious?

She knew what she'd become.

"No," Sharon told him. "It's never going to be alright again."

Varkanin didn't argue with her. Instead he helped Sharon stand up— being very careful not to touch her except through the blanket—and led her out of the little room. A pile of clothes was waiting for her in the kitchen. They weren't the ones she'd been wearing when they'd gone hunting for werewolves, and she realized those must have been pretty well shredded when the wolf attacked her. They were a man's clothes, but they were clean and warm. Sharon pulled them on hurriedly. People very rarely got naked in the Arctic unless they were showering or going to bed with each other. Having no clothes had made her feel utterly vulnerable. Varkanin gave her a cup of hot chocolate and some caribou jerky to chew on. Between the food and the clothes, Sharon was feeling almost human again by the time Varkanin led her into a sitting room.

It looked like the front room of every hunting lodge Sharon had ever seen. Rustic furniture made of untreated wood, gun rack on one wall, trophy heads of caribou, elk, and even one very old and ragged polar bear staring down at her.

"Nanuq," she said.

"I beg your pardon?" Varkanin asked. He sat down on the arm of one of the chairs and tried to meet her gaze, but she just kept looking down into her cup.

"That was Nanuq who screwed up your plan. I wasn't expecting that." She put the cup down and stared at her hands for a while, expecting them to turn into paws at any moment. "The elders around here tell a lot of stories. You grow up listening to them, whether you want to or not, but you don't really believe them. It's like Santa Claus or the Tooth Fairy. Even when you're a kid you know there's something too weird about them to really be true. Then something like this happens . . . it was Nanuq."

"This is some god of your people?" Varkanin asked.

"We don't have gods, except Jesus. We're Christians in Umiaq."

The Russian nodded politely.

"What we have, are spirits. I guess maybe souls is a better word. It's like, imagine all the polar bears in the world, and they all have just one soul they share between them. Nanuq is that soul. If you kill a polar bear, or if you just survive when one attacks you, you thank Nanuq. Maybe you just say it under your breath. Or maybe, if you're like my dad or one of the elders, you actually take some food out on the ice and leave it for him. It's a way of making sure your luck doesn't dry up the next time you meet a polar bear. Nanuq is supposed to look after us, then. But instead he was on the side of the werewolves, huh?"

"It would appear so."

Sharon grunted. "I guess that means he's on my side now, too."

"I want to assure you I did not believe this would happen," Varkanin said, clutching his hands together in front of him as if he didn't know what else to do with them. "I knew there would be a certain element of danger in the hunt, and that one or more of you might not survive. However, I—I—"

He stopped because Sharon wasn't listening to him anymore. She was weeping, quietly. She reached up and smashed the palm of her hand into her eyes, trying to push the tears back in. She was not the kind of girl who cried a lot.

He stood up. Came a step closer. Reached for her, maybe intending to hug her and give her some support that she could really use. Then he pulled his hands back as if he was afraid of touching her. As if he was afraid he would catch her disease if he made contact. She couldn't really blame him.

With the edge of her shirt cuff she wiped away the tears. When she'd finished, she reached for her cup again. Put it back down. "I don't want to be like this," she said, very softly. "I want it to stop. I don't like turning into a wolf. I don't like it." She struggled to find more words. To describe exactly how she was feeling. She couldn't find them. There'd never been anything like this in her life before. How could there have been? "What are we going to do?" she asked.

He cleared his throat. "There is one thing. One possibility."

She looked up at him with hopeful eyes.

"I can end your suffering," he told her. His mouth squirmed around the words. He didn't want to say this, any more than she wanted to hear it. "I can do it painlessly. You won't know it's happening."

Ice crystals bloomed in her stomach. She felt like she was going to throw up. "You mean you can shoot me? With a silver bullet? That's the best idea you have?" She threw her cup across the room and it shattered against the far wall.

He didn't even flinch.

She shook her head violently. "No," she said. "No!"

"I understand. I meant only—"

"No!"

"—to suggest it, in case it was what you wanted, but if you decide to—"

"No!"

"—live, that you wish to live with this condition, then of course, I—"

"Not yet," she told him, looking right into his eyes. "Not today."

55

"So the news is bad," Preston Holness said. He sat down on his couch and put his free hand over his eyes. He was in his own apartment, having just gotten in after a very long and frustrating day's work. This was not what he wanted to hear. "You didn't get any of them?"

"I'm afraid not," Varkanin confirmed.

"They're all still alive. Even after I sent you land mines. Land mines, which are more or less banned by international treaty."

"There were complications," Varkanin said.

"I'm going to put you on hold. I may be a while," Holness told him. He muted his cell phone and put it down on the couch beside him. Then he got up and went to his kitchen. To his liquor cabinet. He scanned the various bottles there but couldn't find anything that was going to help. This was going to require bolstering of another sort.

So he went to his closet. Preston Holness had what many Canadian women desired more than rubies or pearls, which was ample closet space. His apartment was a one-bedroom efficiency with a tiny kitchenette, but it did have a walk-in closet big enough to double as a fallout shelter. When he opened the door lights came on automatically, showing him the double row of suits hanging on padded hangers, the serried ranks of gleaming leather shoes, the immaculately organized bins for sweaters, fleeces, socks (dress, casual, and sport, each in their own drawer), and silk underwear.

He picked out an Armani suit, one of his oldest and still one of his favorites. He put on a crisp new white oxford cloth shirt that was still wrapped in tissue paper. Finally he took out a pair of cuff links that had been given to him personally by a prime minster of Canada in a private ceremony.

He felt like a knight putting on his suit of armor. Or a hockey player putting on his protective padding. He felt safer when he was dressed up. He felt like he could handle this.

Then Varkanin told him about Sharon Minik.

"Oh, for the love of gravy," Holness moaned. He wanted to lie down on the floor and curl into a ball. But that might have rumpled his suit. "I hired you to kill three werewolves, and now we have four? I can't believe that—"

"You forget yourself, sir," Varkanin said, his tone darkening.

"What?"

"You never hired me. We are working toward similar goals and have achieved an understanding. That is all."

I will tear out your heart and show it to you, Holness thought. *I will take a shit on your head from a very great height.* But what he said was "Yes, of course. I beg your pardon."

"My plan was foolproof—based on the intelligence I possessed at the time. Its failure was due to the appearance of factors I could not anticipate. Specifically, the operation was complicated by the appearance of a supernatural creature. One of the same order as Dzo, the werewolves' boyer."

"What the fuck is a boyer?" Holness asked.

"One who tends to a camp while the hunters are away," Varkanin explained. "You are of course familiar with the creature I refer to."

"Yeah, he's in the dossier. But we never did figure out what he was. He's not human—we got that much from the fact that the wolves don't shred him every time they change shape. Beyond that he's a mystery."

"I believe I know what he is," Varkanin said, "but I don't think I could explain it to you in a satisfactory way. The important thing to note here is that other creatures of the same type are assisting the werewolves now."

"Okay," Holness said. "Whatever."

"It may become necessary to arm myself against them."

"Uh-huh."

"They do not seem to suffer the same weaknesses as you or I, but I believe there is a way to defeat them. It will require some special assistance on your part, however."

"What do you need?"

"I have read the dossier you gave me, describing the events that led to our agreement. Specifically the events that ended with the death of Robert Fenech. These notes are maddeningly inconclusive, but they offer some subtle clues. When the werewolves entered Port Radium, the creature Dzo did not accompany them. In fact, it appears from those documents that he could not accompany them without putting himself in peril. Therefore there must be something about the Port Radium site that constitutes a hazard to his very existence."

"Okay."

"I believe I know what it was. And if I am correct, it should be relatively easy to produce a countermeasure that will function against this new class of creature."

"This is beginning to sound expensive."

"Not necessarily in monetary terms. Though the required items will be difficult to procure." Varkanin told Holness what he needed.

It was enough to make Holness lie down on the floor after all. He could always have the suit pressed. "You do realize," he said, while Varkanin was outlining his requirements, "that what you're asking for is prohibited by the Geneva Convention?"

"Does that mean you cannot help me?" Varkanin asked.

Holness unbuttoned the top button of his shirt. "No," he said. "That's not what I'm saying. I'll have them shipped to you within the week."

56

Chey rose through a dream of growling, a dream of paws padding back and forth on snow, pacing, searching, of noses snuffling around the ground, of barking, of howling, of—

"Jesus," she said, sitting up very fast. All the blood rushed out of her head and she had to lie back down or throw up. Her body tingled painfully all over. It was worse than any other time she'd transformed back into her human body. It made her want to curl up and die. "Fuck," she moaned.

Carefully, she opened her eyes and looked around. She was lying in the shelter of a pile of rocks that formed walls on three sides. The sky above her was dark blue streaked with very white clouds. She was lying on her outspread parka, which kept her from actually sitting on the cold ground. She grabbed up a handful of snow and scrubbed her face with it, which made her feel a little better.

"Sleeping beauty has awoken," Lucie said. The redhead stood in the open space between two rocks. She was dressed in Powell's coat, as usual, but underneath that she had on a shirt and a pair of jeans that didn't quite fit her. Chey realized after a moment that they were her own, the same clothes she'd been wearing since she left Port Radium. Lucie was wearing her socks and boots, too. "I was beginning to wonder if you were not altogether lost." Lucie's smile was colder than the snow on Chey's face. "Such a shame that would have been. Monty would have been so upset, *non*? But of course I would be there to console him."

"Not yet," Chey said. "I'm not gone yet."

"Non," Lucie agreed. "Yet it won't be much longer, now."

A sudden thought made Chey wince. "How—long?" she asked.

"How long have I been out?" When Lucie blinked at her in incomprehension she demanded, "How long has it been since we changed back?"

"Only the better part of an hour," Lucie assured her. "This time."

"This time?"

Lucie's smile creased at the corners, turning into a frown. "But of course, you will not remember. It has been three days since we last spoke. Since you were last, ah, yourself."

"No way," Chey insisted.

Lucie shrugged. "For the last three days, your body changed, but always, when we approached you, it was the snarling and the biting. You tried to kill us one morning in our sleep, but thankfully, we were able to fend you off. You seemed so much like poor Élodie—though of course, we were always able to rouse her eventually. You never broke through. I think you are one good shock away from madness. Utter madness."

"Powell won't let it come to that," Chey said. Though she knew better. She knew he wouldn't be able to stop it alone. It occurred to her that she couldn't hear him anywhere nearby, couldn't smell him. Her eyes narrowed. "Where is he?" she asked.

"Hunting," Lucie said. She turned her face up toward the sky. "Dzo scouts ahead, and he lies in wait for the prey. They left me behind to protect you." She chuckled. "I suppose in desperate times . . . and these are desperate times. A proper sacrifice must be made for the spirit, and game here is very scarce. One wonders what he will find that Tulugaq will find acceptable? Perhaps nothing. Perhaps this is the end of our journey."

Chey pushed herself up to her feet. "Give me my damn clothes back."

Lucie shrugged and reached up to unbutton her coat. "If you insist. Though—will you actually wear them, I wonder?"

"Of course I will," Chey said. Though honestly she wasn't so sure. It felt good to be cold. Her blood was racing through her body and her forehead felt like it was glowing red hot. The idea of putting on clothes didn't appeal all that much. She just didn't like the idea of Lucie wearing them. "You'd like that, wouldn't you? If Powell couldn't find anything to get Tulugaq to come. Then I'd go insane and you'd have him all to yourself."

"How callous I would be to want such a thing. *Jeune fille,* I think only of your well-being." Lucie unbuttoned Chey's pants and wiggled her hips so they dropped off her legs. She kicked them over to Chey, who bundled them up in her arms.

"Bullshit. If you could think of some good way to kill me and make it look like an accident, you'd do it right now," Chey said. "Don't fucking lie and say otherwise. Hell, if I could do the same to you I would. Then I'd tie a big red ribbon around your corpse and leave you for the blue guy to find. Maybe then he'd leave us alone. He doesn't want us, just you."

"I suppose that is the truth," Lucie allowed.

"So why don't you do us a favor and leave? Go find him, settle the score personally. Instead of hiding behind Powell and me."

"*Jeune fille,* your words are like barbed arrows, that strike at my heart." Lucie took off Chey's shirt and threw it to her.

Chey grabbed it and tossed it to the ground. Then she stomped over and slapped Lucie across her porcelain cheek.

Blue fire exploded behind Lucie's eyes. Her lips drew back from delicate little teeth that Chey knew could bite through a plank of wood. At her sides, Lucie's fingers crooked into the shape of vicious claws.

"Speak the truth for once in your misbegotten life," Chey demanded. "You're only here because you need Powell's protection. And you're going to sabotage any attempt to cure me."

"You are incorrect," Lucie said, very carefully.

Chey reared back to slap her again.

Lucie's hand shot out and caught Chey's wrist. It was all Chey could do to pull out of Lucie's supernatural grip.

"I long for this cure," Lucie said. "If it exists. It will make you human again. A weak, snot-nosed little human girl. And then Monty will see you for what you really are, and he will turn away from you in disgust. He will realize what he truly is, and then he and I will run together again. As life-mates. Do you understand? If there is a cure, I will cherish it. And if there is none, if you are doomed to the fate of Élodie, then this is even better. He cannot love a wolf. You see how much he hates the one within himself."

"And what if we find a cure—and he takes it, too?" Chey asked.

"He will not," Lucie said, as if it were the most obvious thing in the world. "He would never hurt me so."

"Ha! You can't believe it, can you? That he might like me better than a psychopathic redhead who kills people for fun."

"Don't you understand? The love he and I share is meaningful. It is a force of power. I made him a wolf. I made him to be my mate." Lucie stared deeply into her eyes. "What of you? You were an accident. A little girl, lost in the woods. The wrong woods, at the wrong time. He feels some obligation to you. Some guilt he must rid from himself. But when that is done you are nothing to him. Just as you are nothing, less than nothing to me. The grit I crush beneath my heel."

Chey grabbed for Lucie's arm, planning to twist it up behind her back so she could force her stupid French face down into the snow. Or even better, smash it against a rock. Lucie made no attempt to avoid the grapple—but with her other arm she reached up to snatch at Chey's face, maybe to rake her eyes out with her nails. It would have devolved quickly from there—except they both froze when they heard someone approaching from the other side of the rocks.

It was Powell. He came climbing over the rocks with a dead seal slung over his shoulder. From behind him Chey could see Dzo looking down at them.

For the first time Chey realized that both she and Lucie were completely naked. She put her arms across her breasts.

"What have you two been doing?" Powell asked, a smile on his face.

"Just talking," Chey said.

"Talking, only," Lucie said, at exactly the same time.

57

"I had to go all the way up to the coast," Powell said, slinging the seal down on the ground next to the fire. "I'm sorry I left you here for so long."

"What's it like up there?" Chey asked. She had managed to button the shirt over her chest, but it had been hard. Her body didn't want to wear clothes anymore. They felt weird and unnatural and constricting, as if she couldn't breathe in them. As if she couldn't run properly.

"It's cold," Powell said with a shrug. He sat down next to the fire and she sat by his side. "Icy. It's nearly November and even the sea is starting to freeze over. The water is about as thick as soup—what the locals call grease ice. There are towns up there, too."

"What, really? People actually live up here? Mostly Inuit, right?"

He nodded. "Whaling villages, old trading posts, mine outposts. Most of the people living north of the Arctic Circle live on that coast—the ocean is the only source of food around here." He shook his head. "When I first came to the north country, I came to get away from people. As people moved into western Canada, I kept moving farther and farther north to get away from them. This is it, though. This is as far as I can go. Any farther north and I'm right back to civilization—and putting innocent lives at risk. I don't know where we'll go next."

She leaned into him and laid her head on his shoulder. "Hopefully we won't have to," she said. Across the fire she could see Lucie, staring into the flames with a certain intensity. "Hopefully this cure will work, and we can go live normal, healthy, human lives together. That's what you want, isn't it?"

He looked down into her eyes. "More than anything. More than I want to take my next breath," he told her, his voice very serious.

"I believe you," she said, as if there had been some doubt.

She looked across the fire at Lucie again. The redhead glanced up with a frown.

"Powell," Chey said, very softly, "I appreciate everything you're doing for me. Really. Even if it doesn't work, if Tulugaq doesn't have what we're looking for—"

"He will."

She smiled at him. "Even if . . . even if I don't last long enough to benefit from the cure. I want you to know how grateful I am. How much it means to me that you did all this. Powell . . . will you take a walk with me?"

He glanced down at her carefully. "It's warm here by the fire," he said, "and I've been freezing cold all day. I don't want to get up unless there's a good reason."

"Oh, there is," she said, and gave him a very warm smile.

As the two of them rose from the fire together, Chey gave Lucie one last meaningful look. The redhead understood perfectly, she could tell by the way Lucie's nostrils flared.

Powell led her away from the light and heat back toward the rocks where she'd woken up. They passed Dzo, who was standing watch, and told him to go over to the far side of the camp. The musquash spirit shrugged and did as he was asked, clearly not understanding why but not curious enough to ask. When the two of them were alone inside the shelter of the rocks, Chey began slowly to unbutton Powell's shirt. She leaned forward and planted gentle kisses on his collarbones and throat, tangling her fingers in his chest hair. He started breathing heavily and after a moment he grabbed her hands and held them away from his body.

"It's been a really long time," he said. "I might be a little rusty—"

"It's okay," she told him.

"—the first time," he went on. "I also don't want to give you the wrong impression. I liked what you were doing," he said, "kissing me like that," though he sounded slightly uncertain.

"But?" she asked.

"But you might want to brace yourself." He grabbed her then around the waist and threw her down to the ground. He buried his face in her throat as he fumbled with the zipper of her jeans, then yanked her pants down around her ankles. She helped by kicking them off—they hadn't felt right on her anyway. She wasn't wearing any panties. When her legs were bare he grabbed her face in both hands and kissed her passionately. Then he scooted down on his knees and grabbed her hips. His mouth buried itself in her pubic hair and her back arched convulsively.

For a guy who was born in the nineteenth century, he knew his way around the female anatomy, she thought. He found the right spot the first time and knew what to do when he arrived. It didn't take long before her body caught fire and in the midst of her climax she barely even noticed when he moved up her body and started kissing her mouth again with lips that tasted like the ocean. Then he was inside her, and it kept getting better, and better, and then she came again, and couldn't open her eyes to see what else he was doing to her. The power in his body—the strength of hers, to receive it—made her cry out loud enough to split the Arctic night.

"Oh my God." She laughed. "Werewolf sex is awesome!"

"Why haven't we done this before?" he demanded, and she had no answer.

As good as it was, he was right, though. He didn't really catch his rhythm until the second time around.

58

The moon rose the next morning, but it set within a few hours. When the silver light left Chey lying only a few dozen meters from the camp, she quickly took stock of herself and found that the wolf had let her be human for once. She could feel it panting at the back of her mind, but it didn't try to take control. Her body didn't even hurt as much as it usually did after a transformation—and she didn't have any of the soreness she usually felt after a night of good sex.

Powell found her stretching in the snow, naked to the sky. She raised her eyebrows in invitation. He smiled, but shook his head. "We need to get moving. The moon will be down for five full days and I don't want to waste any of that time."

"I wasn't suggesting we waste it," Chey said, but when she saw he was serious, she grudgingly let him help her up to her feet. Together they headed toward the campfire, where Dzo had laid out their clothes to warm on a sunny rock. Powell dressed quickly. When Chey took her time about pulling on her clothes, he turned away so she wouldn't be ashamed of how much of her had turned to wolf. She forced herself to button her clothes together and pull her parka on, though she left it unzipped.

They found Dzo where they'd left him, standing guard. He said he hadn't seen anything, and Powell thumped him on the back and said, "Good man."

"You sure you want to go through with this?" Dzo asked.

"Hmm?" Powell said.

"Finding Tulugaq. He's a tricky bastard, and he won't give you what you want without getting something in return."

"That's what the seal is for," Powell told him.

Dzo shook his head. "He ain't that cheap." He would say no more, though. Instead he flipped his mask down over his face and got to work scattering the ashes of their fire and hiding all traces of their passing.

The three of them headed west, then, and found Lucie a half kilometer away. She was crouching in a snow field, arms stretched out to either side. Her eyes were closed. Powell gestured for the others to stop and they waited until she pounced, throwing herself forward on the ground, her hands thrusting down into the snow. She came up with a lemming that screamed as she fondled it.

"Put that out of its misery," Powell told her. "It knows what you are."

Lucie looked up at him and smiled. "And I know it, as well. I know it is my breakfast."

"We're heading out," Powell told her. "We'll make this *inukshuk* by lunchtime, and you can eat then." He started off across the snow again, then, and Chey hurried to keep up with him.

"You know where the *inukshuk* is?" she asked him. "Exactly where?"

He nodded. "I saw it when I went for the seal. It's tall enough you can see it for miles, which is the point. The ground where we're going is flat and when there's snow on it, all of it looks pretty much the same. The Inuit build *inukshuks* as landmarks, so they don't get lost out here. It isn't far off."

She nodded and fell into an easy rhythm walking beside him, her bare feet sinking effortlessly through the packed snow. She looked behind and saw Lucie and Dzo a couple dozen meters back, out of earshot. "So," she said, suddenly feeling sheepish. "About the other night."

"It was glorious," he said, not turning his head to look at her.

"Yeah," she agreed. "I wanted to talk about why it happened."

He nodded. "Good. Yes. We should discuss that. We should talk about how much we love each other."

" . . . Oh," she said. She had planned on talking to him about Lucie, and the delusion the redhead was living under—that Powell intended not to take the cure himself, and that he would return to Lucie once Chey was out of the picture. She had wanted a little validation that his plans were quite different.

Instead it seemed he needed his own assurances. "I've loved you for a long time, Chey. Longer, I think, than I was willing to admit to myself. At first I thought my feelings were just based on guilt, for the things I've done to you. I can see now they run a lot deeper. The other night, you proved that you love me, as well. You couldn't have given yourself to me so completely if you didn't feel like I do."

"Yeah," she said. "Yes. Yes. I did that."

If he noted her hesitation he didn't show it. "I needed that," he told her. "Chey," he said, turning to stare into her eyes, "what comes next—it won't be pleasant."

"No?"

"We're headed toward darkness, of one kind or another. I can't tell you what will happen. Not yet. But we need to be prepared. I'm going to do things you might not approve of."

"You will?"

"But you have to know I'm doing them for you. That they're motivated by the love we share. You have to promise me you'll remember that. And that you won't tell me to stop, no matter how ugly things get."

"You're kind of scaring me," she told him.

He nodded. "I understand. Still. I need that promise."

"I promise to remember," she told him.

He leaned over and kissed her quite softly on the lips. "When this is over, I want to marry you. Don't answer me now. I want to propose to you as a human, on one knee, with a diamond ring, the whole ritual. And then we'll have a lifetime together. Not this eternal cycle of moon and sun. A human lifetime. Maybe we'll have a little house, somewhere civilized. In an actual town. Maybe we'll be blessed with children. We'll get jobs, and have friends—human friends—and—Jesus—we can go bowling one night a week. Do people still bowl out there? It was the biggest fad when I was human, before I met Lucie. Do you like to bowl?"

"I . . . do. That sounds great," she said, which was the first honest thing she'd said.

He nodded and started trudging forward again. They were silent after that, but sometimes when they were walking over even ground and the snow was shallow enough to make walking easy, he reached over to hold her hand.

In less than two hours they came in sight of the *inukshuk*.

It stuck up out of the ground like a signpost, alright. Like a landmark. It was about twelve feet high and in that flat country it could be seen for kilometers in any direction. It was made of piled gray stones, in the rough shape of a human form—two tall stones made its legs, with more stones laid flat atop them to create the body. Halfway up its height a pair of flat stones stuck out straight at either side like arms. The wind had brushed it almost clean of snow.

It was massive and silent and powerful. To Chey's eyes it was an incredible work of art—half natural and half manmade. She thought it was very beautiful.

When they finally reached its base Powell dropped the seal carcass at its feet. It landed with a thud, having frozen solid overnight. The sun had not been able to defrost it. "Okay," Powell said. "Let's start searching for wood. There have to be some bushes around here buried under the snow. I want to build a fire so we can thaw this out."

"Then what?" Chey asked.

"Then we wait for Tulugaq to come."

59

Dzo grew increasingly agitated as they waited around the fire. He would pace back and forth for a while, then plop himself down in front of the blaze with a dramatic sigh. Then he would get back up and start pacing again. "I can't believe this," he kept saying. "Tulugaq. It had to be Tulugaq."

"Relax, old man," Powell told him, but Dzo just shook his head.

"Listen," Dzo said. "Just—just be careful. He's smart. Really smart. Whatever he says to you, think about it real careful. Figure out what he actually means. And before you say anything to him—just know, he'll decide what you really mean for himself. And it won't be what you meant to mean."

"We've dealt with other mischievous spirits, you and I," Powell said. "Do you remember the time we spoke with Coyote the Trickster?"

"What happened then?" Chey asked.

"This was about thirty years ago, when I was actively looking for a cure. I had already learned something of what Nanuq told us—that Amuruq, the wolf spirit, was the origin of our curse. Coyote was her little brother," Powell explained. "I thought he might know a way to free her. So I sent Dzo to go find him. It turned out Coyote was living on a ranch in America, in Colorado, where he raised sheep."

"I brought him up here to meet Powell," Dzo said. "They drank some beer and things seemed to be okay. They had a few laughs, told a bunch of old stories."

"Nothing useful, really, just stories about Amuruq's youth. But it was nice to have someone else to talk to, and I thought it would be nice for Dzo to be around one of his own for a few days. So I invited Coyote to spend the night."

"Big mistake," Dzo said. "In every story where somebody lets Coyote spend the night in their house, they regret it in the morning."

Powell shrugged. "I knew that Coyote had that reputation, yes. He is what folklore experts call a trickster figure. A hero who overcomes obstacles and defeats threats to the community through guile and intelligence, rather than strength or brutality. Odysseus was the trickster of Greek myth, for instance. The Trojan Horse is a classic trickster strategy. Every culture has such a figure. In Africa they tell stories of Anansi, the spider, who—"

"I get it. What kind of trick did he pull on you?"

Powell looked down at his hands as if he was embarrassed, but he was still smiling. "I figured Coyote would behave himself around another spirit. I was also more than a little drunk when I finally went to bed that night. In the morning I couldn't find Coyote anywhere in the house, so I went to the front door. That was when I saw that he had taken every roll of toilet paper I owned and used them to make streamers that hung from the branches of the trees out front."

Chey waited to hear more, but Powell was done with his story. She laughed in disbelief. "That's it? He TP'd your trees?"

"He also stole my truck," Dzo added. "I had to chase him down to get it back. He was joyriding around on the logging roads and totally threw it out of alignment."

"Most vexing," Lucie said, rolling her eyes.

"If that's the worst we can expect from Tulugaq," Chey said, "then suddenly I feel a lot less worried."

"Oh, no," Dzo said, with a snort. "Tulugaq's different. He's a trickster, alright, just like Coyote. But he has a much nastier sense of humor. This one time, back in the old days, back when the old stories were first being written, I ran into him. I don't even like thinking about it now." He shivered violently. "It was winter. Maybe the first winter, I don't know."

"Back when there were wooly mammoths and Neanderthals?" Chey asked.

Dzo's face puckered as he thought back to that time. "Maybe before that. Like I keep saying, time is funny. It was a long, long time ago, let's say. And it was very, very cold. So he comes across me down by the water, where I've been diving, and his teeth are rattling and he's turned kind of blue, and he says, 'Hey, musquash'—this was before the Dene people gave me my name—'Hey, musquash, I'm really cold. You look warm in that fur coat. Do you think I could borrow it?' I said no, of course, like, three times. Finally he asked me if I was getting enough to eat. I said it was tough, because all the plants were frozen. He said if he could borrow my coat, just for a little while, he would go find some food that wasn't frozen and bring it back. Sounded like a good deal, right? So I loaned him my fur."

"Did he bring back some food?" Chey asked.

"Sure. Loads of it. Only, I couldn't eat. See, I was just standing there in the water with no fur on. Just my bones and stuff hanging out in the cold air. So I froze like an ice cube. I couldn't even ask him for my coat back because my tongue was frozen inside my mouth. He left me there for months like that. It was horrible!"

"I can imagine," Chey said.

"Let's be fair," a new voice said. There was a fluttering of wings. "I gave your coat back after I stole the sun and invented summer."

Chey had experienced enough weirdness since she'd become a were-wolf that she did not immediately jump up and run away. Instead she held very still and turned her head slowly to look around and see who had spoken.

On the far side of the fire, a massive raven had perched on top of the dead seal. It was as big as a dog, with untidy feathers forming a ruff around its neck. It took a step forward on its reptilian feet and then bent down to pluck at one of the seal's eyes with its wickedly sharp beak. As Chey watched in horror it dragged the eye out of its socket and swallowed it whole.

"Am I correct in believing this is meant for me?" the bird asked, in a croaking voice.

"Yes, Tulugaq," Powell said. "Thank you for coming."

60.

The raven hopped down to the ground and fanned its wings before the fire for a moment. "It would be improper for me to refuse your summons." With one wingtip it pushed upward on its beak, which swung free to reveal a human face underneath. It wasn't an Inuit face, but Chey couldn't have said what kind of face it was. The skin was kind of brown, but light enough that it could have belonged to a Caucasian with a tan. The eyes weren't almond-shaped, but they weren't exactly round like her own, either. They were brown, and the bangs that hung down beneath the beak were black, but the hair was neither curly nor truly straight. She wasn't even sure if the face was male or female. "When a pack of shape-shifters and my dear old friend Musquash call me, it would be rude not to at least show up." The raven shifted its wings around and suddenly it was wearing a cloak of black feathers, and human hands emerged from beneath the cloak. At some point—she could not have said when—the raven had become human sized as well. The beak had become a carved wooden mask, painted black and red, that stuck up from behind the spirit's head like a miter.

"Is our sacrifice acceptable?" Powell asked.

"Yes. Though a trifle fresh for my taste," the spirit said, prodding at the seal's nose. "Usually I prefer my dinner well aged. The meat grows tender when it's left out in the sun a few days. But it's rude of me to complain. This time of year game is hard to come by, in any condition. You must think me rude to say anything."

Dzo opened his mouth to speak, probably to agree, but Powell reached over and grabbed his arm. Dzo settled back down. He stared at the raven spirit, though, with a brooding intensity.

The raven ignored him and started skinning the seal with a pocket knife. When he got to the meat underneath the pelt he tore off a long strip and popped it in his mouth.

"Tulugaq," Powell said. "I—"

"You shouldn't call me that."

Powell blinked. "I'm sorry? Did I address you improperly?"

"Not at all. But that is only one of my names. I have so many of them. You're not an Inuit. Would you prefer to pick a name you can actually pronounce? Like Munin. Or how about Bran?"

"I don't suppose it matters what we call you," Powell said, "but—"

"Kakakiw? Hrafn? Kangi Tanka? Cuervo? Fiach? I was always partial to Cigfrain. That's my name in Welsh. Or Watarigarasu, which is Japanese."

"He's trying to impress you," Dzo muttered. "Just because people tell stories about him all over the world, he thinks that makes him a big deal. Talking all fancy like some kind of big shot, you ought to just call him Mr. Fancy Pants."

The bird spirit looked over at Dzo as if he was vaguely amused. "That would be a new one."

"Raven," Powell said. "How does Raven suit you?"

"Nicely." Raven shrugged and picked another strip of meat off the seal.

"Good. Now, I wanted to ask you a favor, which is why—"

"Vron."

Powell looked confused. "Ah . . . ?"

"That's what they call me in Russia."

"I see." Powell laid his hands in his lap and smiled wearily. "Perhaps we should let you eat before we talk."

Raven shook his head. "No need. I can do two things at once. I am not limited to linear time like a mortal."

Powell nodded. "Alright, then. I had hoped that I could ask you for a favor. In exchange for this meal."

Raven stopped eating. "No."

"Please, it's very important."

The bird spirit inhaled deeply. "Yes, of course it is. Would you have called me all this way if it was something trivial? It doesn't matter, though. Believe me, I would gladly oblige you if it were that simple. You summoned me, and I came. Payment in full."

"Be reasonable," Dzo insisted. "These are my friends!"

Raven gave them all a weak smile. "That makes very little difference, Musquash, and you know it." He turned to look at Powell again. "I'm afraid I'm hampered by the stories that are told of me—I must live up to my reputation. In those stories, I don't give away anything for free. If you desire something more, we must trade for it. Though I will warn you—I make hard bargains."

"Even for the descendants of your sister, Amuruq?"

"The wolf?" Raven shook his head in the negative. "I never much liked her. She was well on her way to becoming a trickster spirit like me, once. She had some excellent stories—you must know the one about Fenrir, the wolf who had to be bound with magical chains so he wouldn't swallow the moon. That was one of hers. And there was the one where she devoured an old woman and then wore her skin so she could eat her granddaughter, too."

"You mean Little Red Riding Hood?" Chey asked.

Raven waved away the thought. "The red cloak was a much later addition, something to do with menstruation, I believe. In the original the girl gets eaten. Wolf's stories always ended with somebody or something getting eaten."

"So you tricked her into letting an *angakkuq* chop her up," Powell suggested. "And be eaten herself. Why? So she wouldn't compete with your fame?"

Raven stared across the fire at him. "That's a very hurtful thing to say."

"Is it true, though?" Powell asked.

"Well, that depends on how you define truth," Raven said, with a sly smile.

Lucie stood up suddenly and glared across the fire. "Enough! Enough of this babble! Answer his questions honestly and simply, or it will go very hard for you."

Raven dabbed at the corners of his mouth with the end of his sleeve.

"Will you talk like a normal person, or will you continue with these pointless digressions? Will you do as we ask?"

"Yes, granddaughter," Raven said, with a twinkle in his eye. "I will . . ."

"Good." Lucie sat down.

" . . . for my price."

Lucie growled and started to get up again, but Powell raised his hands for peace. "I'm prepared to pay any reasonable price for the information I seek—"

"Excellent!"

"—however," Powell went on, "I will be the one who decides what is reasonable."

"Ah." Raven looked dejected for a moment. "I suppose that is acceptable."

Powell nodded. "I need to know the full story of what happened to Amuruq. And I need to know where, exactly, it happened, so that I can find that place again. What price will you demand for this information?"

"It must be a reasonable price, you say."

"Yes."

"Hmm." Raven looked down at the seal. He touched its head with one finger, pointing out its empty eye sockets. Then he looked back up at Powell. "Well, as you can see, I'm partial to eyeballs."

61.

"What?" Chey asked. "You mean—metaphorically, or something. You can't possibly mean you want our *eyes*."

Raven looked confused. "Why ever not?"

"Because—that's just horrible," she said.

"Better than your skin," Dzo pointed out.

"Okay," Powell said. "How many?"

Chey grabbed his arm. "Wait!" she said. "Wait—just—this isn't cool. What the hell kind of spirit are you, Raven? You're not like Dzo, or Nanuq. They would never ask for something like that."

Raven sighed dramatically. "It does seem—untoward, doesn't it?" he asked. "But I assure you, it's strictly necessary." When that didn't seem to mollify her, he added, "It's part of who I am. I feast on the eyes of the fallen. On battlefields, in desolate forests, out here in the frozen tundra, all the stories agree. For myself, I'm not very fond of them. They're not very nutritious, but they're soft and easy to get to and so ravens, the actual birds, do eat them first when they find a nice piece of carrion. So I do it too. And when I eat somebody's eyes, I can see what they've seen. In this case, it will allow me to know exactly what you're looking for."

"Bullshit. We already told you that," Chey said.

Powell rubbed her hand where it lay on his arm. "Sometimes you have to follow the rules," he told her. "How many?"

"Two should suffice. Are there any volunteers?" Raven asked.

"I refuse," Lucie said. Chey was not surprised.

"I guess I—" she started to say, but Powell interrupted her.

"You can have mine," he said. "Both of them. They'll just grow back, anyway, the next time I change."

"That's not for five days," Chey pointed out.

Raven shrugged. "Even so, he has a point. Would someone be kind enough to hold him down?"

Chey couldn't watch it happen. There was some screaming, though not much. Powell always had been a tough son of a bitch. When it was over she was surprised to see there wasn't much blood. However Raven had done it, Powell's eyelids had been left intact and he kept them closed so she didn't have to see what was underneath. She tore off a strip of her shirt and tied it around Powell's empty sockets. "I would do anything for you," he whispered while she stroked his hair. It made her heart sink when he said that.

"Let's make sure it was worth it," she told him.

Dzo had moved around the fire to stand over Raven and started shouting at the bird spirit. "Don't you try anything tricky," he said. "Don't you even think of backing out of the bargain now."

"Oh, I wouldn't dream of it," Raven assured him.

"I'm watching you now. I'm watching you like—like an eagle."

"I would expect nothing less," Raven said, and laughed. It was a nasty cawing laugh, totally at odds with his previous demeanor, and Chey wondered if it had all been a trick—if they had just played right into Raven's hands.

"Now," Chey insisted. "No subtlety, no tricks, no games. You got what you wanted, now tell us what we want to hear."

"I'll go one better, and tell you what you need to hear," Raven said. He drew himself up straight and looked deep into her eyes. "I'll tell you how the first werewolves came to be, and where it happened. Exactly where it happened, so you can go there and undo what was done."

62

Raven's voice dropped an octave as he began to tell the story. The werewolves and Dzo all craned closer to pick up every syllable, to catch every nuance. Chey expected another abstract retelling of an old myth, a tale couched in the vague language of folklore. But Raven was true to his word and gave them all the nasty details. "This isn't a story you're supposed to learn from," he told them. "There's no happy ending, and no easy moral to glean. This is about the facts, about what I saw with my own eyes, not anybody else's.

"It happened more than ten thousand years ago. There were people here then, though they left no traces that remain today. Archaeologists speak of the ancestors of the Inuit, called the Thule people. Before the Thule they speak of the Dorset culture. Inuit today retain stories of people even older than that—the Tunlit, a name that means 'the first people.' The Tunlit were giants, they say, but feeble-minded giants, simple people who spoke a language no more complex than that of infants. The Tunlit were docile and were easy to drive off their lands, and the Inuit erased all sign of them. But even before the Tunlit there were people here—the Nean-derthals, who first told stories of animal spirits, and who summoned Musquash and Raven and Polar Bear and all the others with their songs.

"They did not call themselves Neanderthals, of course. They called themselves the Sivullir, a word that means 'people with red hair.' The Sivullir all had red hair and brown eyes. They looked much as you do, though their brows were a little more prominent, their jaws a little more square. They were a little shorter than people are now, but everyone was shorter back then.

"They lived on average for thirty years. By the age of twenty a Sivullir looked very old. They had homes they carved out of the ice, whole warrens connected by wide passages. They wore fur parkas that they never removed, as anyone must who lives in this land. Especially in that time.

"This was during the ice age, when the ocean was lost beneath great glaciers, and the valleys between massive mountain ranges of ice were always filled with snow. It was a time when there was only winter, and the sun was dimmer than it is today.

"It was a harsh time, a brutal time. The Sivullir were tough people. They had to be to survive. Their ways would seem drastic to you, or even to modern Inuit. They lived on what meat they could catch, and they kept their numbers small enough that they could survive each vicious season. They had very strict laws about this. When someone had grown so old they could no longer perform useful work, or when they had lost all their teeth and could no longer chew meat, they were expected to hang themselves so as not to become a burden to others. When too many babies were born to a family, the mother would smear the bile of a bear on her nipples, and let the newborns suck. Bear bile contains massive amounts of vitamin A, and death would follow within minutes."

"That's horrible," Chey said.

"That's survival," Raven told her. "Always these people tottered on a thin edge between life and extinction. They had only the crudest of tools, and only what metal the glaciers gave them, which was very little. They could not have survived very long, if it hadn't been for their one great advantage: us.

"They were the ones who created us. Among the Sivullir there were shamans—the word will probably make you think of New Age nonsense, but back then they acted more as doctors, and psychiatrists, and especially as musicians. The Sivullir had such wonderful music. They made bone flutes and drums out of animal hides and they played such songs that we were compelled to leave our animal bodies behind just to come closer and listen. Their songs made us immortal, and gave us power over the environment, and over the animals we represented. In exchange we interceded on behalf of the Sivullir, making sure their hunts were successful and leading them home when they got lost out on the ice. These shamans knew how to talk to us, and how to make bargains with us, and sometimes how to fool us into doing what they wanted.

"With our aid the Sivullir survived, long after they should have died out. By the time of my story they were the last of their kind. Yet they had no sense of the passage of time, nor any way to know they had outlived their own history. Their world was one of constant change as the ice groaned and shifted and spilled over into new valleys, or cracked and split open to reveal brief rivers that had been buried for millions of years. We helped the Sivullir anticipate those changes, but there was a change coming even we could not predict. A threat to their very way of life."

Raven fell silent as he pulled a strip of meat off the seal carcass and stuffed it in his mouth.

"What was the threat?" Powell asked finally, as if urging the spirit to continue his story.

Raven swallowed noisily. "Global warming," he said.

63

"The Earth was warming back up as it crawled out of the last ice age. With each year that passed, there was a little less snow, and the air was a little warmer. Exposed water didn't freeze as quickly. Animals changed their migration patterns. It was the little things like this that told us the world was about to end. The world as they knew it, anyway."

Raven shrugged. "Over the centuries, as the ice thawed in the valleys, new passes were opened through the glaciers. There were reports of new animals seen by the hunters, animals that had never stalked the ice before. And then there came the new people, from the east."

"From across the land bridge?" Chey asked, remembering what she'd learned in school.

"Originally, yes. The newcomers had traveled from Russia across the land called Beringia, which was a thick isthmus connecting Asia and North America, a dry strip of land that the ice never got a hold on. By this time, however, the land bridge had sunk back into the sea. The newcomers were as much Alaskans as they had ever been Russians, by the time my story begins. They weren't Neanderthals, these new people. They were Cro-Magnons. They were short and stocky and very hairy, but genetically they were indistinguishable from you modern humans. These called themselves the Bear People, because they worshipped a giant bear. Everywhere they went they left their shrines, which were caves wherein lay the skull of their god. They lived in small huts made of mammoth bones, which could be packed up and moved very quickly. They practiced ritual scarification, cutting elaborate spiral patterns in their cheeks and foreheads with flint knives. They came from a more pleasant land, where wood was plentiful, and they had better tools and weapons than the Sivullir.

"What they did not have was us. They knew no spirits from their old land. Here their god forbade them from even speaking with us, much less propitiating us for our assistance. So it was a long while before they were able to make a life here, even when the ice began to shrink.

"The Sivullir did not hate the Bear People on first meeting them. There was no precedent for their arrival. The Sivullir had always believed themselves to be the only people in the world—but rather than reacting with fear on meeting the newcomers, they welcomed the Bear People into their ice warrens, and gave them food, and saved them from death when they were found stranded on the ice. In return the Bear People offered the Sivullir the great revelations of their bear god. The Sivullir were largely uninterested, but they did not try to stop the Bear People from practicing their religion.

"Not at first, anyway.

"The world was changing faster and faster. The ice was receding and suddenly there was a new season in the year, something you would be hard pressed to call summer, but that is what they called it back then. A time when some of the valleys were clear altogether of ice and snow, and plant life began to take hold. Some of the animals the Sivullir relied on for sustenance flourished. Others migrated even farther north, to keep up with the withdrawing glaciers. The diet of the Sivullir changed and this brought diseases. Other sicknesses came with the Bear People, though no one made that connection at the time. What they did know was that people were living shorter lives and more children were dying every year.

"The Bear People took advantage of this tragedy. They had never practiced the strict child laws of the Sivullir. They encouraged their people to have large families, with lots of children. Many sons made the hunt easier, and spare daughters, they believed, could be sold to other tribes."

"Ugh," Chey said. "I take it this was before feminism was invented."

Raven shrugged. "I'm not a mortal, so I can't judge them. At the time I was as horrified as any of the Sivullir when I saw Bear People families with seven or even more children. The Bear People were breeding the Sivullir out of their own lands.

"It seemed the Sivullir would vanish from the Earth, swallowed up by these interlopers. The shamans, who were the last defenders of the old ways of the ice age, knew that something had to be done if those ways were not to be lost forever.

"So they did what they had always done before, in times of crisis. They turned to us, their cousins. They asked for our help."

"That's where we come in, I imagine," Powell said, his voice a growl.

64

Raven chewed quietly for a while. He asked for a drink of water before he went on. "Don't give him anything. That wasn't part of the bargain," Dzo insisted.

Raven shrugged. "This paranoia doesn't become you, Musquash," he said. "I liked you better when you trusted everybody."

"Sure. Because that made it easier for you to take my skin."

Raven laughed. "Believe me, if I wanted it now, I could have it." He turned to face the werewolves again. "I was always the smartest of the spirits, you see," he explained. "That was why the shamans of the Sivullir came to me when they knew they had no other hope. There were six of them at the time—all that remained of their number. I was shocked when I saw them. Three of the shamans were withered old men, maybe thirty-five years old. They should have hanged themselves long before they grew so old. One was a boy, barely a teenager, who looked terrified, as if he'd never seen a spirit before. I was told he'd been chosen as a replacement at the last minute by a shaman dying of some fast-acting pox. The other two were no less strange. One was a woman. That had been unheard of, until right before the end, when there weren't enough shamans to go around. She was middle-aged and fat and she smiled a lot but she never spoke to me. The last one, the shaman who addressed me by name when I came into the cave, had white hair and white skin. His name was Vull. It was a common name among the Sivullir, but it seemed particularly appropriate in this case, since it was also their word for freshly fallen snow before anyone steps on it.

"Vull tried to flatter me with compliments and by regaling the others with some of my best stories. He was trying to distract me, of course, so I wouldn't notice as the others placed a ring of small black stones around my feet."

"Pitchblende," Dzo said, as if it were a profanity.

Raven nodded. "Everything that is supernatural in this world has a weakness, some substance it cannot abide. Pitchblende—and similar minerals—is ours. In its presence we weaken and suffer. The Sivullir used to wear necklaces of the stuff for protection from the less friendly spirits, but never before had they thought to use it like this. Encircled by poison, I was trapped, unable to fly away. When it was accomplished, Vull apologized profusely. He knew this would anger me. He was quite correct in that. He explained, however, that he had no choice. Something had to be done to drive away the Bear People before the Sivullir were wiped out. They intended to use the one weapon they had left at their disposal, the power of the spirits, to achieve this, though he admitted he was not sure how it could be done. He thought I might have some ideas.

"I was being given a chance to save myself. I curbed my anger, and instead I praised him for his clever trick. I said it made sense he should choose me, the most intelligent of spirits, and that I understood what he had done. But I suggested that perhaps what was needed in this case was not intelligence, but fear. The Bear People were afraid of certain animals. I suggested that the spirit of the dire wolf—Amuruq, though that was not the name she had then—would be far more likely to terrify the Bear People than myself. I also suggested a way her power could be used to best effect, and Vull agreed it was a very cunning plan.

"He released me so that I could summon her. She had never been very close to the Sivullir, for they feared her as much as the Bear People did. It was rare for a shaman to call upon her and rarer still that the shaman was not devoured for his efforts. I used this to my advantage. I found her tearing apart a mammoth up in the heights of the glaciers and I spoke with her at length, telling her all about the wonderful gifts the Sivullir had given me, and all the kindness they had shown me."

"Nanuq said they tricked her by offering to show her how well they treated their sled dogs," Chey said, remembering the polar bear spirit's version of this story.

"Nanuq is very old, and forgetful. The Sivullir never domesticated the dog," Raven told her. "My lies had the same effect, however. Amuruq came with me back to the ice warren and there she came before Vull, who had laid out a great feast for her. She was always hungry, and never sated, and she was glad for the bounty. She did not even look at the food before she pounced on it, and so she did not realize it was stuffed full of powdered pitchblende. When she did realize it, it was far too late. As I watched, for the first time I understood fear myself. Her shape began to grow indistinct. As the dust poisoned her she tried to change into her animal form, thinking this would save her. She grew very sick. Her fur fell out in great clumps and her eyes clouded over.

"While she was halfway between forms, the shamans came upon her with ropes to hold her down. She fought them savagely and two of them were killed, torn apart by her claws and teeth. The boy shaman ran from the cave howling in panic and went quite mad. The others could barely hold her, but they managed to keep her still long enough for Vull to reveal what he hid under his parka. This was the gift of another spirit, the spirit of the giant moles that lived in that time who burrowed under the ground, who had knowledge of stone and metal. That spirit had given him an *ulu* made of silver."

"What's an *ulu*?" Chey asked Dzo, quietly.

"A crescent-shaped knife," he explained. "The Inuit still use them."

"The *ulu* was unlike any knife the Sivullir had ever possessed before. It was not a piece of sharpened bone or rock, but supernatural metal, and it possessed powers unknown until that moment. Vull used it to carve Amuruq into pieces while she was still changing," Raven went on. "Her blood stained his skin so that he spent the rest of his life with red hands. He didn't stop, even when she was dismembered. He ground her bones to powder and burned all her fur. Her eyes and her tongue were placed together in a bag and—"

"Please," Chey said. The story was making her queasy. "Maybe we can skip what they did with her eyes and tongue."

Raven shrugged. "You wanted the whole story. It was important that everything but her meat was destroyed, you see, because if it wasn't then she could have just reformed herself from the pieces that remained. The meat was put into a pot and cooked to make a stew. The female shaman spiced it with her own moon blood, which was the last part of the spell they were performing."

"By moon blood," Dzo tried to explain, "he means—"

"I've already figured that one out," she told him, patting his arm.

Raven waited for them to be quiet before he went on. "When the stew was finished cooking, they took it out of the ice warren and down to the valley below."

"And fed it to their warriors," Chey said, nodding. "Nanuq told us that, too. So they could fight the Bear People, and defend the ice."

Raven laughed. "The Sivullir had no warriors. They were hunters, but they were forbidden to ever kill one of their own kind—or one of the Bear People, either. No, they had no desire to transform themselves.

"The two of them—Vull and the female shaman—took the stew to a camp of Bear People. They said it was a gift in return for the great gift the newcomers had given them, the gift of the bear god's revelation. It would have been rude to refuse such a gift. The Bear People of that camp ate it right away, while the shamans watched. The shamans made sure they finished every drop. Then they went back to the warren, to watch and wait for the moon to rise. They knew exactly what they had done, and what would happen next."

65

Night had fallen as Raven told his story. The fire light flickered across the shiny black feathers of his cloak as he went on.

"I doubt I need tell you in great detail what happened when the moon rose that night," Raven said. "Those of the Bear People who had partaken of Amuruq's flesh were changed. Awakened by the magic in the female shaman's moon blood, they transformed—just as we had watched Amuruq transform in her final moments. She was not dead, but only dispersed. Those afflicted by her spirit found themselves consumed by hatred and rage and a desperate need to slay any human being they could find—Amuruq's rage was unquenchable. We made our curse very carefully, and she had no desire to harm a single Sivullir, but no human was safe. It was a night of horror, as the wolves fell upon those who were truly their own kin, slaughtering and ravening without cease. Bodies were torn apart, cries for mercy went unheeded. Chaos and panic reigned and only when the moon sank below the horizon again did it end. The Bear People had no silver weapons. They could fight against the supernatural wolves that appeared without warning in their camps—but they could not destroy them. Those they killed, the wolves ate, just as Amuruq devoured everything she could find. Those who somehow managed to survive were usually so terribly wounded they were not expected to live through the following day.

"Yet something occurred which even I had not foreseen. The wounded did survive. Vull and his shamans had thought only to make a demonstration of their power. But the terrible peace of the Bear People camps that day was not to last. That very night, Amuruq emerged again— and this time there were more bodies for her to possess. Those wounded

Bear People who had been taken back to their tents to die were transformed as well. The curse we had created was spreading.

"For you see, Amuruq was far from dead, and in some way she was aware of what had happened to her. Her spirit was divided, spread among many bodies, but still it longed to coalesce again, to take her original form. When she could not do so, she took every body she could lay her claws into. And so it has continued for more than ten thousand years."

"But the curse—did it work?" Chey asked. "What did the Bear People do?"

"Most of them died," Raven told her. "Vast numbers of them were slain and they did not rise again. Those who survived eventually fled the ice lands, just as Vull had hoped they would. They spread out to the south, into new lands. And they took the curse with them. Within a millennium or two, there were werewolves everywhere on Earth. There was no way to stop it. It wasn't until the invention of metallurgy, and the refinement of silver, that the first weapons were made that could slay the lycanthropes. Only the metal that had carved Amuruq's flesh originally could harm her."

"What became of the Sivullir?" Lucie inquired.

Raven shrugged. "They had won a small victory. Yet they had addressed the symptom of the change that was destroying them, and not its cause. The ice age was over, and with it, their way of life. Within a generation they were extinct. Similarly, the dire wolves that once haunted the glaciers had lost their soul. Without Amuruq to keep them alive, they grew listless and weak. They were easily destroyed by other predators, or simply allowed themselves to starve to death. Even as the last of the Sivullir died, the dire wolf vanished from the world as well. The spirits, whom the Sivullir had originally summoned forth, lived on, of course. We live forever, whether we want to or not. Yet things had changed even for us, with the passing of the Sivullir. Our cousins were gone. That was the end of the time of stories, and it is now the end of my story as well."

66

Raven rose easily to his feet. He grabbed up the remains of the seal and tucked them under his arm, then turned as if to go. "Well, it's been a pleasure," he said, and reached up to pull down his mask.

"Not so fast," Powell said. He stirred himself up next to the fire and reached for Chey's hand, which she gave him. "That's half of what I wanted."

"I'm tired after talking so long," Raven whined. "I'll come back later and tell you the rest, if you like. But right now I need to rest."

"This is how he does it!" Dzo said, jumping to his feet. He jabbed a finger at Raven. "He says that, and then it's months before he comes back. It's always some trick with him. He thinks it's funny!"

"Take it easy, old man," Powell said. With Chey's help he stood up. She turned him slightly so he was facing Raven. "I paid you in full. I expect you to keep your bargain."

"And so I shall. When I have rested," Raven assured him.

It was then Chey noticed that Lucie wasn't sitting by the fire anymore. At some point during the story she must have gotten up and slipped into the shadows. Now she pounced, jumping on Raven's back and throwing an arm around his neck.

"Do what he asks," the redhead growled, "or I'll tear off your wings."

"You can't do that," Raven said, as if he were addressing a child. "No human can. I'm immortal. I—"

"I'm not human, am I? You just told me I have the spirit of Amuruq inside me. I bet I can make you hurt," she told him.

Raven's mouth pursed at the thought. "This is silly. I can just change my shape and fly away."

"Try it," Lucie suggested.

Raven let out a deep sigh. "Listen, werewolf," he said to Powell, "she can't really hurt me. But I find this tiresome. If I give you what you want, will you call off your dog?"

"Tell me if the curse can be undone," Powell said.

"I asked for an assurance that—"

"Can it be undone?" Powell demanded.

"Yes. Magic can always be reversed."

Chey felt something strange bubble up in her stomach. It made her feel a little dizzy. She eventually identified it as hope. For the first time it seemed even possible that Powell was right—that there was a way to save her humanity. She held tight to the feeling, not letting it consume her. It couldn't possibly be as easy as that. Could it?

"Now tell your defender here to—"

"What do I need to undo the curse?"

Raven rolled his eyes. "Well, obviously, you need the silver *ulu*. Once you have it you can—"

"I know what to do with it. But where is it?"

"Exactly where Vull left it. Where it was used," Raven told him. "In the lowest cave beneath the glacier."

"And where is that?"

"On Kitlineq," Raven said. He looked down at the fire. "I really shouldn't be telling you this. You'll get no happiness out of—"

"Where on Kitlineq?" Powell demanded. "That's Victoria Island, right? It's a big place. Where exactly is it located?"

"I seem to have forgotten my GPS tracker," Raven said, exasperated.

"I don't even know what that is," Powell told the spirit. "Most likely Chey does, but it doesn't matter. Tell me how to find the silver *ulu,* and I'll let you go."

"I only know what it looks like from the air. If she lets me go, I can draw you a map."

"You forget I don't have any eyes to see it," Powell told him.

Raven gasped in frustration. "Your wives here can see it. Or Musquash. Look, there's no good way to just tell you. I need to draw a map, and I can't do that with a werewolf hanging on my neck."

"Alright. But if you try to fly off before I'm satisfied, you'll regret it."

"I'm sure," Raven said.

Lucie dropped down to her feet and let Raven go. Instantly the bird spirit tried to slip his arms inside his cloak so he could transform back into his animal form. Lucie didn't need to be told what to do. She grabbed one of his arms and twisted it up behind his back—hard enough that if he'd been human she would have dislocated his shoulder. Raven cried out pitiably and tears rolled down his cheeks.

"Please! Please! You've won," he moaned.

Chey looked over at Dzo, who just shook his head. He wasn't buying this act.

"Twist it again," she told Lucie.

Lucie complied.

"Alright! Alright! I'll draw your damned map. Then you let me go."

"Alright, Lucie," Powell said. "That's enough."

Lucie let go of Raven. The bird spirit shook his arm out, but it didn't appear to be broken. The tears were instantly gone from his face and he did little more than mutter as he grabbed a twig from the fire and started drawing in the snow. The light was bad, but Chey studied every aspect of the map as best she could.

"Here, there's a lake. It looks like a whale's flukes from above, yes? There's a hill over here, on the north side, and over here there's a pile of rocks sticking up out of the ground that resemble fingers."

"Is this what it looks like now, or what it looked like ten thousand years ago?" Chey thought to ask.

Raven scowled and scrubbed out the map he'd been drawing. "You can't blame an old trickster spirit for trying," he said. He started drawing again. The lake's shape had changed considerably, stretching itself out across the terrain. The hill was gone altogether, but the fingerlike stones remained. "Of course, they're smaller now, and this one, the index finger, has fallen over. Now, there's an island on the lake, and there's a cave on the island. At the bottom of the cave you'll find the *ulu*—and everything else you have coming to you. Got it?"

"I think so," Chey said.

"Good. Farewell!" Raven shoved his arms back into his cloak and it became a pair of wings. With a sarcastic "Caw!" he jumped into the air and turned into a bird. A bird that flew away at top speed.

Chey knelt down in the snow over the map, memorizing every line, trying to imprint every detail on her brain so she wouldn't lose it.

"I think—I think I can remember this," she told Powell. "I think we can do this! I don't believe I'm saying this. But I think we can find this thing. We can find the cure."

"Maybe we can," he told her. But there was something wrong with his voice. He didn't sound particularly happy. If anything, he sounded like his worst fear had just come to pass. He rolled over and turned his eyeless face away from her.

67

Chey was suddenly energized, excited at the prospect of the cure. She could be human again—even better, she could reverse the madness that had been consuming her, the depredations of her wolf on her humanity. She tried to ask a million questions about Victoria Island, and the best way to get there. Powell was very tired, though, and his wounds bothered him so much that he just wanted to curl up and rest.

"We've learned something valuable, yes," he agreed with her. "Though there are still problems to overcome. It won't be easy to find this place."

"What are you talking about?" she asked. "It should be easy. We have a map, now."

"We know it's on an island in a lake on Victoria Island," he said. "That's actually less useful than you seem to think. We still don't know exactly where this lake is."

"We don't? How many lakes can there be on one island?"

Powell grimaced. "Victoria Island has hundreds of them. It's a bigger place than you think it is."

"How big?"

"It's the size of England and Scotland. And we don't have a map."

Chey refused to have her mood dampened. "So we just need a guide. Dzo—what about you? You must know the place pretty well, right?"

Dzo waved his hands in the air. "Don't look at me. There's no musquashes on Victoria Island. Haven't been for a very long time. I've never been there, myself."

Chey frowned. "Well—we just have to get a good map, then."

Lucie laughed. "And how shall we do that, *jeune fille*? Perhaps we find some nice Eskimo nearby and say, give us your maps or we tear out your throat? A solution that has worked for me before, I will admit, though I doubt Monty will allow it."

"You know damned well I won't," he agreed.

Fuming with frustration, Chey sat down hard by the fire and hugged herself. "This would be so easy if we could just Google it."

The rest of them stared at her as if she'd suddenly started speaking in Sanskrit.

She stared back. "What?" Then she shook her head, realizing she was the only one in the camp less than a hundred years old. "Right. None of you have ever used the Internet. You've probably never even heard of it."

"Is it like one of those . . . GPS boxes Raven mentioned?" Dzo asked.

"*Non, non, non.* I think—yes, I believe I heard something of this Internet, when I was in Russia," Lucie admitted. "It is a new kind of television, yes? It was all the rage."

Chey laughed. "Yes, that's exactly what it is." She scrubbed at her face with her hands. "Oh, my God. Look, there's this program—this—this Web page—" She stopped because she was getting a lot of blank looks. "Okay, imagine a map, a really, really good map of the world. It's based on satellite images, so it's up to date and it shows everything. You know what satellites are, right?"

"Oh, yes," Lucie said, beaming. "Like Sputnik."

"Yeah," Powell said, sitting up a little. "I remember Sputnik. Drove the Americans crazy. They thought it would rain bombs on them. That didn't ever happen, though, right?"

" . . . Right," Chey confirmed. "This is going to take a long time to explain. They have a lot of satellites now, and some of them have cameras on them, to take pictures of the Earth from above. By combining all those pictures they can make a photographic map of the entire planet. Including Victoria Island. With a computer, you can access those pictures. If we could get to a computer, we could look at the pictures of Victoria Island and find this lake. It would be pretty easy, actually."

"You would have to pore over thousands of pictures with a magnifying glass," Powell said, shaking his head. "It could take weeks."

"No it wouldn't," Chey said. "There are some benefits to progress, really." She hugged her knees against her chest. "Listen," she said, because she'd had a sudden thought. "Powell, when you went hunting for that seal, you said you saw there were towns up on the coast."

"Yes," he agreed.

"Well, any of those towns would do. Any of them is likely to have at least some kind of Internet connection."

"Really?" he asked. "Are you sure? A lot of them don't have running water or sewers. And there are no roads up here."

"Trust me, even a place that still uses outhouses will already have the Internet. People have to get their porn somehow. If we could go to one of those towns, we could ask to borrow somebody's computer for a couple hours. We could find this place on Victoria Island, figure out exactly how to get there. Then we just leave, and nobody gets hurt."

"What if we don't find it before we transform?" Powell asked. "I don't think this is a very good idea."

"It's going to be four more days before we change again," Chey pointed out. "Trust me, that's more than enough time."

"I don't know," he said. "It's dangerous. I don't think I can allow this."

Chey felt anger flush through her. Her cheeks burned as she stood up and loomed over him. "Listen," she said. "When we're wolves, you're the alpha pack leader head honcho whatever," she told him, "but right now I'm human, and I don't need you telling me what to do."

"You don't?" he asked. He honestly looked surprised.

"I'm going. My mind's made up. I'm doing this. For once I'm going to be the one in charge. You can try to stop me, but it'll be pretty hard tracking me without any eyes."

"That's a cruel thing to say," he told her.

She didn't bother addressing that. "Lucie—you watch him while I'm gone. If anything happens to Powell before I get back, I'm holding you personally responsible."

"I shall nurse him back to health, like my own baby," Lucie assured her.

"Creepy. But I guess it'll have to do. Dzo, you come with me. Do you know where the nearest town is?"

The musquash spirit shrugged. "Yeah, I guess so. There's one about twenty kilometers east of here. Just a couple hundred people, almost all of them Inuit. They're probably all buttoned down for the winter."

"Perfect," Chey said, and without further ado, she started walking east through the snow.

68

Chey and Dzo trudged on in silence for a while, covering a lot of ground. She was in a hurry to get to this town and find a computer. He kept up with her easily, his feet barely sinking into the powdery snow. He looked sad, though, and after a while she had to ask. "What's up?" she said. "We're finally on the right track. Isn't that a good thing?"

"I guess," he said.

"So what's wrong?"

He shrugged and pulled down his wooden mask. It was something he did when he felt like human weirdness was getting to be too much for him, she knew. "I'm very happy for you and Powell," he told her. "Really. I just wonder what's going to happen to me after you're gone."

"We're not going anywhere," she told him. "We're just going to be human again."

He shrugged. "Sure. And maybe—maybe you'll let me come stay with you? I'm not real good with cities. Too much stuff going on all at once."

"I imagine we won't be moving to Toronto anytime soon, either," she told him. "I've almost started to like this place. Well, not this tundra." She looked out across the frozen waste. She saw little but a barren snow field stretching to the horizon. There were a few hills to the south, but they did little to break up the monotony. "We'll go back to Great Bear Lake. Maybe we'll head down to Yellowknife every once in a while for a beer. You can definitely come along." It was a rosier picture than she really believed in, of course. She and Powell had done enough horrible things that they were more likely to be sent to jail as soon as they set foot back in civilization. But eventually they would be let out again, if they were model prisoners and showed real remorse, she thought. "We'll live together like a happy family."

"Sure," he said. "Until you die."

She stopped in her tracks. "What?"

"You'll be human. You'll be mortal again." He threw his hands up in the air. "Do you even understand how long I've been alive already? How much longer I'm going to live? It's like, forever. That's years and years yet. I'm sure you two will be real nice to me, but you'll be gone before I even notice, really."

Chey exhaled long and hard. Then she rushed over and hugged him, her arms sinking into the depths of his furs. He stood stiffly in her arms for a moment, then laid his head against her chest.

"We'll have good times before then, I promise," she said. "And . . . and maybe you can hang out with, you know. Our children."

Now there was a crazy thought.

It was weird. Chey had been doubtful at best about this cure when Powell had mentioned it before. Now she believed in it—completely. She was certain that she would be human again, and that it wouldn't be long in coming.

The wolf in her brain howled at the thought, but her good mood was enough to keep it from getting out.

They stopped after a couple hours and rested for a while, or rather, Chey rested while Dzo stood guard. He didn't sleep, as far as she knew, nor did he ever tire. She supposed there were real advantages to being the collective soul of a rodent species.

When they started up again, dawn was breaking—a long, drawn-out process that involved lots of pink clouds. The early light made the snow buzz a fluorescent blue that made her head fizz just to look at it. Before the sun was fully up, however, she caught her first sight of the town.

It didn't look like much. Just a couple dozen low, square buildings, half buried in snow. The rooftops were completely covered except for where chimney pots and radio aerials stuck up out of the accumulations. There were roads, or at least places where someone had plowed the snow back, leaving wide striped tire marks in the white. At every corner a light on a tall pole loomed over the buildings, shedding sickly yellow illumination that bounced off icicles and windows alike.

As the two of them walked cautiously into the town's main road, they didn't see a single human being. Occasionally they heard a snatch of music from a distant radio, and once they had to step back into a snowdrift to let a rumbling pickup truck glide past. Chains on its tires jangled and its lights painted the walls it passed by, but there was so much half-scraped snow on the windshield that they couldn't see the driver.

Chey found herself glad that they'd arrived so early. The fewer people they came across, the less likely they were to get into trouble. Powell had been a jerk for telling her she couldn't do this, but she knew he was right—this was a dangerous mission behind, in a sense, enemy lines. She kept her head down in case anyone was looking out of a window, and she studied the buildings they passed, anxious to get this over with.

It didn't take long to find the place they were looking for. It was one of the largest buildings in town and it had a handicapped ramp out front of a wide pair of double doors. The brown-painted front of the building was adorned with a hand-painted mural that showed a smiling Inuit family, dressed in parkas with fur-lined hoods. In the middle of the mural was a big sign in yellow type that read:

HAMLET OF UMIAQ, NU
Town Offices, Fire Brigade,
Post Office, Northern Store,
Community Center, Health
Clinic & Public Library
-welcome!-

She shook the snow off her feet and headed inside, Dzo trailing after her.

69

It was so weird to be *inside* again. It was warm inside the community center, far warmer than the air outside. She couldn't hear the wind. There was no snow on the floor. But most important—there was a roof over her head, and walls all around her. Electric lights that hummed quietly on every side. Glass and metal and bricks.

The last building Chey had actually lived inside was Powell's cabin down by Great Bear Lake, near Port Radium. That felt like a lifetime ago. Now she was once more in a place built by and for human beings. She felt afraid to touch anything in case she got it dirty.

That was silly, of course. She cleared her head and looked around. She was standing in a broad foyer with doors that led off in various directions. One glass door was labeled "Library." Through it she could see a couple of shelves lined with paperback books and three Internet stations next to a circulation desk. The lights were off inside but the computer monitors were on, cycling through screensavers that showed pictures of life in the Arctic. She reached for the door and found that it was locked. It had a solid metal frame but she figured she could pull it open—as a werewolf, she was pretty strong. Maybe she could get in, get on the computer, and get this done before anybody came in to work. *The perfect crime,* she thought, until she heard a door open behind her.

"Library's closed, hon," someone said. The voice was gentle but firm.

Chey spun around, a big smile on her face. The voice belonged to a middle-aged woman in a turtleneck sweater that made it look like she had no neck at all, as if her head were just fused onto her shoulders. She looked Inuit and she wore enormous cat glasses.

"Hon?" the woman asked again. "You feelin' alright?"

"Hi," Chey managed to say, finally. It had been so long since she'd spoken to someone normal that she felt like she'd forgotten how. "Um, I need the Internet. Are you the librarian?"

"Phyllis Oonark," the woman said. "I do lots of things."

Chey nodded and thrust out her hand so Phyllis could shake it.

"Like I said, it's closed. Come back about nine-thirty. No, better make it ten—my husband's just due home then from the plowing, and he'll want some breakfast."

"What time is it now?" Chey asked.

Phyllis squinted at her. "Just after seven. I wouldn't be here myself 'cept the post needed sorting. Hon? Did something happen?"

Chey frowned, not comprehending. Then she noticed Phyllis was looking at her feet. She had, of course, forgotten to put her shoes on before leaving the camp at the *inukshuk*. "Oh," she said.

"You're not from town, or I'd recognize you," Phyllis said. She looked more concerned than afraid, which was something. "Plus you're white, which is pretty rare in Umiaq. I know I shouldn't just question strangers, it isn't polite, but I'd really like to know what's going on."

"It's—it's complicated," Chey tried. "I just need to use a computer. Just for a little while. I don't have any money, but—"

"You're trying to bribe me? So I'll let you check your e-mail?"

"Mrs. Oonark," Dzo said, then. He'd been standing in the shadows by the door. Now he moved to Chey's side. Phyllis just about jumped in the air. "It's important, alright. Do you recognize me?"

The librarian blinked a couple of times. Her face didn't change much, but she did take a step backward. "Not . . . as such," she said.

"But you know what I am."

Chey looked over and saw that Dzo had his mask down over his face.

"Now, that's . . . that's difficult to say," Phyllis told him. "Maybe I should put some coffee on."

"Coffee?" Chey asked. "Seriously? That would be so awesome, I can't even tell you."

"Sure. Anything you need." Phyllis edged around the two of them as if terrified of touching either of them, even though she'd already shaken Chey's hand. She unlocked the door to the library and switched on the lights inside. "Have you eaten?"

"We're not hungry," Chey said. It seemed to come as a distinct relief to the human woman. "But I can't tell you how much I would love a hot shower."

"Speak for yourself," Dzo said. "I'm a vegetarian, so you know."

Half an hour later, with her hair still wet and stinking of shampoo (her lycanthropic nose could be too sensitive sometimes), Chey finally got to sit down at the computer. Phyllis typed in the password and launched up the Web browser for her.

"I—I don't know what you folk need with the Internet," she said, "but we've got a filter going to stop you from looking at adult sites and such," she told Chey. "You don't need that turned off, do you?"

"No," Chey said, "that won't be necessary."

"Alright, then," Phyllis said, and left her to it.

Chey navigated to a map site she'd used a very long time ago and found that the interface had completely changed. She figured out the new system easily, though, and started a search for satellite images of Victoria Island. She quickly realized that Powell hadn't been lying. Victoria Island was the eighth largest island in the world, she learned, and the biggest island in the Canadian Arctic Archipelago—a triangular mass of islands curling from the northern coast up toward and around the north pole. A helpful little text box came up telling her that it had a population of less than two thousand people, most of them in the town of Cambridge Bay, and that it was shaped like a stylized maple leaf. She squinted at the picture on the screen but couldn't quite see that. Clicking on the on-screen arrows, she zoomed in on the island and found that it was liberally dotted with lakes. Hundreds of them, some no bigger than ponds, some big enough to surround their own archipelagos. Almost none of them had names, according to the map software.

She sighed. She had no idea how big the lake she was looking for might be—or how small. She was going to have to zoom in on every single one of them until she found one that matched the outline Raven had drawn in the snow. Well, at least it was possible, if laborious. She started at the northwest corner of the island and zoomed in until she found the smallest lake in the view. It was the wrong shape. She panned over to the next one.

It was also the wrong shape.

So was the third lake she looked at. And the fourth. She sat back in her chair and sipped at the coffee Phyllis had made for her. It was heavenly. The caffeine buzzed in her bloodstream and helped her keep her eyes wide as she looked at a fifth lake. And a sixth. Which didn't have any islands in it.

Some time about the fiftieth lake, the library opened for the day. Phyllis came in and put some new magazines on a shelf, then went out again without saying a word. Chey panned over to the fifty-first lake. Eventually people started coming into the library. They stared at her—the town didn't get many strangers coming through to use the Internet—but she was able to ignore them. They picked through the magazines or the paperbacks, checked their e-mail, left again. The seventy-fifth lake looked kind of right, except there was no island and its southern shore was too round. Someone sat down at the Internet station next to her, but Chey didn't even glance at them. The seventy-sixth lake was all wrong.

The eightieth lake was promising . . . but wrong. The eighty-first— well. Well, the outline was very close. And there was an island in the middle of it. She zoomed in further on the northern shore.

"Ahem," the person at the next Internet station said. The voice was female and very harsh. "Hey. You."

Chey lifted her head but kept looking at the monitor. She took a sip of her coffee. "Mm-hmm?" she mumbled. There was a rock formation on the north shore of the lake that looked just about right. This lake was definitely—

"Are you stupid, or just deaf?" the woman at the next Internet station asked.

Annoyed, Chey looked up and saw the woman. She was young, maybe not even twenty. She was Inuit, but unlike other Inuit women Chey had seen, her hair was cut very short, almost cropped down to her scalp. Her eyes were full of rage.

She grabbed Chey's coffee cup out of her hand, then dashed the lukewarm contents in Chey's face.

"I've been sitting here twenty minutes trying to get your attention," the woman said.

Chey was too surprised to react.

"I want you to look at me when I beat the shit out of you," the woman said, pushing her chair back and getting to her feet.

70

Chey jumped up from her chair and grabbed the only thing at hand—the keyboard of the computer she'd been working at. As the stranger's fist came whistling toward her face she brought it up high like a shield.

The fist smashed right through the keyboard. Broken keys and bits of green circuit board went flying, but the fist kept coming. It collided with Chey's chin hard enough to send her spinning backward.

Chey threw out her hands to catch herself. The stranger swept them out from under her with one booted foot.

So she was strong. Incredibly strong. And faster than any human ought to be. Good to know.

The stranger brought a boot down on the back of Chey's neck—hard—as Chey tried to struggle up from the carpet. Chey's face hit the floor.

"Who are you?" she asked, her voice muffled by the carpet. She was starting to wonder where Dzo had gotten to.

"My name is Sharon Minik. You wouldn't know that," the woman said. "You didn't bother to ask, the last time we met."

Chey's mind worked overtime to understand. "Sharon," she said, "I'm—"

Sharon grabbed one of Chey's arms and started dragging her out of the library.

"Stop that," Chey protested. "Listen, the last time we met I'm guessing I didn't look like this. Right? I looked like a big wolf?"

Sharon kicked open the library door and hauled Chey through. She didn't answer the question. Chey could see the foyer of the community center flash past. Phyllis Oonark was standing in a doorway, talking to someone on her cell phone. Chey tried to call out to the friendly librarian, but suddenly Sharon's hands were under her armpits and she was being hauled up to her feet.

"I don't want to mess this place up," Sharon said. "I live here."

"Okay, I'm cool with that," Chey said.

"So we take it outside." Sharon kicked Chey hard in the chest and sent her sprawling backward. Chey's back hit the double doors of the community center, and she stumbled out into the street.

The sun had come up and lit up the town. There were people around—most of them standing back in doorways or keeping their distance, but they were watching this and not helping. Chey fought to regain her balance. The people stopped to point and stare when they saw her slipping around on her bare feet.

"Somebody call the cops," she said. Though as soon as she thought about what she was saying she realized it was a terrible idea. Cops would have questions, questions she couldn't even begin to answer.

While she was pondering that, Sharon Minik erupted from the community center doors like a human harpoon. She slammed into Chey's side and sent her sprawling again, arms flailing, sliding down the street like a toboggan. Chey grabbed at anything solid that flashed past her—a light pole, the side of a house, the tire tracks in the snow. She scrabbled to get her feet under her and then she jumped back up to a standing posture. Ten meters away, Sharon Minik stood outside of the community center, breathing heavily.

"You're good at this," Chey said. "Tough. And fast." Too tough, she realized, and way too fast, to be human. Which could only mean one thing.

"I'm a hunter," Sharon shouted back.

"You're a werewolf."

"Thanks to you."

Chey nodded. She dropped her hands to her sides. Shook them out. Dug her toes into the snow. "We can talk about that," she said. "Or we can fight."

"Guess which?" Sharon asked.

"Thought so."

Sharon came running at her, charging with her head down and her fists up to defend her face. She knew Chey wouldn't just stand there and take the next hit. Chey tried to kick out low, to hit Sharon in the knees, but the hunter was ready for that and turned sideways at the last moment, stepping inside Chey's kick. She threw a punch while Chey was still following through, and it took every bit of Chey's supernatural speed to block it with her forearm. Sharon hooked her left fist around and there was no way for Chey to block it, so she took a nasty jab in the ribs.

Damn, Chey thought. *She's tougher than me. A much better fighter.*

Her body insisted that she double over in pain and she had no choice but to lower her head. Which let Sharon bring down her right fist hard on the back of Chey's neck.

Sparks lit up the inside of Chey's skull. Sparks that woke something that had been sleeping.

Chey's wolf understood it was being attacked, and it wanted to fight back. It howled to be released. It begged to help her.

Just as it had the day she'd first met Lucie. She hadn't understood its power then, and she had let it out. Let it fight. She'd still gotten her ass kicked, but the wolf had been fierce and desperate. It had given her energy and strength she didn't know she had.

Sharon brought her knee up hard into Chey's chest. Bone snapped in Chey's side and she felt like she was being stabbed in the liver by her own shattered rib. It hurt.

Jesus, it hurt.

The wolf was panting in her head.

Letting it out now would be a mistake, she thought. It already had so much power over her. Every day it was getting stronger. Letting it fight for her now would mean surrendering more of her precious stock of remaining humanity.

Sharon laced the fingers of both her hands together and brought her entwined fists around like a club that slammed into the side of Chey's neck. Chey's head snapped around and she felt her vertebrae pull apart under the force of the blow. Her spinal cord didn't snap, but it was a close thing.

The wolf whimpered. And whined. And grunted in frustration.
She needed it. She would have to make the sacrifice.

"Okay," she whispered, her eyes clenched tightly shut.

"Okay what?" Sharon demanded. "You think I'm done?"

"I wasn't talking to you," Chey said. And let the wolf loose.

71

The gray wolf inside Chey's brain leapt out of its confines and immediately seized control. It took the wolf a moment to take in its surroundings and understand what was going on—and even longer to adjust to the fact that it was inside a human body. But then it turned and saw the other human drawing back her fist for a nasty punch at the wolf's face.

Growling wildly, it rushed at Sharon Minik, its shoulder low to catch her in the chest. It dug in hard with its feet and shoved her backwards, up against the wall of a house. Sharon's breath went out of her in a puff of crystallizing vapor in the cold air. She tried to bring her hands up to protect her face, but the wolf just grabbed her by her collar and her belt and threw her bodily across the street.

Sharon went down in a heap. Almost immediately she was up on her feet again—she was very fast—but the wolf was charging again, one hand up to rake at Sharon's eyes. It was a feint and Sharon fell for it. The wolf body-slammed her into another house, sending a miniature avalanche of snow sliding down from its roof.

Sharon coughed up blood that flecked the wolf's face. She wasn't finished, though. She brought up one hand to chop at the wolf's throat, a blow that would easily have crushed the wolf's windpipe.

So fast. But the wolf was faster. The wolf grabbed Sharon's fingers and splayed them backwards until the little bones inside popped, one after the other.

The wolf didn't fight fair. It didn't fight dirty, either. It fought like an animal trapped in a corner for too long.

Sharon tried to headbutt the wolf. The wolf swung its head around and dug its teeth deep into the skin of Sharon's neck. Sharon screamed as the wolf's mouth pulled free, taking a mouth full of skin and blood with it. The wolf leaned over a little to spit, and Sharon took the opportunity to break loose and dodge down the street.

She was running away.

The wolf's bloody lips split in a wicked smile. The wolf loved it when prey tried to run. It was good exercise, for one thing. And the thrill of a good chase made the prey taste that much sweeter.

Toes spread wide for maximum grip, the wolf dashed after Sharon, intent on catching her and tearing her to pieces. Sharon ducked around a corner and the wolf followed, pushing off the snow and leaning into the turn. Sharon looked back over her shoulder and nearly tripped over a pile of snow in the middle of the street. She recovered gracefully, but it slowed her down for a split second.

It was all the advantage the wolf needed. It shot forward and sprang, legs pumping, muscles straining nearly to the breaking point to launch its borrowed body through the air. It didn't care if Chey's body got hurt as long as it killed this enemy.

The wolf threw its arms out in midair and scooped Sharon up at the top of its trajectory. It ducked its head under one arm as the two of them smashed into the rough plank wall of a house—and then through the wall, boards snapping under their weight, hundreds of splinters gouging their skin or pattering off their clothes like dry rain.

Someone screamed. A human scream—a sound the wolf loved.

Inside the house a woman in a housecoat dashed out of her kitchen as the two tumbled across the linoleum tile floor. Sharon smashed up against a stove and dented the steel oven door with her face. Moaning in pain, she rose stiffly to her feet.

The wolf was already standing, silhouetted in the hole the two of them had made in the wall. Stray flakes of snow drifted past its shoulders and face. It panted a little when it saw blood dripping from Sharon's left ear. It wanted very much to lap up that blood. And then bite Sharon's face off. The wolf took a step forward.

There was a pot of boiling water on the stove. Sharon grabbed it one-handed and tossed the water in the wolf's face.

It hurt. There was no denying it. The water scalded the wolf and made it want to whimper in pain. It held back the sound, reached up, wiped the water off its cheeks and away from its eyes. Took another step.

Sharon had jumped over the kitchen counter into the parlor beyond. Somewhere along the way she'd grabbed up a wooden block full of knives. She flicked one at the wolf's eyes.

The wolf reached up and batted the knife out of the air. Its edge sliced through the skin of her knuckles, but she ignored the sudden pain. Took another step.

Another knife, aimed low this time. The wolf leaned to one side and the knife missed it altogether, imbedding itself in the wall behind the wolf and thrumming there as it vibrated back and forth.

The wolf took another step toward Sharon.

Sharon had saved the biggest carving knife from the block. She didn't throw this one. Instead she waited until the wolf was close enough, then stabbed wildly, bringing her hand up from a low position so the wolf couldn't see it coming.

The wolf was capable of admiring a strong attack. It panted wildly as the blade came right for its belly. There was no time to move aside, so instead the wolf stepped into the blow, turning slightly to take the cut in its hip instead of its entrails. Blood poured down the leg of Chey's pants and pain burst like fireworks all up and down her side and leg. She had to close her eyes and squeal a little just to handle it.

When the wolf opened its eyes Sharon was running for the far side of the house. The wolf chased after her and through the front door, back out into the snowy street. Sharon's eyes were wide and full of terror when she saw the wolf still coming after her, hands stretched out to grab for hair, or arms, or whatever the wolf could reach. The game was winding down, now. Sharon had played very, very well. But she couldn't match the ferocity of the wolf, or its willingness to sacrifice its human body for the win.

The wolf's shadow loomed over Sharon as it came on like inexorable doom. Just one more step and—

—and—sniff—the wolf's nose twitched. Something—something in the air—

—silver.

There was silver nearby. A lot of it. The wolf turned on its heel to look. It was vaguely aware that behind it, Sharon dashed around a corner and was gone. It could track her down later, as soon as it figured out where the stink of silver was coming from.

A blue-faced man stepped around the corner of a nearby house.

"This has gone on long enough," he said. He had a silver chain in his hands, as thick and heavy as a truck's tow chain. It gleamed in the snowy morning light.

The wolf's eyes narrowed and its nostrils flared. It stamped its feet and then shot toward the man, head low and arms up to dash him to the ground. He didn't shift an inch as it charged him. At the last second it brought one fist around in a powerful hook that would smash his jaw to bone chips. He was no werewolf—he was human, weak and fragile and easily destroyed.

The wolf's fist connected with the blue man's chin with enough power to pulverize concrete. There was no way human skin could withstand that much pressure, no way human bone could take that much shock. Yet something strange happened. Something the wolf could not have imagined.

When its fist touched the blue chin, every bone in every finger shattered. Muscles in the wolf's forearm split and kinked. Blood dripped from broken skin and the wolf dropped to the ground and howled in agony, clutching its crippled arm close to its body.

The blue man wasn't so much as bruised.

The wolf's pain was so enormous that it did not notice at all the raven standing on the roof of the house across the street, cawing raucously.

72

The wolf continued to rage in pain and anger for a long time. Chey, buried deep inside the wolf's consciousness, was barely aware of what was happening as it was hauled away in silver chains. The people of Umiaq came to watch as it was loaded onto a snowmobile and carried out of town.

By the time the snowmobile reached Varkanin's cabin, Chey had started to reassert her control over her own body. When Varkanin dragged her inside and fastened her chains to a couch in his sitting room, she was able to speak again. "How?" she asked. He seemed to understand what she meant—how could he stand up to a rampaging werewolf without getting his hair mussed? How was it that when the wolf attacked him, all it got for its trouble was multiple fractures of the arm bones?

"Colloidal silver," Varkanin told Chey, as he sat down with a grunt on a chair opposite her couch. "Perhaps you have heard of it? No?" He sighed. "When one fights monsters, one must array one's self in proper protection. In the Middle Ages, werewolf hunters wore chain mail made of silver links. When I began to hunt Lucie I looked into having such a suit of armor made for myself. I was told how much it would weigh, and how much it would restrict my movements. I knew I required a better solution. I did much research on silver and one day came across the story of an American who was running for governor of their state of Montana.

"He was having difficulty securing votes. Not least so because his skin was blue." Varkanin's eyes lit up. "He was a believer, you see, in alternative medicines. Looking for some more natural type of antibiotic, he'd found colloidal silver. There is nothing particularly unnatural about it. It is simply purified water in which a certain amount of silver has been placed in suspension. It has been marketed as such for quite some time, though obviously the advertisements tend not to mention the one unfortunate and quite permanent side effect. It turns your skin blue, all over. Like mine." He held up his hands to show her, first the backs, then the palms. "Of course, this man in Montana did not mean for this to happen to him.

"It took some work to find a dealer of colloidal silver—the stuff has fallen out of favor with the public—but when I acquired enough of it, I found it had no unpleasant taste and no bad side effects beyond changing the color of my skin. It worked quite well for what I had in mind. Every square centimeter of skin on my body now contains very small amounts of silver. More than enough to protect me from any werewolf attack."

"You did this intentionally," Chey said, with a cold realization. "You wanted to kill Lucie that badly—that you turned yourself permanently blue."

"Yes," he said, as if it was the most reasonable thing in the world.

"That's commitment."

He nodded agreeably. "I have devoted the remainder of my life to her destruction." He brought his arms up before him and flicked his wrists. A pair of silver knives emerged from his sleeves and landed easily in his blue hands.

Chey gasped.

"These are for her, not you. Do not worry. She will suffer before she dies."

"In God's name, why?" Chey asked. "I understand she's hurt a lot of people. But who deserves to be tortured to death?"

"The same woman who killed my three lovely daughters," Varkanin told her. "Who made them suffer, before she allowed them the release of death."

"That's rough. But—but . . . she was a wolf at the time," Chey insisted. "Wasn't she?"

"Yes," he confirmed.

"We can't control what our wolves do. Listen, I'm not a big fan of Lucie either. But you have to understand. We know about the curse. We know what's going to happen when we change. That's why we live in secluded places, like here, or Siberia. So we won't run into people and hurt them when we can't control our behavior. I'm sure Lucie didn't mean to do that."

Varkanin closed his eyes and breathed deeply through his nose for a while. "My daughter Irina, yes? My youngest. She lived in Magnitogorsk, with me. She was the first to die. Three weeks later my Varvara was found in pieces in Chelyabinsk. Hundreds of kilometers away. The last to perish was Lyudmilla. She lived in Novosibirsk, where she worked as a doctor. The wolf may not have known who the victims were. But Lucie did. She tracked them down, learning their addresses from a phone book. She put herself in their paths, just as the moon was set to rise."

"I'm—so sorry." It was all Chey could think to say.

"You tell me the wolves are not responsible. They cannot be blamed for what is bred into their bones." He frowned and shook his head. "I say who else can be blamed? The one who made you a werewolf, this Montgomery Powell. I am told that was not his first crime. He killed your father."

It was Chey's turn to close her eyes. "Yes."

"In fact, he partially ate your father."

"Yes."

Varkanin leaned forward in his chair. "I do not say these things to be cruel. But I must ask you—you have forgiven him for this? You have accepted that it was his wolf, and therefore his soul is spotless?"

"Not . . . entirely," she had to admit.

Sharon Minik came through the door from the kitchen. Her face was dotted with bandages and she walked with a distinct limp. She had a steaming pot in her hand. "I haven't forgiven anything," she said. She lowered the pot so that Chey could see it was full of oatmeal. "You hungry?" she asked.

Chey figured she knew what was coming, but the fact was that she was starving. "I could eat," she said.

Sharon came closer and held out the pot. Chey's hands were bound behind her but she leaned closer to smell the oatmeal. Sharon had laced it with sugar and cinnamon and it smelled amazing.

Leaning forward, Sharon spat blood and what looked like a tooth into the pot. Then she stirred it with a wooden spoon. She held the spoon toward Chey's mouth. "Have a bite," she said.

"Sharon, please," Varkanin said, sounding disgusted.

"Eat it, bitch," Sharon said. When Chey turned her head away, Sharon dumped the contents of the pot in Chey's hair. It burned where it touched her skin, felt slimy where it dripped down her face. She couldn't even wipe it away.

73

"One thing I don't get," Chey said, while the oatmeal dried in her hair. "How did you even know who I was?"

"The good people of this town have reason to keep a watch for were-wolves," Varkanin told her.

Sharon scowled. "You wolves killed two good kids from this town, Jimmy Etok and Leonard Opvik. You almost killed me." Her face went very still.

She sat down on the floor next to Varkanin's chair and he put a hand on her shoulder. Apparently the layers of shirts and sweaters she wore were enough to protect her from the silver in his skin. "Shortly after our return, we alerted Umiaq's citizenry that you were in the vicinity. We told them what had happened to James and Leonard. What was still happening to Sharon. This is a small town where everyone knows everyone else's business," Varkanin said. "They look after one another."

"When Mrs. Oonark over at the library figured out what you were, she called me right away. She figured I would want to know you were in town. She stalled your friend the *tuurngaq* while she waited for me to show up. Turns out she didn't need to. Crazy spirit ran away the second I hit you the first time. That's the kind of loyalty someone like you deserves, I guess."

"Dzo didn't run away," Chey said, looking at Varkanin.

The Russian nodded. "He went to get help."

"That's why I'm here, isn't it?" Chey sighed. "I'm the bait. You're hoping Dzo will go get Powell and Lucie and that they'll come in here loaded for bear. Then you'll just pick them off when they show their faces."

"The bonds between members of a wolf pack are not easily broken. Mr. Powell will think he has no choice but to come and rescue you, no matter how dangerous this might be. I doubt Lucie will come happily, but she will do as he says. Is that not so?"

"She will," Chey agreed. "You sure you can handle them? Last time we faced off with you, we won."

Sharon bristled, but said nothing.

"The last time you were aided by the spirit of the polar bear. This time you should expect to rely on no such assistance," Varkanin told her.

And she believed him. She could tell by the look on his face that he wasn't bragging. He had thought this through, very carefully, and considered every possibility. If Powell and Lucie came for her, they would be walking into certain death.

"And then . . . what about me? Once I've served my purpose, obviously you're not going to just let me go."

"No," Varkanin confirmed.

"Are you going to ship me down to Ottawa, so they can put me in jail for life? Or maybe you're going to take me back to Russia with you."

"Ms. Clark—"

"—make me be some kind of special forces assassin for your army, is that it? Or hell, I don't know, maybe you're working for some evil corporation, and they want to put me in a lab, and—"

"Please, Ms.—"

"—do experiments on me, maybe even dissect me? Is that it?"

Chey looked down at her legs. They were trembling so hard that her feet were drumming on the floor. She tried to force them to stop, but that just made it worse. Her teeth started chattering in her head and she felt like her body was going to shake itself to pieces. This was fear, she knew. True fear, born of desperation. Because she knew that all of those guesses were wrong. She knew exactly what he had planned.

"When the time comes," he told her, something like pity in his blue eyes, "I will place two silver bullets in your brain. That is all. I will do it when you are in your wolf shape. I will do it as humanely as I know how." He shook his head. "I wish it could be another way."

Chey bit her tongue to try to keep her teeth from clacking together.

The back of her head felt cold and wet, as if he'd already shot her. She felt like she might wet herself in terror. This was it. This was the end.

Across the room, Sharon Minik laid her head gently against Varkanin's knee. She wasn't smiling. She didn't laugh in wicked excitement. She just looked satisfied. Content. Chey's death would be enough, it seemed, to soothe her rage.

74.

They left Chey alone after that. There was no way for her to get free of the silver chains that bound her—especially not when her arm felt numb and useless, the bones in it broken so she couldn't even twitch her shoulder or make a fist. It was all she could do to keep her shirt cuffs between the metal and her skin. Every time she shifted on the couch the chains around her wrists slipped down and made contact. Their touch was like being burned by acid.

Eventually she managed to swivel around so she could lie down. The position was not quite as uncomfortable as sitting up had been. It took some of the pressure off her injured arm, anyway. She tried to sleep, but the fear wouldn't let her. All she could do was lie there and imagine what it would feel like when the bullets entered her head.

Varkanin had said he would do it when she was in her wolf form. Was that better or worse, she wondered? Her human mind wouldn't feel the pain. But she would know—when she transformed, he would be waiting. She would see the silver light that marked a transformation and in that last instant she would know she would never return.

Perhaps it would have been better to just surrender before that happened. To let the wolf in her brain take over—to give up on humanity altogether. Yet when she reached for the wolf she couldn't find it. It was as if, having been hurt when it tried to attack Varkanin, it had gone to sleep and didn't wish to be disturbed.

In the morning she felt like hell. No sleep and the chafing burns on her wrists made her want to just curl up and disappear herself. She wasn't given the option. Varkanin came out of his bedroom with a key. "I am not a cruel man," he said. "I expected them to attack during the night. If I had known they would bide their time, I would not have left you trussed like this." He unlocked the chains and let her get up from the couch. She was surprised that he would give her that much freedom. "You think I am being foolish?" he asked. "You already know that you cannot hurt me, nor Sharon. I see no reason we cannot permit you a small degree of freedom."

She glanced at the room's windows. She couldn't help herself. If she could get a running start, she could throw herself through the glass, roll into the street outside and dash for safety in the snow. But of course, he must have thought of that.

"Go and take a look at the house next door," he told her. When she hesitated he waved one hand dismissively. "Go ahead."

She went to the window and looked out through the curtains. Across the street was a house much like Varkanin's. There was an old man sitting next to the window, watching her back. He had a cup of coffee sitting next to him and a hunting rifle across his knees. When he saw her he picked up the gun.

Chey drew back from the window.

"Sharon is going door to door, teaching each person in this town what she knows about how to kill a werewolf. I have a patron, in your government. He has been most generous to the people of Umiaq, and provided for their safety with silver bullets in a variety of calibers. Of course, they already had the necessary firearms. Everyone up here owns a gun of some sort, if only for protection from moose and polar bears." He shrugged. "They know what is happening. They know your face. If you were to leave this house you would be gunned down. Many times. Is this clear?"

"Yeah," Chey said.

Varkanin nodded. "Very good. I see you are a reasonable woman. Will you answer a question?"

"Depends."

"Of course. And perhaps this is one you will not wish to answer. Can you tell me why your lover has not come for you yet?"

Because he doesn't have any eyes, right now, Chey thought. It wasn't the kind of thing she thought she should share.

"Maybe he thinks I'm already dead," she told him.

"No, I doubt that. Your friend the animal spirit will have told him what happened. And he is smart enough to know that I will use you as bait." Varkanin went to the kitchen and poured himself a bowl of granola. He glanced at her, then made a second bowl, and filled them both with milk. He put a spoon in each bowl and then brought them back out. "Please. To show I am not going to poison you, you may pick which bowl you will eat from."

She glanced at the bowls in his hands. She couldn't deny that she was starving. "Let me guess," she said. "Those are silver spoons."

His eyes went wide. "Wonderful! Such a wonderfully clever idea. But as I said, I am not a cruel man. I have no desire to torture you or cause you pain. Please. Take one."

Hunger won out over defiance. Chey grabbed the bowl out of his left hand and dug in. The spoon was stainless steel, and there were no nasty surprises in the granola.

"Perhaps," Varkanin said, "your lover waits for the moon. Perhaps he thinks he has a better chance of rescuing you in his wolf shape."

She shook her head. "No. There would be too much chance of accidentally hurting somebody innocent, then."

"Very good. Then, when the moon rises tonight, I will not worry." Varkanin smiled at her.

"Tonight?" The time had gotten away from Chey. "I'm going to change tonight? Is that—is that when you'll—when you—"

"Do you really wish to know exactly when death is coming?" he asked. "Perhaps it is more of a mercy to have it come unexpected."

She shut her eyes and set her bowl down on a coffee table. "Maybe."

"But no," he said. "Not tonight. Not until he comes. He seems a smart man. If he learned somehow that you were, truly, dead, then he would not come, would he? And he would not bring Lucie with him. So you have a temporary reprieve."

"Great," she said.

He left her alone most of that day. Just before the moon rose, though, he took her to a little room at the back of the house. "I apologize for this," he said, and opened the door. Inside, Sharon Minik was crouching on the floor. She had a silver collar around her neck and it was chained to the wall.

She didn't look happy. A second collar lay next to her on the floor. "It is the only way."

Chey did as she was told. What choice did she have? She sat down next to Sharon, who wouldn't even look at her. She let Varkanin put the collar around her throat. It was very loose—but of course, her wolf's neck was thicker than her own. He had thought of everything.

When she was secure, he left the little room and closed the door. Almost instantly the air inside grew stuffy and thick.

Sharon closed her eyes and started muttering to herself.

"What are you saying?" Chey asked. "A prayer?"

Sharon shook her head. "I'm trying to talk to my wolf. I'm telling it to tear your guts out for me when I'm not here."

Chey sighed. "They don't listen to us. They can't understand language."

Sharon shrugged. "It can't hurt."

75

The silver light came, and changed Chey's body.

But not her mind.

She sat up on the floor of the small room and blinked in confusion, unsure what had just happened. Her vision was blurred and the colors seemed washed out—but her nose was assaulted by a million smells she couldn't begin to process. She could smell wolves and silver and wood and metal and Varkanin's aftershave and . . . and . . .

She looked down and screamed. The sound came out of her throat like a squeal. She didn't have hands anymore. She had paws. Big furry paws with inch-long claws.

She had let her wolf inhabit her human body for the fight with Sharon. It had relished the opportunity and it had possessed her with glee, only to be horribly injured when it attacked Varkanin. Now it must be tucked away in some corner of the brain they shared, licking its wounds—and it had decided not to come out when the change occurred.

Chey felt as if her hands had been chopped off and her throat had been scrubbed out with sandpaper. She couldn't talk, couldn't make any human sounds at all, no matter how hard she tried. The body she was in felt alien and wrong and she barely knew how to coordinate its muscles to move at all. She started to panic and tried to fight against the silver collar holding her to the wall, but that was a bad mistake. When her body changed her clothes had fallen away, so now there was nothing between her skin and the silver but fur, fur that crinkled and died at the softest pressure from the collar. She felt her throat rub up against the metal as if acid were eating away at her skin.

From the far corner of the room—only two meters away—Sharon's wolf growled at her. It was a beautiful creature, but a terrifying one, almost all black except for a few patches of tan fur on its face and legs. Its teeth were enormous. Was that what Chey's wolf looked like? It had been so long since she'd seen a dire wolf that she was horrified all over again—as scared as she'd been when Powell's wolf attacked her and gave her the curse. She pressed herself tight against the wall of the little room to get away from Sharon's wolf, but that just put more pressure on the silver collar.

It wasn't long before Sharon's wolf realized there was something strange about Chey.

Whining and whimpering, Chey could only cringe away as Sharon's wolf lunged at her, again and again, jaws snapping. Sharon's paws swatted at the air as she pulled and yanked at her own collar, trying to get free, trying to attack, to kill—

The only thing that saved Chey from madness, that night, was the fact that the moon set barely three hours after it rose. When the silver light came again, she had never been so grateful for the change.

She woke up on the floor. Human in shape. She touched her face, her skin. She was still in control of her own body. The silver collar had left a wide swath of burn tissue around her throat, but she could breathe. She could think, and even see colors again.

She remembered what had happened, though it had been so terrifying that she thought her brain had shut down at some point and spared her any further horror.

That was probably a blessing, she decided.

Sharon was nowhere to be seen. Her collar lay abandoned on the floor. It was a while before Chey figured out how to remove the cotter pin that held her own collar shut. Removing it meant burning her fingertips, but she was just glad to be free of the thing. She picked up her clothes from the floor and studied them. Her claws had torn her shirt in a couple places as she had scrabbled around on top of it in her panic, but it was still in one piece, as were her pants. She pulled them on and went to the door of the little room. It swung open easily when she pushed on it.

Outside of the little room was a kitchen. Sharon was leaning against the counter, running an electric razor over her head. Her eyes were wild.

"It keeps growing back," Sharon screamed. "Why the fuck does it grow back? I was overdue for a haircut when this happened. Now I'm stuck with long hair for all eternity, is that it?"

Chey shook her head. She didn't know what to say.

"I can't live like this! I won't! I'd rather be dead. What the fuck have you done to me?"

Chey took a step backward as Sharon waved the razor at her. It couldn't hurt her, of course, but she couldn't bear the weight of the accusation.

"What the fuck are you? Why couldn't you just die, the first time? He poisoned you, and you didn't die! He laid down land mines and you didn't even step on one! What the fuck are you?"

Chey could only run away in fear. She dashed into the parlor of Varkanin's little house—and got another surprise. This one was a little more pleasant.

Dzo was standing in the parlor, talking quietly with Varkanin.

"Ah, there you are," Varkanin said, gesturing for her to come in.

76

"Your friend," Varkanin said, gesturing at Dzo, "arrived a few minutes ago and asked to see you. I told him you were still sleeping and I didn't wish to disturb you, and he said he would wait. We've been having a very pleasant chat."

Chey stepped into the room without comment. She didn't know what to do, whether she should sit down on the couch or scream or . . . something. "Hi, Dzo," she said, because it was the only thing that felt like something she ought to do.

"Hi, Chey. I've come to rescue you," he said, with a big smile.

"Thanks," she told him.

For a while no one spoke. Dzo just stood there, smiling, looking very proud of himself. Varkanin waited patiently. He had one hand in his pocket and he didn't take it out, even as he moved over toward the couch and sat down.

"Alright," he said, finally. "If no one else will ask, I will. How do you plan on doing that?"

Dzo squinted for a second as if trying to remember something. "Oh, yeah," he said. "I'm supposed to say that Chey and I are going to walk out of here right now and there's nothing you can do to stop us. You can't hurt me, um," he thought about it for a second. "Because . . . you can't hurt me because I'm an immortal animal spirit and none of your weapons will affect me. Is it affect or effect? I can never remember."

"You got it right," Chey said.

"Oh! There was one more thing. If you hurt Chey, Powell will kill you. He'll hunt you down for the rest of his life. Or maybe it was the rest of your life. But anyway, he won't stop. Ever." He looked over at Chey and gave her a wink.

Something in her chest started to flutter like a bird taking wing. It was hope, which she thought had died inside her. "What do you have to say to that, Varkanin? Can I go?"

The blue man shook his head in apology. "Let us not be foolish. Not now. Of course you can't go. You are my prisoner, and you will remain so until I decide on your disposition. Now, Mr. Dzo. I'll give you a chance to leave my house peacefully. Alone."

"Not going to happen," Dzo told him.

"I was afraid so. Alright. Let's discuss another matter, then. I've been studying you, my friend."

"Really?" Dzo asked. He looked flattered.

"Indeed. After my plans were thwarted by your friend Nanuq, I requested all the information the Canadian government had on you and the other animal spirits. There wasn't much. The government's position is that you do not exist. That you are only a story told by less sophisticated people. A bit of folklore."

"Kinda, sure," Dzo said. He shrugged.

Varkanin smiled warmly. "However, there was a very thin report on you dating back to the events at Port Radium. You may remember that incident, Ms. Clark—that was when you and Montgomery Powell killed Robert Fenech and his associates."

"I remember about half of it," she agreed. The half that she'd experienced as a human being. "It's not something I like to dwell on."

"Understandable. I'm not interested so much in rousing feelings of guilt, however. I was far more interested in learning about Mr. Dzo's participation in those events."

"I wasn't even at Port Radium!" Dzo said. "I can't even go there. Just can't—if I tried, it wouldn't work. The water there is too polluted for me to swim in."

"I know," Varkanin confirmed. "Specifically it's polluted with radionuclides. Tailings and runoff from the former uranium mining operations there. You would have liked to go there, to help your friends, I'm sure. But the background radiation that pervades the Port Radium site precluded this."

"Yeah," Dzo agreed. "But what does that have to do with anything?"

Varkanin took his hand out of his pocket. There was a square little gun there. It didn't look like it had much stopping power, but Chey felt terrified at the sight of it anyway. Was it loaded with silver bullets? Was this the moment he was going to kill her—as he'd promised, when she least expected it?

"Put that away," Dzo said. "You know it can't—"

Varkanin shot Dzo in the stomach. The noise of the gunshot was enormous in the small parlor and it made Chey jump. Dzo stopped talking to grimace in annoyance, but he didn't even take a step backward. The bullet seemed to ruffle his furs, but there was no blood, nor any other sign of an injury.

Varkanin ejected the gun's clip. Then he placed gun and magazine on a side table. "I apologize. I assure you it was necessary."

"Oh, come on," Dzo said. "That was just silly. Bullets can't hurt me. I told you that already! I'm immortal. I'm—"

Chey felt her face go slack in terror. She watched as Dzo grew pale and some of his fur started to fall out. He looked like he might throw up.

"I—I don't know what—you hoped—to." Dzo couldn't seem to finish his sentence. He blinked rapidly and looked around the room as if he was having trouble seeing straight. "Chey? What—was—"

"No," she said. She shook her head violently. "No, no, he couldn't have . . ."

A thread of blood erupted from Dzo's mouth. "Pitchblende?" he asked.

Chey remembered Raven's story. How the Sivullir had used pitchblende to poison Amuruq and make her vulnerable. How even its presence could trap a spirit and leave it defenseless.

"A little more than that. Pitchblende is the ore from which uranium is processed," Varkanin told him. "The bullet I shot you with is made of depleted uranium. It is mildly radioactive. Much like the water around Port Radium."

Dzo dropped to his knees. "I have to get out of here. I have to find— oh, boy."

"Dzo," Chey said, rushing over to hold his shoulders. "Dzo? Are you okay?"

He shook his head. "This really hurts. I can't remember the last time something hurt. I guess when Raven took my fur. Chey, I'm sorry." He staggered back up to his feet and rushed for the kitchen, where Sharon Minik was boiling a pot of water.

"I'm so sorry," he said, and then he dove into the pot. He seemed to hang in the air for a moment, a kind of furry blur across Chey's vision, and then he shrank down to nothing and was gone.

"You killed him," Chey said, turning to stare at Varkanin. "You killed Dzo."

77

She shouted in outrage. She stormed around the room. She wanted to attack Varkanin, beat him down with her fists, but she didn't dare. It would just break her bones and burn her skin. So she raced back and forth like a wild creature stuck in a cage. "Do you even understand what you just did?" she demanded.

"I fear I may have doomed the muskrat to extinction," Varkanin said. There was a deep sadness in his voice that startled her. "That is how it works, is it not?" He shook his head. "I don't enjoy doing these things."

"Then stop," she screamed. "Just stop! Let us go. Let us go and we will never bother you again. Please! Please just stop this!"

He opened his mouth to speak, but a sudden noise made him stop.

It was a gunshot. A distant gunshot. Somewhere out in the town someone had just fired a gun.

"Oh, God, no," Chey said. "No—Powell!"

Powell and Lucie must be coming for her. They must have realized that Dzo's rescue attempt had failed—or maybe they just thought it was taking too long. So they had come to Umiaq to do it themselves. To save her.

And now they were going to die.

"Please," she begged. She dropped to her knees and clenched her hands together in front of her chest. "Please! I've never asked anyone for anything before. I've never done anything to hurt you!"

"Not me, perhaps," Varkanin said. "But Sharon—"

"Keep begging," Sharon said, stepping into the parlor. "Come on. Tell me what you'll do for me if we let you live."

"Please," Chey said. It was all she could manage.

Another gunshot sounded out in the town. A cell phone in Varkanin's pocket started ringing out the strains of Tchaikovsky, a quiet, tinny music that made mockery of Chey's horror. She stared at him as he answered it. He spoke quietly into the mouthpiece for a few seconds.

"Very good," he said, and closed the phone. "Montgomery Powell is near the community center. Now it is only a matter of time. There has been no sign of Lucie yet." He sat down on a low bench and mopped his forehead with a handkerchief. "Sharon? Could you bring me a mineral water?"

"I'm not done with her yet," Sharon told him. She looked down at Chey. "I think I told you to beg some more."

Chey swallowed with some difficulty. "Please," she said. "I will do anything you ask."

"Like what?" Sharon said. "Will you give me money? Huh?" She kicked Chey in the ribs. Chey flinched but managed not to fall over. "Are you going to offer to have sex with me or something? Or maybe him. You gonna suck his silver-plated dick?"

Chey blinked away tears. "Anything. Just—just tell me. Please. Tell me what you want and I'll do it. Anything, if you stop this."

"There's one thing I actually want," Sharon admitted.

Outside they heard another gunshot. Then three more, one after the other.

"Whatever it is, I—"

"I want to be human again," Sharon said. She kicked Chey again, this time in the leg. Chey slumped down to sit on the floor. She started another kick, aimed at Chey's head. Chey reeled backward and Sharon laughed, putting her foot down. "I want to be human. All human, none of this wolf bullshit. You gonna make that happen? You think you can do that for me, you little bitch?"

Chey's eyes went wide.

"Yes," she said.

Varkanin's phone rang again. He stepped into the kitchen to answer it. Outside the sound of gunshots was almost constant now.

"Yes," Chey said again. "I can do that. There's a cure."

"Bullshit," Sharon said, and grabbed Chey by the hair. She hauled

Chey across the room and smashed her face into one leg of the couch. "No fucking way you can do that! Don't lie to me, bitch!"

"It's what we've been looking for," Chey insisted. "Why do you think we came so far north? There's nothing to eat up here! Why else would we come?"

"Don't," Sharon said, "you," she grabbed the back of Chey's head, "fucking," drew it back, "lie," and shoved it hard into the wooden frame of the couch.

"I swear it!" Chey moaned. Blood erupted from her nose where it had shattered from the repeated blows. "I'm telling the truth! There's a cure! There is a cure! It's on Victoria Island!"

Varkanin leaned in from the kitchen. "Sharon, please. I really think that's enough."

Sharon grabbed Chey's hair and hauled her up to a sitting position. "It's enough when she dies! That's the only way it will ever be enough!"

Varkanin's phone rang once more, but Chey could barely hear it for all the gunshots.

"On Victoria Island," she whimpered, her voice broken by the blood pouring down the back of her throat and the sobbing tears coming from her eyes. "Victoria—Island, it's there—the silver *ulu*—Raven—Raven told us, he took—took Powell's eyes, and—and told us—told us about the—the silver *ulu*—and—and Amuruq, the—the wolf spirit, and—"

Sharon released her. Chey fell in a heap on the floor.

For a moment there was no sound but the constant gunfire as the townspeople of Umiaq unloaded silver bullets into Powell's location.

"Wait," Sharon said. "Who told you this?"

"Raven," Chey sobbed.

"Raven who?" Sharon demanded. "You mean Tulugaq? I don't believe you."

"Nanuq told us how to find him. He—he ate Monty's eyes."

Sharon brought one hand up to her face and rubbed the back of her hand across her mouth. She shook her head for a moment, but Chey could tell she'd gotten through. Sharon believed now.

Sharon looked up at Varkanin. "There's a cure," she said.

"Ms. Minik," Varkanin said, "I have other things to worry about right now."

"Only Powell knows how to do it," Chey said.

"There's a cure," Sharon repeated. "If Tulugaq told them, then—there must really be a cure. I don't have to be like this. Varkanin!"

The Russian raised one finger for silence. He was busy dialing a number on his phone. Sharon rushed over to grab his arm, but he pulled away from her.

"Varkanin—you owe me this," Sharon demanded, staring him in the eye and refusing to let him look away.

He met her gaze, finally. His face was very still. But then he sighed.

"Cease fire," he said, when his connection went through. "Immediately."

78.

Chey wanted to go out into the town and bring Powell in herself, but Varkanin wouldn't allow it. So she had to shout to him through the window and convince him she wasn't being forced to trick him into revealing himself.

Eventually he believed her—at least, enough to step out into the street. Instantly she saw that he was wounded. At least one of the gunshots she'd heard had hit home. She could only shout encouragement to him as he staggered closer, every step seeming to cost him immense agony.

There was a bullet hole in Powell's shirt. Blood foamed from the wound and his face was pale. He looked like he was about to collapse as he stepped inside Varkanin's cabin. "This has to be a trick," he said. He gasped for breath and staggered over to one wall. He put a hand against the plaster and lowered his head for a moment. "Right?"

"No," Chey said, rushing over to cradle his face in her hands. "He's willing to listen, anyway. If you can convince him the cure is for real, then—"

"Then what?" He shook his head. "Never mind. We're out of here. Where's Dzo?"

Chey grimaced. "He's dead," she said.

"Not likely," Powell said.

"Varkanin shot him with a uranium bullet."

"Depleted uranium," Varkanin amended.

Powell's eyes were glassy and his pupils were tiny. At least he had eyes in his head again. He leaned toward Varkanin, perhaps intending to attack, but the strength visibly drained from his limbs as he tried to move. "I need to sit down."

He moved heavily into the room, his feet barely shuffling across the floorboards. Everyone was staring at him. Eventually he looked up and met Varkanin's eyes.

"If you want me to live long enough to talk, I need to get this bullet out of my belly."

"Certainly," Varkanin said. "I believe you'll require a pair of forceps." He stepped into the kitchen and disappeared, leaving Sharon to watch them. The Inuit werewolf had a gun in her hand but it wasn't pointed at anyone. She watched Powell with a certain fascination.

Powell nodded and stumbled into the parlor. He dropped onto the couch and closed his eyes. For a while he just held his breath and didn't move. The pain must have been incredible.

"Don't die yet," Chey begged him. She could hardly stand to see Powell so weak. "Is it . . . bad?"

"Yes," he admitted. "Rifle bullet . . . it's in my guts. Hit something vital. I can taste bile in my throat, so maybe my liver." He shook his head. He was so pale. "I'll die if we don't remove it soon."

Sharon stepped closer and bent down to look at the wound. "How is he still breathing? I thought if we got shot with silver bullets we just keeled over dead," she said.

Powell looked over at Chey. "Who is she?" he asked.

"That's Sharon. Apparently I gave her the curse, back when we were wolves. She's the one who convinced Varkanin not to kill you."

He looked up at Sharon with a curious expression. "Thanks, I guess." He glanced down at his shirt. "Silver doesn't kill us all at once. It's like poison. Takes a while to work. Hurts like hell the whole time. I can feel it in there, burning me."

Sharon nodded and stepped back as if she expected Powell to jump off the couch and attack her at any moment.

Varkanin returned with the forceps and a spool of gauze. "No need for antiseptic, in this case, but I'm sorry, I have nothing for anesthetic. Not even a bottle of vodka. This will be painful."

"Yeah," Powell said. "I know."

"I would do this myself," Varkanin said, "but I'm afraid I would touch your skin unintentionally, and this would only make matters worse."

"His skin is impregnated with silver," Chey explained. "That's why he's blue."

Powell frowned. "Argyria? You did that to yourself on purpose?"

"Yes," Varkanin agreed.

"That's . . . a really clever idea. Here." He reached for the forceps.

"Don't be stupid," she said. "You can't do it yourself."

"I'm going to try." He took the forceps and tried to open them, but they fell out of his hand. They clanged against the floorboards. "Damn."

"Let me," Chey said. She picked up the forceps off the floor. "Help me get this shirt off." Powell could barely lift himself up off the couch enough for her to slip the sleeves over his arms. The wound under the shirt was ragged and crusted with blood clots. Fresh blood sluiced from the wound every time Powell moved and every time he drew a breath.

"It's deep," he told Chey. "You're going to really have to get in there and dig for it. Don't worry about hurting me."

"Don't be such a baby, then," she told him. His eyes went wide, but when he saw her smile he calmed back down. "You want something to bite on?"

"I understand a bullet is traditional," he told her. "But no."

"Okay. If you need to scream, just go ahead," she told him.

Her bravado was patently empty, but she knew she had no choice but to do this and do it right the first time. She got the nose of the forceps into the wound without difficulty and then shoved the instrument in hard, until she felt it clink off the bullet. She tried to open the forceps a little so she could grab the bullet, but Powell jerked on the couch and he did scream. It was not a very manly sound.

"Jesus, you moved it," he said, his breath ragged in his throat.

"I need you to stay still," Chey insisted. Powell didn't even seem to hear her. She held her own breath and steeled herself to what she needed to do. As quickly as she could, using all of her supernatural strength, she cranked open the forceps and jammed them around the bullet, then dragged it out into the air.

Powell screamed again. And again. And again.

Chey stared at the silver bullet she had removed from his abdomen. It was as long as the first two joints of her little finger. Ribbons of smoke wafted off its surface wherever Powell's blood touched the silver. It hadn't deformed much inside the wound, and it looked intact—normal lead bullets often shattered inside human bodies, she knew, and she'd been very worried that there might be pieces of it still inside Powell's viscera, but it looked like she'd gotten it all.

Powell kept screaming, for a long time. She used the roll of gauze to bandage the wound, but blood leaked through the thin fabric almost instantly. If she was right and she'd gotten it all, he would be okay once he transformed again. If even a minute amount of silver was left in his body, though, he wouldn't survive the change. There was no way to know until it happened.

79

Eventually he stopped screaming. Clearly he was still in a lot of pain and his eyes were wild, but he was able to talk.

Varkanin's first question was predictable. "Where is Lucie?" he demanded to know.

"Somewhere safe," Powell told him. "You think I trust you now? Just because you stopped shooting at me? I'm not going to tell you that."

"Very well," Varkanin said. "So tell me about this cure, instead."

Powell glared at Chey as if she'd let him down by telling Varkanin what they were after. It had been the only way, though.

"I've been looking for a way to remove the curse almost since I got it," he told Varkanin. "I tried a lot of things. None of them worked. It looks like this is the real deal, though. The spirits gave me the information I needed."

"How is it done? I wish to know exactly, please," Varkanin said.

"Forget it," Powell told him. "You killed Dzo. I'm not going to give you anything."

"Powell," Chey said, "if you don't tell him, he won't help us."

"Or," Powell suggested, "if I do tell him everything, then he'll just kill us and use the information himself. What the hell do you want a cure for, anyway?"

"For Sharon," Varkanin admitted. "Honestly, I do not care very much what happens to the two of you. I want Lucie in my custody, so that I can dispose of her as I see fit. And I wish to restore to Sharon her humanity."

They all glanced at Sharon, then, but she just looked away.

"In the interests of justice, I suppose you should be killed," Varkanin said. "Yet I am an old man, and a Russian. These two things make me a pragmatist. You turn over to me Lucie. I will take her back to Russia with me, and after that her fate is none of your concern. Sharon will remain here with the two of you."

"What?" Sharon asked, suddenly paying close attention.

Varkanin shrugged. "You seek a cure. If you agree to take her with you, to cure her as well, then I will offer no resistance."

"No," Powell insisted.

Varkanin sighed wearily. "Mr. Powell, I can kill you right now, should I so desire. You are too weak to resist me. I can kill your Ms. Clark as well. Surely you can see I do not wish to deceive you now?"

"I won't give you Lucie," Powell said.

"Please," Chey said. "Just think about this. I know—you know what he's going to do to her, I'm sure. It isn't pretty. But maybe she deserves it. She's a killer, Powell. A sociopath—do you honestly think she deserves that kind of loyalty?"

"No, I don't," he told her. "The relationship I have with Lucie is complicated. But I have no problem letting her die if it means saving you." He looked Chey right in the eye. "I'd kill her myself, for you."

Varkanin looked confused but pleasantly surprised. "Then we can reach an agreement, surely?"

"I can't just give her to you," Powell explained, "because we need her to make the cure work." He winced and sat up on the couch. "She has to die so the rest of us get our humanity back. The cure requires a werewolf sacrifice."

"Oh," Varkanin said.

"It . . . does?" Chey asked.

Powell grabbed her hands. "I told you it was going to get darker, the closer we got to the end," he told her. "You still with me?"

part three

victoria island

80

It had been a mild autumn in Toronto, and the grass in Queen's Park was just turning yellow under trees that still showed their brightest colors. Preston Holness waited on a bench, sitting quietly with his hands folded in his lap. He had a Burberry overcoat on top of his suit jacket. Lying next to him on the bench was an unmarked shopping bag with a drawstring.

He had been waiting for hours. Demetrios had summoned him, demanding he come at once, and then left him waiting there long enough to start wondering if he was ever going to show. Holness understood the game that Demetrios was playing, and received the message this lateness was intended to send.

He had fucked up. Royally.

He had been feeding Demetrios daily progress reports since early October. The lawyer had grown increasingly upset every time he received one of these detailed e-mails, and had not restrained himself from showing his displeasure. Holness had carefully read each of the lawyer's replies and then deleted them from his hard drive, after checking to make sure no copies remained on the e-mail server. That was standard practice for any communication he received, but he especially wanted to be rid of the insults, threats, and demands that Demetrios sent him. Some of them were quite creative. Others were simple. They all boiled down to the same thing.

The oil company that Demetrios represented was now on the verge of pulling all of its interests out of the Canadian economy. When that happened, Holness would lose his job—if he was lucky. He might end up in jail. This worst case scenario didn't worry him too much, however.

Unemployment would be bad enough. He could not produce a résumé, because nothing he had done in the course of his career had any kind of official sanction or recognition. He would enter the job market unable to account for years of his adult life. He would most likely end up working in retail.

For a man with the expensive fashion tastes of Preston Holness, that would be worse than jail. It might actually be worse than death.

He shouldn't joke, he told himself. It could come to that.

He sighed and watched a group of young girls pass by, talking animatedly on their cell phones but not to each other. They were wearing lightweight coats and all of them had those furry boots that he detested so much, but that were apparently the "in" thing. When they had passed out of his field of vision he looked back down at his hands.

Demetrios was sitting next to him. "I'm here," he said.

Holness didn't jump. He was technically a spymaster, and in the James Bond movies, M never seemed surprised when James Bond just showed up somewhere, so Holness had trained himself not to react under similar circumstances. "Hi," he said.

"I didn't get a progress report today," Demetrios told him. "I'm guessing that means there's bad news." The lawyer didn't look particularly angry. He almost looked happy. That might be another part of the game, calculated to put Holness off his guard.

Or it might be the smile of a wolf descending on some unfortunate prey animal.

"Well," Holness began. "Yeah. I guess you could say that. I received a phone call from Varkanin last night. He said our arrangement was at an end."

Demetrios raised one professionally plucked eyebrow. "Which could be interpreted as meaning the werewolves are all dead."

"Yeah, but no," Holness said. He reached over and with one hand he squeezed the plastic shopping bag lying next to him. It gave him a little strength. "They're all still alive. He was able to kill the muskrat spirit."

"Impressive, but not part of the plan," Demetrios said.

"Right. He said that he no longer wished to work in cooperation with my government. He said he wouldn't be returning any of the toys we sent him, either—which includes a parcel of custom-cut depleted uranium bullets. I'm going to have a really hard time accounting for those, since technically Canada opposes their manufacture or use." He shrugged. "I'm sure you have better things to worry about than my troubles."

"Unless they become mine. Go on."

"There's not much more to tell," Holness said. "He's doubled on us. That's spy lingo. It means he's become a double agent, working for the other team."

"Varkanin? Working with the werewolves? I saw his dossier."

"I don't have any explanation."

Demetrios nodded. "I see. I think you know what this means. Unless you have some amazing card to pull out of your ass, I think our association is also at an end."

Demetrios started to stand up.

If he stood up and walked away, Holness's life was over. Kaput. He would be working at a department store, selling men's pants, before he could blink. So Holness grabbed Demetrios's hand-tailored sleeve.

The lawyer looked amused. And also like he was ready to break Holness's arm any second now with a judo chop. "Yes?" he asked, quietly.

It was Holness's turn to smile. Though he didn't feel particularly happy. "I'm an espionage agent. Of course I have another trick to play." He dragged the shopping bag onto his lap. It was very heavy. "Varkanin is still a foreign national on Canadian soil. By taking this step he has declared himself engaged in interests that are counter to Canadian security and the public welfare. You see where this is going?"

"Maybe."

"My bosses wouldn't give me any troops to play with, not when we were fighting werewolves. Now we're fighting an armed foreign national who entered our borders with violent intent. Do you understand?"

Demetrios's eyes went wide.

"Yeah," Holness said. "We're fighting a terrorist."

He let that sink in for a moment.

"That means there is no problem whatsoever with getting what I need. I've been cleared to take a company of Special Operations Forces personnel—the tan berets—and whatever equipment I require up to the frozen north to deal with this threat directly. If that equipment happens to include silver bullets, nobody's going to ask any questions."

Demetrios actually looked impressed. "Do I understand correctly? You're going to be leading them yourself?"

Holness opened his shopping bag. Inside was a thick navy blue combat vest with lots of straps and quick release buckles. He held it up so Demetrios could see. "Hundreds of layers of interwoven nylon fabric. Guaranteed to stop a knife blade—or a werewolf claw."

Demetrios whistled as he ran the thick fabric between his fingers. "Very nice," he said.

"I just wish it came in black. Black goes with everything," Holness said.

81

"**Keep an eye** on him," Powell told Chey, when they were still half a kilometer from the *inukshuk*. "I'm going to have my hands full when we arrive." Varkanin was following behind, keeping a gun trained on both of them. Obviously, he didn't exactly trust them yet.

Not that Chey felt too sure about the Russian, either. But they didn't exactly have much choice. If they wanted to live they had to play by his rules.

To prove they were all on the same side, Powell had to get Lucie to come back to town with them. Chey wasn't sure exactly how Powell planned on doing that. She figured she would just back his play, whenever he revealed it to her.

Varkanin was walking far enough back that if they whispered he couldn't hear them. That had to count for something, Chey figured. It meant he trusted the two of them not to turn on him without warning.

"This is kind of fucked," Chey said. "What's to stop him from killing us as soon as he figures out how to cure Sharon?"

Powell shrugged. If anything, he seemed less paranoid than she was. "I've spoken with him. And I've seen the way he operates. He's a man of honor."

"You buy that?"

Powell glared at her. "He'll keep his word. As long as he gets what he wants, he has no reason to hurt us."

"I hope you're right." Chey hugged herself, though she wasn't particularly cold. "He killed Dzo without blinking an eye. And I think he actually *liked* Dzo. If we can't deliver what he wants—"

"We will. Okay, stop here."

They were only a couple hundred meters from the *inukshuk*. Chey could see the remains of the camp where they'd met with Raven. There was no sign of Lucie.

"There's something you should know," Powell told her, while they turned around in circles, scanning the barren snowfield all around them. They headed into the camp but there was no sign of Lucie anywhere. "When I went to rescue you, I asked Lucie to come with me. To help me. She said no."

Chey shrugged.

"She said you'd gotten yourself in this mess and you weren't worth saving."

"I'm really not surprised," Chey told him. "She'd be happy if I died, because then she could have you all to herself."

Powell's face hardened. "Is that really what you think? That if you were dead, I would turn to her for consolation?"

"No," Chey said, looking down. "But I know for a fact it's what *she* thinks. Where the hell is she?" There was nowhere for her to hide in the empty landscape. She wasn't lurking behind the *inukshuk,* nor in the rocks nearby. "You think she just ran off?"

"No," Powell said. He turned and waved at Varkanin. "She isn't over here," he shouted. "Do yourself a favor, and—"

Lucie didn't wait for him to finish his warning. She had been lying in wait under the snow, probably not even breathing. Without a sound she rose up out of the ground cover, the white snow that fell away from her only slightly more pale than the color of her skin. Chey could only recognize her because of her red hair—otherwise she was a blur as she streaked across the open ground and launched herself at Varkanin.

The Russian was only human. He couldn't react fast enough to stop her. The gun in his hand went flying as Lucie knocked him to the ground. Had it been anyone but Varkanin, death would have been certain.

Lucie laughed and darted her head forward, her mouth open wide. She was going to try to tear Varkanin's throat out with her human teeth.

"Oh, boy," Chey said. "That's going to hurt."

Lucie reared backward and then rolled off of him, clutching at her bleeding mouth. She moaned in agony as she spat out broken teeth.

"You okay?" Powell shouted. Varkanin raised one hand in an affirmative wave.

"Lucie," Chey said, "you can't hurt him; he's—"

Lucie had never been the type to give up easily. She tried to grab Varkanin up off the ground, perhaps intending to throw him far enough and hard enough to break every bone in his body. Wherever her hands touched him, though, her strength just melted away. Varkanin struggled to sit up, then get to his feet. Lucie tried one last desperate punch to his jaw.

As far away as she was, Chey heard Lucie's knucklebones pop and crackle as they shattered. She definitely heard Lucie's screams.

Eventually, when the redhead had calmed down, Powell went to her and picked her up out of the snow. He put an arm around her shoulders and helped her walk off some of the pain. "Our plans have changed," he told her.

82

The plan was to leave for Victoria Island immediately. Then the weather turned bad.

The wind came howling out of the north, bringing with it fine sheets of snow like shaved ice. Those few people who braved the streets walked bent over, their faces covered completely with scarves and goggles. It never seemed to start snowing for real, not like in the storm the wolves had slogged through, but the snow that did fall didn't melt. It built up in enormous windswept drifts, great slopes of it leaning against every building, tons of it piling up atop every roof. The roads, which to begin with had just been places where the snow had been scraped down, filled in and disappeared.

Inside Varkanin's cabin, the werewolves and the Russian were forced to wait.

Victoria Island lay no more than a hundred kilometers from the town of Umiaq, but it was separated from the mainland by the Dolphin and Union Strait, a stretch of water thirty kilometers wide at its narrowest point. It was impossible in the winter to travel across that distance by boat, because the water was frozen solid. Traditionally the best way across had been by dogsled, but these days most people chose to fly. There were airstrips all over the north, one for every town of more than a hundred or so people. Umiaq had one and so did both Cambridge Bay and Ulukhaktok, the two towns on Victoria Island.

Planes couldn't fly when it was snowing, however, or even when the wind just kicked up. It was hard enough keeping an engine from icing up on a clear day, and radar was almost useless in a place with so few landmarks, so visibility had to be perfect or the bush pilots would refuse to take off.

"I have quite a bit of money," Varkanin suggested. "Surely we can convince someone to take on this challenge."

Sharon shook her head. "People up here are poor, but they aren't crazy."

"So what do you do when you have to get somewhere in a hurry?" Chey asked.

"We wait," Sharon replied. "In the winter, up here? There's no such thing as a hurry. If somebody gets hurt real bad, and they need to be flown to a big hospital, well," she shrugged, "we do our best. But if the weather's bad enough, they just have to wait, too."

Chey sighed and stared out the window at the snow coming down. It just didn't look that bad. She was anxious to get started, to be cured. To go back to real life. She was learning that weather was something you had to take seriously this far north.

"Without Varkanin, we could press northward on foot," Lucie said, coming up behind her. "We could cross the ice like wolves."

Chey turned and stared at the redhead. Lucie would never really accept the change in alliances, she knew. She might be crazy, but she wasn't stupid enough to think that Varkanin had forgiven her. Chey didn't think she could lie convincingly, either, and convince Lucie that she was going to come out of this alive—Powell had warned her not to say a word on that front. Still, there was one way to keep Lucie from trying to run away. One thing that would convince her to play along.

"This is what Powell chose," Chey said. Lucie's eyes flashed with deep fire for a moment, but then it was gone.

"I'm hungry," she said, and threw herself across the couch.

Chey had to admit she was starving herself. She hadn't eaten since they'd returned from the *inukshuk*. She headed into the kitchen and found Sharon there, already preparing a bunch of sandwiches.

"Slice up some of that meat," Sharon said, indicating a haunch of caribou that she'd taken out of Varkanin's freezer. A long chef's knife lay next to it. "Use a cutting board so you don't mess up the countertop."

Chey stepped over to the kitchen counter and picked up the knife. "You trust me with this, now? A couple days ago you wanted to tear my guts out."

Sharon looked down at the table, where her hands were busy shredding a head of lettuce for the sandwiches. "I wouldn't say I'm thrilled about how things are now," she admitted. "I wouldn't say I *like* you now."

"Okay," Chey replied. She shared the sentiment.

"Up here, though, we don't really believe in grudges. Back when we used to hunt whales, just for food enough to last through the winter, we had a sort of unwritten law. It didn't matter if somebody was sleeping with your husband, or they stole all your money, or you just didn't like the way they looked. The captain of the whaling boat had to trust that everybody would work together—if they didn't, they would *all* get killed. You had to rely on the guy next to you that he was going to paddle like crazy. You had to rely on the guy with the harpoon that he was going to throw it right. And you definitely had to rely on the people back at camp who kept the fire going. If you couldn't trust all those people, you would just have to starve. So no matter what grievances anybody had with anybody else, they got put on hold—just so we could live long enough to work things out later. Even if—"

Sharon stopped in the middle of her sentence and stared at Chey's hand.

"What?" Chey asked. Then she looked down and saw the knife trembling in her grip. She hurriedly put it down and smiled as brightly as she could.

"You okay?" Sharon asked. It didn't sound like friendly concern.

"I'm fine," Chey said. She turned around and faced the caribou haunch in front of her. She didn't understand why her hands were shaking so badly. She felt fine, she really did. She felt okay, at least.

The haunch before her was dripping with blood. It was raw and red and the bone sticking out one end was filled with creamy marrow. Chey had to clamp her mouth tight to keep from drooling.

"I think maybe you should sit down," Sharon said.

Chey shook her head. She was absolutely fine. She felt perfectly—completely—

Her hand reached down and grabbed the bone. Chey couldn't stop her hand. It brought the haunch up to Chey's mouth and she took a bite out of the meat, the blood smearing on her lips and cheeks.

She wasn't controlling her own body.

"Get—guh," she tried to say, but her mouth was full of meat. "Get Powell!" she managed to gasp.

She could hear people running around in the cabin. She could hear voices calling, but she couldn't understand what they were saying. Her vision grew dim and she heard a high-pitched ringing, like an air raid siren going off in her head.

Then it was as if a light switch had been flipped inside her head, and her consciousness just . . . went out.

83

"No!" Chey screamed, and she reared upward, gasping for breath. Arms were wrapped around her chest, holding her down, suffocating her, and she fought wildly, scratching and punching without thought, just trying to get free. Tears burst from around her eyes and she could hear herself moaning in panic and fear.

"Chey! Chey, calm down," Powell hissed, right next to her ear. The arms that held her were his, she realized. "Be quiet! You can't let them hear you. Please—just calm down, calm—"

"I'm okay," she lied. She dropped onto her back and curled into a ball, unable to do anything but breathe, sucking air into her lungs as if she'd woken up underwater, drowning and weak.

She heard someone ask, "Is everything alright back here?" It was not a voice she recognized.

"She's just a nervous flyer," Powell responded.

She heard a door closing and someone walking away. And underneath that a persistent humming sound, a throbbing mechanical drone. The sound of an engine laboring away. She looked around herself and saw metal walls, curved like the fuselage of an airplane. Boxes and crates were stacked everywhere, secured with bungee cords to keep them from shifting in flight.

"We're in the air already?" she asked.

Powell stroked her hair. "The weather lifted and we caught a lift on a cargo plane headed to Cambridge Bay," he told her. "The others are up front in the passenger section, but I figured it would be safer to keep you back here with the cargo. Varkanin didn't want to travel at all with you in bad condition, but I told him we didn't have any choice."

Chey closed her eyes and ran her fingers through her hair. "How long was I gone?" she asked.

"Three days."

She squeezed her eyes shut even harder. "It was different this time. My wolf took over—I mean, that's happened before. But always in the past I felt like I could fight it. Like I could somehow get control back." She shook her head. "This time there was no warning, and not a thing I could do to stop it. Was I—did I cause any problems?"

"You tried to attack Sharon. She didn't take it well, even after I explained why it happened. After that we kept you in restraints."

Chey opened her eyes a crack and looked down at her wrists. A band of red skin on either forearm told her they'd had to use silver manacles. So it was bad. Really bad.

"I think I may have done something really stupid," she told Powell. "When I was in Umiaq, when I first met Sharon and we were fighting in the street—I let my wolf out. I asked for its help."

Powell pressed his body close against hers. It was a comfort. Not least because he was human, human-shaped anyway. If she sniffed hard enough she felt like she could smell her wolf still lingering on her skin.

"That was probably a mistake," he said.

She nodded. She'd figured as much. She'd let the wolf out and now it felt like it could take over whenever it wanted to.

"I'm running out of time."

"We need to move quickly. That's why I didn't want to wait until you came back to us," Powell confirmed.

"This must be what Élodie felt like, at the end," Chey said.

"Don't say that. You still have time," Powell insisted.

She had a hard time sharing his optimism. "Even if we find the cave, and the silver knife—what if I'm already gone by then?" she asked. "What if my wolf figures out what we're doing, and decides she doesn't want it?"

"That won't happen."

Chey grimaced. "It's fine to say that, but—"

"It won't happen. I won't let it," he told her.

84

They set down outside of Cambridge Bay but didn't stick around that tiny town for long. Chey knew they were in a desperate hurry—on her behalf—but it saddened her to see buildings and people on snowmobiles and electric lights go by and know that soon they would just be a memory again, when she was out on the wild tundra. Her time in Umiaq had not been a lot of fun, but just the simplest experiences of being in civilization—walls around her, rooms warmed by central heating, even using the Internet again—had been so exciting after the time she'd spent in the wilderness. Now here was the world of people again, and then it was gone in the blink of an eye.

Varkanin drew the usual stares and pointed questions when he showed his blue face in town, but he was able to hire the use of a snowcat, a big vehicle with a square yellow cab that stood on top of four massive treads. It roared and rumbled as its diesel engines were fired up and then lurched forward when he threw it into gear. He and Sharon—both of them armed to the teeth—sat in the seats up front, while Chey, Powell, and Lucie rode in the cargo area in the back, bracing themselves against the walls of the cab as best they could.

The ride tossed them around pretty badly when they were in town, but as soon as Varkanin got them out onto the unbroken snowfields beyond things settled down quickly. The four giant treads each had their own separate suspension. The snowcat's motion wasn't like the jouncing, rattling, up-and-down roller coaster ride of Dzo's old pickup truck, but more like the rolling pitch of a ship on the ocean. The snowcat's chassis was always in motion, but it was a gentler, almost regular motion.

Except of course when a tread went over a boulder buried under the snow, when the whole vehicle felt like it was going to flip over and they were all thrown together in a heap. But those occasions were somewhat rare.

The cab was lined with windows on all four sides and it gave an excellent view of Victoria Island. Chey spent the first twenty minutes or so of the ride staring out at the snow and the ice-covered lakes and the distant peaks of mountains the same color as the white sky.

Eventually, though, she grew bored. It looked an awful lot like the snowfields around Umiaq, or anywhere else in the Arctic for that matter. She turned around and looked at Powell and Lucie. He was curled up as best he could manage in one corner of the cab with his eyes closed, perhaps trying to catch up on a little sleep. She knew he hadn't gotten any in the three days her wolf had possessed her body—he had told her he had stood guard over her the whole time, refusing to part from her even for meals or hygiene. Even when he had transformed into a wolf, he'd been chained to her, the better to protect her and to wait for her return to humanity.

She considered waking him up for conversation—she could certainly have used some of his resolve just then—but couldn't bear to wake him. Instead she turned to look at Lucie.

The redhead was staring into the middle distance while she chewed on the nail of one index finger. It was a strange gesture for Lucie. Chey had never seen her rival at anything less than full confidence and self-possession. To watch Lucie fidget nervously now was almost shocking.

"What are you thinking about so intently?" Chey asked.

Lucie looked up with a start. *"Jeune fille,* my thoughts are not for you," she said. "Who are you to even ask for them?"

Chey rolled her eyes. "I'm just trying to make small talk," she suggested. "If you'd rather sit and brood, that's fine."

Lucie gave her a shrewd look. "Perhaps, when it is put in this way," she said, "you have a point. It will help pass the time, yes?"

"That was kind of the idea."

Lucie nodded. "I was thinking of lovers' obligations. Of what we owe those we love. It is strange, *non*? One reaches out for the object of one's desires, thinking, I will possess this. It will be mine. And then we learn that it is ourselves who have been possessed."

"I guess I don't think about love the same way you do," Chey told her. They chatted away about it for a while, Chey only paying half her attention to the words. In her mind she was only watching Lucie. Studying her.

This is the woman I am going to betray, she kept thinking. *She's horrible. She's a monster. And we are going to murder her.*

She hadn't really stopped to think about it before. There had been little time for reflection after Powell revealed what he intended to do. How long had he been living with that knowledge, she wondered? Since he had spoken to Raven about how the cure was achieved? Or maybe ever since Lucie arrived in Canada.

There had been times when she had wanted to kill Lucie herself. Times when rage had so consumed her she couldn't look at the redhead without imagining tearing her to pieces.

But this was different. This was in cold blood.

And it was the only way Chey could save her own life. Did that make it like self-defense? Did that make it justifiable?

She couldn't be sure.

" . . . you see lovers as equals, then, separate beings who share some arrangement of emotions," Lucie scoffed. "Like merchants exchanging goods and services. I think perhaps you have never truly loved. *Non, jeune fille,* real-love is like fire. Its warmth draws you in, little by little, until you do not know it but you are burned. It is the fire that consumes us. Destroys us, utterly. And yet we would have it no other way. This is why *mon cher* dallies with you, do you see it? Because you are safe. You cannot hurt him. Yet his heart knows what it requires. What it cannot resist. And in the end he will make the decision rightly, and I shall have at last what I deserve."

"I suppose that's one way of looking at it," Chey agreed.

85

Eventually the big vehicle ground to a halt in the middle of a snowfield dotted with patches of highly reflective ice. Varkanin summoned Chey forward to the front of the snowcat, while Sharon climbed over the seats to sit in the back with Powell and Lucie. She kept a gun in her hand the whole time. It was, of course, loaded with silver bullets. Neither Powell nor Lucie bothered to react to the threat. Lucie kept chewing at her fingernails, but it wasn't because she thought Sharon would shoot her. Lucie and Sharon had exchanged no more than ten words in the whole time they had been aware of each other's existence, but already it was clear that Lucie wasn't afraid of the Inuit girl.

Chey wished she could have shared that confidence. As she sat down in the passenger seat to look at Varkanin, she was astonished as always at how she had gotten to this point—not quite the Russian's prisoner, but never his ally either. Yet he needed her help, just as he needed Powell's, if he was to achieve his ends. So for now the détente remained in place.

"I want to discuss two things with you," Varkanin said. He took a large folding map off the dashboard and showed her where they were. "Here, is Ovayok Territorial Park," he said. "These three hills. We passed over this one, one hour ago."

"We did? I didn't see any hills. All this land looks the same."

Varkanin shrugged. "To a southerner, I can understand why this would be so. To those who are raised on the tundra, like Sharon, many small landmarks present themselves. Rises of land which to you or me would be only hillocks, to them are like mountain ranges." He shrugged again. "It does not matter; the GPS will find the way for us. But I want you to look here, and tell me if this is the place."

Chey studied the map. "Yeah. This doesn't show the rock formation that Raven drew for me—when we see that, then we'll really know we've found it—but the shape of the lake is right, and here's the island."

"Very good." Varkanin folded up his map and put it away. "It is only a few kilometers away, now. We would arrive in an hour, if not for one thing."

"Yeah? You need to take a bathroom break or something?"

"No. I refer to the fact the moon is coming up in one hour."

"Oh." Chey hadn't considered the fact that until they actually had the cure, the cycles of the moon were still going to be an issue. "How—how are we going to handle that?"

Varkanin frowned. "I would be willing to let you and Mr. Powell run free. I have little doubt you will return. Lucie, however, cannot be given such privilege. She must remain with me, chained securely. This may present a small problem."

Chey glanced back over her shoulder. Lucie was staring out the window, not paying attention.

"If she's the only one chained up, she'll know something fishy is going on," Chey whispered. "Yeah, I get it. So Powell and I need to be chained as well. But not Sharon."

Varkanin looked as if she'd surprised him. "Why would she not be chained?" he asked.

"Well—because she wouldn't want to," Chey suggested. "I mean, her wolf won't want to be chained. They go a little crazy when they can't run free."

"But why would she or I care what her wolf feels?"

Chey was really taken aback by that. She didn't know what to say.

"The wolf is an abomination. An unnatural thing. The sooner we are rid of them, the better the world will be for it." Varkanin shook his head. "I understand that you and Powell will not feel this as clearly as I do. After all, he has been half wolf for a very long time and it will have worked on his belief of who he is. You, I know, are in a losing war with your wolf, so you must imagine it as some fearsome competitor. A rival for your soul. As for Sharon and myself, we see the wolves for what they are. A disease."

"That's—that isn't—it's a flawed metaphor," Chey insisted. "Being a wolf isn't all that bad. It's not, not unnatural, for one thing."

"If lycanthropy is not a disease, why do we go to such lengths to find a cure?" Varkanin asked her. "You will not tell me that there is some part of you that wants to remain afflicted. Such thinking is not—"

He was interrupted by a sudden noise loud enough to shake the cab of the snowcat. A thundering, throbbing sound, much like the snowcat's engine—but louder. Much louder. And it was coming from overhead.

"What the hell is that?" Chey asked.

"That is a helicopter," Varkanin announced. "A military aircraft. It is a UH-60 Black Hawk, I think."

"Out here?" Chey was totally confused. "What would a military helicopter be doing way up here in the middle of the winter?"

"Obviously, it has come for us." Varkanin sighed. "I was afraid it might come to this. Strap yourself in, please. I will attempt to evade it." He threw the snowcat back into gear and stepped on the gas.

86

The snowcat was not built for speed, or maneuverability. It was in essence a civilian tank, built to climb slowly over terrain that would defy any other vehicle. Varkanin nearly tipped it as he swung it around in a tight circle, the treads on Chey's side whining as they came free of the snow.

"Everyone to the right!" Varkanin called. Chey leaned as hard as she could over to the side, while in the back the other werewolves grabbed whatever they could to haul themselves up the rapidly sloping floor of the cab. With a flat whooping noise the snowcat dropped back down onto all four treads and grabbed at the ground, lurching forward on its new course.

"Where are you headed?" Chey asked, staring out through the windows, looking for any sign of the helicopter. "Who are they? What do they want?"

"For any cover I can find," Varkanin said, answering her first question first. "I go now for the hills over there, unless something better presents itself. As for who follows us, they are soldiers, certainly. My contact in your government told me he could not send soldiers up here. The fact that he has now done so tells me the details of our arrangement have changed. I am now one of the hunted."

"Nobody's fired a shot at us," Powell insisted. The wild maneuvering must have woken him up. "Are you sure that's what they're here for?"

"Perhaps," Varkanin insisted, his voice calm as molten steel, "you would wait for them to land, so we may ask them?"

Powell didn't respond to that.

Varkanin kept the throttle wide open, even when the engine started to chug ominously. He dodged down a shallow valley between two low hills, but even Chey could see the cover they offered was marginal at best. As if to mock his attempt at subterfuge, the helicopter buzzed over them again, so low this time it made the snowcat rock back and forth on its treads.

"They are attempting to make visual confirmation," Varkanin announced, as if he knew exactly how this worked.

"What are we going to do?" she asked him.

"There," Varkanin said, and pointed through the windshield. Chey saw a scattering of rocks ahead, most of them the size of her fist. Some were larger boulders, big enough to hide behind, but not many. It was a typical glacial esker, of a kind she'd seen all over the Arctic. A kind of landlocked sandbar, created where once a river had flowed under the ice until it choked on rocks and silt. "If we can get among the rocks, perhaps we can establish an ambush zone, with clear fields of fire, or even set up some manner of trap to—"

The helicopter shot overhead again, and the snowcat fishtailed on the loose snow.

"Or perhaps," Varkanin went on, "we must only fight for our lives." He looked over his shoulder at the werewolves in the back. "Mr. Powell," he said, "there is a storage locker near your left foot. Inside you will find a hunting rifle, a very good one, which you will give to Sharon. There is also a Beretta 92 pistol, which I would like you to take for yourself." He reached down and took a sidearm out of the holster he wore on his thigh. "This," he said, turning to face Chey, "is for you. Do you know how to use it?"

It was a Glock 23. "Fourteen bullets, right? Thirteen in the clip, one in the chamber."

"I do not keep one loaded where it might go off like that."

Chey had trained in the use of handguns back when she had first come north, when she had thought she was going to kill Powell and then go home to a happy human life, kept warm at night by thoughts of revenge achieved. Things had changed.

"They are all currently loaded with silver ammunition," Varkanin announced. "This will not do. Mr. Powell, you'll find magazines for each weapon in the locker, all loaded with conventional rounds. I have inscribed a small red hash mark on each with a grease pencil, in order to designate it such."

Powell did as he asked. "You were prepared for this," he said.

"What do you mean, please?"

Powell handed him a speed loader for the revolver he still wore under his left armpit. "Why bother with lead bullets at all, if you only came up here to kill wolves?"

"In business, strange bedfellows can be made. One does not always trust one's associates as much as one would like," Varkanin said. He shrugged. "My contact in your government was what you call an asshole."

The word was startling coming from the eloquent Russian. Chey pressed a hand to her lips to keep from laughing.

"He is also some kind of spy, in the espionage business at least. Just as I was, once. I would never trust him, not totally."

Chey looked down at the gun in her hand. "But you trust us. That seems like a major risk."

"I trust that you need me as much as I need you. Mr. Powell, it is at this time I will remind you of the deal we made. Also, I will remind you that the *ulu* you seek is made of silver. You will need someone to hold it for you."

"I remember," Powell grumbled.

"What about me?" Lucie asked, from the back of the cab. "Do I not get a gun, with which to defend my poor self?"

"No!" everyone said, in chorus.

87

The helicopter swung around in the cold air, its nose turning to point right at them as Varkanin poured on every ounce of speed the snowcat had. It made no attempt to fire at them. Chey studied its dark insectile shape as best she could through the cab's windows, but she couldn't see any machine guns bristling from its hull. "It must just be a troop transport," Varkanin said, "or we would already be cut down. Be ready, now, please."

Chey gripped tight the Glock in her hand and reached for the door release at the same time. When Varkanin stepped on the brakes, she pushed the door open and rolled out into the snow. At the back of the snowcat Powell threw open the rear door and the others spilled out as well, long before the treaded vehicle slid to a stop.

A hundred meters away—no more—the helicopter began to settle toward the ground.

"Over here," Powell called, and the werewolves followed him toward the esker, Varkanin bringing up the rear. He couldn't run as quickly as the supernaturally strong werewolves, but he did his best.

Chey kept her head down and tried not to panic, but as the first gunshots rang out, she allowed herself to yelp a little. She forced herself not to look back until she'd reached the shelter of a boulder as large as a house. Other, smaller rocks stood around it, providing cover from a number of different angles. It looked like the perfect place to hide. Powell, Sharon, and Lucie were already there, curled up to make themselves as small as possible. Pressing herself behind the boulder, she peeked out and saw pale figures spilling out of the helicopter, which still hovered a meter above the ground.

"It can't land here, not without becoming stuck in the snow," Varkanin explained as he threw himself to one side of her and crouched in the shelter of the big rock. "They must come to us on foot."

A bullet struck the rock not far from where Chey crouched, making a flat whining sound as it ricocheted off into the snow. She pulled her head back instantly, but her need to see was too desperate to just hide and wait for death to come. She peeked out again.

The ten soldiers rushing toward them wore white coveralls—Arctic camouflage—and tan berets. Their faces were hidden behind ski masks and tinted goggles. The assault rifles they carried had white-painted stocks, but the barrels glinted sharply in the sunlight.

They came on in rough formation, a running wedge of men who stopped every few meters to get off a shot before dashing forward again. They were firing silver bullets, which were laughably inaccurate at that range—most likely they didn't expect to hit the werewolves. They were just laying down suppressing fire, enough bullets to keep their targets from making a break for it.

It was working.

Chey had fought men with guns before, at Port Radium. Both in her human body and as her wolf she had defended herself against them. Those had been civilians, though. They'd been poorly organized and they'd known little about fighting lycanthropes. She didn't imagine these would be so easy to pick off.

Sharon crawled up on top of the rock that was their only shelter, exposing herself to the bullets that kept coming, one after another, but she didn't flinch as they struck the rock like hammer blows. Instead she stretched out her hunting rifle, bracing it against the stone, and lined up a shot.

She glanced down at Varkanin, as if for confirmation.

He nodded. "They will take no prisoners. We have no choice."

Sharon bent down over the rifle's scope again and squeezed her trigger.

Fifty meters away, a red splotch appeared on the sleeve of an oncoming soldier. He twisted around and dropped to the snow, clutching at his arm.

This was it, then, for real. They were fighting for their lives. Chey checked the action of her weapon, but Varkanin held up one hand for patience. "Not until it is necessary," he said.

He lifted his chin and she understood he was telling her to listen. The sound of gunshots had stopped.

"It can't be that easy," she sighed.

He told her, very quietly, "They are not fools. Now they know we are armed, and they know we have them at range. Our lead bullets are much more accurate than their silver bullets. They will take their time approaching again, and make sure they have us covered."

"I . . . I don't know if I could shoot them anyway," she whispered. "They're Canadians. And anyway—how can that possibly end well? Even if we could kill them all, they would just send more, right?"

"Yes. Though by that time, we will have reached the island. This lot understand why they have been sent here. They know the dangers. When the time comes, you must fight. Do you understand?"

She looked down at the gun in her hand.

He glanced at his watch. "Ah," he said. "Perhaps it will not matter if you are ready. I am certain that your wolf will not hesitate."

88.

Up in the helicopter, Preston Holness stared through binoculars at the ground below, watching the soldiers fall back outside of range of the hunting rifle. He grabbed at the microphone attached to his radio headset and growled, "I thought they were tan berets!"

Sergeant Matthieu came to crouch next to him in the open side hatch of the helicopter. His words were torn away by the icy wind, but Holness heard them in his headphones. "They're obeying standard operating procedure. No need for them to get themselves killed before they even reach the targets."

"If the targets get away now we'll be chasing them until spring. It is essential, sergeant, that we catch them now, and kill them, *now.*"

"Certainly, sir. However, if I might suggest a more measured approach—the troops can encircle this position and keep the enemy pinned down. We can take them at our leisure, then."

"Fine. You don't want to do your job right. I'll just have to use *my* skill set, then." Holness swore under his breath and grabbed a stanchion to pull himself up. The inside of the helicopter seemed strangely empty without any soldiers inside. He walked up the double row of seats, holding on to nylon straps that dangled from the ceiling. When he reached the cockpit he tapped the shoulder of the copilot, who flinched wildly.

"You. Tell me. Is there a loud-hailer system on this crate?"

The copilot's face started to cloud with confusion. Holness didn't have time for the idiot to figure out what he was being asked, so he turned to the pilot. "There is one, right? Just switch it on to my headset."

The pilot flipped a couple of switches on the radio board. Holness cleared his throat and even over the noise of the rotors he could hear his phlegmy roar roll out across half the Arctic.

"This is it, Varkanin," he said.

There was no sign of movement from the pile of rocks where the Russian and his pet werewolves had gone to ground. Holness supposed he shouldn't be surprised. Varkanin was a classic tough guy, the kind that had pretty much gone extinct in the twenty-first century. He'd also, though, seemed like a reasonable man when Holness met him.

"There's nowhere for you to go," Holness said. He let the echoes die down, then went on. "I'm not going to pretend you can walk away now. But you and your friends don't have to suffer. Just give up!"

He watched in vain for any sign of reaction. Ten seconds went by. Twenty.

Then something happened. The barrel of a rifle lifted above the rock where they were hiding. Holness hoped it would have a white flag tied to it, but nothing—nothing in life was ever that easy. Instead the barrel jabbed out at the sky. Specifically at one point on the horizon. The gesture was repeated again, more emphatically, and then the rifle was withdrawn.

Holness made a gesture at the pilot, who switched off the loud-hailer. Then Holness frowned and squinted down at the rocks.

What the hell was Varkanin trying to tell him?

When it finally occurred to him it was almost too late. He dashed back to the belly of the aircraft, where Sergeant Matthieu was waiting for him. "Attack now," he ordered.

Matthieu sighed audibly. "Sir, as I said before—"

Holness glared at the Quebecois sergeant. "I gave an order and I expect it to be carried out. I told you to storm that position. You don't know anything about lycanthropes. I do. The moon will be up any minute! They're tough as hell to kill right now, but when they change they're *monsters*."

"With all due respect, sir, unless they can fly—"

"I wouldn't put it past them. Send your men in *now*."

Matthieu stared into Holness's eyes for far too long. Then he saluted and grasped his own microphone. "All units, advance," he said. "Return fire at will, but take the position at once."

Down on the ground, the white-clad soldiers jumped up from their ready positions and did as they were told. Shots rang out from the rocks but they just ran serpentine patterns as they fell on the rocks en masse. None of them were hit as they approached the big rock, the one the enemies were hiding behind. One after another of the soldiers got his back up against the rock, then dashed around either side of it while a squad hung back to provide cover.

Holness saw smoke leap up as shots were fired—he didn't know by whom. He couldn't hear a thing. He thought about going forward to ask the pilot if the helicopter had any listening devices. But then he saw red blood jet out from behind the rock—followed closely by a head in a tan beret. The head rolled across the tundra like a football before it came to a stop, slowly spinning on a patch of ice.

On the horizon, the rising moon was a white blur.

89

In the esker, chaos ruled.

The gray wolf bit and clawed at the men who came rushing at her. She did not discriminate between bodies—any arm or face or back that presented itself to her had to be attacked. There was no room in her mind for doubts or questions. Beside her the white and the male fought just as hard, tooth and claw.

Another wolf, one she did not know, stood with them. Her coloration was mostly black. What she was doing there was a mystery that would have to be solved later—when all the humans were dead. For now the gray simply admired the savagery that drove the black. She had a human by the arm and was swinging him around, her rear paws dug deep into the snow for leverage as she twisted her victim one way, then the other. The human screamed and then his head struck a rock and he stopped screaming.

The gray didn't get to see how the black finished him, though. Motion flickered in her peripheral vision and the gray reached for an arm that flashed past her. It was holding a big piece of metal and wood that it dropped when her teeth met inside the human's flesh. She wheeled around, wrenching her teeth out of the wound and ripping open bloody tissues. The human screamed and the gray's eyes blazed with excitement. Another human stood not three paces away, raising its own metal stick in her direction. The gray pounced, launching herself through the air. Halfway to the human's throat a piece of silver, moving very, very fast cut through her lip and buried itself in the ground behind her. The pain was enormous, but it did nothing but make her more angry, want the human's blood even more. She crashed into his chest and knocked him backward, her claws sinking effortlessly through the woven fabric that covered his ribs. Her teeth flashed forward and snapped closed and she tore the goggles and the mask off his face. Underneath his features were pale white and terrified. She lifted her snout to howl at the air, just for the pleasure of it, and tore open his guts with her hind claws. He died stinking of excrement and fear.

Then silver tore through the air all around her with a noise like thunderbolts smacking a mountaintop. She spun around, looking for her attacker, and found that the male had already brought him down. The human struggled weakly, trying to smack the male wolf in the side of the head with the butt of his weapon. The male tore the human's throat out with one twist of his powerful neck and then leapt away, looking for a next victim.

But it seemed there were no more. Six human bodies lay bleeding and torn on the ground. The wolves were not unscathed. The black female was bleeding copiously from a wound in her side. The male had a new hole through one ear that looked like it had been burned through with a hot iron. The cut on the gray's mouth wasn't healing. But they had survived, and the humans had not. The humans were all dead.

Except—

A seventh human was suddenly there with them in the rocks. During the battle he had hidden himself away in a crack in the largest boulder, but now he emerged and stared down at them with blue eyes. His skin was blue, too. The gray wolf dimly remembered him. He had been there when the polar bear spirit rescued them from the hunters. What was he doing here now? She had attacked him, then. Tried to bite his arm.

Her teeth hurt when she tried to remember. It had not gone well.

The male looked from one to another member of his pack, watching their reactions. He wasn't sure what to do about this new human threat. The black wolf, the outsider, crouched on top of the rock staring down at him.

There was no fear in the blue human. Not a drop of it. The wolves didn't know what to make of that. The very purpose of their being, of their creation, had been to strike fear into the hearts of human beings. Now here was one, admittedly one who looked different from the others, who seemed unaffected. He stood alone in the middle of a ring of blood-thirsty wolves, and did not cower or tremble.

The male took a step closer. Sniffed at the wind. Growled. The message should have been clear. The human was about to die. The least he could do was show proper respect and drop to his knees, or sweat profusely, or cry out in a wavering voice. That was normal. That was what was expected.

Instead, the human spoke to them. The wolves could not understand his words. He shook his head, almost sadly. Then he brought his hands before him and slowly removed one of his gloves. The naked hand underneath was as blue as his face. He held it out toward the male, very much like a human extending a hand to a tame dog so the dog could receive his scent.

The gray whimpered out a warning, but it was too late. The male lurched forward and tried to bite the human's hand off at the wrist.

The human didn't even flinch. The male, however—the alpha, the leader of the pack who had seemed omnipotent before, who had seemed like he knew everything and never was at a loss for what to do next—jumped back with his tail between his legs. Bloody drool fell from his mouth in long steaming ropes, and he cried out in agony.

The white female had been lurking behind some stones until that moment. Now she leapt forward to defend her alpha, her blue eyes very, very bright. They looked like burning sapphires. Before she could strike, however, the gray wolf signaled a warning by growling at her. It was not the white's place to attack next. It was not for her to decide whether they attacked at all.

Warring instincts and desires fizzed inside the gray's brain. This was a human! There could be only one course of action—she must kill it! Kill, kill, kill—any way, any how, just kill! Yet clearly attacking him was a terrible mistake. He stank of silver—of death, of pain.

The human solved the dilemma for her. Striding forward, he came to stand directly in front of her. For a moment they stared into each other's eyes. She did not understand what she saw in his gaze. Then he jumped, spread his arms out wide, and hollered at her with angry noises.

She dropped low to the ground, spreading her paws for better traction on the snow. She shot one querying glance at her alpha, but he wasn't even looking at her.

The human pulled his leg back to kick her like a disobedient pet. The gray snarled—but she also turned tail and ran, dodging out of the rocks, not caring what direction she headed in, just trying to get away.

The shame of it burned her worse than the wound on her lip. But not so badly as her fear of what a silver-plated foot would do when it connected with her rib cage.

90

"What the hell just happened?" Holness asked.

Nobody on his radio channel had an answer for him.

The helicopter circled the esker slowly, its rotor noise drowning out all but the most immediate thoughts. There was blood down there. A lot of it. Dead bodies. The wolves—all of them, one after the other—jumped down out of the rocks and dashed away, headed north. It took a while before Holness thought to look to the south, where his four remaining soldiers were dug in, waiting to cover the raiding party. One of them looked up at the helicopter and pointed at his ear. He must be waiting for further orders.

Soldiers. Soldiers needed orders. They did what you told them to, even if it got them killed. But you had to tell them, first.

Holness grabbed his microphone. "Go after them," he said.

"Sir," Sergeant Matthieu said. "Sir, if I can suggest—"

"Go after the fucking wolves! Shoot them!" Holness screamed. "They're getting away!"

Down on the ground the remaining four leapt to their feet and started running north, at last. The wolves were already a hundred meters ahead of them and their weapons were useless at that range. The wolves could run faster than the soldiers. It was pointless. But now they had their orders, and they were going to follow them, to the letter. They would keep running until they were ordered to stop.

"Screw this. Break off the pursuit, it's pointless. You, pilot," he shouted, looking forward toward the cockpit. "You chase them. They can't outrun a helicopter!"

"Sir," Matthieu said, again.

"What?" Holness demanded, spinning around so fast that his spittle slapped against his own cheek.

"I'd like to suggest, sir, that we still have men down on the ground, as well as an unknown situation among those rocks."

"Yes? And? What is it? Tell me already!"

"Leaving them here without support might be a mistake."

"A mistake." Holness throbbed with the need to chase after the wolves. But Matthieu was right. It would be a mistake to just leave his last four soldiers here while he went haring off after the wolves. Especially since, when he caught them, he would have nobody left to shoot them for him. He certainly wasn't going to go down there and do it himself.

Of course, setting down, collecting the soldiers, and taking off again would take time. Time during which the wolves would get farther and farther away.

He smacked the fuselage of the helicopter with the flat of one hand. Damn it. The wolves were getting away and he had to let them go. For the time being, at least.

"Sir. Would you like me to have the pilot set down so we can collect the men?" The sergeant waited patiently for an answer.

Holness closed his eyes and nodded. "Yes, I think that would be a very good idea at this time, sergeant. Why don't you do that?"

Holness stared down at the esker again. For the first time he really thought about what might be down there. Where was Varkanin? He didn't see any blue faces among the scattered body parts down there. "Tell them to shoot anything that moves. Make sure we don't have any more nasty surprises coming."

Matthieu turned away and spoke into his own microphone. "They have confirmed receipt of your order," Matthieu told Holness.

"Tell them to be careful!" Holness bellowed.

The look on Matthieu's face was carefully composed. This was not a man who would be insubordinate with his commanding officer, not even if that CO was a civilian consultant like Holness. But he couldn't keep his eyes totally under control. Somewhere inside that steely gaze Holness read exactly what Matthieu was thinking.

Bit late for that. Sir.

91

The wolves ran north. It seemed to the gray as if they had always run north, as if something had been pulling them to this place, a lodestone coded into their DNA as surely as the pack hierarchy or the hatred they felt for humanity. Before, when the male had led her north through the blizzard, she had been confused, unsure of where he was headed.

Now she knew.

There was a place, somewhere very close. A place they must reach. A place where something wonderful was going to happen. Something terrible. She could not know what it was, but she didn't wonder what it might be, either. It was her destiny. How could she possibly refuse its call?

When she looked to the others, to the male, to the white female running beside her, to the black wolf who was not even part of the pack—she saw it in their eyes. They felt it just as strongly as she did.

So they ran. Because their bodies told them to. The danger behind them didn't matter. Future dangers could barely be conceived. Only this one goal had any weight. They ran.

They ran, in fact, until the black wolf dropped. She stumbled forward, into the snow, burying her muzzle up to her eyes. Her legs worked beneath her without strength. She was trying to rise. To run farther. But she couldn't.

The gray would have abandoned her there. The black wolf wasn't one of their pack. They owed her nothing. The male, however, seemed to feel otherwise. And what the male, the alpha, chose, the pack chose.

The gray stopped where she was, watching him as he trotted back to where the black wolf lay. The gray looked to the north. To their destination. It was as if an invisible aurora shimmered there, calling her. It took real strength of will to turn away, even for a moment. To go back and join her alpha.

But wolves never lack for willpower.

The black lifted her face out of the snow as the pack approached. She snarled a warning. They should stay away. She was not one of them.

The male took a step closer. Off to one side, the white female cut a wide circle around the prostrate black wolf. Getting behind her—just in case. The gray came up by the male's flank, where she could support whatever move he made.

The black wolf growled, now. Barked at them like a dog. They should stay away—she was making it quite clear she did not want them near. The male took a tentative step closer, then looked off to the side. His face, his ears, his tail showed boredom. The saddle of fur on his back lay flat.

It was an offering. He was giving the black female the opportunity to join his pack. To come under his protection. She need only come forward and lick his chin. Show deference.

The white wolf stood up very tall, stretching her legs. She didn't like this, didn't want the black female in the pack. As the most submissive wolf in the pack, she would be suspicious of any newcomers, of course. She would worry they would force her even farther down the pecking order.

The male didn't acknowledge her concerns. He just stood there, waiting. The gray lowered her head and licked at the snow, her eyes drinking in everything. She was ready if the black wolf tried to challenge the male's dominance—or to just attack.

The black wolf got one leg underneath her. Pushed herself up out of the snow. It stuck to her fur, flakes getting caught in the long guard hairs that stuck out above her thick undercoat. Her eyes were glassy. She got another leg underneath her. Stood up.

That was when the gray saw why she had faltered. The wound in the black wolf's chest was soaked in blood. The fur there had fallen out in great clumps, and the skin around the bullet hole looked charred and cracked.

Silver, the gray wolf thought. She had silver inside her body. Soon she would be dead.

There was still a chance for her to save herself. If she could somehow get the silver bullet out of her body, she would heal when next the moon changed her. It wasn't something she could do on her own, however. There was only one way for a wolf to get a silver bullet out of her body. The male would have to bite it out. Tear it free with his powerful jaws and enormous teeth. The pain would be extraordinary for both of them, but the gray knew the male would do it, if the black wolf would only agree to join the pack. She knew it because once, the male had done it for her. It had felt like he was killing her. Like he was tearing her to pieces.

It had been a gesture of love. Of the feelings one wolf of a pack shared for another, which were more profound than any human words could convey.

He would do this for the black wolf. She had only to submit. Join him.

Still acting as if he didn't care one way or another, the male started walking toward the black wolf, sniffing at the air, twitching his tail back and forth. As if he had better things to do. The laws of the pack made it clear he could not show any sign of concern. He could not evince the slightest desire for the black wolf to join the pack. Yet because he was resisting the siren call of the north, and because he had already ignored the black wolf's growling, it was obvious to them all. He wanted desperately to save the black wolf. To accept her.

She had only to submit.

Yet her eyes, her ears, her tail, sent all the wrong signals. She growled low in her throat. Her saddle stood straight up, and her tail was tucked tight between her legs as if she was afraid the white female was going to bite it off. She turned to the left, then to the right, as if looking for an escape route. Some direction she could run that would get her away from the pack.

The male let her make all these signs without challenge. What she was doing was the height of rudeness—or it could symbolize true aggression, true hatred. He was letting her burn off her excess pride.

But there was a limit to how far this could go. The male yawned, his long tongue curling out of his mouth, his eyes squinted shut. Shaking his head, he walked over to the black wolf, well within range of her claws and teeth. He turned to face her and suddenly the intensity of his gaze would have melted ice. He walked up beside her and pushed at her side with his forehead.

She was so weak that she fell over. He shoved at her legs, at her ribs, trying to get her to roll onto her back. Maybe he intended to bite the bullet out even without her consent—which would be unthinkable.

All she had to do was lie down and lick his chin. The gray wolf leaned forward on her legs as if she could urge the black wolf to obey, to submit, by only desiring it.

The black wolf didn't submit. Instead, she wheeled around with the last of her strength and tried to sink her teeth into the male's throat.

He jumped back easily and her teeth snapped shut on empty air.

The white female growled. The gray's eyes went wide. If he gave the slightest signal, the two of them were ready to fall on the black wolf and punish her severely for her transgression.

But instead, he just trotted away. Headed north. As if nothing, whatsoever, had happened.

The black wolf had been given her chance. She would not get another.

The three of them, the pack, headed north without a glance back. They left the black wolf there, dying in the snow.

Because she'd made it very clear that that was what she wanted.

92

The moon went down again, and the wolves changed back to human.

Some of them.

"Leave her," Lucie said. "This is our last chance. You and I, *cher,* we can go away together. Where they will never find us. But we can't take her with us. It will be like Élodie, again."

"No," Powell said.

Chey could hear them. She couldn't open her eyes or move, but she could hear them talking.

Then their voices faded away. Everything faded away. Her sense of her body. Her sense of time. The cold, the air on her face.

All gone.

For a while there was nothing. Not even a self. Then she returned.

Chey found herself standing in the snow, staring at her hands. They looked like paws. No. They were hands, with fingers, with—they looked like paws. She felt fur bristling all over her body. She felt herself start to drop forward, to land on all fours.

"Stop it," she begged. "Just—just give me one more day. Let me be human one more time." Tears started to roll down her cheeks. Her fur caught them, soaked them up.

Her hands—her paws—flexed, the claws—the fingers—stretched out before her—the claws scratched at the air.

"Please," she said.

Her ears twitched. Her tail—she didn't have a tail.

"Please."

And then, in a sudden burst of clarity, of light, the wolf was standing in the snow, and the woman stood facing it.

Two of them. Separate bodies.

It was a hallucination. It was very convincing. They stared at one another, both understanding. This wasn't real. It couldn't be. The wolf licked her lips, showing her enormous teeth.

The wolf was going to devour the woman. Tear her up and eat the pieces. The blood would be slick in her throat. The flesh would go down in thick gobbets. The wolf would crunch the bones they shared, break them open and suck out the marrow. The wolf would eat her, her hair that was not fur, her tiny little round human teeth. Her human eyes. Her human tongue.

"No," the woman said. Chey said. She fought to hold on to her own name.

Wolves don't have names.

"No," Chey said again. Louder this time. The wolf's ears went back. It snarled low in its throat.

Fascinated, Chey crouched down to look deep into the wolf's eyes.

This wolf had a name. A soul. She was a soul.

"You," she said. "You're Amuruq," she said.

The wolf blinked.

"You're—you're afraid of me," Chey said.

The wolf started to fade. To vanish.

"I can help you," Chey promised.

The wolf crouched. Ready to spring. Promises. The wolf had heard promises before. She had been betrayed, before.

"Please. Give me one more day. I'll make it happen. No matter what it costs."

The wolf was gone. Amuruq was gone.

Chey opened her eyes. She was lying on her back, in the snow. Powell was kneeling next to her, holding her hand. Lucie stood nearby, not looking at Chey. Chewing on her perfect little fingernails.

They were all naked.

"She wanted us to come here," Chey said. "The only way she could make that happen was to possess me. To take over. She wasn't trying to destroy me. She was trying to push me in the right direction."

"What?" Powell asked.

Chey blinked and tried to sit up. Moaned. She hurt all over. "What?" she asked.

He smiled at her. Rubbed at her wrist with his thumbs. Hard enough to hurt, a little.

"You said something, just now," he told her. "I couldn't quite make it out."

"You were mumbling," Lucie told her. "Raving in your sleep."

"I . . . don't remember," Chey said. The dream was there, the vision. The communication with—with someone. Something else. But as she reached for it, she lost it. She'd made a promise, or maybe a threat? She'd named something . . . it was gone.

She sat up and buried her face in her hands. "How long was I gone this time?"

Powell shook his head. "A while. No wristwatch to time it." He held up his bare wrist and smiled.

She smiled back. "Where are we?" she asked.

"Take a look for yourself."

She pushed herself up farther on her arms. Looked around.

They were on the snow-covered banks of a frozen lake. A big lake, with an island in its center, just a pile of yellow and brown rocks. On the far side of the lake a formation of gray rocks stood up in the shape of a hand with broken fingers.

"We made it," she said. "This is it."

"The wolves brought us right here," Powell told her. "They knew. They wanted us to do this."

"No," Lucie insisted. Shaking her head. She put her index finger to her mouth again and chewed vigorously on the nail. She knew something was up, obviously. Knew she was the only one who still didn't know what was going to happen.

"We've won, almost," Chey said.

"No," Lucie told her. More determined, this time. "We have—"

Powell stood up suddenly, interrupting her. "Look, over there," he said.

They all turned to look where he pointed. Out into the snowfield, into the ice glare. A figure was approaching, a human shape in a heavy parka and snow pants. His face was blue. Over his shoulder was a body, the body of an Inuit woman with long black hair that hung down at his side. She was wrapped in a white blanket thick with red blood.

Varkanin, and Sharon Minik. Except Sharon was dead.

93

Varkanin laid Sharon's body down on the ground near the water. The snow didn't melt against her cheek.

He sat down beside her and looked out at the island. His blue eyes were hollow and he didn't speak. Chey took a step toward him, thinking she could comfort him somehow, but before she could reach out to him he got up again and turned to face them. "I hid until they were gone, then followed you on foot. Your tracks were easy to find. Footprints in the snow and . . . and blood trails." He reached up and pinched the bridge of his nose. "The soldiers will be here soon."

"Cher," Lucie whispered. "Now, perhaps."

"Forget it," Powell told her. "Listen, Varkanin, I want you to know—"

Varkanin waved one hand at him in abnegation. "There is nothing to say. You have arrived here, as I said you would. Now you must go inside and find your cure. And hurry, please. The moon will rise again before long. Your wolves will not know what to do—and then all will be lost."

"The only reason he let us live was to cure her!" Lucie grabbed at Powell's arm. When he brushed her off, she put her fingernail to her mouth again and bit down hard. "Do you think he will just let us go? Do you think he will let me live?"

Varkanin turned to stare at her. His eyes were perfectly focused now. "I would break every bone in your body with my bare hands, if I could. I would flay you from the top of your head to the soles of your feet, and laugh at your screams. But I made a promise."

"Promises," Lucie said, "are worth no more than the wind that carries them. I think, sir, that we will go into that cave and find this cure, and when we come out you will be waiting for me. To have your revenge all the same."

Varkanin glared at her for a while. Then he turned to face Powell. "I'll hold off the soldiers as long as I can. That will not be very long—and the moon is coming. Go, now."

"Give me your word, that you mean me no harm," Lucie mocked.

"Lucie—this isn't the time," Powell said.

Lucie lifted her finger to her mouth one more time. Chewed off a piece of fingernail and spit it out into the snow. "Help me kill him," she said.

"Lucie!"

Chey laughed. "Haven't you figured it out, yet? We can't even hurt him. And I for one don't want to. Hasn't he suffered enough? Haven't you made him suffer enough?"

"I have done nothing to deserve his hatred, or the dangers he has brought down on us," Lucie said. Even Powell had to laugh at that. "It was my wolf that injured him, not me. You think this a joke? Tell me, Cheyenne—tell me how you came to forgive Monty. How you forgave him for slaughtering your father, and cursing you?"

Chey opened her mouth to speak. But she couldn't answer.

Was Powell responsible for what his wolf did? If he wasn't, then what did that say about Lucie?

"You hunted down his daughters," she said, finally. "When you were human."

"I defended myself after he tried to kill me. Always I have sought to find a way to release myself from his pointless vendetta. I came to you for help, when I could not defeat him myself. Only to have you make an alliance with this man, who wishes to torture me to death! But I have kept my peace. I have understood, I must defend myself, as always. I have been watching him, for some time. Studying him. Is it so strange?" Lucie asked. "He is my enemy. I have looked for his weaknesses. His blue skin is like iron to us. We cannot hurt him where he is blue."

Varkanin pulled the blanket over Sharon's face. He didn't even seem to hear what Lucie was blathering on about. Some of it must have gotten through his grief, however. Finally he stood up and faced them.

"I have noticed one thing," Lucie said. She flexed her hand in front of her, as if testing its strength. "I have seen that his tongue is still pink."

Varkanin looked puzzled as to why she would care. He opened his mouth to speak.

And that was when Lucie struck.

Chey understood what was happening even as she realized she couldn't stop it. Lucie hadn't been chewing on her fingernail because she was nervous. She had been sharpening it. Biting it down to one razor-fine point.

She lunged forward and stuck her index finger in between his teeth. He tried to reel backward away from the attack, but she was too fast for him. His eyes went wide even as smoke puffed out of his mouth. Lucie withdrew her finger—Chey saw it was burned down to the bone where it had touched Varkanin's lips—and spun around with madness in her eyes.

Behind her, Varkanin dropped to his knees, clutching at his mouth. Bright blood leaked from one corner of his lips.

"Now I have given you my curse," Lucie told him, her back still turned to him. "Even the slightest scratch will suffice, *non*? But what will become of you when the moon rises, I wonder? What happens to a were-wolf who transforms when every cell in his body is suffused with silver?"

He stumbled trying to get back to his feet. Chey looked at Powell, but he seemed as shocked as she was, and as unable to do anything to help. What could they do? Lucie was right—even a small scratch could transfer the curse.

"Will you explode when you change?" Lucie asked. "Will you simply disintegrate into a pile of ash?"

Varkanin's shoulders shook wildly, as if he was going into convulsions. He managed to get to his feet. He reached for the gun at his hip.

"Perhaps you will hurt. Perhaps the pain will be unimaginable," Lucie said, her nostrils flaring. She turned around and waited for him to draw the gun from its holster. Then she reached over and plucked it effortlessly from his grasp.

He could only stare down at his empty hand, as if wondering what had happened.

"You bi—" he tried to say, but before he could finish the profanity his mouth filled with blood and he had to spit it out.

Chey started to rush to his side, but she stopped when she realized that Lucie had the gun trained on her chest. Slowly she raised her hands.

Lucie didn't speak to Chey, however. Instead she addressed Powell. "Come with me, *cher*. The time for silly games and little infatuations is over. You must have known, even from the start, it would come to this. Every time you let your human heart take the place of your brain, it comes to this. Everyone dies. Except us."

"No," Powell said. "We're going to cure ourselves. We're going to be human from now on. No more bloodshed. No more guilt!"

Lucie swung the gun around to point at him. "But I don't want to be cured," she told him. "Did you suspect, even for a moment, it was otherwise?" She watched his face for a while. Studying him, perhaps trying to work out the right words to make him join her. For the first time Chey thought perhaps Lucie really did love Powell. That she wasn't just obsessed with him, or thought of him as her possession. That she wanted him to be happy. That she wanted him to want the things she did, and that it caused her pain when he did not.

It was the only way she could find to explain why Lucie stared at Powell so intently that she didn't notice Varkanin coming up behind her.

The blue Russian was clearly crippled by pain. The curse must already be at work inside him, transforming him, fighting with the silver in his body. But he was not the kind of man who let pain control him. He had managed to get to his feet. He had managed to drop into a crouch. And somehow he found it within himself to tackle Lucie, knocking her to the ground and sending the gun flying.

"You two, go on," he insisted, as he struggled to hold her down.

Chey and Powell did as they were told, because it was their only chance. Together they raced out onto the ice of the frozen lake, and headed for the island, and whatever was there, waiting for them.

94

Chey's bare feet slid on the ice. Under a light powdering of snow it was as slick as glass and she kept falling onto all fours. Every time she landed on her hands and knees, she looked down and thought she saw paws.

Don't, she told the wolf inside her head. *Just don't.* The wolf could barely hear her, though. It was so close—close to what, Chey didn't know. But it could taste this place in its oldest memories. It remembered this lake, this island, so vividly that it was panting loud enough to deafen her.

Powell was calling to her, from ten meters away. He was reaching for her as if he wanted her to come to him. She shook her head. She couldn't hear what he was saying. Struggling, slipping, she got back on her feet. Two feet, like a human being.

For the moment. She looked up at the horizon and though there was nothing to see there she knew—knew, in absolute factual terms—that the moon was coming back. If it came before she reached the cave, what then? Varkanin would die. The soldiers would come and find her, and Powell, in wolf form. They wouldn't hesitate or make any blunders this time. They would shoot them from the air, like Americans did in Alaska, shoot the wolves from on high. And that would be an ending.

An ending. Any ending seemed welcome, now.

But there could be a better one than that.

She slid her feet forward across the ice, keeping her balance by flailing her arms. Caught up with Powell and climbed with him up onto the rocky shore of the island. There wasn't much to it, just a pile of smooth black rocks dusted with snow. No plants grew on the island, not even lichens or brush. There were no bird droppings or animal tracks to suggest that anything living ever came here.

Of course not, she thought. *This is a place of death.*

It wasn't her thought. Yet it wasn't a wolfish thought, either—her wolf couldn't think in English.

"Stop," she said, to Amuruq. Ahead of her Powell turned around, a look of annoyed puzzlement creasing his face.

"No, no," she said. "Not you."

His face cleared. "She's talking to you," he said.

Chey put a hand to her mouth, ashamed. Ashamed by her weakness, by the fact that the wolf had grown so strong inside of her and she couldn't keep it contained.

"She spoke to me, once," he told her. He held out one hand and helped her scramble on top of a huge boulder. "Just the once. She told me how to do this."

Chey nodded. "She wants this. But she's afraid, too. Afraid it won't work."

Powell licked his lips and studied the rocks before him. There was no sign of a cave entrance.

What if the rocks had collapsed and the cave was inaccessible now? What if it was full of old snow, a hundred meters deep? Snow never melted up here; even in midsummer it lingered in the shadows. What if— what if they couldn't—because—

"We can't do this without Lucie," she said, because it was a terrifying thought, and saying it out loud was the only way to fight it.

He picked up a boulder as big as his torso and flung it away from the heap. Grabbed another, and then another, rolled them down onto the ice. Soon he had revealed a tunnel, a dark den entrance just wide enough for a wolf or a human being to wriggle through. A smell came wafting up out of the hole that startled Chey. It smelled like her mother's freezer. Like dead meat, frozen so long it started to rot even at subzero temperatures.

This is a place of death, the wolf said, inside her head. *This is a tomb. My tomb.*

"Powell," Chey said, to get the noise out of her head. "Powell, did you hear me?" He was already reaching inside the hole, searching it with his hand, checking to make sure it went all the way down. The smell hadn't been enough to convince him, but Chey knew. Knew for sure, this was the way. "I said, we can't do this without Lucie."

"No," he told her.

"No—just—just no? We can't? We're wasting our time here?"

He withdrew his arm and looked at her for a long time. His eyes were hungry. He wanted to devour her. Wanted to seize and possess her, right here, even now. Wanted something from her she had refused to give him. This wasn't about him. It was about her, about Chey. About the lengths he would go to for her.

"No," he said again, "as in, no, you're wrong. We can still do it. With or without Lucie. Let's go."

95

Varkanin was dying, cell by cell.

The curse fought with the silver in his body. It raged and fumed and snatched at him, piece by piece, trying to change him, destroying itself even as it grew and fought. His human body could not withstand that onslaught.

He writhed on the ground, his limbs twitching as he fought for control. As he pushed himself past his own limits, just to roll over on his side. He vomited explosively onto the snow. He curled around his stomach as it heaved and heaved again. Sweat slicked his face and the palms of his hands.

Death was coming, and it would take from him his last chance of revenge.

That must not be allowed to happen.

He could not see Lucie. She must have run off. But he intended to find her again before he drew his last breath.

Somehow he got up onto his knees. He clutched at his face, because it was burning. He clutched at his chest because he could feel his heart racing so fast it might tear itself loose from its moorings. He cursed and spat and turned every ounce of his considerable willpower just to stopping the trembling, to keep himself from shaking to pieces.

Eventually, it worked.

His lungs throbbed like bellows as he worked to calm himself. His eyes stared from his head and then clamped closed as a new wave of pain and nausea swept through him. But he did not fall down. He did not go into convulsions. He did not die.

Not yet.

There was nothing he longed for more than the sweet release of oblivion. Yet his work was not done. He need only look over toward the quiescent face of Sharon Minik to know that.

Sharon—who looked nothing at all like his three lovely daughters. They had been blond, with their dear mother's sharp features and gracefully long limbs. Sharon was short, and squat, and her hair was black as Raven's wings. Yet for a while, he had known a very broken kind of peace, when he had spoken with Sharon. When he had seen the life and youth in her. It had made him weak, of course. Peace always did—it was inner turmoil that gave a man strength, in Varkanin's philosophy. His affection for Sharon had cost him everything. If he had not felt obligated to find the cure for her, he would never have trusted the werewolves.

Now Sharon was dead. He owed her something. Something like what he owed his three perished daughters.

When the helicopter appeared on the horizon, a blurred smudge of darkness like an especially large black fly, when it took a bearing directly toward him, he forced his body to be quiet. The war inside him raged on, but he refused to let it overcome him. He was a man, and there are things in this world a man must do before he dies.

The helicopter came in low and made a cautious landing half a kilometer away. Varkanin had moved by then, taking shelter in the strange rock formation on the far shore of the lake. He made sure not to be too stealthy, too invisible when he picked his hiding place. It was important—vital— that the soldiers in the helicopter knew where he was.

Of course, he need not make it *too* easy for them. They were special forces, trained in tracking and pursuit. Trained in the extraction of violent men from defensible positions. They would be disciplined. They would be very well armed. Varkanin did not even have his pistol anymore, because Lucie had taken it from him. He was only one man, and there were four soldiers coming for him.

But Varkanin had been trained by the Spetsnaz. The special forces of the Soviet Union, whose combat prowess had been legendary. He was older now, and had not fought soldiers in many years. But he thought he remembered a few tricks.

96

The tunnel went down quite a ways. In places the ceiling was so low that Powell and Chey had to crawl. In others it was big enough that four people could have walked through it abreast. It ran straight enough that light from outside streamed down its length, which was good—otherwise it would have been pitch black inside.

Powell did not say a word as he headed down into the depths of the earth. He gestured to Chey occasionally, to warn her to watch her head, or to urge her to hurry onward. Chey tried to match his silence—this was a sacred place, after all, and it felt like any words she spoke would disturb its ancient and very sad peace. But then she tripped over something and scraped her hand badly on a rock as she fell forward.

"Fuck!" she shouted.

The obscenity echoed up and down the tunnel, rolling along the ceiling, coming back as echoes louder than the original profanity. Powell swung around to stare at her.

She bit her lip and looked down to see what she had tripped over.

"Oh my God," she said, and danced sideways. There was a skull half-buried in the floor. Another one, a few meters away, caught her eye and she shoved the knuckle of her index finger into her mouth to keep from swearing again.

When you looked for them, bones were everywhere. Not just skulls. Rib cages and pelvises and arm bones and most of a skeletal hand. Some were broken and worn away by time. Some collapsed into dust when she touched them. Others looked almost fresh. One skull she saw still had patches of hair attached to its crown.

"Who—this couldn't be—are these the bones of the last of the Sivullir?" she asked.

Powell frowned. He picked up one of the skulls and studied it carefully. "No," he said. "These are the bones of werewolves."

Chey stared at him.

He came over and showed her the skull in his hand. The jaw was stretched forward and the teeth were pointed and wicked. The eye sockets looked human, though, and the braincase was round like a human's. It was half wolf and half human.

Chey shook her head. "No, that's not possible."

He raised one eyebrow and held the skull out toward her.

"When we change, we go directly from our human shape to our wolf shape. There isn't some weird half-and-half form in between. It's just a flash of silver light and then it's done."

Powell nodded. "I know."

"So what is that thing?" she demanded.

He set the skull gently on the floor of the tunnel, exactly where he'd found it. "I'm guessing we aren't the first werewolves to come here, looking for the cure. I would be surprised if we were. But no one has ever done it right. Maybe if you do it wrong—this is what happens."

His eyes went very wide, then, startling her. Had he seen something behind her? Was one of these hybrid abominations lurking back there, waiting to grab her, or—?

Then she felt what he had felt. She felt Amuruq pacing madly back and forth inside her skull. An animal trapped in a cage.

Do it right, the wolf spirit said. *Do it now,* she demanded.

Then she was gone.

Chey covered her face in her hands. "You heard that, too?"

"Yes," Powell told her.

"Okay."

Without another word they headed deeper into the tunnel. The light was growing very thin by the time they reached the bottom, but at least one stray beam of sunlight touched on the cave down there.

It was not as big as Chey had expected. Maybe five meters across, the ceiling like a dome that made her feel very hemmed in and claustrophobic. The dome was painted everywhere with pictures of animals and people, but time and moisture had so damaged the paint that it was impossible to make anything out clearly.

The floor was covered in bones. They crunched under Chey's feet as she stepped inside. She couldn't begin to guess how many skeletons were strewn around the floor. There was nothing else in the cave. No remains of Sivullir magic. No old fire rings or even old broken pots. The silver *ulu* was nowhere to be seen.

"It must be here," Powell said. "Raven said it would be."

"He's famous for lying every time he gets the chance," Chey pointed out.

Powell shook his head. "I know that, but he lies by twisting the truth, not by making things up. The *ulu* must be here somewhere. There should be something else, a little leather bag." He started stirring through the bones, because if those objects were anywhere they must be hidden under the pile. "Help me find it! We don't have much time."

Chey didn't want to touch the weird twisted bones. Just looking at them made her feel funny. But he was right, they were on a deadline—the moon would be up, soon. And the soldiers were still coming for them.

She got down on her knees and dug in.

97

Up in the helicopter Preston Holness watched it all through binoculars. Standing next to him, Sergeant Matthieu relayed his instructions through the radio.

The four soldiers spread out around the rock in perfect formation. They kept their weapons up and ready and covered one another's field of fire in textbook fashion. Periodically each of them checked in over the radio, so they all knew where the others were, and they could not be surprised. Sergeant Matthieu seemed pleased with their discipline. Holness didn't give a shit, as long as they killed Varkanin.

The Russian must have chosen this spot, Holness thought, because it was so similar to where everything had gone wrong the last time. Where six of the soldiers had died. These rocks were similar to the ones where the werewolves hid back then. They provided plenty of hiding places, and they would be difficult to storm. The soldiers knew that. They were not going to make the same mistake again and attack it en masse.

The helicopter drifted slowly inward, toward the rocks, to provide visual intelligence. "Keep us out of pistol range," Holness told the pilot.

"Give him a reason to move," Sergeant Matthieu said, into the radio.

One of the soldiers raised an arm in the air and threw a hand signal. The others shifted position, moving in to cover him. He clambered up into the rocks, then jumped back down in a hurry, trying to draw Varkanin out.

Nothing happened. The radios squawked again. The soldiers held their positions.

"Anything?" Holness asked.

The lead soldier climbed back into the rocks. "I heard something," he said. "Something moved. Somebody come up here and cover me."

A second soldier climbed up beside him. Together they scanned the rocks with their weapons. The lead unit moved a little further in. The pile of rocks was like a maze. There were footprints in the snow, he said.

"Up ahead of my position, about five meters," he went on. "That would be a great place for an ambush. Sight lines are limited."

"You know what to do," Sergeant Matthieu told him.

The soldier nodded—Holness was watching him from above. He reached down to his belt and detached a smoke grenade. "I'm going to try to flush him out. Everybody move back, but be ready to catch him when he runs for it."

The radios bleated a confirmation.

The lead soldier popped the pin off his grenade and tossed it into the labyrinth of rocks. It hissed and spun around as it pumped out hundreds of cubic feet of sweet-smelling smoke. The fumes billowed out of the rocks in thick clouds that hung nearly motionless in the still air.

"He doesn't have any breathing gear, we're sure of that?" Holness asked. The radio confirmed that none had been seen on Varkanin's person.

Sergeant Matthieu gave a tight little nod. Sweat had formed on his upper lip. "Okay, he'll either run or suffocate. Stand by to—"

Suddenly the soldier was gone. Vanished. The soldier covering him rushed forward to catch sight of him but he was just—gone.

Inside the smoke cloud someone screamed, just for a moment. Then there was silence again.

Preston Holness itched all over. The tactical clothing he wore was made of nylon—manmade fibers!—and it didn't breathe. He was sweating inside his werewolf-proof vest and he had a sudden urge to loosen his neck tie, even though he wasn't wearing one.

The radios went wild, squawking and beeping as the soldiers tried to understand what had happened, what could possibly have gone wrong. "Give me information, dámn it," Holness shouted. One of the soldiers was foolish enough to lower his weapon as he tried to answer. There was a gunshot and then a red blotch appeared on the hood of his parka. He collapsed in a heap.

"No!" Holness shouted. Sergeant Matthieu started yelling for the ground units to return fire.

The remaining two soldiers responded instantly, shooting blind into the smoke. "I can't see him!" one of them shouted. "Where the hell is he? He's using our own smoke for cover—who the hell is this guy?"

He never received an answer to his question. A bullet caught him in the chest and he was dead before his body could fall to the snow.

"Come on," Holness grunted. As if he could make Varkanin appear by yelling for him. But the Russian stayed hidden in the smoke.

The last remaining soldier turned and ran. He kept his rifle low and ready in his hands, and he glanced behind himself frequently, but clearly he was far more intent on getting away, escaping, than in watching out for the killer in the rocks.

Finally Varkanin emerged from the smoke, his face covered by the respirator mask of the lead soldier. The first one to die. In his hands he held the assault rifle he'd taken away from that same soldier, after he yanked him into the smoke. Holness had no doubt that soldier was dead.

Taking his time, Varkanin ejected the weapon's magazine. It was loaded with silver bullets. He let the clip fall to the ground. Holness understood why he did that. Silver bullets were notoriously inaccurate and useless at any kind of range. Nor were they needed for this target. There was another magazine, this one full of traditional lead ammunition, taped to the receiver of the assault rifle. Calmly, with hands that had performed this action a hundred times before, he pulled the replacement magazine free, then slapped it into the weapon and locked it home. Then he lifted it to his eye.

The soldier running away from him fired back over his shoulder, burning through his own ammunition in one furious burst. The silver bullets pinged and bounced all around Varkanin, but none of them came close to hitting him.

"Shit," Holness barked.

The Russian waited until the other soldier was done with his pointless attack. He adjusted his own weapon for single fire. Then he took aim and squeezed his trigger. There was a cracking noise, and the last of Holness's soldiers dropped to the ground, lifeless.

Varkanin lowered his weapon. Then he looked up at the helicopter. To Preston Holness, up there in the helicopter, it felt like the Russian was staring him right in the eye. Varkanin lifted his rifle to his eye again and fired. One bullet. Two.

"Move," Holness told the pilot. "Up, up, go up!"

The helicopter's engine whined as the pilot grasped for more altitude. The big aircraft wasn't built for fast maneuvers. Varkanin lined up another shot. Took it.

"Jesus, can he hit us from there?" Holness's heart was pounding in his chest.

Sergeant Matthieu shrugged. "It's unlikely, a tricky shot even for a marksman, but—"

A bullet struck the bottom of the helicopter's fuselage. It sound like a stone being tossed into an aluminum pot, an almost comical sound, but it made Holness scream like a little girl. "If he does hit us?" he demanded.

"If he hit a fuel line, or worse, the hydraulics," Sergeant Matthieu said, "it could—"

Another bullet cracked one of the side windows.

"Get us the fuck out of here," Holness shouted at the pilot. He had just ruined a very expensive pair of silk boxer shorts.

"But the objective," the sergeant insisted.

"Do I look like I fucking care about werewolves right now?"

98

"**What was that?**" Chey asked, but she knew already—the sound she'd heard, which boomed inside the echo chamber of the cave like pounding surf, was the noise of gunshots. "They're here."

A cold wave of dread went through her.

"Don't stop," Powell demanded.

She hadn't, though. She was still digging through the pile of bones, though her hands were scraped by the sharp edges of the broken skulls and spines and arm bones. Though her back hurt from stooping so long.

So far she'd found nothing—except enough to disturb her. Rooting through the bones, she'd had no choice but to look at them. She'd realized quickly enough that they were not normal. It wasn't just that they belonged to both wolf and human skeletons—often each individual bone was a perverted combination of the two. A human femur would thicken and twist as it curved from one end to the other. A rib cage would splay outwards, the ribs like broken fingers grabbing for something they couldn't reach. The skulls were the worst. Mostly the jaw bones had fallen away from the crania, but sometimes they were intact—horribly intact.

It was evident from the state of the bones that when the werewolves who came here died, they died in agony. In horrible, twisting pain, wracked from within as two competing anatomies struggled for dominance inside their bodies.

"When we find the silver knife, you know what to do with it, right?" she asked, patting the stone floor of the cave under the bones. There was nothing down there. "You know the proper ceremony? So we don't end up like these?"

"I know it," he told her. "Keep looking."

The sound of more gunshots came rolling down the tunnel. Inside the dome-shaped cave the noise was immense. It made her lungs hurt and her ears pop. She forced herself to keep looking. "If they find us like this, they—"

She stopped, because her hand had touched something. Powell looked up at her, suddenly very alert. She reached around under the bones and her hand closed on a leather bag. She brought it up to the light. It was smeared with bone dust, but it looked surprisingly well preserved for something that was ten thousand years old. The stitching that held it together had not come undone. The leather itself hadn't rotted at all. "How is this possible?" she asked.

"Magic," he told her. As if that explained everything. "Good. Now we just need to find the *ulu.*"

She studied the bag in her hands. It was held shut by a tightly knotted piece of leather thong. She picked at the knot with her fingernails and it started to come loose. "What's in here?" she asked, as the thong came undone.

"No, don't!" he shouted, and stumbled toward her across the bones. "Don't open it, not yet!"

Then two things happened all at once. The bag came open in her hands. It felt like it had opened itself, like it had a will of its own and it *wanted* to open. She wasn't sure if she could have stopped it. Inside were a bunch of small black rocks, two eyeballs, and a long thin piece of pink flesh. Like a tongue. It curled in her fingers and she dropped it in horrified surprise. The little black rocks flew everywhere.

At the same time, Powell's foot sank deep into the bones and he cried out in torment. Drawing back in horror from the eyes and tongue, Chey rushed over to him and found him hopping on one foot. He held the other in his hands. It was missing some toes.

"The *ulu,*" he said. "I must have stumbled on—"

He didn't finish his sentence.

Chey couldn't have heard him if he had. Amuruq burst out of the darkness in her head and seized control. She dropped to all fours and started sniffing at the body parts from the bag.

Amuruq's body parts.

Raven had tried to tell her what was done with the contents of the leather bag. What the Sivullir had done with it when their spell was cast. She hadn't wanted to hear it. She should have been less squeamish.

For ten thousand years the spirit of the dire wolf had been looking for those last pieces of herself that remained. The pieces the Sivullir had held in reserve, trapped inside a bag of pitchblende to keep her from finding them. Now they were in her reach. She pounced, trying to get them back. To absorb them back into her body.

Except she didn't have a body. She was borrowing Chey's.

"Powell," Chey managed to shout. Except it wasn't a human word that emerged from her lips. It was a snarling, yelping vocalization of the kind a wolf might make.

Amuruq surged forward, straining every muscle in Chey's body. Pushing them past the point of collapse. *Must have them,* she said, inside Chey's mind. *Waited so long. Stop fighting me!*

"Chey, no," Powell called, running toward her. He had something in his hands. A knife shaped like a crescent moon, made of pure silver.

It was too late. Chey felt her bones start to change. To lengthen in places, to contract in size elsewhere, pulling her flesh around, tearing things open inside her. She felt hair burst from her skin. She was changing. Without the moon. And she could not survive the transformation.

99

Varkanin watched the helicopter shoot away toward the south, until it was no more than a dark dot against the sun. Then he finally let himself relax, lowering his assault rifle, letting his shoulders slump.

The curse inside him was winning. He would not last much longer. He was unsure if he would even live long enough to see the moon come up. He would surely not survive the change when it did.

He had come so far. Gotten so close. Now he was going to fail. It was a very small consolation that he had aided Powell and Cheyenne. He hoped, in an abstract way, that they would find their cure. But that was not his fight. His life's purpose lay elsewhere.

It was closer than he thought. As he started to lean forward, thinking he would just lie down and wait for death, he heard someone moving in the rocks behind him. Given the possibilities, it was not difficult to imagine who it might be.

"Have you come to gloat?" he asked, his voice softer than he would have liked.

"I've come to watch you die," Lucie told him.

He spun around with what little strength he could muster. Raised his weapon, even knowing the lead bullets in its magazine would not harm her. He needn't have bothered, of course.

She was faster than he was. She was so much faster than he was, even when his strength was full within him. Now she was a blur in the cold air. She grabbed the rifle by the barrel—careful not to touch him directly, she had learned that lesson—and tore it away from him. Bent the barrel over her knee and threw the weapon toward the lake.

Then she danced backward, getting clear of his reach, all before he could even react. She had his own pistol in her hand. She kept it pointed at his stomach.

"Silver bullets," she said, gesturing with the handgun. "They will still kill a human, *non?* I think they will. Do not try anything, now."

"No. Even if I could." He fought his rebellious body but there was nothing left in his legs. Even the bones felt soft and pliant, like gelatin. He dropped painfully to his knees. Inside him a wolf scratched and bit, again and again, at the silver in his cells.

"You accept that I have won," Lucie said. She looked surprised.

"The conditions of earthly life do not lend themselves to justice," he said. "What is good, what is right, are the province of God in his heaven, and such things are not meant to be expected from flesh and blood."

"Poetry. At this late date. Still, you have not truly surrendered, have you? Put your hands behind your head."

"Very well," he said, and did as he was told.

"You followed me halfway around the world, to come to this. Was it worth it?" Lucie asked, taking a step closer. "I admit, you had reason. I hurt you. Now, in this place, I will accept that what I did to you was perhaps excessive, compared to your crime against me. I can see why you would seek revenge."

"I shot you, to protect my community. You slaughtered my children in return," Varkanin said, his voice flat. "I had no choice but to act as I did."

"Choice," Lucie said. She came closer still. Daring him to make an attack. When he did not she stepped even closer. "It is good to have choices. That is all I wanted. The choice of where I should live, the choice of how I should live."

"Even if that choice meant death for human beings."

"Especially if it did! I am a werewolf, Varkanin. I am meant to kill you and your kind. Damn Powell and his moralizing. We are made for this purpose, and this alone. You would take that away from us, our right to choose our lives. But I will give you a choice. A choice of death. You may wait for the moon to rise. I have no doubt the result will be entertaining."

"For you. For me it will be quite painful," he said, seeing where this was going.

"Exactly. Your other choice is simple . . . to kiss my feet. Lick them, with your tongue. Like a wolf. No, like a dog. If you do this simple thing, I will make your death effortless and without pain. You see? I am not without mercy."

He managed to tilt his head back. Looked up at her face.

"Which one first? Left, or right?" he asked.

She smiled. She bared her teeth. Who could say which was the more apt description? She was enjoying this.

Which was the only reason Lucie ever did anything, he knew. Because it felt good, at the exact moment she chose to do it. She could understand nothing more than that.

"You may choose that, as well," she said, with a little laugh.

Varkanin unlaced his fingers and placed his hands down on the snow so he stood on all fours like a dog. He lowered his face toward her left foot, putting all his weight on his left hand. He had so little strength left that his left arm began to tremble and falter.

His right arm did a little better.

He flicked his wrist. A silver knife jumped out of its sheath. He brought it down to his hand in a practiced motion, smooth, very smooth, and then stabbed upward without even looking. Buried the knife in her belly before she even saw it.

She screamed and drew back, ready to bolt, to run. He tried to push harder, to lodge the blade in her guts, where she would not be able to get it out.

"I choose to wait for the moon," he said, even as she ran away, into the snow, desperately trying to escape the burning pain he had given her. "So that I may watch you die."

He did not have long to wait. Even at that very moment, the moon was beginning to rise.

Neither of them, Varkanin nor Lucie, exploded when its silver light touched them. There was some screaming, and some blood. But it did not last long. When it was over their eyes, blue and white, stared up at the moon from faces that were still human, but cold and still and dead.

100.

Chey's teeth were like daggers in her mouth. Her arms were changing shape and the agony of it was beyond description. All the while Amuruq was panting and whining in her head, so loud she could not hear anything else. Didn't the wolf spirit understand? This was the wrong way—the way that had claimed so many werewolves before, and left their bones rotting on the floor of the cave.

The moon—the moon was up, the transformation was beginning. It would not stop what was happening to her. Only one thing could.

This must be how it always happened. And Chey knew exactly who to blame. The Sivullir hadn't wanted Amuruq to find her body again so easily. That would have spoiled their sadistic plan for driving out the Bear People. So they had created this trap, this safeguard, to keep it from happening.

"Chey," Powell shouted, right in her ear. It sounded like a whisper underneath the snarling, mewling cries of the wolf. "Chey, hold on, I just need to—"

He shouted then in pain and distress. Silver light flashed in her eyes and she thought—she thought the moon—all thoughts were torn away from her, a wind blew through her head and everything was gone, everything—everything lost—

Slowly she opened her eyes.

She saw the room full of bones, with just a few stray beams of sunlight coming down the tunnel, streaking through the bone dust in the air. She saw the tongue flapping on the ground, next to the pair of eyes. Blood splattered them, fell in huge drops that pooled around them. Almost as soon as it touched them, the blood was absorbed. Sucked into the eyeballs and the tongue as if they were drinking it.

Blood.

Chey's chest hurt. Her face was a mask of pain. She touched her arms, her legs, and found them shaped like they always had been. Human shaped.

Blood.

She tried to close her eyes again. Tried to look away. She did not want to see where that blood was coming from. Because she already knew what she would see.

"Chey," Powell said. "There was no other way. No time left."

"I know," she said, her voice breaking. She was going to start crying if she looked. If she accepted what had happened.

"I fell in love with you, Chey. I think—it must have happened when we—when we were still trying to kill each other, actually. Before Port Radium. At first I thought I was just lonely. That I was just glad to have someone share my solitude with me. Later I came to understand. What I feel for you is bigger than that. It's bigger than me. I don't regret this."

Chey reached up to wipe tears from her eyes. Before they flooded her vision and made it impossible to see, she looked up. She owed him that.

Powell was standing very close. The silver *ulu* lay at his feet, stained with his blood. His face was pale, but his wrists were open and red and pouring out his life.

"It has to be done this way," Powell said. His voice was already fading. "She tried to come back to life inside your body, but—that would have killed you. She needs her own body back. What's—left of it, anyway. Her blood runs in our veins. She couldn't be whole again, not without her blood. I had to give it back."

She surged forward to hold him, to save him somehow, but he shook his head.

"Don't. If you touch me—it'll be—bad, I think. She'll take your blood, too."

She could barely control herself. The need to embrace him was so strong. "What can I do?" she asked. She knew already there was no way to save his life. He'd lost too much blood. "What do you want most, right now?"

"I want—I want you—to say you love me."

"I do," Chey gasped. "Oh, God, Powell, I've never loved anyone like this—"

"You're lying," he said. His mouth twisted in a complex smile. "I loved hearing that. But I know it isn't true. I'm the guy who killed your father."

"No," she said. "It wasn't you. It was your wolf."

"Thank you, Chey," he said.

It was all he had the strength for. He sank down to his knees, somehow keeping his wrists directly above the eyeballs and tongue on the floor.

Her tears did obscure her vision then, so she could see nothing. She wept for a very long time, her chest seizing up with sobs, with cries of grief. She didn't love him. She didn't forgive him. But those were absolute terms, words that could not convey the shades of gray, the complexities of how she felt, and the sacrifices he'd made.

Eventually she wiped her tears away. Eventually she could see again. Someone else was in the room, someone who hadn't been there before. She was not surprised, though she should have been. She was not afraid, though she should have been terrified.

It was a woman, a very beautiful woman with gray hair, wearing a fur cloak that draped around her bare feet. The woman reached up over her head and pulled a wooden mask over her face. It had an open, gaping mouth, perfectly round like a circle.

The woman didn't speak. She just looked down at Powell's bloodless body.

"Amuruq," Chey said. "He freed you. You owe him a debt."

The woman did not answer. Instead she knelt down on the bones as if she were about to start praying. But that wasn't what she had in mind at all. Instead she leaned over Powell's body and—

"No!" Chey shouted, but it was already too late.

Powell's body was gone. Swallowed up.

The woman rose to her feet again. She gave Chey a piercing look, with eyebrows raised. "Of all the bodies I was trapped in, I liked his the best," she said. "I'll take him with me. Make him part of me. That is what I owed him."

"That's not enough—"

"Think of what is owed to me, little ape. Think what I deserve after so long. Do you wish to join him, inside my belly? Maybe I deserve you, too."

Chey shrank back, clutching her arms across her chest. The woman nodded, once. "I did not think so," she said. Then she walked up the tunnel and out into the daylight. In the distance, very far away, Chey heard wolves howling in joy. In triumph.

Amuruq was back. The spirit of the dire wolf. Did that mean they had returned from extinction, too? Chey couldn't begin to guess.

It was then that Chey began to feel cold. Not just chilly, but bone-searingly cold. She had a desperate urge to put some clothes on.

It had worked. It had seemed impossible. But it had worked.

She was human, once more.

Human. And a long way from home.

"Okay," Chey sighed to herself. "Okay." The sound of human words broke the spell. Hearing a voice, even her own, made her feel less alone and defenseless. She zipped up the parka she'd taken from one of the dead soldiers, and stood up. Her feet felt as if they were on fire, even inside the soldier's socks and boots. Her body was cramped with the cold. It had been a long walk from the tunnel mouth to the rock formation on the far side of the lake, where Varkanin had made his last stand. A long walk on bare, human feet. She wasn't sure how badly her feet had been damaged by the cold, but she figured if they still hurt, that was a good sign. It was when they stopped hurting that you were in trouble, she thought. But oh man, did they hurt. She had to stop for a second and wait for the roaring in her ears to die down. The next step hurt slightly less.

"Okay," she said. Louder. More confidently. The hard *k* sound was the part that helped. "Okay, you little idiot. You're going to be okay."

The tundra swallowed her up without comment. Her slow pace made it easier, actually, to cross the rough ground. She had plenty of time to look and see where each foot should go, to avoid the rocks and the deep snowdrifts. She had time to listen to the sound of snow squishing and crunching under her feet, to the squeak of old ice as her boots sank down through it. She could smell the snow, too, smell how clean it was. Smell the blood that stained the front of her parka.

So many people had died. Varkanin had died—she'd found his body. Lucie, Sharon, Powell.

Powell.

She'd come so close to telling the truth when she said she loved him. She walked for an hour, as best she could tell. Then she stopped to rest.

Sitting down on a dry rock, she pulled her knees close to her chest and looked back the way she'd come. There was no trail or path there—she felt really proud for how she'd covered so much unbroken ground. Then she looked up and saw the lake behind her, and the cluster of rocks like a broken hand behind it.

It stood no more than a half kilometer behind her. In an hour that was all the distance she'd covered. The town of Cambridge Springs was fifty kilometers away. Assuming she could find it. Assuming she didn't just keep walking south until she died.

Tears exploded in her throat. Chey bit them back, sucking breath into her body. "No," she said, though she didn't know what she was rejecting, exactly. "No!"

She was lost.

She was alone.

Her feet fucking hurt.

She knew how to add up those figures. She knew what the sum would be. Those three variables were what separated happy, healthy young human women from corpses no one would ever find. Her body would fail her, the life drained out of it by the cold or the wind or by hunger or lack of water. Whatever animals actually lived up here would find her, after she died, and eat her corpse. In time her bones would bleach white and then even they would decay, and no one would ever know where she'd gone to. Maybe a million years from now, she thought, she would be a fossil, and some future paleontologist would dig her up, and wonder what she was doing there, so far from any human habitation.

"Goddamn it, no!" she shrieked. "I won't stop here! Not when I've come so far!"

Her shout echoed around the snowfield. A drift of snow slid off the top of a half-buried rock.

"I won't," she said, as if saying it aloud could make it so.

In the distance a bird called back to her with a high bell-like note she didn't recognize. A bird? Up here? She hadn't seen any birds. It must not have been a bird at all. It sounded almost mechanical, actually, less like an animal sound than something man-made. It sounded almost like a fork clinking on a metal plate.

She closed her eyes and concentrated, and heard the clinking sound again. If she concentrated, really concentrated, she was pretty sure she could hear something else, too—the tearing sound of ice cracking open.

Chey rushed forward, using up all the strength she had left. Ahead of her, something bright caught the sun, so bright it hurt her eyes. A tiny pond, the frozen surface of a miniature lake. As she got closer she saw a spiderweb of white lines snaking across the ice. It was cracking, breaking up. Suddenly a piece of ice popped out of the web of cracks and spun away. She heard water splashing underneath. More ice broke up and then a hand reached up out of the black water. An arm, wrapped in thick furs.

Water cascaded down from Dzo's furs as he climbed up out of the ice. He had his mask down over his face. For a second the two of them just stood there, staring at each other. Then he lifted the mask and smiled at her.

"What did I miss?" he asked.

She grabbed him and hugged him and asked a million questions. How had he survived after Varkanin shot him? Where had he been? What was he doing here? She barely heard his answers. She got the sense that the depleted uranium bullet had hurt him—badly—but that he had just gone deep enough into the water until he didn't have a real body anymore. That down there he'd been safe, and that now he was fine, having reincorporated in a new body. She had no idea how that worked, very little idea what he even meant. She didn't care. She hugged him and he was warm and he smelled—he smelled like campfires, and cooked food, and, and, yes, deep in his fur she caught a whiff of Powell. Of the way Powell used to smell.

Powell.

Powell, who was gone, now. Dead like all the rest.

Chey broke down and cried, then. Really hysterically wept, like she never had before in her entire life. Her entire human life. Dzo waited for her to get the worst of it out of her system. Then he asked her what they were going to do next.

"I have to go back to civilization," she said. "But I don't even know what direction town is in, and I don't think I can walk that far anyway. I think I may have survived just long enough to get myself killed."

"There's an abandoned snowcat over that hill," he told her, waving one arm. "I saw it when I was looking for you, trying to figure out where to come up out of the water. I think I can drive it. You want me to give you a lift?" he asked.

She stared at him in total surprise.

He just stared at her, his face wide open.

"That," she said, "would be very nice of you."

acknowledgments

When I finished *Frostbite,* I always wondered where the wolves were going. I'd like to thank Julian Pavia, my editor, and everyone at Three Rivers Press who made it possible to find out. I'd also like to thank my agent, Russell Galen, for believing there was more to life than the vampires and zombies.

about the author

David Wellington is the author of *Monster Island, Monster Nation, Monster Planet, 13 Bullets, 99 Coffins, Vampire Zero, 23 Hours,* and *Frostbite.* Born in Pittsburgh, Pennsylvania, in 1971, he currently lives in New York City with his wife, Elisabeth, and his dog, Mary.

For Cheyenne Clark, there's a bad moon on the rise ..

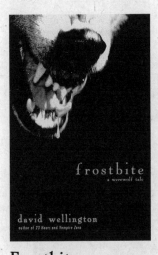

Frostbite
A Werewolf Tale
978-0-307-46083-7
$14.00 paper (Canada: $17.99)

When a strange wolf's teeth slash Cheyenne's ankle to the bone, her old life ends, and she becomes the very monster that has haunted her nightmares for years. Worse, the only one who can understand what Chey has become is the man—or wolf—who's doomed her to this fate. Yet as the line between human and beast blurs, so too does the distinction between hunter and hunted . . . for Chey is more than just the victim she appears to be. But once she's within killing range, she may find that—even for a werewolf—it's not always easy to go for the jugular.

13 Bullets
A Vampire Tale
978-0-307-38143-9
$13.95 paper (Canada: $17.95)

99 Coffins
A Historical Vampire Tale
978-0-307-38171-2
$13.95 paper (Canada: $16.95)

Vampire Zero
A Gruesome Vampire Tale
978-0-307-38172-9
$13.95 paper (Canada: $15.95)

23 Hours
A Vengeful Vampire Tale
978-0-307-45277-1
$14.00 paper (Canada: $17.99)